THE INVISIBLE TRIBE

THE
INVISIBLE
TRIBE

What a Man can't Know, the Eagle Sees

TEAM TUCHINA

ADRIAN ROMAN

A Novel

MILL CITY PRESS

Mill City Press, Inc.
2301 Lucien Way #415
Maitland, FL 32751
407.339.4217
www.millcitypress.net

© 2012, 2020 by Adrian Roman

ADRIANROMAN42@gmail.COM
DreamCatcher Entertainment and IronHorse Books

Printed in the United States of America

Paperback ISBN-13: 978-1-9382-2346-4
Ebook ISBN-13: 978-1-9385-6442-0

DreamCatcher Entertainment & IronHorse Books

ADRIANROMAN42@GMAIL.COM

Photo by Adrienne N. Roman

PREFACE

"I am invisible, understand, simply because people refuse to see me."

Author Ralph Ellison 1952

I n his first novel, The Invisible Tribe, Adrian Roman embarks on a formidable quest, namely, writing socially responsible fiction in an America blind to the plight of its indigenous people. As Sancho Panza to his Quixote, I'm proud to offer this preface.

It's been more than thirty years since I answered an ad placed by High Energy Entertainment. Its chief, Adrian Roman, a black belt master and jack of all trades, hired me as a musician and convinced me to back an Elvis impersonator. Later, he would drive me from Dallas to his birthplace in Oklahoma. Along the trip, he related stories that became lyrics to The Ballad of Tall Bear.

Roman had bigger dreams though. A fan of John Grisham, he longed to write a mystery thriller. His realistic fiction would introduce John Wilkerson Tall Bear, a full blood Choctaw battling the social inequities, which affect a contemporary tribal nation.

As an English tutor familiar with his songwriting, I was secretly skeptical. Nonetheless, Adrian's fearless determination outweighed his literary liabilities. In 2012, he published the first edition of The Invisible Tribe. Despite less than enthusiastic feedback, Roman had already thrown himself into an even more ambitious sequel, IronHorse the Medicine Man.

As Chief honed his writing skills, he trusted me to proofread the sequel via a prolonged email correspondence. Like The Invisible Tribe, the second book was filled with believable characters, realistic dialogue, and intriguing plot twists. My objective was to tighten its grammar without disturbing the author's spirit or intent. Chief patiently tolerated nine months of revision.

Believing the tenuous process was worthwhile, Adrian convinced me to revisit The Invisible Tribe as editor. Here, I admit to identifying with Joseph Grand in Albert Camus' The Plague, a dreary civil servant who spends his free time polishing the first sentence of a prose-perfect book he dreams of writing.

I pray any revisions born of my inherent prejudices do not dilute the significance of this work. Events as recent as the Standing Rock protests of 2017 convince me that even fictionalized accounts such as The Invisible Tribe are both relevant and necessary.

Hopefully, readers will find universal truths in Tall Bear's journey, insights that leave them neither defensive nor resentful. Only our imagination allows a written narrative to transcend its pages and touch the soul.

PATRICK WICK...aka Tone Arranger

This book is dedicated to the memory of my two sons,

RANDELL MARLON ROMAN

August 4, 1963 ~ February 17, 2011

Shortly after completing my new novel, *'The Invisible Tribe'*, I lost my oldest son to an overdose of prescription medication. Randell always wanted to be a soldier and eventually joined the Army and served a tour in Korea. He came home suffering from PDSD because the military ask him to do hostile actions that went against his moral code. He was crying out for help for the last time, and we can only guess if this episode was an accident or whether he truly meant to leave this earth. Having the answer wouldn't change anything, as nothing can bring him back.

When Randy was about twelve, he convinced his mother to let him come and live with me. Shortly after that, his younger brother, Reagan Lee, followed, and we were all together, once again, united as a family. I began teaching them martial arts at an early age and both achieved Black Belts rank in American Kenpo.

However, music was Randy's true passion until he died. Shortly before his death, he completed an original song, Firehouse Funk. His recordings give me comfort hearing his fingers move over the strings. He loved to play and sing the blues. His rock idol was Eric Clapton, and he was halfway through Clapton's autobiography at the time of his death. Randell enjoyed the music industry enough to become a professional at his craft. Another hobby was scuba diving in the Caymans.

During my career as a martial artist, he would teach class in my schools. Randy and his younger brother Reagan Lee would film and produce my DVD's. While filming and producing my material, Randell knew what I knew, but didn't perform. He showed no interest in the martial arts until shortly before his death, when he requested I teach him the Red Warrior movements and forms. He thanked me for sharing our Native art with him. He had plans to begin teaching, should the opportunity come about. He was a gifted son and teacher. I miss him!

Randy was a generous soul, caring and giving. He was an ancient warrior from a different time and place. He had the values of our ancient ancestors. I wish we could all be more like him.

Twelve years ago, while Randy was in Talihina Indian Recovery Center, he and I spent a day together there. He taught me how and why our Indian people participated in Sweat Lodge Ceremonies. It was wonderful time, a son teaching his father. He took me into the mountains in Talihina, OK where I was born, and showed me an actual Sweat lodge, where he participated in. Randy taught me a lot about the ancient culture of our people, and for that I dedicate this book in his honor.

I was blessed to have both of them for the years I did, and I am eternally grateful for their presence on this earth. I will hold both of them in my arms again someday.

I'm the proud father of Randell Marlon Roman, Army Airborne Ranger/Choctaw Indian

Reagan Lee Roman

March 13, 1966 ~ Sept 2, 2016

During Randy difficult journey, Reagan Lee was drinking heavily with him and developed Cirrhosis of the liver. When Randy overdosed Reagan began his downward spiral and was gone in five years. He was in and out of hospitals, we would almost loose him and he would recover. He was like a cat with nine lives. In the end, I realized Reagan had a death wish for he could not continue on without his brother. Reagan Lee was his older brother wingman, gifted athlete, a writer, deep thinker, a joker and life of the party. I marvel at his abilities to master American Kenpo Karate and become a black belt at 11 years old. Scuba diving at 110 feet in the Caymans was one of his great loves.

Shortly before his death, we drove by car from Dallas to California to visit his sister Adrienne and niece Peyton. We had long talks and shared stories. We spent a day in Tombstone, AZ walking in footsteps of long ago cowboys. We played our last round of golf in Irvine together. Shared a breakfast at Laguna Beach overlooking the ocean. Regan Lee was a unique individual. Now looking back, I sensed the end was near but never wanted to acknowledge it. It frightened me. It was difficult as a father to watch him slip away and I could do nothing. I was blessed to have both of them for the years I did, and I am eternally grateful for their presence on this earth. I will hold both of them in my arms again someday.

I'm the proud father of Reagan Lee Roman/Choctaw Indian

ACKNOWLEDGEMENT

First I want to give honor to my parents, who took the time to teach me the ancient ways of our people, the Mississippi Choctaws. My mother, Ada Wilkerson, was the love of my life and, because of her struggles in raising ten children, gave me the strength and fortitude to believe I could overcome anything. I honor my brothers and sisters, Roy Lee, Martha Jo, Debby Jean, Jimmy, Buddy Mack, Linda Sue and Dorothy Ann who have passed on to the Great Mystery. My remaining brothers Bobby Joe, and Harry Lee are a living testament to our wonderful mother.

I want to acknowledge my children. My eldest son Randell Marlon Roman age 47 passed on Feb 17th, 2011 and Reagan Lee Roman who passed on Sept 2nd 2016. Randy's insight, knowledge and teachings allowed me to write about Ceremonial Sweats. Reagan Lee taught me how to forgive and be patience. His life was so difficult to maneuver in the end and he never complained. I'm not man enough to endure what he did. And I admire him for that.

My daughter Adrienne Nicole Roman is truly a father's gift. What she has admirably accomplished in her young life, under stressful circumstances, shows a sense of dignity and resolve beyond her years. She is a wonderful mother to her daughter Peyton. I'm blessed to be a part of their life in the autumn of mine. They are the light in my life.

My granddaughters, Peyton, Cassidy, Madison and my great granddaughter Blakely are a grandfather's delight. Their future is so bright, and I know they will accomplish great things.

I'm fortunate to have a lasting friendship with my second wife Sandi Geuike.

Last, I want to give honor to my friend of 30 years, Patrick Wick, aka Tone Arranger who has collaborated with me on musical projects, song writing and editing this novel.

The Invisible Tribe

By Adrian Roman

For some reason I felt a need to attend my mother's church this particular weekend. I had participated in an American Indian Ceremonial Sweat the previous weekend and experienced a strange vision, so it seemed. In my vision, I saw an ancient Roman Soldier and an American Indian Warrior riding horseback side by side on a mountaintop. I saw a herd of buffalo, in a valley surrounded by lush woodland. Leading was a magnificent white buffalo. I thought I saw a white wolf stalking. The Sacred White Buffalo is significant throughout American Indian culture. Were the two warriors on a buffalo hunt together? I noticed red streaks down the flank of the White Buffalo. Had he been wounded? This would have been a tragedy, for the birth of a white buffalo happens once in a lifetime. Then my vision faded away.

John Wilkerson Tall Bear

CHAPTER ONE

The red Allante convertible roars north on highway 75 out of Dallas, just under the posted speed limit. This two-seat roadster is a collector's item, which competed with the Mercedes 450 of that era. Ferrari designed, it was made by Cadillac, shipped to Italy in a 747 for assembly, then back to the United States with a $65,000 sticker, an astronomical price for a car in 1993. Ahead of its time, the stout, small tank, still complements the man behind the wheel.

John Wilkerson Tall Bear is a strong looking man with a dark complexion. He wears his hair pulled back, Indian style ponytail. In his late 50's, he easily passes for a man 15 years younger due to good genes and workout ethic. After living for centuries in an area now Mississippi, his people moved at the turn of the century to south-eastern Oklahoma. On a frigid morning in January, John was born at the Talihina Indian Hospital. Tall Bear is a proud full blood Indian. He is, to be more specific, a Mississippi Choctaw.

John left Oklahoma at seventeen when the Bureau of Indian Affairs (BIA) persuaded his family to move to Dallas. The infamous Relocation Program of the late 1950's was a last ditch effort to uproot Indian families and place them in major cities to sink or swim. BIA agents were great bad car salesmen and enticed Indian families to move. The BIA promised to pay for everything and, jobs making lots of money. Like governments treaties they failed to stand behind their word. Closer to truth, it was another scheme to divide and isolate the Choctaws with tragedy written all over it.

In Dallas, he graduated from high school and spent some time in the military, before settling permanently in Texas. Tall Bear is twice divorced with three children. He has worked at many jobs, however, one remained consistent, his teaching of martial arts. Since his youth in Oklahoma, he has fought prejudice against American Indians to survive.

John began his formal education in traditional martial arts after his first divorce, looking for something to occupy his mind and time. He excelled and went on to become a Master, even forming his own system based on Native fighting principals learned as a young boy from his father and grandfathers. He is successful and is acknowledged by his peers as a gifted instructor. John Tall Bear has appeared on national magazine covers and has had numerous articles written about him. He finds enjoyment with his three children, grandchildren, and playing golf.

Today, he is on his way to a small Indian church in Oklahoma just north of the Red River, the border separating Texas from Oklahoma. In 45 minutes he will be in Indian country. After crossing the river, he turns east on state highway 91 for a short 15-mile trip into a tiny town called Achille. His mother was born and raised here. Passing by the high school, he remembers her talking about good times she had there. She had played on the girl's basketball team in grade school. Tall Bear could only imagine his mother playing one position, point guard. She was a short woman even as an adult, just barely five feet. He wishes he could have seen her play.

Nearby is the bus stop where they said their goodbyes when fresh out of high school. He was leaving for military duty, and when it was time to go, she accompanied him to the stop. They had only a short time to visit before the bus pulled away. He remembers seeing tears flowing down her face and thinking. *'Mom, I'm just going off to Lackland AFB for military training.'* The Vietnam War had just begun to escalate, and John now understands what his mother must have been thinking. Would this be the last time she sees her young son? But until you have children of your own, you cannot begin to understand the significance of saying goodbye to your first-born.

It's been 10 years since John's mother came to her final resting place. She is buried in the local cemetery. Tall Bear has made this journey many times in the decade since, and several years ago officially joined his mother's church. He always has mixed emotions on arrival, but leaves with a sense of peace, after attending church services and visiting his mother's grave. Three of his brothers and three sisters are interred here, in the Achille Indian Cemetery. He comes to speak, calls to all, and confesses the loneliness and listens. Spirits are awakened. This gateway to the afterlife is as close as he can get. As the Allante roars by the cemetery John calls out "Halito Mom," which means 'hello' in his Native language. "I'm late for church. I'll be back later for a long visit."

A mile down the road he turns left, pulls into a small gravel lot, and then parks on the grass. A sign over the front door of a building that might hold 75 people reads Achille Indian Baptist Church. Behind is a smaller wood frame camp house, not much more than a kitchen and a dining room with tables and chairs for maybe 25 people. Like most Sundays, a late lunch is served for the congregation after church. It is a casual time to mix, mingle and catch up with the Indian community gossip. The camp house also prepares and serves food for family members after funerals and burial services.

John Tall Bear sits in his car for a few moments and reflects back on last weekend's sweat ceremony. It was the first he had participated in many years, and experienced a vision. Ceremonial sweats have been an important part of Native tradition since the beginning of the Creator's work. After the 'white man' came, sweats were used to fend off the corrupting effect of alien contaminants. Re-purification from alcohol, sugars, grains, and inhumane treatment was foremost. Those urgent for traditional ways of living found answers in the sweat lodge ceremony. With the help of medicine men and women, they could repair the damage done to their minds, bodies and spirits. The sweat lodge is a place of spiritual refuge providing mental and physical healing. Answers and guidance can be gained through spiritual entities, totem helpers, and the Creator. In rare cases wisdom and power are granted. Sometimes, if one is in harmony with the Great Spirit, a vision will come.

The joyful sound of pounded piano keys and the congregation singing a favorite hymn prompts Tall Bear to exit his car and walk to the church. As he enters the front door, the congregation is standing and well into their first song. John is greeted by one of the older deacons, Glen Wilson. Glen, a white man in his late seventies, has been a fixture in the community for as long as John can remember. He and his wife, a local Indian woman, were faithful church members. Glen is alone now, his beloved Emma died years ago.

"Tall Bear, what a surprise to see you," he says with a smile in a low whisper.

"Halito Glen, it's so good to see you this morning. I would come more often but the gas is getting so doggone expensive."

"I know what you mean. Are you're staying for lunch?"

"If you're serving fried potatoes, I am. You know us Indians, we got to have fried potatoes."

"We can, but you got to peel them."

"I'm not above peeling potatoes, count me in," as Glen hands him the Sunday church pamphlet.

Tall Bear takes a seat behind an old friend, Rosella Gibson. She had remembered his last birthday and bought him a new Choctaw Hymn Book. He has been making an effort to remember his language and, of course, singing the songs helps. The pastor typically asks for a song from all the Choctaw singers. As always, a small group of 8 to 10 singers will make their way onto the stage and sing a couple of selections. This is one of the ways to keep the language alive. Tall Bear felt a little shy at first, but with Rosella's constant encouragement, he has begun to enjoy singing in the group. His mother would be proud of him today for making an effort to preserve her language.

Tall Bear's mother attended Chilocco Indian School in her youth. Chilocco opened its doors in 1884 and tens of thousands of young Indian children in her era were forced to attend. The federal government operated 100's of these schools throughout the country. All tribes largely remember it as a time of abuse and desecration of Indian culture. John's mother often spoke of how difficult boarding school was for her and her friends. The federal government's goal was to stamp out their language and culture. "Kill the Indian. . . Save the Child!" was their motto.

Speaking the Native languages was forbidden. That underlying thread was embedded in his mother when he was born, therefore it was easy for her to let the children speak English. Up until the time Tall Bear was six years old, they spoke Choctaw in their home. His mother and father were wonderful teachers of the language. When he began school as a first grader, things began to change. Slowly, the language slipped away. If only he could have realized the significance of losing his first tongue. But at such a young age Tall Bear could not have known this. As the only Indian family living in a small town in Oklahoma, his mother wanted John and his siblings to fit in, and thus the language was lost. Even as an adult, when his mother was alive, he saw no need to relearn the language. It was only after her death, he realized what he had lost. He had the perfect teacher under his nose. To this day, Tall Bear beats himself up, not taking advantage of her knowledge.

"Now, it's time for a couple of songs from the Choctaw Singers!" calls out Pastor Jonathan Tubby.

Jonathan is a wide body, as Indians say, and has a jolly disposition about him. He came from the northwest a couple of years ago and is a blessing to this church. He is a recovering alcoholic and a humble man because of it. He often interweaves some of the bad experiences from that life into his presentation. He has a commanding voice and can be very funny at times. His voice and presence are just what this church needs. Since he became pastor, church membership and new life has grown in Achille.

Following the songs and an inspiring sermon, the congregation retires to the camp house for lunch. True to his word, Glen hands Tall Bear a knife and a bowl of potatoes when he enters the camp house. John sits down at a small kitchen table with several Indian women, who are engaged in conversation about the local community. Soon, the question and answer session begins to be directed toward him. Most of them knew his mother, so Tall Bear is fair game for teasing, as Indian women like to do. If Indians like you, they will tease you.

One of the ladies says, "Now don't cut your finger, those are the only potatoes we have!" It wasn't long before they are trying to fix Tall Bear up with one of the eligible ladies from the church. Not a minute too soon, he makes his exit to the dining room. He joins a table where the pastor is holding court with a few members of the congregation.

"Tall Bear, I was waiting for lightning to strike the church when I saw you walk through the front door!"

"Very funny, Jonathan! It's almost as funny as some of those lame jokes in your sermon today."

"John, in my next life, I'm going to be a standup comedian, so I need to try my material on my congregation," says Jonathan as serious as he can.

"Jonathan, let me give you a little advice. As a good pastor, you have a sense of humor and a quick wit. In your next life, as a standup comedian, you'll going to need a second job."

Jonathan and everyone at the table burst out in laughter, and he says, "Well, in any event it is good to see you. How's everything in Dallas with you and the family?"

"Life is good, the children are working, my new granddaughter is walking and my golf swing is getting better."

"What's your handicap these days?" asks an unfamiliar man at the table.

"It's old age and short term memory. Thank goodness, my momma gave me a set of strong knees!" Extending his hand to the man he doesn't recognize, "Halito, I'm John Tall Bear."

Tall Bear instantly feels a sense of connection. *'Have I seen this young man before?'* Tall Bear sometimes, well many times, forgets names, but he never forgets a face. Perhaps in another lifetime Tall Bear knew him and his wife.

"I'm Roman Billy and this is my wife, Tammy Lynn. We're first time visitors today and wanted to come and hear your preacher speak. We've heard some good things about him. I've heard good things about you, too, and we were wondering when we might get to meet you."

"Has Jonathan been telling you wild tales about me?"

"A little, but we've seen the magazine covers and looked you up on the Internet."

"Wow, doing some homework."

Tall Bear is a little puzzled by their interest, but then the pastor's wife, Edna, announces lunch is ready and to get in line. Indian tradition feeds the visitors first and then the older men and women. John is ushered near the front of the line, behind the Romans, and next to his future wife, courtesy of the potato-peeling group.

Tall Bear spends the next hour stuffing himself with fried potatoes, green beans, fried chicken and lots of Indian tea. One of the reasons Indians suffer from diabetes is because of our super sweet Indian tea. Indians love their biscuits and fried bread as well. Most do not acknowledge the wisdom of their ancestors now referred to as "hunter/gatherers." If they followed this, they would be eating mostly small game, fish, nuts, fruit, berries, vegetables and drinking lots of water.

Before the white man came, the American Indians were lean and healthy. Diabetes did not exist. Hypertension and heart disease were non-existence. These were white man's diseases. The Indians had no flour, grain or white sugar. Hunting for food and fighting for their lives, they were fit as well. In the last few years, Tall Bear has adopted this philosophy. He wants to give honor to the wisdom of his people and insure good health for a long life. It is working for Tall Bear for he is in great shape for a man of his age. Today, he has taken a small step backward. He deviated from his healthy diet, but it was well worth it.

The last half hour is filled with engaging conversation from the rest of the group. Tall Bear doesn't want to leave anybody out as he moves from table to table. This is what his mother would have done. He is his mother's son and wants to be a good representative for her today. Finally, he says his farewells, for he has another important visit to enjoy. After an emotional stop at the cemetery, he leaves Achille, for Dallas. There is still plenty of light, to play 9 holes of golf before dark. Life is good.

As the Red Allante turns south on U.S 75 and roars toward Dallas, Roman Billy is pulling his pickup out of the church parking lot onto highway 78 towards Durant, OK. Tammy looks to her right and sees a tribal patrol car parked on the shoulder. Roman sees it also. As he speeds away, the patrol car pulls onto the highway and begins to follow. They look at each other, but neither says a word. They can't imagine why the tribal patrol car was just waiting on a lonely two-lane highway on Sunday afternoon. Nobody was out except a few church people.

After a couple of miles, Tammy begins to get nervous. Then, after four or five miles the patrol car hits its lights, and the squawk from the patrol car siren startles them both. Roman eases the pickup onto the shoulder and both vehicles come to a stop. Roman retrieves his wallet from his back pocket, and he and Tammy wait for a long minute or two. The driver appears to be on a cell phone. The second officer in the passenger seat appears to become agitated and animated. The patrol car abruptly backs up, and pulls quickly onto the highway and speeds away.

Roman looks at his worried wife and says, "What was that all about?"

"Honey, I have no idea. You know the tribal police. They can do as they please."

"Maybe they got a more important call."

The night before, their young son, Michael, and his friend were on their way home from the bowling alley. A tribal patrol car had stopped them for no reason. Both were handcuffed and questioned for 30 minutes on the side of the highway. The two officers found nothing to hold them on and let them go. Michael had complained the cuffs were so tight his fingers became numb. Most of the tribal police officers are white and some don't hesitate to harass the local Indians.

"Do you think this has something to do with Michael and his friend getting stopped last night?" asks Tammy.

"I'm not sure, but it appears that we are being watched."

"Now I'm getting a little scared. Maybe you should mention this at tonight's meeting."

"I will, but I don't want to get everyone upset."

CHAPTER 2

Almost back to Dallas, John steers the Allante directly to The Old Course at Freewheel in a northeastern suburb. Golf is a relatively new passion he can enjoy on the spur of the moment. Make a shot and then suffer the consequences. Decisions, obstacles, maneuver, solutions, all in a walk through lush fairways, among the trees and creeks, and shared with the squirrels, ducks, bobcats and yes, snakes.

Tall Bear is a natural athlete and plays the game well, believing the sport allows the weekend golfer the same thrill as a pro. Alone on the tee at the fourteenth, a 195 yard par 3, he pulls out a new Titleist Pro V1 ball, selects a 5 iron and tees up. He acknowledges the danger of the bunker on the left, the line of houses on the right. Because of the low light, his depth of field is not as good as it once was. With the setting sun on his back, he makes his final adjustments, swings and releases the ball to its unknown destination.

Once a $4 Pro V1 leaves the face of the club head, once you release the butterfly from the safety of your palm, hand your car keys to your 16 year old daughter, know you have stepped through another doorway and are no longer in control. He tracks the flight, sensing on impact it had good possibilities. The Titleist hits the front of the green, rolls some twenty feet toward the back right flagstick, and then disappears from his view. Did his eyes fail him, or did he just make a hole in one? John looks around for someone to validate or celebrate his moment of glory. He walks down to the green to confirm the shot. John and the Creator know the Pro V1 found sanctuary in the hole.

John, seeing no reason to finish the round, strides to his red Allante and drives home.

John Wilkerson Tall Bear is a man from two different worlds. He is a product of an era when the federal government was doing everything in its power to strip the American Indian of his identity. John's mother and father had already experienced the same thing, but on a more complex level. Prejudice was alive and well in Oklahoma where John grew up in the 40's & 50's. His was the only Indian family in a small town and, like any young person this affected his outlook on life. In some cases there were two sets of rules, one for him, one for his white counterpart. He quickly had to learn which set of rules to follow. He didn't think it was fair and couldn't understand the discrepancy, but adjusted as best he could. Challenged daily because of his heritage, he used ancestral teaching to endure the pain and suffering.

For much of his first 17 years, John actually believed there was something wrong with him. He was made to feel inferior and ashamed to be an American Indian. Even today, though mature, sophisticated, and supposed to know better, those humiliating early years are hard to forget.

Most vividly, one Saturday at the town square, a drawing was held, for several baskets of food from the local grocery store. The only requirement was to possess the winning ticket. And his numbers matched that eventful morning. He was so happy you'd have thought he'd just won a million dollars. Compared to the US Government food commodity the family received once a month, the basket of store-bought food was going to be a treat for his family of nine.

As his heart danced with joy, he ascended the stairs of the town square gazebo to present his ticket to the town Sheriff. The requirement suddenly changed. The winning number was acknowledged, but he was briskly told he wasn't old enough to win. Turning away he couldn't help but search the sea of white faces for a friendly set of eyes, hoping someone would come to his rescue. Each and every one of them knew his family needed the food more than anyone else there.

His panic was met with bowed heads and vacant stares. Standing alone, John realized no one cared. The Sheriff quickly called another number. Who was he, just a little Indian boy?

As he descended those stairs, tears began to well in his eyes. He grew up a little bit. If only he'd had the courage to challenge the sheriff, he would have asked, '*Why, just a week ago, did a girl younger than me win a basket of food for her family?*' She was white and he was an Indian boy. The memory of a sign, at the outskirts of this small Oklahoma town, flashed through his mind. '*Nigger don't let the sun set on your back.*' He didn't belong here, his hometown.

What little acceptance he eventually got, was due to the athletic prowess he displayed on the basketball court, baseball diamond and in the boxing ring. Black children were feeling the same oppression John was experiencing in the Deep South. Had he only known, he might not have felt so alone. Though little consolation to the boy, the day would come when John, blossomed. He would hold his head high, proud to be an American Indian and proud of his racist nickname.

Chief, staring at the big clock on the wall on the last school day, he was oblivious to the chatter and excitement of fellow classmates, inattentive to his 3rd grade teacher, giving last minute instructions. When the bell rang to end the day, heart pounding, Chief could feel his stomach begin to knot up, not with boyish anticipation, but with fear. He took his time packing his things, and was last to leave the room.

As he plodded down the hall to the front exit, his friends raced by to get home and play. School was out for the year, and many were ready to dive into summer vacations. Chief could not see that far ahead. It was the next fifteen minutes that concerned him. He felt scared to death not wanting to go outside, knowing soon the principal would be locking the door. He had no choice but to leave the building. He lived only three blocks from school, but the daily trip seemed an eternity. What he feared had happened before, in fact, almost every day since starting public school. About halfway home,

Chief's personal bully, with his gang in tow, was lurking in wait for the Indian boy.

At the time, Chief didn't know why he was being picked on. To this day he can't remember the bully's name. Nor may the adversary know he helped transform John Tall Bear. The defining moment was unforgettable. The bully found Chief's weakness when he delivered a punch to his stomach. Chief would crumble to the ground. It was over for a day.

That afternoon would be like many arriving home late and scuffed up. His mother would be there to listen to his problems. He would tell her what he was experiencing while she would comfort him in her loving arms. She disapproved of fighting, explaining in time, his problems would go away. Occasionally, his bruised ego was soothed with an extra piece of pie or cake. And his problem did go away, this time literally. The bully went to California for the summer. Chief spent the whole vacation without fear of getting beat up.

It finally occurred to him to ask his father for some fighting tips. On weekends their family would travel south to Atoka, OK, to participate in weekend gatherings of worship and socializing. It was a time for him to try out wrestling techniques with other cousins and friends. Throughout the summer, he began to gain more confidence in his fighting and wrestling ability. He also grew a few inches taller.

The last month of the summer, the family traveled south to the cotton fields outside of Honey Grove, Texas. Chief's father had contracted with a farmer there to live on property and pick his cotton. Living in a broken down shack with no electricity or running water was nothing new. They would pick cotton from sunup to sundown. The long hours and demanding work was a character builder. The hard work built up his stamina, and he grew stronger and more confident as the weeks went by.

On Saturday they would go into Honey Grove for clothing and enough food for the next week. He was the oldest of ten and his brothers and sisters looked forward to weekend trips into town. Buying pop and candy maybe see a movie made their weekend. Chief was allotted a new pair of Levi's, two t-shirts, socks and underwear for his wardrobe to start the school year. With an eventful summer almost over, John's family broke camp and started for home. The long trip home gave him time to ponder what might happen when he met his adversary next. He went over many scenarios in his mind and, for the first time, realized he was no longer scared. In fact, he was eager for that encounter.

Arriving home, the very small one bedroom house with a wooden front porch looked like a palace. There was a kitchen, a larger living area and a small room in the back. He and his brothers shared the back bedroom. It felt comforting to sleep in his bed. Their parents slept in the main room of the house with the girls on the other end of the room. Crowded? Chief didn't think so, because they didn't know any better. They were all just happy to be home.

A schoolmate announced to Chief his adversary was back in town. One evening after dinner, he decides its time to get the eventual meeting over. The malt shop across from the school is where he will find him. The bully is sitting in one of the booths with a group of friends. He is laughing and having a good time. Chief didn't know where the courage came from. He just walked up to him and challenged him. Chief ordered him outside to the basketball gymnasium, and walked out the door.

Chief could imagine what was happening back at the malt shop now. When a fight is imminent, everyone stops what they're doing and gather to watch. Chief knew he was coming, because it would have been unforgivable for him to back down to an Indian. Chief had brought just one friend along, and he was only there to watch. As a growing group of boys and girls crossed the street, Chief's adrenaline began to pump. He was a little scared, but at the same time he felt confident.

With his friend Freddy Boner, he walked to the west side of the gymnasium. There was a large grassy area bordering the length of the gym. Chief had selected an area he wanted to defend, and turned around to watch the crowd choose their places. A group of about twenty boys and girls formed a crescent behind Chief's bully. It looked like a scene in a Hollywood movie. The two postured for a few moments eye-to-eye, saying nothing. The bully moved closer and threw his favorite weapon, a right hook to Chief's body. This had worked for him many times over the last years. Chief moved to one side, evading the full force of the punch. Chief had caught a glancing blow, but assured had he taken the full blow, he would still be standing. He knew he would win this battle.

Chief countered quickly with a left jab and a right cross to the face sending the bully stumbling backward. The right punch busted his nose, and he began to bleed a little. He regained his balance and charged. The two met in a clinch like wrestlers, each with hands on the other's upper biceps. This close, Chief could see, his right to the face had also caught the corner of the mouth, and caused bleeding. Without thinking, Chief released his left hand, circled it around his opponent's neck and pulled him in close like you kiss a girlfriend. Chief stepped, with his left foot across and in front of the bully's left leg, his buttocks in front of the his left hip in position for a takedown. He lifted him off his feet. Then, turning a little clockwise, Chief slammed him hard to the ground, timing it to fall on top the opponent who's landed on his back.

In modern day fighting techniques, this movement in the US, would later be more widely known as a Judo hip throw. Chief had never witnessed any form of martial arts, which was in its infancy in the western world. His family had no television in the early 50's, so where would he have studied such a move? He called it 'Talihina' and it became one of the anchors in the system Chief would eventually name 'Red Warrior'.

When the bully hit the ground he made an awful sound. The force of the fall had knocked the air out of him. As he seemed to wilt in Chief's arms for a moment, Chief felt relieved. He could hear the crowd yelling in the background trying to rally the groggy bully to victory. Chief wasn't going to let that happen. Just as the boy on the bottom regained some fight, Chief released his hold on his left hand and sent a flurry of right punches to his face. It was over. Chief could tell the crowd was angry he had beaten one of theirs badly. As he got up and walked away, he stared at hateful piercing eyes. Chief had seen this look, years ago, at the Saturday morning town square drawing for a food basket. At seven, he had felt sad and confused. Now, angry and arrogant, he smiled and walked away.

Chief's new reputation as a street fighter was born that night. The fighting didn't stop it only got worse. Now everybody wanted to fight the 'Chief'. Consequently, his destiny was shaped. Many today, study in schools called dojos. What Chief learned in street fighting was survival and acceptance. As a student of hand-to-hand combat, he developed fighting techniques for real life situations and became teacher, ultimately, the master.

———————

After showering and a healthy dinner to replenish lost energy, John winds down the evening watching a little television. There is nothing of interest on, so his thoughts replay Sunday's events. It was great to visit the church, to hear Tubby preach. His message was exhilarating. He had fun lunching with all the church members, especially those who had known his mother. Still, his meeting with the Roman Billy family puzzled him.

CHAPTER 3

J ohn will come to know Roman and Tammy Billy were childhood sweethearts. They'd known each other most of their lives.
Everybody knows everyone in Bokchito, Oklahoma, a tiny town in
the heart of Indian country. In Choctaw, Bokchito means 'big creek'.

Their families had long been involved in the church. After graduating high school, the couple married, just before Roman enlisted in
the Marines. That year, while he was away on his first tour, their son
Michael was born. Tammy worked at the local Wal-Mart and began
raising the baby. With the help of family and friends, she attended
college at Southeastern State in nearby Durant, OK and studied to
become a teacher.

During her third year of school, Tammy gave birth to their first
daughter, Martha Jo. The new addition placed added responsibilities
on the family, so Tammy put school on hold for a year. By this time
Roman had made sergeant and received a pay increase. They moved
to a military base in southern California to be together again. Tammy
was able to complete college and receive her degree in elementary
education. As Roman's tour was winding down, the family decided,
when it was over, they would return home to Bokchito. Tammy began
teaching at the local elementary school, and Roman working as a loan
officer at a bank in Durant.

Durant, OK, thirty miles west of Bokchito, is headquarters to the
Choctaw Nation. The Nation has a huge impact on Durant's economy,
especially the two casinos that bring in millions of dollars every month.
They have Choctaw Casino satellite locations throughout the Nation.

This area is thriving with great economic success and home to 16,000 people. The city is rich in Choctaw history.

Roman and Tammy Billy didn't smoke or drink, and attended church on a regular basis. Their young family has been a wonderful addition to the Bokchito community. They did okay financially, by adhering to a tight budget. Both were full blood Choctaws and tribal members most of their lives. When needed, they utilized services the Choctaw Nation offered. The Nation, thriving from the gaming industry, was building and providing more services in their hospital, dental clinic, and wellness centers.

A famous movie line, "If you build it, they will come" took on a precautionary tone with the arrival of the uninvited 'white Choctaws'. It's not that these people were entirely to blame. They simply took advantage of the Choctaw Tribe's inadequate membership requirements. The Chief and its administration shared fault for not imposing stricter guidelines.

After four or five years, while using many of the Nations services the Billy's began to notice things were not right. They began to witness injustices against their people by the staff members of the Nation. This prompted questions of fellow Choctaws at church and other functions. Others had witnessed similar things, mounting issues, and feeling isolated spurred charges of systemic impropriety. Discussions took place at sewing groups, at dinner outings, and soon a network began to form.

Alerted to rising speculation, they didn't know how to respond or even if they should. As their number became larger, they considered how to better organize. They had to be careful for the Choctaw Nation and its Chief were very powerful. Those who worked for the Choctaw Nation were afraid to speak out fearing of losing their jobs. Unaware they were birthing a new movement, they felt invisible among their own tribe.

Roman, the former Marine, and Tammy, a schoolteacher, soon became the unofficial leaders of this cadre. Because of their success in life, they were thrust into leadership roles. The couple for a year has attended small secret meetings. In the beginning, most were held in homes throughout the thirteen counties that make up the Choctaw Nation. As conferences grew larger, Indian churches hosted them, most, out in the country on gravel roads.

These small churches have few members, on average, between fifteen and twenty-five. Indian people love to sing gospel hymns and attend gatherings, called 'singings'. Many form quartets and traveled from church to church to keep the songs alive and gain recognition. Singing events held every week is a perfect cover to hold secret meetings. Small groups of elders meet behind the scenes to talk politics.

Roman makes his way, driving down a red dirt road, maneuvering the potholes from thunderstorms the night before. He and Tammy are on their way to a church compound in the country called Bacon Springs, famous for killing a hog on Saturday and serving it to all the people who attended on Sunday.

These weekend events grew so large Bacon Springs built three camp houses. These were wonderful gatherings alive with women preparing meals, children running about, and music from the church filling the air. On Saturday afternoon the young men and boys would play baseball or softball on a nearby open field. At the same time, an older group of men would kill the hog and pit roast it to feed the congregation. In the middle, a fire ablaze with a huge iron cooking pot created a savory aroma you could smell for a mile. An underground spring spouted crystal clear and ice cold waters even in dry summers.

Observing the scene Tammy says, "Roman, It looks like we're going to have a good crowd tonight."

"It does appear the crowds are getting larger. We've got some momentum going."

"We're going to need all the support we can get."

As they approach the front door, they hear pounding of piano keys executed with precision. "That's got to be Buddy Mack Billey playing the piano tonight!"

Buddy Mack is a distant cousin from Hugo, Oklahoma, who can fire up a congregation and masterfully keep singers in tune for hours. After about thirty minutes of songs, Roman and Tammy, observe some select people making their way out of the church. It's time for the meeting to begin.

They proceed to the camp house where coffee and donuts are being served. In a separate room in the back, a dozen elders plus have gathered. They are waiting for Roman. As he makes his way to a small table in the front, he shakes hands and greets everyone along the way. The former marine is perfect for his role in these meetings. He is not afraid to take charge if needed. He is also a kind and friendly guy, who doesn't want to impose his will on anyone. He stands about 6'2", 220 an imposing and commanding figure. Yet, among his people, Roman is a teddy bear, well liked and respected."

"Halito Chukma, I want to thank all of you for coming tonight. I know time is short, so I will get to the point of this meeting. As you know, we have been considering who should lead us on our journey.

This morning, Tammy and I met the man many of you have agreed on. Our meeting was short, but after watching him interact with the people at his church, Achille Indian, I can tell you without a doubt he's the right man for our mission. I want to thank our research committee for your efforts. We have all seen the magazine covers and articles, read his philosophy on web sites. We could not have picked a better person.

"John Wilkerson Tall Bear's life story is something all Indians, regardless of tribal affiliation, should be proud of. He grew up in a small town just up the road, Kiowa, Oklahoma, if I remember right. His family moved to Dallas in the Relocation Program. Well, if he survived that, he's got to be a good man. He went on to become some-what of a celebrity in the martial arts world. He has raised several children, doesn't smoke or drink, and looks like someone our children can look up to."

"Do you think he will be interested in what we have to offer?" asks one of the elders in the front row.

"I'm not sure. What I have read on his web site gives me a feeling he might. He appears to shoot from the hip, and from what I gather, he's not afraid to rattle some cages."

"I make a motion that we invite him to speak at our next meeting. If all goes well, we can ask him then," says someone else from the back of the room.

"I second that," says another.

"I'll see to it the invitation is extended, and before we adjourn, I want to say this, ...I don't want anyone to get paranoid, ...but I have reason to believe some of us are being watched. Tammy and I were stopped after church just outside of Achille Indian. A tribal patrol car stopped us and sat behind us for a few minutes and then sped off. So please be careful when you travel home at night, and be sure the person you are speaking with shares your views and ideals."

After a short prayer, the meeting is adjourned.

CHAPTER 4

The following Thursday morning, Tall Bear receives a call from Roman Billy. Roman refers to their brief meeting the previous Sunday and asks John would he be interested in talking to the congregation at a church the next Wednesday night. John has done a few speaking engagements, but not at churches. When he expresses reservations, Roman counters convincingly an Indian audience will find John's life story compelling. Roman makes a point he might help redirect some misguided individual to follow in his footsteps. John can't say no, and accepts the invitation willingly.

Wednesday evening, John is on his way to Indian Country again, the town of Atoka, OK, the county seat. His father was born and raised nearby, in Bentley. As a boy, John joined his family hundreds of times there for singing events. People would travel hundreds of miles to attend these functions. The two lane black top highway, now in bad need of repair, was a dirt road back then.

John thinks back, amazed their old Pontiac survived trips like those. He contrasts the $65,000 two-seat Allante he's driving with the old $100 Pontiac that carried a whole family. He embarrassed and a little ashamed his parents couldn't experience a nicer car. Approaching the small of town of Bentley, he reminisces a lifelong journey in the martial arts. In his writing, John refers to those joyous times as the Movement of Life.

Turning left into the compound and inching down a small hill, he takes time to observe several familiar houses situated to his right. John tries to remember which family lived where, concluding most are dead and gone. Several years earlier, doing research, he had visited and consulted with an old Indian named Chata Jim, a master in the art of the Choctaw blowgun. John thinks perhaps some relatives of the old master might still live here. To honor and respect his teaching, John must pass that knowledge on.

Despite the parking area being unpaved, the thirty to forty cars outside Macedonia Indian Church were parked in orderly fashion. Guest speaker John Tall Bear is impressed with the good turnout and begins to get excited. Walking toward the church, he notices an arbor on the north side, a weather shade like the one 40 years ago, though he is sure it has been replaced many times over. The logs look freshly cut. There are six poles, about eight feet apart, that support many small branches with smaller limbs and leaves still attached. The arbor is used at outdoors meals, a place for friendly conversation. It serves as good cover from the hot summer sun, even shelter in a light rain.

Thought to be arriving early as he enters the church, he is surprised to find so many people already seated. The interior layout is typical, pews on the left and right with a center aisle. Highly visible, John spots Roman Billy and quickly makes his way to the front, taking a seat beside him.

"So glad you could attend, Mr. Tall Bear," says Roman including a handshake, at the same time he motions another who's onstage, the speaker has arrived.

"Bare with us and we'll announce you very shortly."

John nods confirmation and scans the room. The majority of the audience is dressed very casually. To his right he sees a few people that appear almost out of place. The group of four is well dressed, and professional looking. One of them is a stunning woman in her late 40's with shoulder length dark brown hair. Her presentation is very classy. A stylish light brown dress exposes a pair of toned, shapely legs. She smiles when she turns to see him looking at her. John feels a little silly as he smiles back, then averts his gaze to the rest of the congregation. He notices a few other familiar faces and reviews his presentation notes silently.

Another song, then the director announces, "Our distinguished speaker for tonight has arrived, and I'm going to turn the microphone over. Here's someone you all know, Mr. Roman Billy." The audience immediately applauds.

Roman moves to the podium, clearly comfortable in front of this audience. Still in good shape, his broad shoulders and an engaging smile put everyone at ease.

"Halito Chukma, I want to thank you all for coming tonight. We're going to take a short intermission in a few minutes, but before we do, Tall Bear, will you join me on stage?"

"Many here have read the bulletin. For those who missed it, without further ado, here's Mr. John Wilkerson Tall Bear. Say a few words and save the good stuff for after coffee and cake."

This speaking arrangement puzzles John a little, but during the welcoming applause, he gathers his thoughts enough to present a brief history of himself. Not one for boasting, he keeps the preview short, preferring a slice of cake and meeting some of the audience, especially the attractive lady in the brown dress. The ten-minute intermission is spent with numerous introductions before Tammy Billy calls the congregation to order. John, unable to pass the crowd on the left side of the church fails to chat up the dark haired woman who'd caught his eye. Five chairs have been placed on stage, and Tammy directs him to the center chair.

Tammy is a tiny woman. She stands about 5' 2" and probably weighs no more than 125 lbs. John thinks she looks like a little China doll. She bears a striking resemblance to his first wife who he met in a church very much like this. Tonight, Tammy wears her black hair down to the middle of her back. John remembers the day at the church, when she had it up in a ponytail. She seems the perfect life partner for Roman, friendly and even more outgoing than her husband. In most Indian families, the women usually have the last word.

There are some exceptions. In the Roman family Tammy, the devoted wife and mother, generally defers to her husband.

"Please, please, everyone," Tammy calls out, "have a seat so we can get started." As the audience quiets down, she continues. "First, I want to thank the ladies for the wonderful cake and coffee." She turns to John and smiles, "I know Mr. Tall Bear enjoyed it because he had two pieces."

"That second piece was forced on me."

"Mr. Tall Bear, I want you to hear some stories from the people seated next to you. After they have spoken, we want you to speak and then we will ask your advice and counsel. Our first speaker is one of our senior elders, Mrs. Jim."

Mrs. Jim appears to be in her eighties and needs help getting out of her chair and up to the podium. John immediately recognizes her as one of Chata Jim's eldest daughters. He remembers her as the quiet one. As she is being assisted, he gazes out onto the audience. Something clicks upstairs. He notices there are no mixed bloods Choctaws here, as one sees most of the time. Surprisingly, everyone here is full blood or close to it. He has not witnessed a congregation like this in over forty-five years. *'What the hell is going on?'*

Mrs. Jim begins to speak in a Native rhythm. "When I go to the clinic, I have to sit and wait all day. I sign in early in the morning and watch others who come in after me get waited on. Lately the ladies who work at desk are not so nice to me. I don't want to complain, but at my age it's difficult to sit all day. I'm Choctaw, but I can tell you many of those who get help before me are not Choctaw at all. You all knew my father Chata Jim. As he got older he got very stubborn. When I used to take him to the clinic, he would sit all day and never say a word. I wished he had spoken up. Later, he refused to go to the clinic anymore. He died from a simple infection penicillin could have prevented. He could have lived many more years if he had gotten treatment. But he got condescending treatment at the clinic, and he would not go back. Today, as his oldest daughter, I am speaking up for my father. Old people don't like change, but change is needed at the clinic and those who run it. Thank you." Mrs. Jim makes her way off the stage with help, and resumes a seat in the audience.

Jo Ann James is the next speaker, a lady in her late forties. She is a very nice looking woman, but what looks strange and out of place is a pair of scissors in one hand and a small object in the other.

"Out of respect to my mother, I want to learn to speak Choctaw better," she begins. "I was told the Choctaw Nation is offering classes at a college in Dallas. I enrolled and attended a Choctaw Language class at Brookhaven College there. I would drive down to Dallas three times a week to go to class. The teacher was good, and I was learning once again to speak Choctaw. I was so happy. One week the Choctaw Nation provided some guest speakers to the class. The three speakers included a full blood husband and wife team, and their supervisor, who was part Choctaw. He was very little Choctaw at all, but spoke the language very well. There were about 15 of us class members who witnessed a conversation out in the open for all to hear.

"I'm not sure how the conversation got onto the subject matter, but the full blood Choctaw wife mentioned her supervisor gets faster care when he goes to the clinic, even if she gets there before him. They were joking and laughing because it was common knowledge. I could not believe my ears. The non-Indian supervisor gets faster care, because he identifies more closely with the people giving out the services. He laughed it off. Teasing, he could flirt with the ladies behind the counter. This is another example of perverse discrimination. The full bloods are being treated like second-class citizens in a facility that is there to serve them. This did not make me feel good. To be treated like this by my own people, makes me feel sad and ashamed. I want to feel proud as a member of the Choctaw Nation, but I am not feeling proud." She holds up her tribal membership card and, before she leaves the stage, she cuts her card in half with the scissors. It is a powerful statement.

John starts to feel a little nervous, because he doesn't know why he is sitting on this stage. *'What the hell am I going to say when they call me to speak?'* he thinks, his mind racing, trying to put something together fumbling with his notes. *'No luck, I'll just wait it out and improvise on the spot.'* He begins to sweat a little.

The third speaker is a gentleman in his early 50's. He is dressed in blue jeans, tennis shoes, and wears a red baseball cap with the Choctaw Nation logo on the front.

"Halito Chukma, you all know me, I'm Thomas Sanders. I work for the Nation in their housing division. We all work long hard hours building Indian homes. There are not enough Indian homes to go around. We work as fast as we can, getting them ready for our people to move in. At election time, the Chief requests us to come help build election signs and put them up around the town and the thirteen counties. When he is speaking, we have to come and listen. This is on our day off, and we never get paid for it. We have to attend, because if we don't we will lose our jobs. My health is not getting better, so I may have to quit soon anyway. That is why I am here tonight. What do I have to lose? I see people move into Indian homes, and I wonder who they are. They don't look like you and me. My family has been here since the Choctaw Nation had very little money and no services to offer. It was a good time then because we dealt with Choctaws. I remember Chief Belvin, who served for several decades, was a very great Chief. Today I miss him. Thank you." Mr. Sanders leaves the stage and takes a seat in the audience by his family.

Tammy, returning to the podium, announces, "Our next speaker, and last before Mr. Tall Bear, is my husband, Roman. Doesn't he look pretty? I dressed him tonight!" The audience bursts out in laughter as she signals him to join her. The small church comes alive as Roman takes the stage, looking a little embarrassed.

"Thank you, thank you. This is a serious occasion tonight, so Tammy bought me in a new monkey suit straight from Wal-Mart." He laughs out loud, and the congregation joins him.

"Seriously, tonight is a special occasion, and I'm so pleased to see a good turnout. As you all know, Tammy, my family, my brothers and I have been working with all of you in forming a plan of action. We have all heard the stories. We all have grave concerns about the direction of the Choctaw Nation and how it affects us. Years ago, the Nation was given the authority to build bingo halls, and the casinos you see today. We had to serve many people for us to continue to get federal money. Bottom line is, the more people we have and serve, the more money we get from Uncle Sam. The quickest way to create a larger tribe was to lower the minimum blood requirement to become a member. Originally, the federal government set the blood quantum at one quarter. In other words, all you had to do was prove you were one quarter Indian by using the roll number from the Dawes Act.

"The Federal government didn't want to be accused of setting the standard for 'what is an Indian', so they gave the tribes the authority to decide in 1975, with the Indian Self-Determination Act. I know many of you are Mississippi Choctaw. You will be proud to know the Mississippi tribe requirement is one-half and strictest of all. Because of greed, other Nations have dropped their minimum blood requirement as low as 1/64th. The Choctaw Nation of Oklahoma requires the least Indian blood of all at 'one drop'. The Nation boasts over 200,000 strong. The watered down blood quantum dilutes the tribe to the point we look like everybody else. The membership pool is so large it makes delivery of services to all Choctaws thin or non-existent. But when the Chief goes to Washington and asks for more money, he has a very large voice. In these difficult times, when so many in America have lost their jobs, and homes, the average citizens should be appalled, paying tax money to our Nation and its Chief as they play this numbers game.

"A major problem with this one drop blood quantum requirement is, the sovereignty of the Choctaw Nation could be in jeopardy. One day Washington will look at the Choctaw Nation and say 'Wait a minute, you Choctaw Indians have blond hair and blue eyes, and you don't look any more Indian than we do'. The federal government could force us to disband and revoke our sovereignty. We would lose our leverage for gaming and casinos, or forced to take the federal government as our partner.

"If we were able to average the blood quantum of all the members of the Choctaw Nation, we could guess, the average would be one sixteenth. So in my opinion, the Choctaw Nation, as a whole, is a fraud. They are riding the coattails of the brave, full bloods, who survived the bitter winter on the Trail of Tears, in 1832. Had it not been for those brave and resilient people, there would be no access to services the Nation has to offer.

"I want to read the following from this sheet of paper, so I don't miss anything. This information includes a lot of historical data, and I want to make sure I inform you correctly. We want to assemble a group of Choctaws using the Dawes Rolls to authenticate their blood quantum. We want to be recognized as a new tribe of Full-blood Choctaws.

"The Dawes Commission created the Dawes Rolls, or Final Rolls of Citizens and Freedmen of the Five Civilized Tribes. The United States Congress authorized the Commission in 1893. The Commission was required to negotiate with the Five Civilized Tribes to convince them to agree to an allotment plan and dissolution of the reservation system. In doing so, The Dawes Commission established the Indian blood quantum of each member of the five tribes. Consisting of the Choctaw, Cherokee, Creek, Chickasaw, and Seminole.

Reading further from his cheat sheet Roman continued. "The Dawes Commission was quickly flooded by applicants from all over the country trying to get on the rolls. More than 250,000 people applied for membership, and the Dawes Commission enrolled just over 100,000 Indians. An act of Congress, on April 26, 1906, closed the rolls.

"Our new tribe will make application to the federal government, to be recognized as the real Choctaw Nation of Oklahoma. How could they not acknowledge a tribe made of full blood Choctaws? A Choctaw Full Blood 4/4 is absolute and pure and can never be in question," proudly states Roman Billy as he steps back from the podium.

The audience now roars and jumps to its feet. John's jaw drops and, again, he feels confused. Though he understands and completely agrees with what the other speakers have stated, he knows what Roman proposes is difficult, and has no precedent. It takes years, and in most cases never, for a group of Indians to be federally recognized. He has a sense history is being made tonight in this little Indian church.

CHAPTER 5

Tammy rushes to her husband and they embrace, and then stand back to enjoy the scene. What a team they make. They smile and just let the audience have its way for a few minutes. Eventually, Roman steps back to the podium, and raises his hands to ask for quiet. He looks directly at John and says, "Mr. Tall Bear, our members have researched your life and shared that information to a search group. As authorized nominating committee chairman, I ask will you lead this new tribe, and be its Chief."

John's hands and feet go numb. His blood pressure skyrockets. Flushed for a moment, he can't seem to move or say anything. The eruption of the crowd again gives him time to compose himself. He's been blindsided, but for good cause. Roman's extended hand motions for John to stand and address the assembly. John stands, his legs, suddenly a little weak. He has no idea what he is going to say. Gripping both sides of the podium top just to steady self, he lowers his head and begins to think of his mother. He can picture her sitting in the audience, beaming with pride. To even be considered to lead his people is more honors than he could have imagined. Deliberately gathering his emotions, he raises his head and gazes out over the crowd attempting to make eye contact with some, but unable to see through the tears threaten to fall.

"Thank you, thank you," he says, waiting for the applause to die down. "First, I want to thank you all for considering me. It's a great honor and privilege. This is a total surprise, and I don't know what to say. I consider myself a very spontaneous person and able to make snap decisions. However, considering the enormous responsibility of such a distinguished office, I must decline. I will need more time to consider if I am qualified and even worthy."

Roman quickly jumps up and says, "Why don't we take another short break and let Mr. Tall Bear reconsider. We still have plenty of cake and coffee available."

Everyone again applauds, rising to their feet, beginning to move about, talking excitedly in undertones to one another. There is less interest in cake and coffee than in the subject at hand. Roman grabs John's arm and leads him off the stage, surprisingly in the direction of the attractive lady in the brown dress.

"John Tall Bear, I want to introduce you to one of the most influential person in the state. This is Senator Rachel Jim."

"This is truly a night for surprises," as John extends his hand. "Senator Jim, it's an honor to meet you."

"Mr. Tall Bear, I've heard so much about you. My grandfather spoke of you many times."

"Of course, of course. I remember Chata Jim. I can see the resemblance in your eyes. I really enjoyed my short time with him. I had no idea he had such a distinguished granddaughter."

"I had not run for office at the time you knew him. I had just gotten out of school."

"Well you have certainly made up for lost time. Wow, a United States Senator."

"They really surprised you tonight, didn't they?"

"Did you know about the offer?"

"Yes I did. I was consulted and gave you my full recommendation."

"Well, if you don't mind my asking. How do you fit into all of this?"

"I'll be the new tribe's connection with the political machinery. I have the support of several members of the House and one other Senator."

"Do you think they, we, actually have a chance at being recognized?"

"Anything is possible in this day and age. It's a good time we attempt something. The timing couldn't be better with a new President in office. The tribe needs a mature leader, one who will give them stability and guidance. You would make a wonderful figurehead, Mr. Tall Bear, I hope you will reconsider."

Minutes later the meeting is again called to order. Returning to the stage, Tammy invites questions and statements from the congregation. Someone raises her hand, and Tammy acknowledges her.

"Mr. Tall Bear," a lady in the back of the room rises, "If it's ok, I'd like to read something posted on an Internet blog about you."

"Yes, sure," John settles into his seat not knowing what to expect.

She begins, "John Tall Bear, to me, was a person larger than life. He had a commanding presence, a quiet air of authority and an exotic quality about him that people are attracted to. A man with the confidence level of a lion, who doesn't say much. Yet, when he speaks, he uses straight talk, and when he answers, gives simple answers. When he asks a question, it has a purpose. He was nice looking, a bit stern sometimes when he was concentrating. But then all of a sudden there would be this grin that would spread across his face. His eyes would light up with sparkling glints and for a brief moment you could see the little boy in him."

"Over the next few months, there were times when I thought I knew and understood him. Then all of a sudden, something would happen that showed a new side of him, one I had not known existed. On the surface, he could be a powerful man with an arrogance about him that could stop someone in their tracks from investigating further. What I mistook for arrogance was pride. He was a proud man. He was proud of who he is, for he is an Indian. He is an American Indian, in politically correct terms 'Native American'. I thought, 'so what! So he's Native American'. Some of us are Irish, some are French, and some Asian. It's good to know who you are, to know your roots, but why does he feel so strongly about his ancestry. He tried to explain to me the prejudices against American Indians.

"In my own sheltered little world, I had never witnessed any prejudices and couldn't imagine why anyone would be prejudiced against John's race. They were here first. They had a quiet beauty about them. When they laughed it was like music. When they spoke, there was almost a melody in their voice, and when they were sad, it was a deep sadness you could feel.

"I listened to the stories he told me of his childhood. I listened to the stories he told me about some of the things his own children had endured. I came to know his three children. They began to tell me stories they knew about their father. They told me how often others mistreated them at school because they were 'different'. I learned from them, that too often the rest of us close our eyes and don't see what is there. We are not the ones experiencing prejudice. But if the same thing were happening to you, you would notice. You would remember. You would not forget.

"Now I understand why John has prejudices of his own. It's not against other races. It's on behalf of his race. He is angry no one stands up for the American Indians. No one recognizes the contribution they have made to our country. Some progress is being made, but at a very slow rate. The sad thing is his race continues to be diminished, when it deserves recognition and appreciation.

"So this man I know is quietly and slowly bringing attention to his American Indian heritage. All his life, he tried to prove himself to others by striving to be the best at whatever sport or hobby he participated in. Did he do this for himself? Maybe, but he did it mostly to show people American Indians were just as good, have just as much talent and ability to do anything any other race of people could do.

"As he grew older, he became an expert in martial arts. He wasn't a man who accepted second best. This seemed to be his calling. He did well at other careers and endeavors, but for some reason martial arts was his passion. He became successful at teaching American Kenpo, and had several studios in the Dallas area. Maybe he had become too white, too modern. Maybe his own people thought he had abandoned them and their ways. They were wrong. This man had a purpose in the back of his mind and never forgot his roots. He announced proudly to all that would listen, 'I'm Indian. I'm full blood Choctaw!'"

"He believes there is a purpose to everything, and sees how his life and experiences are pointing to something he can leave behind. Now, with the knowledge of putting together a structured system of martial arts, he can combine it with his knowledge of his people's use of weapons and hand to hand combat and create something new, in order to learn about something old. His people used this knowledge every day in hunting and defending their life and family.

"This is his Native system called Red Warrior–keeping his people from being forgotten. In his own way, if he can bring attention to the American Indian culture, then he feels he has contributed something that will be continued for others to learn. What is this man's name? Who is he? He's just a man, a quiet man, and a man of few words. He's a proud man. His name is John Wilkerson Tall Bear. His friends and students call him, Chieftain. I call him "remarkable". Signed, Joan Stovall."

Joan Stovall is a recent and dear friend. John is stunned, deeply moved by her writing. A few months after he met her, she suffered a stroke. She has been in a nursing home in east Texas for the last ten years. At one time, She had mentioned writing a book, but John didn't know she was on the Internet, or had focused on him.

"Mr. Tall Bear, from Mrs. Stovall's paper, I gather you have faced the same discrimination our people suffer, even as our own Nation inflicts it. We are a proud people. You are too. You want a legacy, so here's your chance. A lance stained with Native blood has fallen to the ground. As warrior among warriors, pick up the lance, lead our invisible tribe out of the darkness and into the light."

From the back of the room someone very softly begins to chant, "Chief! Chief! Chief!" Others join in, the chant becomes louder and louder. John feels the vibrations of the wooden floor in his feet. The whole room stands and continues, "Chief! Chief! Chief!"

His mind races to his Movement of Life paper, recalling its last passage written long ago. '*Sometimes very faintly, almost drowned out by the sounds of the city and daily cares, you have heard the distant rushing of the water. You have never seen it, but you begin to feel it rumbling beneath your feet. The thaw is coming, and the first ice is melting. The Movement of Life and its knowledge are starting to flow. You have asked this questions before, 'Why am I here, and what is my destiny?' Tushkahoma (Red Warrior) calls to the bravest fathers and sons of the land, 'Immerse yourselves in the learning river, be the Tushkahoma of the new century, Falammichi (defend, restore) …*'

John slowly rises from his chair and gazes across the crowded room. He can see the hope in people's eyes through the tears in his own. Destiny has brought him to this small church in Indian country. Everything is so clear. He understands. He wishes his mother could have seen this. Without her wisdom and counsel, he could not have made the journey. Feeling her presence, as if she was advising him again, he knows what he must do.

Aiokpachi (I accept)," comes out of his mouth. The chanting swells, the congregation roars, for they have their new Chief.

CHAPTER 6

———

A Choctaw Nation tribal patrol car sits at the top of the hill, across from the Macedonia Indian Church entrance. Ray Cross is behind the wheel. His partner, Jeffrey, rides shotgun. Ray is one of the deputies in the Nation's tribal police force. He is white-haired, short, overweight, with beady eyes and bulldog jowls. Though his sidekick Jeffrey's features are relatively cherubic, they typically drown in the junior officer's innate buffoonery. Their boss, the Chief of the Choctaw Nation, Paul Wilson, is on speakerphone.

"Chief, I'm sorry for calling so late. Jeff and I are still camped outside that church in Bentley. You did say to call in when the services are over. They're still going on. We're fixin' to stay and follow Roman Billy home," says Ray.

"No don't do that. It's not necessary to follow him home this late. I want to know what's going on inside that church."

"Chief, Jeffrey walked down for a closer look a while ago. He took a peek in one of the side windows but couldn't see very much. Something strange, you know how these Church Singing Indians like to sing. Well, there isn't too much singing going on in there at all. It damn sure looks like they're having some kind a serious meeting."

"How many people do you think are in the church?"

"Chief, I would guess there are about seventy to a hundred crowded inside. Last week, we camped outside the church in Achille, we happened to take notice of a particular tall Indian. We noticed him because he was driving a red Allante convertible."

"So?" the Chief prods.

"Well, Chief, he's at the meeting tonight, and he's on stage with several other people."

"Well goddammit, there's something fishy going on, and I want to know what it is. Get me some answers, or I'll find somebody else who can, you hear me? We know a lot about the Billy's. You follow that big Indian when he leaves tonight. Let's see where he leads us."

"Chief! Chief! Something big must have happened, because they're raising the roof off that old church! People are beginning to come out, so it's over."

"Follow the big Indian, and call me in the morning."

"You got it, Chief."

Ray hangs the phone up and barks at Jeff, "You heard the Chief, he sounds pissed. We need to find out what's going on and follow the big Indian."

John is still reeling in tonight's incredible events. Before leaving, Roman and Tammy offered to visit him in Dallas in a couple of days to fill him in and to get his thoughts on a plan of action. The hour and a half trip back home gives him a chance to unwind. Even as far away as Dallas, he had gotten wind something was not right in the Nation. He had no idea how serious it was. For Indians to get that riled up, concern was extreme. Choctaw people, for the most part, take difficulties in stride, adjust and go with the flow. Tall Bear senses, *a black wind is coming, "mali lusa."*

As he turns the Allante onto the road for the short trip back through Atoka, he notices the tribal patrol car sitting across the street. A few cars pull out immediately behind him, and he sees the patrol car ease onto the highway tailing the line of cars.

He's impressed with Roman and Tammy and the support they have. The former marine is a capable leader. John is puzzled Roman himself didn't take the job of chief. *'Hell, he's better qualified to lead them than I am.'* Thirty minutes later, John arrives in Atoka and makes a left onto highway 69 South for the thirty-mile trip into Durant.

Atoka has always been an interesting name to John. He knew it was Choctaw, but couldn't find anyone who knew what it meant. Attending a local Pow Wow as he often does, a conversation with an Indian elder hit pay dirt. Named for Captain Atoka Ochlatubbe, in the Choctaw language, it is 'hitako' or 'hetoka', meaning 'ball ground'. Ochlatubbe was a great ball player. More importantly, he was a leader in the Choctaw Nation of that era and one of the signers of the Treaty of Dancing Rabbit Creek. This treaty began the process of relocating the Choctaw people from Mississippi to Oklahoma in 1832. Captain Atoka brought his band of Choctaws and settled in this area. His final resting home is near the small town of Farris, Oklahoma.

Leaving Atoka, John notices the same tribal patrol car still tailing behind. Several cars are sandwiched between Tall Bear and his tail. John in no hurry drives the speed limit and figures they're going back to their home base in Durant. But it does seem strange they were sitting outside of Macedonia Indian Church this late at night. Tribal police officers have gotten a bad rap, and maybe it's unwarranted. Maybe they try too hard, or they're not as professional as other law enforcement agency's. John thinks it's the nature of the beast to become power hungry and flaunt its position. In any event, he doesn't want to tangle with them.

Passing through Durant thirty minutes later, John turns south on Highway 75. Just outside of the city limits he passes the Nation's flagship, Choctaw Casino and Resort area. Its bright lights beacon in the night, inviting all to come and leave their money. The Nation boasts most of its revenue comes from out of state, meaning Texas, just 20 miles south. However, the filled parking lot has plenty of cars with Oklahoma plates. It's a place for Indians to lose what little money they have and get drunk on cheap liquor. Across the street, the Choctaw truck stop, gas station and tobacco shop do big business for the Nation.

The Choctaws were an agricultural people, probably the most able farmers of the southeastern region. They employed simple tools to raise corn, beans, sweet potatoes, pumpkins, and lots of tobacco. They usually had a surplus to sell and trade. The Choctaws were the first entrepreneurs of their era.

Some don't like the association of tobacco with the American Indian ingrained in history. To John, it's just another evil drug killing the Nation's people. Thousands of Choctaws die every year from lung cancer. The experts say each time you light up, it shortens your life by eleven minutes. That doesn't sound like much, but on ones death-bed-sucking oxygen, eleven minutes is precious. The Choctaws smoke too much, drink too much, and now gamble their money away in the Nation's casino. This saddens John, for it was really a much better world in the old days. In the 50's, when the tribe received extra money, they would divide it up and send checks to all its members. The checks were not very big, but in those days, small money went a long way.

Leaving the bright lights behind, passing through the small town of Celera, John is aware the vehicle is still trailing him. He's a little concerned, because it's a tribal patrol car. As he approaches the Red River Texas/Oklahoma border, he notices the tail slowing, and the glare of its headlights dimming. Driving onto the bridge, he glances in his rear view mirror and sees the patrol car U-turn and head north, back into Indian Country. He feels relieved. Obviously, they had followed him but it's unclear what made them stop. Thinking they have no jurisdiction out of the thirteen counties which make up the Choctaw Nation, he crosses the bridge and leaves the Red River behind, knowing he'll be safe at home in an hour.

There, he can watch a little late night television, kick back, relax, make sense of what happened tonight and where it all might lead. A door to the future opened, and boy did he step through it! Interesting for sure, even exciting, he's pumped thinking about the possibilities. Anticipating a late night bowl of popcorn and a couple of Dr. Peppers threatens his 'hunter/gatherer' diet.

CHAPTER 7

S everal days later, Roman and Tammy visit John's home in Dallas as planned.

"How was your trip?" John asks, shaking Roman's hand and giving Tammy a warm friendly hug.

"It wasn't too bad. We made of couple of stops to get gas and something to eat."

"Did you stop at Dino's Pies, just this side of the river?" John fishes.

"Damn sure did! You been there?"

"Their fried pies are the best! I stop there coming and going. The blackberry is my favorite. It reminds me of my mother's blackberry dumplings!"

"I like the peach," says Tammy as she and Roman have a seat on the leather sofa. "You have a pretty home."

"Thank you." Just then Johns cat, Harley shows up to see what's going on.

"Who's this?" Harley begins to rub on her leg, and she reaches down to pet him.

"His name is Harley and he's from California."

"He's huge, how much does he weigh?"

"He weighs 21 lbs. He's a hunter, too. He was always bringing birds and other small animals home when he lived in California."

"How did you get him to Texas?"

"When I lost my first cat a few years ago, my daughter thought Harley would be good company for me. I had to promise to make him an indoor cat though. When I returned from a trip last year, I put him on the plane with me. He's doing fine at adjusting to house arrest in Texas."

"How did he come by that name?" Roman continues the pet talk.

"My daughter thought he purred like a Harley Davidson motorcycle." He fixes them all a glass of sweet Indian tea, and they make themselves comfortable.

"Roman, if you will, tell me some of your views of the Nation and any solutions you may have," says John, turning to business.

"Tall Bear, there are hundreds of problems, and many issues to address. First, the Chief within his own nation wields more power than the President of the United States. He uses strong-arm tactics to hand pick council members insuring that most vote in his favor. In general elections, those who oppose him are shut down."

"For instance, several years ago, a candidate with a large voter base ran against the Chief. The challenger had a very good chance of winning until two of his campaign volunteers were arrested at the Choctaw Labor Day Festival in Tushkahoma. One, a 64-year old grandmother, was passing out campaign pamphlets. Another was jailed for videotaping police activity. Thirty minutes later, their candidate, an attorney and Marine Corps Reserve Major, was handcuffed, forced into a tribal police car, and suffered minor injuries. No doubt, this mess was ordered by the Chief."

"How can this be? What were the people charged with?"

"At the time of the arrests, the tribal attorney stated the accused were violating a law prohibiting passing out political literature on tribal land. When it was discovered no such law existed, the charges were changed to disturbing the peace and disrupting a parade."

"Because the rights of the people stated in the U. S. Constitution do not apply to Indian Country, free speech can be punished on Choctaw land," says Tammy. "The lady who filmed the arrest was facing between three and five years in jail."

"The Choctaw Nation is a sovereign nation in treaties with the federal government. The Chief uses sovereign immunity to do as he pleases. And, since judges to the tribal court are appointed by the Chief," Roman's voice trails off.

"How can our tribe punish Choctaw citizens, when our tribal constitution was never granted criminal jurisdiction? If I remember correctly, The Bureau of Indian Affairs has taken the position the Choctaw Nation contracted federal criminal jurisdiction through the Indian Self Determination Act."

"Your memory is good, Tall Bear. You're talking about Public Law 93-638 Contract. In the mid 1970s, Congress passed the Indian Self Determination and Education Assistance Act, which allows Indian tribes and tribal organizations to acquire more control over the management of federal programs that impact their members and governments.

"The 638 compacts and contracts are ambiguous and contradictory. Certainly, 1., the U. S. Constitution does not apply to Choctaw land, even though federal criminal jurisdiction is being exercised. Nonetheless 2., tribal sovereign immunity was applied when civil rights violation suits were bought against tribal officers in federal court, after the arrests. Tribal officers are represented by the U.S. Attorney's Office, in their official capacity, but assert tribal sovereign immunity in their individual capacities. They play both sides of the street," says Roman.

"Would you explain what you mean by that?"

"Here is another example. The tribal prosecutor is also the tribal attorney who represents the executive and legislative branches of the Choctaw Nation. This violates the separation of powers doctrine of the United States and Choctaw Constitutions. The Chief appoints the judge for this court, but federal regulations state that's BIA's domain. Under the Choctaw Constitution, the Chief can replace the judge anytime he wants. The Chief hires and can fire the tribal police for disobeying his orders. The Chief always selects a tribal prosecutor he can control."

"With this kind of set up, the Chief and the council can manipulate the court to their advantage," John says.

"Exactly! The Chief and the Choctaw Nation apply 93-638 contracts when anything impacts his office. Controlling as he sees fit, he constantly oversteps his authority."

"Tribal officers are not held accountable to higher standards therefore the system seems ripe for abuse."

"Tall Bear, without federal court jurisdiction, we are at the mercy of a tribal administration both willing and able to harass and intimidate tribal citizens. Sovereign immunity was intended to be a shield for tribes to become responsible and financially solvent governments. Instead, it has become a sword used against its own."

"Roman, why can't we just vote the Chief out? With the kind of following you have, I would think you've had a good chance. Can you get a copy of the Nation's voter registration list? Or maybe get their mailing list from their newspaper, the Bishinik?"

"Tall Bear, it's nearly impossible to do this because the war chest to re-elect the Chief and council comes from federal funds. This is how it works. The tribe is given federal funds under PL-638 to maintain the Choctaw voter registration list. This list is only available to the administration and candidates of its choice, not to all candidates. The reason given for the secrecy is the Federal Privacy Act. The Office of the Solicitor and a federal court both ruled the Privacy Act does not apply to the Choctaw voter registration list. However, the tribal attorney continues to assert that the Privacy Act prevents release of the list. The tribal attorney is paid by federal funds for his advice, which is clearly against the spirit, if not the letter, of law."

"Withholding the voter registration list was challenged by a candidate in the late 1980's. The district court ruled in favor of the candidate and ordered the BIA to release the list. However, ten days after the complaint was filed, and prior to enforcement of this ruling, the BIA amended the voter registration contract with the tribe, to include names only but no addresses. This was obviously done with pressure from the Chief. Without complete names and addresses, candidates cannot inform Choctaw members about their political platforms. The BIA continues to funnel federal funds into a tribe that diligently denies members basic input into their own tribal affairs, and the election of tribal leaders. That is not self-determination, that is dictatorship," asserts Roman.

"This is insane. I've wondered why, after all these years, the Chief ran unopposed. It sounds like he has the whole system rigged in his favor."

"Here's another thing. Tammy, tell Tall Bear what you found out about the tribal paper and misuse of federal funds."

"Oh, yes. The Choctaw Nation does not allow candidates to place ads in the tribal newsletter, the Bishinik, which is funded by federal dollars. This is against the law. Federal funds are used to violate candidate and tribal members' freedom of speech. We can't sue the federal government and we can't sue the Nation either."

"However, the Chief can use federal funds to mail out campaign literature on his own behalf. You know, …those cards you get from the Chief in the mail? 'Hey look, I'm doing a good job and thinking of you on Christmas and your birthday'. The Nation uses the tribal postage meter to send them. We are talking about thousands of federal dollars used to benefit him."

"But the abuse of federal funds in campaigning does not stop there. Federal funds are used to send out campaign letters for the state governor, a U.S. Senator, state representatives, state judges, county commissioners, and county sheriffs. When politicians owe favors to tribal leadership, members are further at the mercy of same, even in forums outside of tribal government."

John had found Roman's knowledge thought provoking, but hearing Tammy assert herself is equally impressive. He had no idea that the Chief's office was generating such pervasive abuse. It's no wonder these Choctaws are up in arms. Their Chief and their government are disregarding their interests. Changes should be made, but without inside leverage, they are forced to the edge of impossible."

"Tall Bear, I don't know if you know this, but the tribe controls the press in southeastern Oklahoma, directly or indirectly. The tribe has contracts with numerous newspapers for tribal printing. Small newspapers are afraid to print fair and accurate tribal news for fear of losing printing contracts with the Nation. Tribal citizens cannot participate in tribal affairs if they are uninformed. A viable candidate would not be allowed to place a campaign advertisement in these newspapers, as they fear alienating the Chief.

"With this kind of political machinery in place, tribal members have very little chance of voting the current Chief out. Such a regime seeks to eradicate justice and democracy. We need a federal court to review these wrongs or we will continue to be treated as second-class citizens.

"We are smart, intelligent people who want to participate in tribal affairs and invest in a government that looks after all of the people, not just a few. This is not an unreasonable request. Congress set up the system we currently live under, and Congress can change it.

"The Choctaw Nation is a microcosm of what is going on across Indian Country. Lack of accountability creates an atmosphere ripe for corruption and abuse. Which is why we need someone like you to lead us in this effort," concludes Roman.

They are all feeling a little drained by now, and Tammy gives them a great excuse to stop. She has heard about a particular store in a local mall and wants to do some shopping for the kids.

"Listen, I would be a bad host if I didn't take you to one of my favorite restaurants. Do you like catfish?"

"Oh, I love catfish," says Tammy.

"Do they have fried shrimp?" asks Roman.

"They have that and more. I'll give you the directions and we can meet there in a couple of hours. It's not far from here, just off highway 75, so it'll be convenient when you get ready to go home," says John with a smile. He escorts them to their car, describing in detail, and the exit ramp to their dinner rendezvous.

CHAPTER 8

A few hours later, they all arrive at Catfish & More. It's a place John tries to visit at least once a week, spacious, with an outdoor patio. There's a bar with several flat screen televisions tuned to stations with hot sports scores of favorite teams. Dashes of Louisiana Cajun color and rustic flavor give the contemporary varnished wood interior a comfortable atmosphere.

As the trio makes its way to the front counter, John explains the honor system used here–place your order, have a seat at your favorite table and enjoy the dinner. When you are finished, tell the cashier at the register what you had, and pay for it. No questions asked.

"Tall Bear, How ya'll doing and who are your friends?" greets Eric Harper, the owner of the restaurant.

"Hi Eric, you know me, I'm always looking for an excuse to come by my favorite restaurant and get some catfish. I've got a couple of first timers here, from Oklahoma. Say hello to Roman and his wife Tammy."

"Well if you're friends of Tall Bear," he extends his hand, "we're going to take care of you. Let me know how you like the food," says Eric.

"So what's good?" asks Roman.

"The catfish and shrimp are great, and they serve my favorite, a tall delicious shrimp cocktail."

After looking at the menu, Roman orders his fried shrimp. Tammy and John get catfish. John also orders appetizers, three shrimp cocktails to savor, waiting for their dinners. They find a rounded booth back in the corner, away from a small crowd of eight to ten people, where they can talk quietly. It is late afternoon, the perfect time for an enjoyable meal.

"This shrimp cocktail is wonderful," says Tammy after a couple of bites.

"I was hoping you'd like it. It's not too hot, is it?"

"It's just right. I love the avocado and chopped onions in the sauce."

"I like the cilantro flavor in there too," says Roman.

While waiting for the fried catfish and shrimp to arrive, a couple of guys take a seat in the next booth. These are the loud mouth obnoxious types. When you see them coming, you hope they don't sit close to you. The tall heavyset 'Bubba' shirt is cut off at the shoulder, exposing sleeve tattoos that runs to his wrist. He wears a baseball cap and, like his friend, dirty blue jeans and work boots. John assumes they work construction. Bubba has a mug of beer in each hand and a boor's craving to be the center of attention. His partner, a little more reserved, sits down to slurp his glass of ice tea.

"Roman, let me ask you, first, why did the Nation lower its blood quantum to almost nothing and second, who has that impacted most?" John reiterates concerns from an earlier dialogue.

"Under the Chief's watch, the Choctaw Nation boasts a membership over 200,000 courtesy of the diluted blood requirement and yet, we look like everybody else. Our large numbers makes delivery of services to deserving Choctaws thin or nonexistent."

"You remember Mrs. Jim don't you? The elderly lady who spoke the other night?" asks Tammy. John nods he does. "This is exactly what she was talking about. If you can prove you have a drop of Indian blood in your family line, you can become a tribal member. The corrupt tribal leaders run this con. The more people they represent, the more money they get from the federal government."

"Tall Bear, myself and other elders know many of the older Choctaws, the amoma (full bloods) in Idabel, Broken Bow, and other Oklahoma towns are having difficulty obtaining services in a timely manner, if at all. When they visit waiting rooms in the Nation's clinics and hospital, its very apparent white Choctaws are favored. The amoma should have priority. Too often, they give up on getting help. The core existence of this tribe should be directly related to high blood quantum and assistance to the most deserving as quickly as possible," says Roman.

"Hey!" intrudes a voice from none other than 'Bubba' at the next table, "What you people talking about over there?"

John's back is to him, so he turns and replies, "We're talking politics, tribal politics for your information."

"Y'all Indian?" with a chuckle, he looks at his partner.

"Yes, we are."

"Well, I'm part Cherokee on my momma's side," snorts Bubba.

"Yeah, I can see it in your blue eyes. Those Cherokees get around," John needles sarcastically.

Bubba gets a little attitude in his voice and says, "Well, I'm sick of listening to that crap for the last ten minutes, can you keep it down!"

"Sure no problem, we took this corner booth thinking we would be out of the way. Sorry Tammy, Roman, I guaranteed the food would be great, not the company."

They continue their conversation for a few minutes. Suddenly, a half eaten boiled shrimp bounces on John's left shoulder, ricochets off Tammy, and falls to the table. Tammy's white blouse is soiled with ketchup. Roman immediately pops up, but John is even quicker and jumps in front of him, almost at the table where Bubba and his friend are sitting. Out of the corner of his eye, John sees Eric stop what he is doing to observe.

"Look Bubba or whatever your name is, there's no call for rude behavior. Didn't your momma teach you how to behave out in public?"

Bubba is a little slow with his comeback. "What are you going to do about it, Indian?" he snarls.

"All I can say is your mother did a lousy job of raising you."

"Fuck you."

Attending basic military training a lifetime ago, John remembers. When a recruit screwed up badly, the TI would jump in their face and say, 'Boy you from Kentucky or Tennessee?' The TI was never wrong.

"So Bubba, you from Kentucky or Tennessee?"

John knows this will riled him up, and so here he comes, out of his booth.

"I'll teach you not to insult my momma. I'm from Kentucky and I'm going to teach you some manners you fucking Indian," and he throws a right punch.

John has observed his beer drinking and anticipates a punch he has seen a thousand times before. He parries Bubba's right to the left, so John's left hand captures his right wrist. He then executes a heel of palm strike to Bubba's right jaw. John can see and feel the man's legs buckle a little. It is all over. John lifts his arm up and spins counter clockwise under it. He then executes another heel of palm to the back of Bubba's head, and spins him down to the floor matador fashion. From there, John creates an arm lock and applies pressure on Bubba's elbow. Bubba lets out a scream, and his partner moves to assist him.

"Tell Tennessee to back off, or I'm going to break your arm!"

"Get back, George! Get back!" Bubba screams.

"Now Kentucky, if you promise to behave yourself, I'll let you up." The dazed oaf nods.

"But before I do, you're going to apologize to my dinner guests, aren't you?" John tightens the arm lock.

"I'm sorry! I apologize! I apologize!" gasps Bubba as John slightly eases the arm lock.

Eric runs over to John and says, "Tall Bear, I saw it all. He swung at you first. You want me to call the police?"

"No, no, Eric. That's not necessary. Actually, he didn't lay a hand on me."

Bubba gets up, rubbing his sore arm and jaw. He and George are walking to the front of the restaurant toward the exit, with Eric right behind them. Just then, two police officers enter. John guesses one of the other patrons has called 911 from a cell phone. Both officers approach Eric for a short conversation. One officer now begins talking to Bubba, who has moved to the cashier station to pay for his dinner. The other officer comes back to talk to John. He suspects the officer has been told what happened.

Asked if he wants to press charges, John says, "No.., Bubba mistook me for Steven Segal. He wanted me to show him some moves. We were just having some fun and it got a little out of hand, Officer. No harm done."

The cop nods, but asks John one more time if he wants to press charges. Again, John shakes his head, 'no'. As the officer joins his partner, John motions for George, Bubba's friend, to come back and have a word with him.

"I tell you what, friend. The officer wants to take you and your friend downtown, so here's what you're going to do. You're going to pay for my guests' and my dinners, and I'm going to forget about all this," John says, as they're walking to join the two officers and Bubba at the cashier's desk. George quickly nods in agreement.

"Hey Officers. Everything's fine. In fact, my good friend George has agreed to buy everyone in the house their dinner."

George's jaw drops wide open. Then he gives John an ugly look, still nodding. The officers stay to insure George and Bubba take care of the bill, and then watch as they leave the restaurant. John, meanwhile, joins Roman and Tammy back at the table.

"Very impressive! That was something, Tall Bear. I can't wait to get back and tell everybody I saw a Master in action!" says Roman.

"With his big mouth, everyone in our county will know before sundown."

They watch Bubba and his friend get in their pickup, turn in the parking lot and pass by close enough for Bubba to flip them off as he drives by. The three of them laugh so hard, they nearly fall out of the booth.

"Some guys never learn," says John, shaking his head.

They say their goodbyes in the parking lot, and John thanks them for coming. Arrangements have been made for John to come to Bokchito in a few days for another briefing.

"Have a safe trip back, and call if you need me. Chi pisa lachike (see you later)."

"Tall Bear," Roman hollers, "What do you call that move back there?" as both wave goodbye.

"The Choctaw, what else."

CHAPTER 9

His trip to Bokchito a few days away, John recalls a friend he hasn't seen for many months. Years before, shopping at a bookstore, he spotted a man about his age scanning magazines in the sports section. It was the month John was profiled in a cover story of a national martial arts magazine. The other customer was looking at that same issue. The martial artist, using detective skills sharpened during a term as Executive Director of an urban center for Indians who were relocated, or moved themselves, knows each tribe has a distinctive look. This was an Indian, a fellow Choctaw.

John approached him and, referring to the magazine cover, quipped, "That's a good looking Indian. Don't you agree?"

Most Indians don't approach strangers to start a conversation. Startled, Levi Tushka looked at John, then back at the magazine, then at John again, and shouted, "That's you, ain't it?"

"Yeah, that's me. Halito Chukma. Su hochifo uh, John Wilkerson Tall Bear. Chi hon-chifo ut nanta?" After greeting, and saying his name, John was asking the man his name in Native Choctaw.

"Halito. Su hochifo uh, Levi Tushka. Chish nato?"–hello, name, and how are you? Levi Tushka is Oklahoma Choctaw.

Levi works as an independent contractor remodeling homes in Plano. Levi and his daughter were shopping together that night. His daughter attends a small college in Austin, Texas and was visiting him over the weekend. John will later learn Levi is an avid reader, who will turn him on to some of his favorite authors. John respects Levi for having retained the Choctaw language, and held true to the heritage

John is determined to recover. The two exchanged phone numbers promising to stay in touch.

John finds out Levi is somewhat of a wanderer who, at times, can't be located. A ladies' man that gets around pretty good, he would call John to say he was just hanging out at the homes of friends and ex-wives. On his lip, he wears a scar that warns he's a tough man in any Indian bar.

Levi knows everybody! John can't call a name and Levi hasn't met the person or knows some of their kin. He has lived and worked all over Oklahoma and a few neighboring states. He's even worked for the Choctaw Nation, though he became dissatisfied with them in just a short time.

John locates Levi in Shawnee, Oklahoma and asks if they can meet to discus Johns new project. He is pleased when Levi asks if George's Hamburgers on Hwy 69, Durant is still open. They agree to meet there for lunch and ride together to visit the Billys in Bokchito.

———

Hundred ten miles north, in Atoka, Oklahoma, a man hoists yet another beer exposing the swastika tattooed on his inner wrist. He chugs, and then tosses the empty, which clanks atop previously trashed cans piled in the corner of his bedroom. He hurls his military boot into the hallway to attract Sugar.

"Bring me another beer, Sugar," he hollers, searching for his cell phone between the cushions of a dirty plaid lounge chair. He dials the private number of a powerful man thirty miles south in Durant, OK, sitting in a butter soft leather chair, holding court to several aides. When his cell beckons, the office man pushes the incoming button.

"I'm a little busy."

"Hey, I'm busy too. Where's my beer, Sugar?" He repeats his demand attempting to cover the mouthpiece.

"Ok, thanks for returning my call. So have you decided what to do?"

"I'll do it tomorrow evening, but I'm going to need another five thousand."

"I'll agree to that, but no more. Come on down to the usually place. I'll send the five over."

"Now I can afford a pack of marshmallows to take along with the weenies."

"What? Oh, I get it, funny man." He hangs up and turns back to his aides.

———————

George's is a little hole in the wall burger joint near Southeastern State College in Durant, Oklahoma. It's an iconic hang out for students and hasn't changed much in 45 years. Even with all the new competition, they still have one of the best burgers in town.

At the appointed time, Levi and John meet at George's for lunch. After enjoying burgers, fries and a milkshake, they leave for Bokchito to visit the Billys.

Before leaving Durant, John eased the car into a service station across the street from George's to get gas.

"Smell that rain coming John?"

"Yep, it's coming for the west."

"Not a cloud in the sky, so how long?"

"It's a couple of hours away."

As John begins to fill up with gas, he notices a man smoking a cigarette on the next island as he fills a rusty gas can with gas. In stark detail the can wore a faded decal of a 'messenger' emoji symbol.

"Say mister I know it's a little cool now, but on a hot summer day, smoking that cigarette and missing with gas can be awful dangerous."

The man looks at Johns imposing figure before replying, "Thanks for reminding me, I've got a lot on my mind," tossing the butt to the ground and stomping it out.

"Say, if you ran out of gas, my friend and I will give you a ride back to your car."

"Thanks mate, but my rides over there. The gas is for my tractor. Got to get back and do a little work before it rains," as he tighten the lid and begins walking toward a black Mercedes.

"I figure you got two or three hours left, see yah," replies John.

———

The Billy home, a white frame house, with three bedrooms, sits on 4 acres, a quarter mile outside of town. Towering pine trees provide cover from wind and storms that frequent the area. They arrive around 6 p.m. Chu Chu, a Chocolate Labrador, is tending the yard near the front door. He barks several times before they get out of the car, signaling someone has arrived.

Michael and his sister, Martha Jo, open the door and greet them. The young man, now 22, looks like his father. Martha, 20, resembles her mother, only much taller. Both attend Southeastern State College. Michael is a senior and Martha, a sophomore.

———

A hundred yards down the road, parked out of view from the Billy home, sits a tribal patrol car. Inside, the two deputies, Ray Cross and Jeffrey Irwin, sit and watch. They can see several cars parked outside of the Billy home, but don't want to get any closer, fearful of alerting the family dog.

"Ray, I'm getting tired of sitting here waiting on those stupid Indians. They could be in there all night," says Deputy Irwin.

"Jeff, if the Chief finds out there was a meeting tonight, even a small one, and we don't have something to report, he'll have our ass."

"Chances are, the Chief won't find out about this one. Let's go have a couple of cold ones at Lou's."

"Shut the fuck up, Jeffrey. We're staying until they leave. I like my job with the Nation, and I'm not going to do anything to jeopardize it. So, quit your whining."

———————

"Halito Chukma, Michael, Martha. Hey, I want you to say hello to my good friend, Levi Tushka."

They all shake hands, then Michael and Martha guide them through the house to a large den where Roman, Tammy and several others have already gathered. Tammy's older and younger brothers, Jacob and Danny, have been invited, as well as Roman's younger brother, Raymond. John expects a lively meeting with the new members present. Tammy has fixed a large pitcher of ice tea, and they settle down to discuss the business at hand.

After exchanging introductions, Roman takes charge of the meeting, addressing John, "Tall Bear, I want to thank you for coming and bringing your friend, Levi Tushka. And, since you are our new Chief, if it's okay, I'd like to turn the meeting over to you."

"Okay, but on one condition. You drop the Tall Bear and call me John. You make me feel so old," John laughs, and the others join in. John tells the story of how he and Levi met, even sharing their discussion on the way down from Durant. "So, I'd like to hear first from Levi and the rest of your young guests."

"When John first told me about this, I thought he was crazy. After we talked for a while, he asked me what are our chances in succeeding. I told him you don't have a snowball's chance in hell of getting the Chief out of office. But call me crazy, now that I've met all of you, I'd like to be a part of any group that's willing to try. Getting someone else elected is almost impossible, considering how the Chief has the city, mayor, police chief, newspapers and all the politicians in his back pocket. I like the other angle about forming a new tribe. That's exciting and might take a little more time, but if we can pull it off, it will be worth the effort."

After a forty-minute trip down a one-lane highway, the man with the gas can nears his destination. Spring weather in Oklahoma is a mixed bag of the unexpected. A fast-moving front from the west has moved thunderstorms into the area. The rains arrive with heavy thunder and lightning. The storm is so violent he thinks about canceling his plans, but decides the weather will make great cover. He parks his Mercedes AMG, a hundred yard away from the entrance to the target and disappears into the woods. The tall Ninja blends with a darkening terrain.

Having watched too many TV crime shows, he's wrapped his boots with black duck tape, so as not to leave footprints. Wandering through the woods, he approaches a small creek between himself and the target. With added urgency, he quickly climbs down the small embankment toward a place where the water stream narrowed to a couple of yards. He had checked it out days ago and had hoped to jump across, however, he had not anticipated the heavy rains. The leap across is more demanding, but it was a leap he thought he could make even with the gas can. He stepped back from the creek about six feet and made his assault. Though he landed safely on the other side, his right foot slipped and made a splashing sound.

'Oh shit, I'm in trouble.' Sensing nature disturbed. He makes a mad dash up the embankment, dropped to his knees, and listened. A dog howled. He hears nothing for a long moment. Now he can hear paws pounding the dry leaves and ground. It's getting louder.

Inside the Billy home everyone hears Chu Chu barking and wonders. Tammy says, "Don't mind him, he just spotted a rabbit or something. Please, continue on while and I'll quiet him down."

Danny, Tammy's younger brother, who is in his early 30's, speaks up, "I can't speak for all the young people, but I'm concerned about what the Nation is doing about producing more good jobs for younger Indians."

"I know exactly how you feel, Danny." Levi responds. "When I was working for the Nation several years ago, I approached the Chief on a business venture to create jobs for all Indians. You know, catfish farming is big business. Right now, most of that product is coming out of Alabama. With all the Indian land available, we could build hundreds of catfish ponds for very little money up front. The Nation doesn't even have to spend its own money. There are federal grants available to anyone that wants to explore food technologies.

"Properly managed, catfish farms create many good jobs. After stocking the farm, someone's got to feed them on a daily basis. That would be a good job for young kids in high school or college. Other jobs it would create would be harvesting, food preparation, food storage, transportation, and marketing. It's a billion dollar industry. I had enough knowledge and information to get the whole business up and running. The Chief blew me off and never mentioned it again."

Jacob, the older brother remarks, "That sounds like a great business plan, Levi. I can see why John wanted to bring you in. The Chief just wants to build more things to stroke his ego. Seeing his name on everything is getting a little old."

"Well, what about the huge equestrian facility the Nation has out there?" asks Levi. "That's another questionable venture. Talk about wasteful spending of Choctaw and federal money. I don't know any Choctaws well off enough to own a horse or even take advantage of the facility."

"Yeah, what's up with that?" exclaims Roman's younger brother Raymond.

"I'll tell you what's up with that. It's just another toy he can dangle in front of the wealthy white entertainers to come in and hang out with the Chief. You won't see any Choctaws using it."

"Levi, since we're trashing the Chief, I listened to him speak to a large group in Dallas a couple years ago. He boasted about the health programs that the Choctaw Nation has to offer," says Danny. "But if you don't live in the 13 Tribal districts in Oklahoma, you don't qualify for these programs. He bragged about the Talihina Recovery Center saying, no matter where you were, if you needed help, the Nation would put you on a plane and get you to the Center. One big problem is the center only offers a 28-day treatment program. You can't cure alcoholism in 28 days! They need to extend treatment programs to six months or one year. Their success rate would be a lot better."

"Has anybody been to the Choctaw Nation lately?" asks Raymond. "You would think the Chief could hire a few more Indians to work in the administrative offices. Shoot, I don't identify with those people up there any more. Roman, have you told them about your solution to the blood quantum?"

"Oh Raymond, don't get Roman started on that, we'll be here all night," says Tammy, smiling.

Levi laughs and says, "Roman, I'd be interested in hearing about that. I've some ideas of my own."

"Well for starters, I don't think we should ever have gotten away from the Federal Government standard 'What is an Indian'. In the beginning, it was one quarter, and today, that should be the minimum. Search the web for sites listing all the tribes and their blood requirement. The Choctaw Nation is not even mentioned! There're several tribes like the Mississippi Choctaws that require you to be at least one half. A dozen or so require one eighth and others require one sixteenth. Our tribe requires you to prove you have one drop of Indian blood in your lineage and you can be a card carrying member of the Choctaw Nation!" says disgusted Roman.

"I'm American Indian and I want to honor the traditions and cultures that my ancestors paid a huge price for. The whites have taken everything from our people, and now they want to steal our identity. How can we stop this?" asks a defiant Martha Jo.

"Here's a solution." says Roman, "If we're going to have to live with the one drop Indian requirement, I propose their access to services be directly related to how much Indian blood they are. Here's an example. If you are half Choctaw, you get a 50% discount for all services. If you are one quarter, you receive a 25% discount. This will keep one drop Indians out of the waiting rooms of clinics and hospitals asking for free services they don't deserve. This would insure Choctaws with substantial blood quantum get the care and services they are entitled to."

"Hey, I like that! It makes a lot of sense to me. That would eliminate a lot of people wanting to be a member of the Nation in the first place. Let's face it, they're just here for the money and services," says Levi.

"Levi and I are a little older than everyone here," adds John. "Let me give you a little history lesson, and I'm sure Levi will agree with me. Most full blood American Indians face a very serious reality. In the old days, the invaders eventually outnumbered the indigenous people. After taking most of their land, their main goal was the eradication of the Indian Nations as nations. They accomplished this by stripping them of all of the elements that make a distinct people a People. They smothered their history, their languages, their laws and customs.

"It took hundreds of years using boarding schools, missionaries, and corrupt politicians, but the process of being broken had a disastrous impact on Indian people. Something very tragic happens when groups of people become displaced. You cannot remember who you are if you are not among people with a common history. My family was a product of the Relocation Program in the 50's was the last of these programs meant to separate us. It's not you don't have a history, you don't know what it is if not shared." John's words have power and everyone awaits his final thoughts.

"Being stripped of your worth and value causes a spiritual collapse of one's self. If your people's history is not recorded in the history books and accepted as truth, you seemingly do not exist. Not enough indigenous philosophy and culture are included in those texts written by 'white' historians. Identity is crucial to the American Indian for what he has endured. The founding fathers and those who came afterward were very successful in "eliminating" indigenous identities. Today, people display passion about having a small percentage of Indian blood. Belonging to an Indian Nation is a way of being in the world. Money can't buy that. You either have it or you don't."

———

He can hear the dog rapidity covering ground in his direction. He has come prepared as he reaches into his inside coat pocket and retrieves a Nine. The dog gate is getting louder as he attaches a suppressor. He upon him now and can see his teeth as his four feet leaves the ground and becomes airborne. The suppressor muffles the sound of two quick shots and the dog falls at his feet. The dog is silent now as he rises and stands. *'Two bad you're one of my favorite,'* as he looks at his kill. He kicks the dog in the back and watches it tumbles into the creek water. He must act fast now as someone may miss the dog. He begins his assault up the creek bed into the woods and winding among the trees.

The can of gas is getting heavy and he's beginning to feel paranoid. He thinks he hears voices. Under the cover of rain, thunder and lightening, no one can possibly hear him approaching the back door. His long legs tremble as he approaches, hands shaking so badly he strains to keep from spilling the gas. "Don't like this arson shit, but it pays," he chants in a raspy whisper.

The door is locked. He plants a shoulder into the door, which flies open. The adrenalin pumping through his veins boosts his confidence. Sounds of thunder and destruction are one. Eager to get in, he has made mistakes, *'Stupid, stupid, I didn't check for any alarms or surveillance cameras near the back door.'* Working quickly, he splashes gas everywhere covering the floor, chairs and tables. He tosses a match in the puddle of gas and his eyes flare as flames consume everything.

———

Martha Jo decides to enter the conversation, "Wow, that's great stuff, Mr. Tall Bear. You ought to be a teacher. In my history class last year we had to do a paper on the Choctaw Trail of Tears. It is so sad how those people suffered and died."

"Martha Jo, I'm told my great, great, grandmother made that infamous trip. Prior to 1832, the United States Government tried their best to divide, conquer, and kill us off. There were about 21,000 Choctaws who lived and flourished in what we know as Mississippi, Alabama, Georgia, and surrounding states. So the question was, 'What do we do with these Indians?' The settlers were moving westward and needed more land. The Choctaws were forced to accept unfair treaties or face the consequences. These forced treaties lead to moving the Choctaws west of the Mississippi River to Oklahoma Territory. In doing so, the 'Trail of Tears' atrocity was born.

"The blacks have their slavery issues, the Jews have their concentration camps and ours is, The Trail of Tears and Wounded Knee. Wreak havoc, death, and slaughter on the Indian people and maybe they will go away. These reflect a mentality of genocide. Andrew Jackson and his administration produced the Indian Removal Act in the 1830's. The Choctaws and the United States Government agreed to nine treaties between 1786 and 1830. The Treaty of Dancing Rabbit Creek was the last to be signed, agreeing to the final removal of the Choctaw Nation to Oklahoma. Choctaw land was systematically obtained through treaties, legislation, and threats of warfare. In 1832 nearly 15,000 Choctaws attempted the move to Indian Territory. About 3,000 women, children and the elderly died along the Trail of Tears from starvation and many froze from the bitter cold," declares John.

"Hundreds of books have been written about that tragic journey, so I will not dwell on it here anymore than what John has stated very eloquently," says Levi. "Do some research and you will appreciate the Choctaw full bloods' heroic journey. The benefits you enjoy today, if any, are directly related to their efforts to make it to the new territory and survive.

Danny jumps into the conversation. "I heard Hitler used the United States treatment of Indians as a model for his genocide against the Jews."

"You're damn right about that! Let me add a little to what John stated. Here is something else to consider. Assimilation into a society that is not yours is a great health risk to indigenous peoples as individuals and communities. It produces anomie–the absence of values and sense of group purpose and identity. That can be the underlying thread that creates domestic abuse and suicides triggered by alcohol. It sets the stage for inappropriate diet, which leads to an epidemic of degenerative diseases. Being conquered and forced into assimilation was the worst thing that could happen to our people four centuries ago."

"What does anomie mean?" asks Raymond.

Levi is hitting his stride now, and John is glad that Levi agreed to come. His knowledge and contacts will be a tremendous asset.

"Anomie means lawlessness, a collapse of social stability, an erosion of standards, the state of alienation experienced by individuals or a class of people. Pretty serious stuff."

In response to the heavy conversation, everyone is speechless. Just in time, Tammy saves everyone, announcing, "Dinner is ready. Wash up, and 'Impachi' (eat)."

After a wonderful dinner consisting of Indian fried bread, chicken and dumplings, fried potatoes and lots of Indian tea, they finish the evening telling stories and having carefree conversation.

———————

Flames and flashes of lightening illuminate the arsonist's sinister profile. Wild white hair, wet with rain and flame darts dancing in his eyes portray an evil man consumed by greed. The fires spread more quickly than he anticipated. He's not trapped but escaping is going to be tricky. A sudden small explosion diverts his mad dash for the door. He spins to face the room's window partially blocked by a large piano. Scrambling across its keys he completes the devilish interlude by diving head into the glass.

He had noticed freshly mowed grass all around the building when he approached. He's lucky enough to land safely and shoulder roll. Tumbling further, he's covered with mulch. There's an immense heat on his body and his leather jacket is literally smoking. He struggles to his feet. His eyes, adjusting to the smoke, he checks to see his escape route. He jogs quickly back into the woods and sprints to his parked vehicle. He slides behind the wheel of the AMG and drives away. At the top of a hill, he stops and views the flames against the backdrop of the cooling night sky. The occasional flash of lightening is an impressive sight to see. He notices people beginning to gather near the building. As they watch the building go up in flames, he can still make out the sign on the front frame, Macedonia Indian Church.

CHAPTER 10

The heavy evening rain has let up as Levi and John make a gingerly dash to their car. Thru the light rain, the deputies can hear the car engine start, and watch it pull away from the house. As the car passes their hidden position, Ray says, "Well, well, look who we have here? The big Indian in the red convertible! Last time we saw him, he was high tailing it back to Texas."

"Looks like he picked up another big Indian, too," says Jeffrey.

"Now, aren't you glad we stayed? The Chief will want to know about this." Says Ray, as he starts the patrol car and eases it onto the road.

In the car ahead, John asks, "So Levi, what do you think about the meeting tonight?"

"The Billy's are nice people. I can see why you want to get involved and help. That Roman is a big dude. I wonder if he played any kind of ball?"

"Don't know, but I could have used him on my all Indian basketball team years ago. Now I can't get up and down the court short of passing out."

"I know what you mean. I look at a basketball and I start sweating." They both laugh at Levi's remark.

"But as you can see, they're persuasive and passionate people. Wait till you meet some of the others behind the scenes. I'm going to set up a meeting with Senator Jim as soon as I can."

"From the way you've described her, I'm looking forward to meeting her."

"Hey big fellow, don't get any bright ideas. I can tell you the lady is way out of your league."

"Hell, that's just my type, I love to grovel."

"Levi, we need to keep this strictly business. I don't want you messing anything up. Besides, I hear you got a woman in almost every county."

"Represent! Howoooooh, my legend grows."

"Am I gonna to have to stop at Wal-Mart and get a muzzle for you?"

"Maybe a six pack, since I'm spending the night alone."

"By the way, where are you staying tonight?"

"The Days Inn on West Main. Why don't you follow me over, and let's have a cold one before you head back to Dallas."

"All right, you have a cold one, but mines got to be a Dr. Pepper since I'm driving back home."

The deputies watch from a distance, as the two men park the car at the Days Inn and go inside the restaurant. They sit and wait for half an hour until the two finally emerge. After exchanging goodbyes, the big Indian gets into the red convertible and drives away.

"What are we going to do now?" asks Jeffrey.

"Well, we know the Indian in the red convertible going back to Texas. Let's stay with the one in the motel room," says Ray.

As Levi walks to his room, he has no idea he's being watched. After entering, he turns the television set on, just long enough to catch the score of the OU/Kansas State football game, and retires for the night.

Deputy Ray Cross pulls the patrol car into the parking lot just close enough to get the license plate number off Levi's car.

"No sense staying here all night. We'll run the plates in the morning. We can find out who he is and report to the Chief."

The following morning Chief Paul Wilson is already at his desk in his spacious office at the Choctaw Nation. He has just finished a call from Senator James Cody. Rarely does the Senator call before 10 a.m., but this call had a degree of urgency.

Paul Wilson was born and raised in Detroit, Michigan. He came to Durant in his late teens, enrolled in the local college, and received a B.S. in business. In his early 60's, he fits the typical office type, 5 feet 8 inches, about 50 lbs. overweight, and what little hair he has is grey. Half German and half Indian, he has neither the profile nor the bearing of a noble Choctaw Chief. He doesn't speak the Native language, but this is not unusual for men of his age. He grew up during a time when speaking Choctaw, or any native language, was forbidden in the schools they attended.

He had a rough childhood, never quite meeting the expectations of his father, Lt Colonel Wilson. The military man died of a heart attack before his son achieved any success. His mother remarried, resides in California, though Paul rarely sees her having always disliked her new husband.

Chief Wilson, prior to taking office, spent over a decade working on legislation on behalf of the Choctaw Nation in Washington, DC. Long hours were spent waiting in corridors to speak to senators, representatives and other movers and shakers who grease the palms and turn the wheels of government. Without these arrangements, nothing gets done and nobody gets paid. Like Washington, money, and lots of it, is the bloodline of the Capitol.

Wilson is a lonely, bitter man, seeking a father's love, driven to achieve, but lacking self worth. He has been married twice and both relationships failed miserably. The Choctaw Nation and all that it entails is his mistress.

Chief Wilson pushes the intercom button on his phone and his secretary answers. "Jackie, ask my two deputies to come in."

"Morning Chief," Ray and Jeffrey say in unison, as they enter the Chief's office.

"I just got off the phone with Senator Cody. He's concerned something big might be going down under my nose."

"Chief, we done as you asked and followed the Billy's for the last two weeks. You know the big Indian in the red convertible we saw last week? Well he showed up last night at the Billy's home in Bokchito. He brought another big fellow with him, and we followed them both to the Days Inn last night. We think, the big Indian with the red Allante went back to Texas. We ran the plates on the other fellow's car, they came back to an owner, one Levi Tushka of Shawnee," says Ray.

"You don't say? I know Levi. He worked for the Nation for a short time a couple of years ago. Is he still at the Days Inn?"

"As far as I know he is, Chief."

"Go down there and tell him I want to see him."

"What if he doesn't want to come?"

"Convince him," as he picks up the phone and motions for them to leave. "Jackie, get me Senator Cody."

The two deputies drive the quarter mile to the Days Inn, and sure enough Levi Tushka's car is still in the parking lot.

"It's almost two hours from check out time, so what do we do?" asks Jeffrey.

"Well, the Chief didn't say when to bring him in. We don't want to wake him up and piss him off. Let's get some coffee and breakfast. We can watch from the corner table and snag him when he comes out."

At 10:30 the door to Levi's motel room opens, and out steps Levi.

"There he is." says Jeffrey.

Both deputies leave their unfinished meals and move quickly out the front door and into the parking lot. As the two officers approach,

Ray stops about ten feet in front of Levi, and Jeffrey takes a guarded position to Ray's left.

"Sir, may we have a word with you?"

Levi, looking surprised at the deputies' interest in him, replies, "Sure."

"You're Levi Tushka?"

"Yes…, what can I do for you two officers?"

"We've been asked by Chief Wilson to bring you in. He wants to talk to you."

"You're not arresting me are you? It's a little early and I haven't had time to do much harm," says Levi with a teasing smile.

"No, but the Chief still wants to see you this morning."

"Well, you tell the Chief, that I've got other plans, and I'll see him another time." Levi begins to move toward his car.

Both officers take a few steps closer.

Ray getting irritated, "Mr. Tushka, I don't think you understand. We're instructed to bring you in, and I strongly suggest you spare yourself a lot of grief. Get my drift?"

Levi knows of the power wielded by the Chief and his police force, and he didn't need or want any trouble today. After careful consideration, he replies, "All right, but I don't want to leave my car in the parking lot. I'll drive myself over. Fair enough?"

"Sure, but we will be following close behind."

"Hey guys, I wouldn't have it any other way," says Levi, as he gets into his car. He starts the engine, and pulls very quickly out of the parking lot, squealing his tires a little. His quick exit leaves the two officers scrambling to fall in behind him. Levi could see the two officers cursing him through the rear view mirror. Levi, having a little fun, was still careful not to overstep the line.

Arriving at the Nation's headquarters, Levi and the two patrol men climb the fifteen steps leading to the front door of the historic red building. This building had been a women's college for decades. It now houses the administrative offices of the Choctaw Nation. They pass a single security officer manning the entry. The three make their way down a short hallway and turn right towards the Chief's suite. In the smaller reception space, the chief's personal secretary, Jackie, meets them.

"Jackie, would you tell the Chief we're here, and that Mr. Tushka is with us?" asks Ray.

Jackie buzzes the Chief on the telephone intercom.

"Mr. Tushka, Chief will see you now."

As Levi walks through the open doorway to the Chief's office, he remembers the last time he was here. He had discussed with the Chief his plan for a business venture. The Chief was not receptive to the idea, therefore Levi made up his mind to give notice and leave the Nation's employment. The Chief doesn't intimidate him, but still the Chief has been known to make things difficult with uncooperative individuals. He has tremendous power. *'Will he exercise it?'* Levi prefers to avoid that today.

"Levi, it's good to see you again." Chief Wilson stands and extends a hand. "Have a seat." He motions to the chair in front of his desk.

Levi reluctantly shakes Wilsons hand, sits down, leans back and stretches out his legs. He makes himself comfortable as he crosses his cowboy boots at the ankle.

"Chief, it's not every day I get an invitation to come see you, with a police escort."

"Sorry about that Levi, but I really need to talk to you. I hope you'll cooperate and answer a couple of questions for me. I won't be keeping you long. In fact, it's almost noon. I'll treat you to some BBQ down the street. How's that?"

"Fair enough. First question?"

"My deputies tell me, you and a big Indian that drives a red convertible visited the Billy's' home last night. What's going on down there?"

"Is that what this is all about? Why the interest in the Billys, and what do you want to know for?"

"Now Levi, I asked you first. What's going on down there?"

"Ain't nothing going on except talking a little business."

"What kind of business you talking about, Levi?"

"Well, I don't think there's any harm, me telling you. Hell, if you had taken me up on my offer a few years ago, we wouldn't be sitting here playing twenty questions."

"What the hell are you talking about?"

"Catfish farming! I talked to you a couple of years ago about the Nation going into catfish farming. Don't tell me you forgot about our conversation, right here in this very office."

"You mean to say all those meetings been about catfish farming," Wilson's face contorts?

"I don't know about 'all those meetings' you talking about, I can only attest the one last night, and it had to do with catfish," says Levi. He's having fun now.

"I find that hard to believe. Why catfish?"

"As I told you a couple of years ago, catfish farming has great possibilities. It would put a lot of Indians to work who are currently unqualified in the business sector. The Nation already owns enough land, and it wouldn't take a lot of capital to get it up and running," says Levi, as if pitching the idea again. But the Chief is not paying any attention to Levi's remarks.

The Chief throws his palm up like an umpire. He looks at the puzzled deputies, turns to Levi again, and asks, "What's the big Indian's name from Texas, and what part does he play in this?"

"Hey, it ain't no big..., Name's John Tall Bear. He's one of the money men."

"And the Billy's, are they investors as well?"

"Come on, Chief, I don't have all the information. They're going to be very small investors and provide some land. Some others are just contributing the land part. It's moving real slow, and may never get off the ground. You know how Indians are. They get a little excited in the beginning, and eventually drop out. Hell, I might be just wasting time down here." *Levi senses his spontaneous catfish story might allay other suspicions. The sight of a bewildered Chief has made his day.*

"Why you getting all paranoid over a few Indians having meetings about catfish farming?"

"Levi, it's my business to know what goes on within the Nation."

"Hell Chief, you got a death grip on this office, and you ran unopposed the last two elections. I don't know why you're concerned," smiles Levi, playing with the Chief.

"All right Levi, you can go now. But if these meetings are about catfish, they better stay catfish," Wilson asserts his authority, tired of Levi's retorts.

As Levi gets up and walks to the doorway, he turns around, big grin on his face, and says, "Hey Chief, what about the BBQ lunch?"

"It's taken care of. Just give Sonny, the owner, your name." He picks up the phone and gives Jackie instructions to call Sonny, and then, Senator Cody.

"Chi Pisa Lachike", Levi's parting dig at the Chief's inability to speak Choctaw, falls on deaf ears.

Levi calls John later, after a free BBQ lunch. He fills John in about the Chief's insistent request to visit him at his office, and the conversation that followed. He tells him how thinking on his feet, he'd deflected the Chief with the bogus catfish venture. John agrees the tale is a brilliant cover to mask their meetings. John will clue in Roman to spread news the invisible tribe is in the catfish business. They agree to meet tomorrow to visit Senator Rachel Jim in Hugo.

CHAPTER 11

———

"Jimmy Joe, I had an interesting conversation with a fellow who attended one of those meetings you were asking about. The gentleman told me a group of investors and Indian land owners are trying to put together a deal to go into catfish farming," says Chief Paul Wilson.

"That's a bunch of horseshit, Paul. I've got a junior Senator and a couple of Congressmen asking question about those meetings, and it ain't about damn catfish!"

———

James Joe Cody a quarter Kiowa is the senior U.S Senator from Anadarko, Oklahoma. The former University of Oklahoma football star stands 6'6", weighs an imposing 295, and sports the thick black flat top of his college days. Having put on more than a couple of pounds in Washington, he's known as Big Jim.

At home, his family and close friends call him Jimmy Joe. He has a younger sister named Donna, who attended Southeastern State College in Durant. Donna was very popular, a cheerleader who graduated Valedictorian of her class. She would eventually meet and marry the current Chief of the Choctaw Nation, Paul Wilson. From then on, Jimmy Joe Cody and Paul Wilson would be close friends. Their friendship would survive the eventual divorce of Paul and Donna, but in the early days, the three would attend basketball games, go to Pow Wows and dream of good fortune.

Jimmy Joe majored in political science and graduated with a law degree. Just out of college, he capitalized on his football success, ran for U.S. Representative and defeated an incumbent. After one term, he easily won a race for U.S Senator. A fast rising star in the Washington political circles, he is a major power broker in his home state of Oklahoma.

Being part American Indian helps Jimmy Joe in Washington. Too many politicians admit the broken treaties and unfair administration yet deny the billions of dollars the federal government owes Tribes. In the beginning Jimmy Joe did attempt to make a difference. He was able to get more money into Indian country. Sadly, he succumbed to selfish greed like his peers. Eventually he made his way onto the powerful committees that impact the Tribes and gaming policies. Meanwhile, Paul Wilson became Chief of the Choctaw Nation. Two friends conspired, helping the Nation become a driving economic powerhouse and, diverting millions of dollars into personal off shore accounts.

"Jimmy Joe, I know this guy. He used to work for me, and he's being straight."

"Paul, I don't believe it for one fucking minute. My sources have information, which suggests your position as Chief of the Choctaws may be in jeopardy. You better stay on top of this shit. You and I have too much at stake, and I don't want anything or anybody rocking my boat. Get some of your best people on this, and tell them to dig deeper. If you hear anything interesting, give me a call. I've got an important meeting with a couple of our people from the 'golden goose'. You keep me posted," and the Senator is gone.

The Chief of the Choctaw's is a powerful man. As a leader of a sovereign nation, he has a twelve-man council loaded with yes men. He appoints his choice of judges to the Indian court. He has his own police department. He has run unopposed for his office the last fifteen years and is considered unbeatable. His Lear jet is parked fifteen minutes away from his office. However, it is very clear his old friend, Senator James Joe Cody, is the real power man. Chief will do exactly as instructed. He retrieves his cell phone and places a call to his white hair associate at the Atoka Inn.

———

"Chief Wilson, you got another job for me?"

"Maybe, any 'hiccups' the other night?"

"Hey, I'm a pro. Whatever pays? I'd rather be a couple hundred yards away looking down the sights of my Lucille."

"Senator Cody and Houston said you were one of the best! You took out their favorite meeting place. Maybe that will slow this rag tag group and scare away new members too."

"I got to admit, watching the flames light up the stormy night was a turn on."

"Glad you enjoyed yourself. I just got a 'name'."

"Bring it on."

"John Wilkerson Tall Bear."

"Sounds interesting. What can you tell me, other than he's Indian?"

"I know nothing about him, so, your job is to find him, lean on him and slow him down!"

"No problem, that's why you pay me the big bucks."

———

Levi and John are looking forward to the meeting with Senator Rachel Jim. The Senator's office is located in one of the oldest historic buildings in downtown Hugo. Levi and John arrive near her office at 9:30 a.m., thirty minutes before their appointed meeting. This gives them a few minutes for light breakfast and coffee at a small cafe around the corner. They rehearse the topics on their agenda and what they hope to accomplish at the meeting. After sausage and egg biscuits, they make their way into a granite stone building across the street. There, they are met by one of senator aids, and led to the inner office of Senator Jim.

The room is not as large as John had expected. However, it is very tastefully done–not overstated. The plush beige carpet joins up with expensive wood paneling on three sides of the room. There's a working fireplace on one side of the room, with a small statue of a Sacred White Buffalo on the mantle. On one wall hangs a portrait of American Indian War Chiefs. The other side has a large panting of what appears to be a scene from the Choctaw Trail of Tears. A dark mahogany desk is positioned near the center of the room, with two plush blue leather chairs and a matching sofa off to one side. The Senator's desk is covered with neat stacks of papers, and projects an image of someone who is very organized. She thanks her staff member for showing her visitors in, smiles at them and says, "Gentlemen, thank you for coming." She rises from her chair and extends her hand to each of them, then asks them to be seated.

"Senator Jim, thank you for seeing us. What an attractive office you have. I particularly like the painting of the Trail of Tears. My great, great grandmother on my mother's side made that journey," John says.

"I have a few relatives, I've been told, that suffered and died along the way too. When I first saw that painting, I had to have it. It's a visual connection to my past, and a daily reminder why I am here to assist my people."

"I must tell you, your statue of the White Buffalo reminded me of a vision I experienced many weeks ago. Without that vision, I don't think I would be here today. Even now I feel uneasy when I look at yours. Don't know why."

"That's odd, I've been having recurring dreams about a Secret White Buffalo. Maybe we have a connection?"

"I appreciate and share your feelings. If an answer fall out of the sky, I'll let you know. Back to reality now. Senator Jim, I want to introduce you to my good friend, Levi Tushka."

"Senator Jim, Let me suggest a glass of wine before you go to bed. That will help you sleep. All kidding aside, it's an honor and privilege to meet you. I'm glad John invited me to participate," says Levi as John lowers his head from the embarrassing commit.

"Mr. Levi Tushka, that's one of the strangest opening lines I've heard from a stranger. John, I gather Mr. Tushka is not intimidated by anyone, let alone a United States Senator."

"Senator Jim, I'm just as shocked as you are. Levi are you off your meds or something?"

"John, I'm sorry, I'm a little nervous! This office, meeting a United States Senator, you didn't tell me she was so pretty."

"Why, Mr. Tushka what a nice complement, thank you, I think. You're off the hook."

"Senator Jim, I imagine you have a busy schedule so I will get to the point of our visit. A lot has happened since I saw you last. Let me give you a short update. The Billy's visited me in Dallas, and that meeting was very fruitful. Afterwards, I placed a call to Levi, who I have known for several years, and asked him to join us in our efforts. Last week Levi and I traveled to Bokchito to the Billy's home for another small meeting. One of Levi's strengths is he knows every Indian in Oklahoma and then some. He even worked for the Nation for a couple of years. The next day after the Billy meeting in Bokchito, he was politely asked by two of the Nation's finest deputies to accompany them to the Chief's office. There the Chief had a few interesting questions for Levi."

"Well, you men have been very busy. It sounds like things are moving along nicely." She smiles and looks at Levi.

John looks at Levi whose mind is elsewhere.

"Mr. Tushka, can you tell me what the Chief wanted?"

"Senator Jim, all my friends call me Levi. I learned the Chief has knowledge of all the meetings. I assume he has some of his deputies doing some surveillance and reporting back to him. What he doesn't know is the nature of those meetings. The Chief was pretty persistent, so I had to come up with a little bogus story."

"What kind of story?"

"I told him the meeting I attended was about catfish."

"Catfish!" Senator Jim bursts into laughter, her brown hair bouncing off her shoulders. The sheer pink blouse she's wearing rises and falls atop her breasts as she is laughing. Now John's mind is elsewhere. It feels good to see her laugh and feel at ease with them. She is extremely good looking, polished and educated with a commanding presence about her, not to mention, a United States Senator.

"Levi, I love a good catfish story."

Levi continues, "Senator, I told the Chief a small group of Choctaw land owners and some money people were considering going into catfish farming. And, I was interested in helping them get it going and secure a position for myself. He's bought it hook, line and sinker for now. At least it gives us a good cover to continue holding our meetings.

"Hook, line and sinker, I haven't heard that expression in some time. Very impressive Levi! Good thinking on your feet, and I like the cover. What prompted you to come up with the catfish story?"

"Five years ago, working for the Nation, I presented a catfish farming venture to the Chief. Lots of money to be made from catfish and it would create jobs for unemployed Choctaws. The Nation already has the land so start up capital would be minimal. Wilson whined he would take it under advisement. I guess the venture didn't fit his needs or plans at the time. He never asked me about it again." Having impressed the Senator, Levi is beaming full of himself.

"As I said, Senator Jim, Levi knows a lot of people, and we have discussed the possibility of him traveling across the state on our behalf to do some networking. He can gather names and addresses of Choctaws who share our views."

"Levi, if John recommends you, I'm sure you will do a fine job for us. Have you given any thought as to how long it might take for you to acquire some serious numbers? Also, what are you going to need to accomplish the task?"

"Senator, I know my way around the state, where and how to concentrate efficiently. It will take six to eight weeks if everything goes as planned. I promise you, I will do whatever I can to help."

"Senator, this has not been brought up, but this is a time to start doing some serious fundraising. I don't want money to stand in the way of us making progress. Tammy Billy has found us a small building to lease. We can renovate and continue the groundwork for our organization. I'd like to provide Levi with a suitable car, credit card and get him started as soon as possible," suggests John.

"John, that's a great idea. Now let me tell you of some of the information I've acquired. I've asked the right people a few questions, and have been surprised by the answers. There are people whispering about a certain construction company getting favorable treatment from the Choctaw Nation. People in the know say companies are underbidding and still not getting the work. That company then subcontracts some of the jobs out to the losing bidders. There are some unhappy people out there. We are talking about millions of dollars in construction bids. This is very hush, hush for now, so we need to keep it among ourselves. If true, this could be catastrophic for the Choctaw Nation. That said it could work in our favor. A tribe with a noble Constitution...," imagines Senator Jim.

"If's true and that information leaks, the Chief has dug his own grave," says Levi.

"It sounds like things could get a little hot around here," says John.

"Gentlemen, with that kind of money involved, you know there must be higher profile people involved than just the Chief. It could get ugly and downright dangerous."

"What we are attempting to do could create unnecessary confusion in the Nation, and I don't want our people to get caught in the crossfire."

"Absolutely correct, John. You should be very careful what you say and who you say it to. I say this partly because of the fire in Bentley."

"Fire! What happened?"

"Macedonia Indian Church burned to the ground last night."

Her statement sucks the air out of the room. Both men are stunned.

"Damn!" says Levi.

John is visibly upset. He gets out of his chair and walks over in front of the 'Trail of Tears' painting. He stands for a long moment. *The Senator is unaware of my long history with Macedonia. I had spent hundreds of weekends there as a young boy visiting with family.* And then turns, "tell me what happened, Senator."

"I knew this news might upset you John. Local people think it was arson. Atoka County Sheriff is not saying for sure, but you can tell they are leaning that way. FBI is scheduled to come and investigate in a couple of days."

"Senator, you had no way of knowing, but I have been going to that old church since I was six years old. Forgive me for being selfish. You must be feeling a great sense of loss too. It was your home church. I'm so sorry."

"I've had twelve hours to grieve about the loss, now I'm so damn mad. Who would do such a thing? They have no funds in reserve. They can barely keep a pastor full time."

"You mind if Levi and I take a look?"

"Of course not John."

"Somehow, someway we've got to help them rebuild."

"We will! Let's try to meet again in a couple of weeks. Until then, I've got a plane to catch to Washington. Levi, I've enjoyed meeting you and thank you, John, for coming." She rises and shakes Levi's hand, then gives John a friendly hug. The meeting is over.

Leaving the picturesque town of Hugo and its historic buildings, John quietly listens to Levi talk about the meeting and Senator Jim.

Realizing John is deep in thought Levi asks, "Ok big fellow, what's on your mind?"

"The fire of course. Man, why would anyone do that? Macedonia Indian has been there before the turn of the century and serves thirty to forty people at most on any given Sunday."

"I visited it once about ten years ago. Some nice NDN's there, they made me feel at home. They killed a hog that weekend and hundreds came. They didn't know how bad I sang and invited me to sing some Choctaw hymns. Levi laughed and snorted, "Any one who put up with my singing are good people."

"I know a shortcut to Bentley, lets take a drive over and have a look around."

"Lets ride, Clyde," shouted Levi trying to be cool.

Thirty minutes later, John pulls the car onto the dirt driveway to Macedonia Indian Church. The small compound is deserted except for a couple of local dogs sniffing around. There's no yellow crime scene tape surrounding the perimeter like you see on television newscasts. The air is heavy with the smell of pine, burnt lumber and other warring odors. The only thing left upright is the skeleton of a piano, a reminder to sad eyes of the powerful gospel melodies that once filled the air. The two men stand and take in the ugly scene.

"Now I'm here Levi, I have a strange feeling bout this."

"Feeling the same way. Angry spirits in the air."

Back to back, the two men spin 360 degrees looking for clues.

"Not much left John. Looks like they used some kind of accelerant. There was a lot of energy in this building to take it down like this."

"Levi, I can smell the gas. I see something! Look at that can over there. I recognize the shape. The two men make there way over trying now to disturb the chard remains. John used his boot to nudge the can exposing a faint impression of a painted decal.

"Look," pointing at the can.

Levi looking a little puzzled, "hard to make it out, but I'm guessing it's the Pillsbury dough boy."

"The other night! When we stopped in Durant, there was a guy filling this can up with gas."

"How can you be sure it's the same can? There're probably thousands of these cans."

"You're right Levi, but his can had a faded decal, a 'messenger' logo on the side. Can you see it now?"

"Goodbye dough boy, hello messenger. I didn't pay much attention to him. What did he look like?"

"Tall, basketball tall, athletic looking. He wore dirty Levis, military style boots and black leather jacket. But, what made him stand out was his hair. For a young man it was almost white. And he was light skin with piercing blue eyes."

"I remember the black Mercedes-Benz. Don't see too many of those around Indian country."

"It was an AMG model, fast and powerful. We have clues as to who, now I want to know why? Let's get out of here."

When Senator Jim told them of the fire, anger and rage found there way into rational minds. Feelings flared when they actually saw the destruction and felt the angry spirits in the wind. Native Spirits are there to alert, but also to give comfort. As John and Levi, walk away a feeling of calm chases away evil deeds

CHAPTER 12

O ver the next month, small amounts of money are raised–bake sales, collections at singings, and donations from interested parties. A fundraiser helps the people of Bentley rebuild Macedonia Indian Church. Nearly 500 people attend its first Sunday service. John loves the sound of a Hammond B3 organ and donates one to the church. Levi pays for a new piano. Songs of strength once again fill the air and Macedonia is alive.

Levi and John canvass the state, visiting churches to network the Choctaw people. Most of the time they travel together. Levi opens doors and John convinces full bloods to get involved. Levi speaks the Choctaw language fluently and moves in circles that John, initially, could not. More time talking Indian with Indians makes John a better communicator.

He and Levi decide to split up and cover more ground. Follow up visits strengthen old ties and gain new contacts. The Billy's are taking care of the southeastern area, which leaves Levi and John to cover the rest of the state. Through their collective efforts, names and addresses are collected from over twenty thousand Choctaws. They have also added thousands of dollars to the war chest.

Traveling throughout Oklahoma looking for recruits, John visits a county seat seventeen miles north of where he attended school. As young teenagers, John and his friends would load into a car and drive to McAlester to see the sights. The city had bigger movie theaters, drive-in restaurants, and good-looking girls. It was also home to the local paper, The McAlester News Capital. The first time John saw his name in print was in the newspaper's coverage of the local Golden Gloves fights. Even earlier, he had envisioned legendary fighters, the Brown Bomber Joe Louis, Sugar Ray Robinson, Rocky Marciano, Jersey Joe Walcott and others as a young boy when his family gathered around the radio and listened to the Friday night fights.

John's competitive boxing career began in the 6th grade when he lost his first three fights. Alone at night, he would pray, 'God, please let me win a match.' He was so discouraged being a loser. Did Creator have bigger things to do than hear a young Indian boy pleas for favor?

Nonetheless, John entered the Golden Gloves Tournament in McAlester and surprised himself wining his first official bout. To keep order and speed the fights up, promoters had set a chair line for boxers leading to the elevated canvas. You literally sat beside your opponent and moved a pair of seats closer with each bout. This allowed fighters time for friendly conversation or imitation.

John won his second and third fight, which placed him in the finals on Saturday night. It was the first time his father would see him in the ring. He was matched up with a local favorite, Blackie Holden. John was nervous and a little intimidated, because Blackie had fought and won his weight division the year before. He was well known in McAlester, and to John, Blackie was a star.

There they were on a Saturday night, in a semi-dark auditorium, the ring lit up like you see it in the movies, buzzing with the electricity of fight fans, parents, friends and loved ones. After a nervous hour of waiting, it was time for their bout. John climbed through the ropes, then bounced around trying to look like fighters he had seen in the movies. In John's corner was his trainer, a high school senior named Bruce, who had never fought in the ring.

Week after week John would run to Bruce's house, and the two would run around the outskirts of town. The running was to build

John's stamina. He was already in good shape from playing basketball and other sports. The trainer would instruct and watch him pound the heavy bag during their training sessions. He was also coach, and his goal was to mold John into a boxing champion.

During his last week of training prior to the fights, Bruce had introduced him to something the boxing world would eventually know as the 'rope a dope'. In a final round feint, John would covers his face with his gloves, keeps his arms in tight, and lets his opponent tire from ineffective punching. The defender conserves energy and when his opponent ran out of gas, he could come out swinging and win the fight. The plan sounded good to John.

Blackie and John were fighting three-round bouts. The bell rang for round one. They met in the center of the ring and, for the next three minutes, stood toe-to-toe whaling away, steadily slinging leather. They could have fought in a phone booth. It was exhilarating! Listening on the radio, John could hear, but he couldn't see. After the first and second round, John knew he was doing well, and holding his own against this seasoned fighter. He thought it was an even bout going into the last round.

The third round was just like the first and second, in the middle of the ring, fighting toe to toe, and neither giving an inch. Toward the end of the third round, John decided to take his corner's advice and use the 'rope a dope'. He retreated with the rope against his back and covered up. Blackie began to pound away. John was not hurt, but he had made a mistake. Just as he was about to break out and take control of the fight, the referee separated them. Thinking the underdog needed to be protected, the referee stopped the fight and awarded the match to Blackie.

Champions were given a trophy and a coveted Golden Gloves leather jacket. Assured he could have fought another ten rounds, John was devastated. Making things worse, it appeared he had given up and thus, embarrassed his father. Fatal mistakes seem forever etched in minds of second place fighters. He had battled to the title bout only to lose to a hometown favorite.

———

While in McAlester, John decides to get in touch with Blackie. He Google's Holden's name and finds an Ann Holden in the area. He calls information and, on the phone, learns she is Blackie's aunt. John explains he is an old friend and asks, "Where is your nephew?"

Her reply shocks him, "He's in the ground."

Blackie had died a horrible death, colon cancer a few years ago. John shares a bit of himself. To his surprise, she says she remembers him and the fight. She gives John a number for Blackie's sister Mary Holden, who lives, of all places, in John's birthplace, Talihina.

John places a call to Mary, gets her message machine, and leaves his number. She calls back an hour later, and when he speaks about their match, she says she remembers it as well as being mad at him for hitting her brother.

"But Mary, Blackie won the fight."

"I know, but I was still mad at you."

He thinks to himself. *'Yeah, I was winning the fight, took bad advice from my corner man and lost.'*

Mary fills him in on the life of Blackie Holden. He had joined the military and become an officer. He fought in Vietnam and Saudi Arabia, got married and divorced, but led a good' life.

Mary, after a bad marriage moved to Talihina to find refuge in the country. Now 64, she shares a small apartment with her dog. She says she may have the picture of their fight that appeared in the local newspaper. John tells Mary the photo would be a small treasure to him. John asks her, if she finds the picture, to call, he would immediately drive to Talihina and take her to lunch.

John decides to travel to Talihina only two hours away to recruit and, perhaps, visit with Mary. He will finish things up and leave in the morning. He can be there by noon and have the rest of the day to look around. He speaks to Mary again, and relates his plans. She promised to continue looking for the picture. The following morning, John is travelling back to the town where he was born.

The trip takes him eastward past a small town called Wilburton and nearby Roberts Cave State Park. Legend has it this area was the home of the train robber, Belle Starr. There are steep rock cliffs and caves, where she and her outlaw gang are supposed to have hidden. A favorite attraction there is rock formation called Devil Slide. You slide down inside a rock formation and crawl through a small tunnel to an opening on the other side of the mountain. John wouldn't do it today imagining all the rattlesnakes they must have crawled past. Then, they had no fear.

The drive takes John up and down mountains and around hairpin curves. Pine trees soar eighty feet into the sky. It is truly a beautiful area of the state. He arrives around eleven a.m. and has lunch. Afterwards he decides to pay a visit to the Talihina Indian Recovery Center. It's an adequate facility, which can house approximately thirty people. The information director is very kind about showing him around. He wonders why he doesn't see more patients and asks how many are currently in-house and she states there are about fifteen. John gets the impression, if they were really on top of things, they could easily fill the facility up. He perceives the Recovery Center should be serving many more patients. This is information he will pass on to Roman and the rest of the staff.

Next, he decides to pay a visit to the new Indian Hospital. The new building has a white outer shell of modern design. John enters the emergency room area first. Entering the waiting area, it's evident what the elder Jim woman described at the church. A movie producer looking to cast Indians would find few in this waiting room. As Ms. Jim stated, the staff behind the counter cannot relate to a full blood Indian. The balance of care is slanted to favor the whiter Choctaws.

Angered, John turns on his heel and leaves. He finds a Days Inn and checks in on the ground level. After showering, he calls Mary and asks can he treat her to her favorite dinner at a catfish place called 'Norma's' on the main drag. People in Talihina eat a little earlier than most, so the parking lot is full by 5 p.m. He's hungry from having an early lunch.

He arrives ten minutes early and, sure enough, Mary is already where she promised, seated at her window table overlooking a small lake out back. Just as John expects, Mary is one of the nicest ladies he has ever met. He begins telling her his childhood story and includes how he got involved in boxing. They relive the story of the fight and how upset she was with him because he had given Blackie a busted lip. He laughs out loud and tells her Blackie had given him a lot more. It's an exaggeration, but John wants to keep Blackie bigger than life to his sister. Mary hasn't been able to find the photo, but promises to continue looking. They conclude their dinner with the promise to keep in touch, and say their goodbyes. The birth of a new friendship with Mary through brother Blackie is treasured. John returns to his room at the Days Inn, makes a few calls and retires. He is tired from the day's journey and falls into a deep sleep.

Outside, a black Mercedes has been sitting in wait. Its occupants decide John Wilkerson Tall Bear is safe in his sanctuary. They quietly leave the parking lot, cruise through town and pull into Norma's parking lot in search of information and prey.....

CHAPTER 13

Ladies and gentleman, Elvis has left the building.
Thank you and goodnight.

Senator Cody doesn't buy the catfish story. Wary of clandestine activities, he presses the Chief. Wilson relays the same pressure to his deputies. The deputies, desperate to satisfy their Chief, continue to investigate and harass people as they travel to and from meetings.

In the last two months, the movement has tweaked and tuned its organization for efficiency. Seven prominent members from larger cities have been chosen as directors found strength to live in racial harmony for their particular areas. Coordinators are assigned to the smaller towns and churches in each county. Coordinators bridge the people and the directors to solicit names, addresses, and contact numbers from the Indian people, noting their needs and suggestions. At the last monthly meeting, seven directors and 28 coordinators met to report and plan for the weeks ahead. Tonight's meeting is to be held in the Durant home of one of the directors.

Gary and Don Taylor graduated from Boswell High School almost ten years ago. They are the only sons of Samuel and Karen Taylor. Big

Sam Taylor, as they call him, is a full blood Choctaw Indian. His wife Karen is white. Small-minded communities like Karen's hometown, Kingston, still disapprove of 'mixed' marriages. Boswell is not perfect, but the Taylors have found strength to live in racial harmony and been accepted. Both brothers were popular and well liked.

Gary, older, by two years, is a lady's man who loves to party in the clubs and beer halls. He grew up singing the music of Elvis Presley. With his dark complexion and brooding eyes, he looks a lot like Elvis did in his early 20's. After memorizing all the 'King's' songs, he watched the movies, and copied all his idol's mannerisms. He started performing at karaoke bars where friends applauded his impersonation.

Gary will sometimes refer to his younger brother as James Burton, Elvis's lead guitarist. Though more introverted, Don slings a mean Telecaster. They are a talented combination, energetic and well liked, especially by the female audience.

Though now in their early 30's, neither of them has gotten married. Both work at odd jobs, and still looking for a calling in life. A lady friend of Gary first told him about a new Native organization, had asked if he was interested in participating. Don, listening to their conversation, also found the new tribe angle interesting.

When Gary and Don are invited to attend a meeting, they accept without hesitation. They do everything else together, why not this? After their first meeting, they feel part of something exciting. Being half white, the brother's were always pro Indian. This was no disrespect to their mother's race, but a way to appreciate an Indian heritage, too often annihilated by US systems. After their second meeting, they are hooked. Would their charisma, flexibility and enthusiasm qualify them to operate as coordinator in Boswell?

Most of the directors know the Taylor family well. Big Sam and Karen are good people, hard working, and respectable. Gary and Don have had their share of problems, alcohol arrests for drinking and driving. Both have been through the Talihina Indian Recovery Center.

The directors having concerns, voice them to Big Sam. The proud father, eager to see his sons involved in something worthwhile, pledges to monitor their activities and help them stay on course.

The night's meeting had been short so there's still time for Gary to perform his Elvis act at a honky-tonk just north of Durant. Gary likes to sing at Lou Ann's, because they provide a live band. They let Don sit in and play guitar because he knows the Elvis tunes.

A couple of months before, Gary and Don had traveled to a Garland, Texas recording studio and cut a demo. The sound engineer liked it so much, he called the owner of a top Dallas booking agent for critique. The agency told Gary and Don, if they continue to hone their skills, good things would come their way. A promoter was impressed and would get them work in the coming holiday season.

Gary bought an Elvis jumpsuit to complete his Elvis transformation. He had chosen an outfit with a Native design called 'the old Indian', one of the King's favorites. It's well known Elvis was part Indian and had a suit made to celebrate his Native heritage. From across a room, Gary looks so much like Elvis it's scary.

As the lights are turned down, Gary and Don make their way onstage for the last set of the night. They start with a rousing Elvis groove, "Burning Love". The crowd goes crazy. As the song ends, Gary says, "Thank you, thank you very much" in his best Elvis voice.

The audience is on their feet, cheering and clapping. Lou Ann's crowd will not let the Taylor brothers leave the stage until they sing more songs. Gary follows with Blue Suede Shoes, Heartbreak Hotel and half a dozen other songs, closing appropriately with Can't Help Falling in Love With You. 'Can't-get-enough' fans shout for more. It's a breakthrough performance for Gary. The confident siblings are ready for Dallas.

After a few drinks with the band members and fans, the brothers say goodbye and make their way to the exit. Gary still wearing the white jumpsuit walks through the door and into the parking lot. Don renders his favorite impression. "Ladies and gentleman, Elvis has left the building. Thank you and good night." Both laugh as they head for their car.

Gary looks at his younger brother and says with a big grin, "Yeah, and Elvis is leaving alone, with his loaded little brother."

"Am I cramping your style, big brother? I saw how that little blonde was hanging all over you!"

"Right, and if you weren't plastered, I'd tell you, 'See you later alligator'."

"Hey, I'm ok! I can make it home! Just point me in the right direction!" says Don.

"No way! Give me the keys. I'm driving." They laugh, get into the car, and drive off in the direction of Boswell.

Deputy Ray Cross and Jeffrey Irwin watch from an unmarked patrol car, across the street from Lou Ann's. They watch as the Taylor brothers get into their car and begin to drive away. Ray Cross eases the patrol car into the traffic and follows. After turning east on State Hwy 70 to Boswell, the tribal patrol car follows even closer behind. This makes Gary nervous. He's had one too many drinks himself, and the Choctaw Nation patrol car on his tail adds pressure.

"Don, wake up. We got problems. We have a Nation patrol car on our tail. He's been following us for the last ten miles."

Don jumps to attention and makes sure his seatbelt is fastened. "What the hell do them assholes want with us?"

Gary is sensing the anger in Don's voice. "I don't know. Now look, if they stop us, you be cool and don't be a smartass."

The two-lane highway to Boswell has no lights, except for what a full moon provides. It's cold outside, and the heavy breathing from the brothers is beginning to fog up the windows, plus making it difficult for Gary to see. He's having trouble keeping the car in the center of his lane. He turns on the heater fan to clear some of the moisture condensing on the windshield. With the fan on high, the road becomes a little clearer. Gary steadies himself and begins to feel relieved.

In the blink of an eye, a possum crossing the highway stares into the headlights. Gary jerks the car to his left swerving across the centerline to avoid hitting the fat little animal. He quickly regains control and eases the car back into his lane. He's sweating a little, because he knows what's coming. The red lights are now flashing in the rearview mirror.

"Damn!" shouts Gary. He begins to slow the car down and eases to the edge of the highway. There is no shoulder and the car is leaning at an extreme angle to the right.

"I hope them assholes are not Indians, 'cause I'm gonna' kick their asses," yells Don.

Gary turns to Don, grabs his shirt just under his chin, shakes him a little and says, "Don, you just keep your big mouth shut and let me do the talking. You pop off and you're just going to make it worse. Hell, we've been in jail before. One more night in that shithole jail in Boswell isn't going to kill us. So you just mind your p's and q's and let me do the talking."

Deputy Ray Cross opens his door, steps out, and begins approaching the Taylors' car on the driver's side. Deputy Irwin does the same on the passenger side. With a flashlight in his left hand and his right hand on his service weapon, Cross eases up to the driver door. Gary retrieves his driver's license and insurance card. As he turns his head to his left and rolls down the car window, Gary is hit in the face with a light beam. Deputy Irwin's flashlight in search of weapons, penetrating through the rear passenger window, floods the interior.

"Put both of your hands on the dash, driver!" commands Deputy Cross.

"You do the same thing, passenger," shouts Deputy Irwin.

"Well, well, look what we have here deputy! We done caught Elvis the Pelvis!" smirks Deputy Ray Cross.

"Hot damn, I knew he was still alive!" shouts Deputy Irwin, getting in on the act.

"You a long way from home, Elvis! Memphis is due east about 450 miles," jokes Deputy Cross.

Agitated, Don begins to get pissed off.

"Passenger, you just keep fucking still, and keep them hands on the dash!" shouts Deputy Irwin.

"You got a driver's license, Elvis?" asks Deputy Cross.

"Yes, sir," answers Gary very loudly, "Right here," as he hands the license through the window.

"Well you're not Elvis after all! Says here you're Gary W. Taylor. What are you doing wearing that Elvis get up?"

"Come on, officer. I'm a singer and I was doing a show at Lou Ann's tonight. I saw you in the parking lot when we came out."

"Don't be a smart ass, Indian! I smell liquor! Get out of the car!" snarls Deputy Cross.

First Gary, then Don exit the car under observant eyes. They are prodded to place their hands on top of the car, and spread their legs to be searched. Bewilders faces in passing cars witness a costumed Elvis about to be searched.

As Deputy Irwin pats Don down, he grabs his crouch area very violently. Don whirls around and screams at Deputy Irwin, "You filthy rotten pig!" Just as the words escape his mouth, Irwin slams the flashlight toward the side of his head. Don jerks back and the blow catches him on the shoulder. He lunges at the officer, and they struggle.

Deputy Cross, with his left hand on the back of Gary's neck, presses him against the top of the car, shouts, "Don't fucking move Elvis or I'll blow your head off!"

Turned in the direction of the scuffle, Gary is restrained by the threat. He sees Don wrestle an edge, fear in the Deputy's eyes, the flash at the muzzle, all before the exploding gun shot shatters a deadly silence in the night. The bullet pierces Don's chest, just below his heart, catapulting him backwards. He falls into the ditch on his back several feet from Gary.

The ditch is covered with several inches of rain from the night before. Water and mud splatter in all directions. Deputy Irwin takes a couple of steps closer to Don, as if ready to fire his weapon again.

Don clutches his chest, looks at the deputy, and in a faint voice says, "You sorry piece of white trash! The new tribe will take care of you and your sorry Chief. I hope both of you rot in hell!"

Don looks in the direction of his brother and reaches out with his left hand. Their eyes meet momentarily, and then Don closes his eyes. Gary knows he is gone. In a split second, a violent rage comes over him. He jerks free of Deputy Cross's hold.

"Chief Tall Bear is coming!" screams Gary.

He bolts in the direction of Deputy Irwin to render justice in honor of his fallen brother. He hears the 45's thunder, but doesn't see the flash. A split second later he feels the large caliber slug rip into his back. Gone before he hits the ground, Gary falls into the ditch, his head below his feet in the water from last night's rain. Traffic is stopping in both directions. Several get out of their cars and handy IPhones capture the scene.

Red, white, and blue lights flash on the patrol car. Don lies on his back, Gary on his stomach as their young souls escape. Two deputies, and guns in hand, stand over them. By morning, this chilling image will be telecast worldwide.

CHAPTER 14

The Days Inn switchboard operator at Talihina is instructed by an incoming caller to ring John Tall Bear's room.

Startled by the bedside table phone, he squints at the clock radio for time confirmation. Sensing trouble, he grabs the handset from its cradle, "Hello!" he practically shouts.

"John!" He hears Roman's frantic voice in the receiver. "John, we got problems here! Turn on your TV set. It's on every news station you can't miss it. Call me when you're up and ready. I've other calls to make." Tall Bear is confused by Roman's abrupt hang up.

John gets up quickly, splashes cold water on his face, puts in his contact lenses, and turns on TV. The first thing he hears is a report the FBI is coming to investigate the death of two Indian men.

The station replays a video clip of two men lying in a ditch. One, sprawled on his stomach, is dressed in an Elvis jumpsuit. Nearby, a tribal patrol car is parked behind, presumably, the deceased's vehicle. A small group of officers stand around gawking at the odd scene. A caption runs insistently across the top of the screen. 'Elvis impersonator and brother shot dead by Tribal police.' John changes stations to no avail–sketchy information and few details. He tries another channel, same news. *'Who were these men, and how are they connected to us?'*

Retrieving his cell phone from the top of the bedside table, John punches in Roman's number. The call goes straight to voice mail. He leaves a brief message and watches TV for new information. The Sherman-Dennison television station, twenty-five miles south of Durant, across the state line in Texas, has a news crew at the killing site. They show a clip of the Chief of the Choctaws walking up the steps to his office. He is walking quickly and surrounded by tribal police. When asked about the killings, he shakes his head and offers no comment.

Video feed switches back to the killing site, now 8 hours old. The bodies are still in place, waiting for word whether regional FBI will take over the investigation. Everything seems snail paced. *'Why I never wanted to come back to Oklahoma'.* Though the situation screams for the obvious, there is no urgency.

His cell phone rings. He quickly answers, "Roman?"

"No John, its Levi."

"Sorry Levi, I was expecting Roman to call me back. What the heck is going on?"

"Have you been watching TV?"

"Yes, for the last fifteen minutes. I got a call from Roman half past 7. He told me to turn on the TV, and then call him back. That's all I know."

"John, those two men are Gary and Don Taylor."

No! John is stunned. He had taken a liking to the young brothers. Gary had researched Tall Bear prior to their meeting and knew he too was an Elvis fan. What Gary Taylor didn't know was Elvis and Tall Bear studied American Kenpo under the late Grandmaster Edmond K. Parker.

The King was a black belt under Ed Parker, as were the security and bodyguards that traveled with him when in concert. The black guitar Elvis played during his comeback was adorned with Parker's IKKA school patch, a trademark of his Kenpo system. Tall Bear would come to know Parker, and receive a black belt under him as well. Master Parker was true genius, a friend, and legend in his own time.

Tall Bear and Parker, a full blood Hawaiian, had discussed the similarities of their two cultures, their spirituality and deep devotion to family. Both held elders in high esteem, wore elaborate celebration costumes, cooked and prepared meals to honor family and Mother Earth.

At dinner one evening, Parker asked Tall Bear about Indian wrestling, techniques that John might have learned as a young boy. John told Ed he knew a few things but nothing of great significance. Parker related a conversation he had with Elvis, while spending time at the singer's home in Memphis. Elvis had confessed to being ashamed he was part Indian. It was not uncommon for a young boy who grew up in the south to be part Indian, and sometimes not even know it. If a family had Indian blood, it was kept secret and not talked about. In reality, most were ashamed to admit it. After a long discussion, Parker convinced Elvis being part Indian was something very special. From that day forward, Elvis spoke proudly about his Indian heritage. Soon after, Elvis began wearing the elaborate jumpsuits adorned with American Indian designs in concert.

During their conversations, Parker had suggested Tall Bear do something with his Native fighting art. Upon the Grandmaster's death in December of 1990, John, realizing he had dismissed Parker's inquiry too quickly, began to reach in the deep corners of his mind to retrieve the warrior art that was passed down to him orally by his ancestors—father, uncles, grandfathers and friends of the family. Memories run through Tall Bear's mind even as his thoughts go to Gary and Don's parents, Sam and Karen Taylor. *'What must they be going through, losing both of their sons at the same time?'*

"John, are you there?"

"Levi, I'm here. I'm shocked and don't know what to say. Where are you now?"

"I'm in Ada," says Levi, "90 miles northwest of Durant."

"I'm in Talihina, about the same distance away. If we both leave now, we can meet in Durant around 10 a.m."

"OK, I'm on my way."

"When I get to Atoka, I'll call you to set up a place to meet. Phone Roman to see if he has any more information," and John hangs up.

Before leaving his room, he turns the television on for updates on the Boswell shooting. Suddenly one station touts 'Breaking News' across the bottom of the screen. It cuts to a reporter standing outside a small home, announcing another homicide.

'A local woman was found beaten and shot to death last night. This is the first murder in Talihina in ten years. Mary Holden, age 68, was found by her landlord when he noticed Mrs. Holden's dog running free outside her small home. A slightly opened front door explained the dog's escape. Peeking in, the landlord saw the victim lying on the living room floor'. The sheriff and his small team of investigators declared, 'She appeared to have been beaten badly and shot in the head, execution style.' Robbery has been ruled out. There are no suspects and this small town is shaken to its knees. That's all for now, back to the station.'

The news hits John like a sledgehammer. Is this killing random? Sick to his stomach, he runs to the bathroom to throw up. Nothing happens. He composes himself with more cold water to the face. After a couple of minutes, he realizes the killing in Boswell is his priority. He will check with the Talihina local authorities later about Mary Holden.

John quickly checks out of his room and begins his trip back to Durant. He's actually a little further away than Levi, so he has to make up some time. The route he has chosen is a lonely two-lane highway with very little traffic. The Red Allante roars into the Buffalo Valley floor and onward toward Stringtown, to meet highway 75 and turn south to Atoka. Occasionally on this route you might see a fawn and its mother crossing the highway. Wild hogs and other animals roam the valley floor. For John and his people, kinship with all creatures of the earth, sky and water was a real and active principle. Driving through Buffalo Valley, John's mind begins to wander. Death at anytime is complicated. Death in the family of someone you know is always a tragedy. John is yet to realize how the death of these two men will impact the Indian community.

Buffalo Valley is such a peaceful place. It reminds him, in death, there is peace for those who pass on. He perceives some insight into the life of the Taylor brothers. Their life was complicated because they were half-breed Indians. Not many things in their lives were absolute. They were constantly being pulled one way or the other. Their young lives walked a gym's balance beam. The beam is only four inches wide. *'When I fall, and I will, which way will I fall?'* Like flipping a coin, *'heads or tail', 'to be or not to be',* or *'Am I white or am I Indian?'* John knows something of their journey senses both are at rest. He begins to feel a peacefulness coming over his own body. He can feel his blood pressure coming down. *'It is what it is, and now we all must deal with it. We must remain strong for the family.'*

On both sides of the valley floor, the mountains stretch high into the sky. It is so beautiful this time of the year. John can see several bald eagles soaring in the sky. On a high cliff above, a hang glider has just gone airborne from a rock bluff called Eagle's Nest. This is where John was born. It is no wonder he enjoys coming back here. Talihina is a Native Choctaw word meaning 'iron path'. The word describes the train tracks that wind through the valley floor. The Indians in the old days would refer to the train as IronHorse. John can feel the magical pull of his birthplace. He hadn't made a decision yet, but perhaps this will be his resting place one day. This he knew. It would be here or in Achille where his mother sleeps.

There had been no traffic for thirty minutes on this lonely stretch of two-lane highway. His peaceful moment is suddenly disrupted when a dark vehicle quickly runs up behind him. John was doing 70 mph when the black car braked to avoid hitting John's rear bumper. The car backs off 50 yards, and then accelerates again close behind. There's nothing to keep the aggressive car from passing, so John waves him around. Repeatedly, the menace lingers for a couple of miles, each time returning. John can now see a man behind the wheel and a woman passenger. The black sedan is a Mercedes AMG and the driver has wild looking short white hair. *It's the man at the gas station!* John hits the breaks to slow the AMG. Down to 20 mph, he pulls halfway onto the shoulder signaling the nuisance to stop.

The Mercedes roars by. The woman smiles at Tall Bear as they pass, blocking the driver face. She's very pretty, Liz Taylor pretty. John tromps the accelerator and begins chase. His car is no match for the powerful Mercedes and within a minute, it is out of sight. A connection in his brain screams, *'Mary..., you son of a bitch, you killed Mary!'* He doesn't know this for sure, but why was he in Talihina? Why did he burn Macedonia?

As John turns left onto highway 75 toward Atoka, he receives a call from Roman as to when he will arrive. He and John decide Levi, Tammy and some staff members need to meet as soon as possible. Roman says the meeting has a new sense of urgency because of the latest reports about the shootings. No one is saying anything, but a couple of items have been leaked to the press, deputies stated one of the victims threatened a 'new tribe coming,' and the name Tall Bear was mentioned.

"Everyone is just guessing what it means, but the cat is out of the bag, and we must act quickly". Roman concludes. They decide to meet in Durant at the home of Henry Gibson, one of the community directors, at 11 a.m.

John is the last to arrive and Henry greets him at the door. He follows Henry into a spacious den near the back of the house. Roman is on his cell phone, and Tammy and Levi look to be having a serious conversation. A couple of staff members are taking calls on their cell phones too. Tammy and Levi turn at John's entrance. Roman acknowledges him, finishes his conversation, and rises to shake his hand and give him a hug.

"Now we're all here, let's get down to business. Time, for many reasons, is precious," announces Roman. "John, Levi, my cell phone hasn't stopped ringing since the first TV reports this morning. Tammy's been inundated with calls as well. Our two staff members' landlines and cell phones have blown up. Some of these calls are from close friends, family members, and acquaintances of Gary and Don, but most calls are coming from our member-recruiting program. These are from Indians wanting to get involved in our cause. They want to help in any way they can."

"This fact we know for sure, two of our most popular coordinators died at the hands of Chief Wilson's tribal police force. People want to come and honor these two men and, at the same time, show defiance and disdain for the Chief and his officers," offered Levi.

"From the volume of calls coming in, it would appear hundreds of our people might be interested in coming to Durant to attend the funeral. We need to decide how to manage this, yet maintain a sense of dignity for the family. We don't want to take any action that may look like we are exploiting the family's tragedy. John, what are your thoughts?"

John takes a few moments to gather his thoughts, then says, "In any family, the loss of a loved one is tragic and can be overwhelming. The family should not feel they are alone in their loss. It's our loss as well. If the family has no objections, then this is what I suggest. Chahta Amoma Atokoli (full blood Choctaws) will take charge, plan and coordinate the funeral. It would appear the Chief knows our intentions, so it's time to move quickly and establish who we are and what we want."

Everyone looks surprised and pleased at John's statement. The surprise is, he has given their movement and organization a name.

"'Ahchukma', I like the new name, it says exactly who we are. Let me suggest we use the acronym CMA," says Levi. In Choctaw, you can drop the "A" in Amoma and it means the same thing.

"Levi, I like that even better. Agreed?" John asks. Everyone is nodding agreement.

"Tammy will you place a call to the Taylors and get their ok?" Tammy excuses herself and moves into another room to make the call.

"The second matter for us to consider is the shooting looks very suspicious at best," asserts Roman. "We have two unarmed men shot by two armed deputies. We know the Chief and the Durant Police Department are in bed together. I don't trust them to investigate the crime scene."

"John, we need to get an independent investigation unit to take control of the situation before the bodies are moved. The FBI may be investigating but that's purely speculation. They're not commenting on the matter and will not say whether they are involved. The Chief has a lot of power and nobody wants to step on his toes, adds Levi."

"I agree, then we should call Senator Jim's office to see if she can assist us", suggests John. "Levi, I know you'd like to make that call. What are you waiting for?"

"Consider it done." Levi jumps to his feet and leaves the room.

Tammy reenters the room, pauses with feet shoulder width and both hands on her hips, "John, I just spoke to Sam and Karen. They're holding up as best they can, Sam less well. Karen complained he's moody, angry and wants some answers. She's afraid of what he might do. She can handle him for now, but after the funeral, she's afraid. She and Sam have given permission to CMA to make arrangements for the funeral."

Levi rejoins the group. "John, I just spoke with Senator Jim. She says she will call the FBI Regional Office in McAlester and pay a visit to Chief Wilson this afternoon. She agrees the investigation should be turned over to an outside source. She promises to apply as much pressure as needed. John, she seems very angry. I don't envy the Chief when she get in front of him."

As Levi is speaking, John is putting together a team in his head. He will assign staff members a to-do lists as soon as this meeting is over.

"As most of you know, in life, when one door closes, another one opens. The tragic events of yesterday have brought us together to deal with the death of our friends. At this meeting, the formal birth of CMA honors our fallen friends, Gary and Don Taylor. Now everybody get busy! Levi, Roman I'd like a word with the both of you in private."

The three leaders conference in a small room, "We have another huge problem. As I was passing through Buffalo Valley, a black Mercedes AMG pulled up behind me...."

CHAPTER 15

Senator Cody is about to leave for the Hill, when one of his staff members runs into his office and tunes the television set to a breaking news story in southeastern Oklahoma. The news of the death of two Indians is unpleasant in itself. However, when they are shot by one of his closest friend's deputies, he is shocked and furious.

The Senator pushes a button on the telephone desk set and says, "Helen, get me Paul Wilson on the phone!" After waiting a couple of minutes he shouts to Helen again, "Helen, you got the Chief?"

"Senator Cody, I can't get through to them. Their system must be down or jammed."

"Try his personal cell number, but get that ass on the phone."

After another minute, Helen buzzes the Senator, "I got him. He's on line five."

"Paul, what in the hell is going on down there? I don't give a shit if you're standing in the middle of a rattlesnake pit. You take time! The FBI's outside your office? What the hell are they doing there? United State Senator Jim is with them? How and why is that bitch involved? The FBI doesn't have any jurisdiction on Indian land! Tell them to go fuck themselves!"

"Was the shooting justified? What kind of deputies do you have down there? I'm hearing on the news report both of the Indian men were drunk and unarmed. Paul, please tell me those deputies are Indian. They're both white? Oh Lord, help us!"

"Paul, the news just reported the victims shouted something about a new tribe coming and mentioned someone named Tall Bear before they were shot. What's that about? That's the only words mentioned before they died? Are you sure? All right, see what the FBI wants, and be careful what you say to Senator Jim. She's as smart as they come. Remember, she's from that area and she has a lot of support. The way she cozies up to them Senators, she can make anything happen. She's a player Paul, don't underestimate her." He slams the phone down and is off to the Hill.

———————

"Jackie, would you send in Senator Jim and the FBI agents?" Jackie escorts the three into the Chief's office.

"Senator Jim, it's so good to see you." The Chief stands and extends his hand.

"Chief Wilson, I'd like to introduce agent Joe Jackson." Jackson is a tall black man who appears to be in his late 40's.

"And this is agent Karen Rivers." Rivers is a slender white lady in her mid 30's with a southern accent. Three chairs are positioned in front of the Chief's desk, and Senator Jim takes the center seat. It's obvious she's there to take charge.

"Chief, I don't have to tell you we have a very delicate situation here. From initial findings at the crime scene, and the information your two deputies gave, it appears that the shooting was not justified. I'm getting pressure from the family and the media, to intervene and get to the bottom of this. The FBI is standing by and will take charge, if you and your office are willing to step aside. Personally, it would be in your best interest to permit an outside and impartial investigation."

"Senator Jim, we have the Durant Police Department and my staff of deputies taking care of the crime scene as we speak. I don't agree with you. I have spoken to both deputies and they assured me, the shootings, though tragic, could not be avoided. Both have been on my staff for many years and are good family men. They are both remorseful and extend their condolences to the family."

"Chief, I understand your support for your deputies, however, let me say this. Durant is going to be a hotbed this weekend, with the possibility of a few thousand American Indians descending on the city to pay tribute to those two men. I hope you and your officers will take a low profile and let the Durant police take responsibility for policing the city. They will be looking for you and your office to do the right thing. Let's not give them any reason to start marching on your Capitol steps.

Secondly, a few of my colleagues in the House and Senate are expecting me to obtain an agreement with you and your office. They also believe the FBI should take over the investigation. Those are people you will want to be in good standing with when certain bills come before them on the House and Senate floor. Those bills will influence the Choctaw Nation and future federal funding. You have done a wonderful job leading the Choctaw Nation. This is not a time to drive the car off in the ditch," says the Senator.

"Well Senator, I can see how you got elected. You can be pretty persuasive, while you bring up some valid points. Tell you what I will do. I'll instruct my officers to stand down until we get a favorable report regarding the shooting incidents. I don't see why we can't let the FBI take over the investigation. I expect to be kept fully informed of their findings."

"Chief Wilson, I'll be the agent in charge, and let me assure you, you will have a report on your desk as soon as we complete our investigation," says Agent Rivers. "Agent Jackson will be in touch with you and your staff on a daily basis to keep you in the loop. We'll have a full team of forensic personnel on site within the hour. If everything goes well, we should be able to clear the crime scene this afternoon and release the bodies to the funeral home."

"Chief, we'll need to interview the two deputies as soon as possible. Here is my card," says Jackson. "Have them call me, they will be instructed where to report. I suggest you suspend or assign them to office duty until after we complete the investigation."

"Agents Jackson, Rivers, I'll take that into consideration." Paul Wilson stands, and extends a hand to each of them. The Chief is dismissing them to show his authority.

"Senator Jim, it's been a pleasure. I am sorry it was under these circumstances. Perhaps after this is over you might pay us another visit," says the Chief with a winning smile. The Chief has made a sad little attempt to let her know he might be interested in something else.

"Thank you, Chief." Senator Jim and agents remains seated to send a message to the Chief. The meeting will be over when she stands.

"One more thing!" says the Senator. "I have been asked by a new organization called the CMA to ensure this matter is given the highest priority. I'm sure you'll agree we want to see the true facts come out and put this tragic event behind us."

"CMA, I never heard of them."

"You will! I've taken a special interest in Chahta Amoma Atokoli because of what they stand for. I will be very unhappy should they not succeed in their endeavor. I'm hoping you and your office will assist them in the event they need your advice and counsel. They are a faith based church organization and they have the ears of many Choctaws here in the thirteen counties. Indians helping Indians is the neighborly thing to do. As for the invitation, I'll see if my schedule will accommodate it."

Senator Jim stands ignoring the Chief's outstretched hand, and says to Agent Rivers, "Agent Rivers, I just love your shoes, where did you buy them?" Senator Jim's message gets across to the Chief, and the three leave the office.

'That bitch! Who does she think she is?'

"Jackie," as he presses the intercom button on the phone, "Try and reach Senator Cody."

Chief Wilson still fuming sits at his desk wondering. *'Why that bitch Senator is involved with, 'What did she call them?' CMA. Could the new group trouble him and his plans with Senator Cody?*

"Chief, Senator Cody is on line seven," says Jackie.

"Jimmy Joe! That Jim Bitch and two FBI Special Agents just left my office. They wanted me to turn over the investigation of the shooting to the FBI. Well yeah, after some consideration, I decided to let them take over. Jim, Jim! You weren't here in the meeting, so give me some fucking credit. She made a good argument for letting the FBI takeover. They're going to keep me informed if anything new comes up. I've agreed to have my officer's stand down for the weekend, because there're expecting hundreds of Indians to come to the funeral. I get the impression they're looking for blood, and I don't want any of my officers involved.

"Fuck you Jimmy Joe! I'm not lying down. I'm just trying to do the smart thing here. It makes good sense for the FBI to find my officers clean. That way, they'll be seen doing their job. I want this thing over and done with too. With what we have in the works, I don't need any more trouble here.

"But we have another little problem to consider. You were right about the meetings those Indians are holding. All right, all right, so you told me so! Senator Jim just came out and told me! She stated she has a personal interest in this new group called the CMA. That crazy bitch even asked me to assist them if they call me. Who the fuck does she think she's dealing with here? Jimmy Joe, you're getting on my fucking nerves! Quit being a smart ass. Hell, you were the one who told me she was pretty sharp. Now that their little group is out in the open, we can finally find out just what kind of threat they are.

"I've already got our man working behind the scenes. I've instructed him to turn up the heat. I'll call you just as soon as I get more information."

"I'll be careful Jim, I know the Nazi son of a bitch is crazy. Hell, I'm half German too, so I know what he capable of doing. I don't want him turning on you or me. Hey, he's your fucking guy. He's a pro Jimmy, he just want his money and have a little fun at the same time. I know the thieving Senator Houston referred him to you. Don't turn your back on Houston either. Later!"

CHAPTER 16

Charlie White and his wife Beverly have been married for twenty-five years. Janice, their only daughter, is a sophomore at Southeastern State studying for a medical degree. Since she was a newborn, Charlie has worked for the Choctaw Nation. He started as a janitor under the former Chief. When Wilson took over, he was moved to the Chief's home to oversee house activities there.

The Choctaw Nation built a small estate for Chief Wilson half-a-mile from the city airport, where two Lear jets face the horizon beyond the last hangar. One belongs to the Chief and the other to the Choctaw Nation. A road was built to link the airport to the Chief's new estate. The Chief is an avid horseman and owns a half dozen Arabians. He keeps them at a state-of-the-art barn and riding stable adjacent to the main house. One of Charlie White's main duties is to make sure the Arabians are well cared for and ready at a moment's notice, should the Chief bring in a VIP to show off his prized horses.

Charlie has seen all kinds of people come and go. Visiting Senators, Congressmen, lobbyists, and middlemen do business with the Chief. Seedy underworld characters, drug dealers, thugs, pimps and prostitutes frequent the estate. Charlie has witnessed enough to bring his boss down. Blinded by power, the Chief doesn't feel threatened by what his hired hand knows. It never occurs to him Charlie could be a problem one day.

"Jackie, find deputies Cross and Irwin and tell them, I want them here, ASAP." Not long after, the two deputies enter the Chief's inner office.

"The FBI and their team are taking over the investigation, and I'm putting you two on administrative leave until it's over. Here's Special Agent Jackson's card. He needs to interview both of you. It shouldn't take very long. In the meantime, I want you to go over to my place and see my nigger. He'll tell you what needs to be done."

"Aw Chief, I don't want to be taking orders from no nigger," says Ray Cross.

"You're not taking orders from a nigger, you're taking orders from me! I've already called Charlie and he'll fill you in and get you started when you get there. Now get moving!"

The deputies arrive and Charlie relays the Chief's instructions for the day. After exercising the Arabians, they are to make sure a new stainless steel refrigerator is installed properly in the barn's western loft.

Near the middle of the barn is a doublewide staircase to a landing that reverses higher. At the top, the Pavilion beacons, a spacious and lavishly decorated lounging area. Plush dark brown leather sofas face two flat screen televisions. The new cooler will fill a far corner along side the snack bar. Three doors, to men and women's restrooms with shower stalls and a small room with a queen size bed, line the rear wall. Nearby a short back bar boasts vintage liquors.

Across the room is a snooker table with tables and chairs all around. A large picture window overlooks the training track and offers a prominent view of the countryside.

Despite its first class amenities, the Pavilion's luxury mocks a fool with too much money and little time to use it right. The loft has mostly entertained the Chief's VIP's, serving as hideaway for sexual traffickers. Bound by his job, Charlie kept this tent of wickedness ready. He has witnessed, on several occasions, women in over their heads. Many were pros; some just made the mistake of being in the company of powerful and corrupt men. No doubt, there was crime, but Charlie never dared to speak.

———————

With the Arabians tended to and the refrigerator tucked in place, the two deputies call it a day. Neither is in a hurry to leave, they decide to watch a little television and play some snooker. The refrigerator is filled with different brands of beer. There's hard liquor on a back bar. After an hour and a half, they rack the cue sticks and sit relaxed.

"What a fucking day! You know, my family comes from a long line of plantation owners in the South. My great, great granddaddy owned fifty niggers, and here I am taking orders from one! Ain't that a bitch?" says Deputy Cross.

"Ah shit, Ray! Charlie isn't bad. He's was just relaying the Chiefs orders," says Jeffrey Irwin.

"Hell, my family owned some Indians, too. Those were some good old times back in Alabama."

"Ray, is it true back in those days you could kill Indians and get paid for it? I heard there was some kind of bounty on Indians back then."

"Hell yes, Jeffrey, that's true! That's where that slogan came from, 'The only good Indian is a dead Indian'. If this was still the good old days, you'd been paid some big money for killing that Indian boy the other night. Hey, you feel bad about shooting him? You know you didn't have to kill him. Why didn't you just use your Taser on him?"

———————

Climbing the stairs to the pavilion, Charlie White had reached the landing turnaround, when he heard conversation. He has heard enough incriminating talk over the years. You don't want these people to even think you heard something that might come back to haunt them one day. He'd wait, quiet as a mouse, till talk was over, before walking up.

"Ray, I know you're right, but for a long, long time I've wondered what it would be like to shoot someone. Hey, it was just a fucking Indian. And, what about you? You didn't have to shoot that other fucker in the back. That was cold blooded murder."

"Fuck you, you son of a bitch! I was just covering your stupid ass! You think I was going to leave the other one alive to tell everybody what happened? We would have both gone down."

"Ok, but I'm not stupid," countered Jeffery.

"Sure you're not. I like my job here and we've got a good thing going! The Chief's got a good thing going, too."

"Ever wonder how much money he's worth?" asks Jeffrey.

"I bet him and that crooked Senator Cody have millions stashed away in off shore accounts."

"I heard that they are skimming off the top of the casino money," says Jeffrey.

"You know they are making a shit load of money from being the hidden owners of Sinclair Construction too," says Ray.

"Man, if those other construction owners knew what was going on, the shit would hit the fan," says Jeffrey laughing.

"They are the secret owners of several companies," adds Ray.

"You know, with the information we have, we could make some serious money from businesses that lost construction bids."

"Jeffrey, you'd be dead in a week. You don't want to fuck over the Chief. I would hate to see your skinny ass tied buck naked on an ant hill."

Charlie, still on the landing, accidentally drops the wet towel he had draped over one shoulder. Both deputies hear it hit the floor.

"What was that?"

Jeffrey runs to the head of the stairs and sees Charlie bending down to pick up the towel.

"Charlie, how long you been standing there?" Ray Cross has moved along side Jeffrey.

"Not long, Mr. Irwin, I just got here. I was waitin' till you finished talkin'. I didn't want to interrupt or have you to think I was eavesdropping."

"That's exactly what you're doing! You get your black ass up here!" shouts Ray, who grabs Charlie by the shirt lapel and jerks him around near the top of the steps.

"You know what we do to eavesdropping niggers? We hang'em! You tell anybody what you heard and we'll fuck you up good. We'll come and get that pretty little daughter of yours and have a fucking party! I could use some young black pussy."

"Please Mr. Cross, I swear, I didn't hear a thing," cries Charlie.

"The hell you didn't!"

Ray slaps Charlie on the left side of his head. The blow catches the caretaker in the eye. Off balance, he strikes his head on the railing and falls back down the stairs. He tumbles all the way to the landing and lays sprawled on his back, one foot snagged in a staircase strut. The deputies creep down and hunch over him.

"Jeffrey, he's out cold and his breathing is shallow! You better call 911 or we're going to have one dead nigger on our hands."

CHAPTER 17

F rom the meeting, which birthed the name CMA, Levi and John drive to comfort the Taylor family in Boswell. John speaks what he has in mind and Levi agrees. Thirty-minutes later, they join half-a-dozen cars parked in front of the Taylor house, and twenty to thirty people milling inside and out.

John first pays respect to the assembled extended family, then asks for a private meeting with Sam and Karen. Levi and John follow them to a small den near the back of the house. The room, decorated with Taylor family photos, tastefully celebrates Gary and Don. Framed awards for academics and attendance sit atop a dresser. Football and basketball trophies from their high school days line a shelf. One wall is covered with poster size photos of Gary performing on stage as Elvis. Don is seen in each playing guitar, accompanying his big brother. Mother and Fathers are rightfully proud of their son's accomplishments.

John Tall Bear pulls his chair up very close in front of Sam and Karen. He grabs Big Sam's massive right hand with his left and offers his right to Karen. Accepting the circling gesture is as important and sincere as the speaking and the hearing of words, "I want you both to know you have my deepest sympathy."

"Words cannot take away the pain you feel in this moment. I've had great losses in my life, and I can empathize what you must be feeling. For me the big question is always why? Why was it necessary for Creator to take them so young? There is no answer to that question, we only guess and wonder. This world is such a difficult place to journey, and some can only endure so much pain. It's my personal belief Creator felt they had suffered enough and wanted to bring them home. My mother will greet them and show them the way. We are not alone in the Great Mystery. After a moment of pause while tears are wiped away, John continues.

"They were here for a short time yet, Creator gave them a purpose in life. They are still here in your heart and in fond memories you have of them. This room is a testament to that. Karen, you and Sam will hold your sons in your arms again one day. You will be united again in a place where there is no pain, suffering or sorrow. Sam, I know it's difficult not to be angry and vengeful. Gary and Don would not want that for you. Grieving is healthy, but be joyful for their time on earth and their time with you.

Pausing, still holding their hands, Tall Bear says, "Levi, would you voice a prayer?"

On one knee Levi Tushka takes Karen's hand, then, with all hands joined, expresses a wonderful prayer in Choctaw. Everyone feels better and stronger hearing the words.

"Karen, Sam, we have something for you to consider. The loss of your sons has struck a chord. Hundreds, if not thousands, of our people will journey to Durant to attend their funeral. We need a place convenient for all. I haven't talked to my pastor, Jonathan Tubby, but I am sure he would permit us to hold the services at Achille Indian Baptist.

"The church sits on ten acres of land, and we can set up several large tents to accommodate a large service. We can secure burial plots just down the road at the Achille Indian Cemetery. It has two camp houses so the women can prepare food for all that attend. We can bring a catering company to cook and supply more food and water if necessary. CMA wants to do this for you cause your loss is our loss. With all the attention this tragedy has gotten, I'm sure the media will be covering the services. We want to show the people how we take care of our own. Gary and Don were good warriors for their family and CMA. Symbolically the lance they were going to carry has fallen to the ground. CMA wants to pick it up and move forward in their honor. Can we do this for you and your family?"

Karen and Sam look at each other and nod as they embrace. Levi and John surround them with their arms and hold them for several minutes until the crying stops. John senses Karen will be fine. He pulls Karen aside and pledges, if she needs any assistance with Sam, they will come in a heartbeat. With assurance, Levi and John depart for Achille Indian Baptist Church to speak with Pastor Jonathan Tubby.

Achille Indian Baptist is an hour's drive away, back to the outskirts of Durant, and then another twelve miles south on Hwy 78. Tall Bear contacts Pastor Jonathan Tubby, and asks if he and Levi can drive down and speak with him? Anticipating the nature of their visit, Jonathan calls his assistant Pastor, Junior Simon and one elder deacon, Glen Wilson. After they arrive, all five gather in the pastor's small office. John introduces Levi to the pastors, and finds they have many acquaintances in common. Levi feels at home.

"Jonathan, gentlemen," John addresses the group. "Levi and I have a big favor to ask of you and the church. I know you've heard of the tragic deaths of Gary and Don Taylor. It's been all over the news. Gary and Don were two of the young coordinators working for Chata Amoma Atokoli. We have spoken with Sam and Karen Taylor, and they would like to hold the funeral services here at Achille Indian Baptist. Our organization will make the arrangements for burial at Achille Indian Cemetery. We have offered the services of CMA to coordinate and take care of all expenses."

"John, we had a feeling you might ask this. Prior to your arrival, we discussed that in detail. I don't have to tell you how we feel about you." Jonathan looks at Glen and Junior, "We all agreed, if you ask to use our church, we will say yes. We will be honored to have the services here at Achille Indian Baptist."

"John," says Junior. "We do have some concerns about whether the church can adequately accommodate so many.

John looks at Levi. Not missing a beat he says, "Junior, we expect several hundred people. I'm sure we can bring some of our volunteers here to help you coordinate everything. CMA can handle all the financial needs and will be completely at the church's disposal."

"John, we all know the situation and local conflict within the Nation. Having said that, this is a service for the family. We don't want it to turn into a political event," says Jonathan.

"We don't want that either, Jonathan. Some things we cannot control, but most we can. That's one of the reasons I wanted to get the services away from town," states Tall Bear. "You have ten acres at the back of the church, and it can accommodate a lot of people. There is plenty of parking out in the field. Since its private property, we can control who comes in. With your permission, we would like to gather names, addresses and contact information for all who come through the gate. You would ask this if the services were held inside the church. The family will want this information to thank all that attend. Our organization can use that information as well. Is that agreeable?"

"John, we don't have a problem with that. In my early years of scuffling around in the Seattle area, I got involved in grass roots politics, and boy, things could get ugly. I know your organization is church and faith based. But there are Choctaw elders in the church who I know would frown on any political undertones."

"Jonathan, gentlemen, we understand. But let me say this, the world is watching, interested to see how our people respond. It's imperative that CMA, Achille Indian Baptist, and our community display a positive image. We have all come a long way. We are small in numbers, but let's remind them that we are Indian, a proud people, and we take care of our own," says John.

"Gentleman," says Levi. "I'm told there will be dancers from many cities wanting to come in and have a service like the old days. They'll be willing to bring their families and set up teepees and create an Indian village. Those participating can express traditional Choctaw ways by singing and dancing in honor of the fallen. It is an important part of our heritage."

"We must do this right," says Glen the elder deacon, "everything necessary to make it a cultural event. Pastor, Junior and I suggest the funeral be held Saturday afternoon at 2 p.m., if that is acceptable with the Taylor family."

"Jonathan," John says with a big grin, trying to lighten the conversation, "you realize you're going to have a captive audience on these grounds when you speak on Saturday. After they hear you speak, I know many will want to attend your Sunday morning services as too. It might be the largest congregation of your pastoral career. I suggest you go to Wal-Mart and buy a new suit that fits. Take your wife along, cause I know she got better fashion taste than you."

"John, I'm delighted my message may lead many to the Lord on Sunday. And if I can help save you, I can help anybody!" He roars with laughter and the others join in. "I didn't know your momma, but many of the old Choctaws here did, and they say you were a rascal!"

"All right, meeting adjourned," says John quickly. *'Realizing he doesn't have a snowball in hell's chance matching wits with Jonathan Tubby.'*

CHAPTER 18

Tammy has leased a 2200 square foot building for CMA on east Main Street. Chahta Amoma Atokoli Resource Center suits their needs. It's clean, has a fresh coat of paint, and furnished. A sign has been ordered from a company in town, and ads announcing the grand opening phoned to the newspaper office. Everyone works together for the cause. A double portrait will be hung prominently in the building to recognize the work of fallen coordinators Gary and Don Taylor.

Levi and John take a trip to Atoka to talk to the CMA Director, coordinators, and volunteers there. It was to be a quick 30-minute brainstorming to get everyone on the same page. They are about to start the meeting when John's cell phone rings. It's Tammy Lynn. She says, soon after arriving at CMA's new headquarters, the leasing agent dropped by to inform them the owner is terminating their lease. The reason given is 'failure to fully disclose the nature of business.' They have twenty-four hours to vacate the premises, and a full refund will be given. The leasing agent expressed her sorrow for the inconvenience, but complained that the owner is firm about his decision. John tells her he and Levi are on their way back and to sit tight. They quickly conclude their meeting with the contacts in Atoka and leave for Durant.

Forty-five minutes later they walk in the door of CMA, where everyone is visibly upset.

"John, we have more problems. The papers called and informed us they could not print our ad and they are refunding our money. The sign company also called and barked they don't have the time to build our sign. Something about too many signs on backorder and not enough builders to fill the orders," says Tammy.

"It's the Chief, says Levi! "I told you in the beginning the Chief has this town in his hip pocket. He's a powerful man and he controls many of the small businesses. With all that casino money, everybody wants to do business with the Nation. If they do business with us, the Chief will cut them out. I'm pretty sure the Nation is part owner in the newspaper. All he had to do was make a call to the sign company."

"How can we run our organization here without cooperation from the town's businesses?" asks Tammy. 'She is visibly upset.'

"Hold on now!" says Tall Bear. "This is not the end of the world! We knew this wasn't going to be easy. First thing we need to do is find another building, even if we have to buy one. Over the last two weeks we've taken in a lot of funds. We can use some of that money to buy a small building. Moving to another town is out of the question. We have to make our stand in Durant. You know the old saying. 'Keep your friends close, but your enemies closer'. The Chief is the enemy. We need to keep that in mind when we consider everything. We're going to step on some toes by being here in Durant. We can get another sign company in say, Sherman, Texas, to make one and bring it here. It's just going to cost a little more money. I assume since the Chief owns some of the newspaper, he may have an interest in the local television station as well. We'll have to find alternative ways to get our message out to the public. But first things first, we've got to be out of here in 24 hours, so let's get busy and secure another building."

By the end of the day, Tammy has found an even better building, one they hadn't considered when they were leasing. The freestanding building has excellent visibility with plenty of parking on the side and rear. When you enter Durant from the north on Hwy 69, you have to turn or run up to the front door.

Tuesday morning at a law office in town, the purchase of the building from an out of state investor is completed. CMA is the proud owner of its own building in the heart of Choctaw country. Later that day, Roman finds a sign company in Sherman, Texas, to measure the building for a new sign. Roman is promised the sign will be up and lighted within 48 hours. Roman promises a bonus. The sign company owner thanks Roman saying a bonus isn't necessary.

On Wednesday morning, CMA begins moving into the new facility with renewed enthusiasm. Plenty of sandwiches, pizza, salads and cold beverages are made available to keep everyone's energy level up. Never mind the calories, there is much work to be done. As promised, the sign is mounted before Thursday evening, when Choctaws and other tribal members begin arriving to attend Saturday services.

Over the next twenty-four hours, a tremendous amount of work is accomplished. Volunteers are assigned to assist Achille Indian Baptist Church. Tents, lights and sound equipment are ordered from Sherman and as far away as Dallas. A catering company is secured to provide food. Indian people always provide a big dinner for the family after the service is completed. The caterers are instructed to have plenty of sweet ice tea. Printed flyers direct visitors to Achille Indian. Volunteers take turns outside the building, greeting drive by visitors with brochures.

Roman asks his friend Buddy Mack Billey, music director at Hollywood Methodist in Dallas, to play piano for the service. He also enlists a long time musician friend from Dallas, Willis Wallace, to assemble a small rhythm section. Willis and Buddy Mack gather voices from all churches represented to form a choir. Roman and Tammy are trusted as event co-directors, to up-date information and keep things moving. Personnel are assigned to help direct traffic into and out of Achille Indian. Bright red t-shirts are ordered for staff and security personnel displaying a new logo designed for CMA. After all their planning, staff members feel they have everything covered.

The weather is cooperating wonderfully. A high temperature of 73 degrees and sunny skies are forecast for the rest of the weekend. By Friday afternoon, it becomes clear they had underestimated the numbers of attendees. A steady stream of arrivals late Thursday afternoon intensifies the following day. Over a thousand Indian visitors fill every hotel room in the city. Many have arrangements to stay in homes of family and friends. Hundreds are directed to makeshift campsites behind the church. Actions are made to bring in more water and other necessary supplies. The church engages with the farms on each side of it to run water hoses to accommodate the sites. More volunteers are recruited to provide security at the campsite.

On Friday afternoon, the young people organize a 'stickball' game. The Choctaws invented this ancient game called Kabocha-toli. It is the oldest game played in the United States. The modern day game of Lacrosse is a more civilized version of Kabocha-toli. Others decide to participate in Itishi, a form of Indian wrestling that turns into a 'toughest Indian contest'. Eventually, security halts this activity before someone is badly hurt. An injuries list documents busted noses, bloodied lips, and wounded pride.

The campers plan a Choctaw Stomp Dance for Friday night with Cherokee Dancers from Tahlequah, Kiowas from Anadarko, Chickasaws from Ada, Creeks, Seminoles, and other tribal members all participating. This dance celebration lasts well into early Saturday morning. After each dance, money is collected to help the immediate family and the host Achille Indian Church. There are several dances to assist CMA for their expense in planning the event. CMA didn't solicit this, but Indian people know where help is needed and are willing to give. John has attended Pow Wows in Oklahoma and Traders Village in Dallas, but has never attended one this large. Even the Choctaw Nation Labor Day Festival, held every year at Tushkahoma, paled in comparison. This is a cultural event that truly honors the Choctaws and neighboring Indian tribes.

The city of Durant is alive with people from all over the state. Several magazines that cater to American Indian readers assign representatives and writers to cover the event. Television stations from Sherman-Dennison and Atoka have sent additional camera crews. Something big is happening. Hotels and motels are booked solid for the weekend. Visitors gawk and talk at restaurants downtown. Parking spots are hard to find at the Sonic and George's Drive-in.

It is now obvious CMA's existence is out of the bag. Their new office remains open until midnight, directing people and passing out information, tirelessly obtaining names, addresses and contact information from all that come by. CMA is going to play hardball now. The gloves are coming off.

CHAPTER 19

———

Charlie is taken by ambulance to Ada Indian Hospital northwest of Durant, OK. He is checked over by the emergency staff and diagnosed with a concussion and a bruised hip. His wife Beverly is notified and he's placed in a room on the third floor. He is unconscious most of the night, but wakes to a severe headache, shortly before the doctors make their rounds the next morning. They convince the Whites that Charlie will be fine but should stay in the hospital for a few days. After Beverly leaves for work, Charlie enjoys a little breakfast, and then turns on the TV to watch the morning news.

All the stations are covering the shootings of the two Indians. The roadside footage is shown again and again. The use of deadly force is questioned. Charlie sees his boss, the Chief, interviewed about the two deputies responsible for the shootings. The Chief says he will have a statement when the investigation is over, when he has all the facts.

Tall Bear is seen talking to Channel 8 Dallas regarding funeral arrangements. They want him to confirm that hundreds, if not thousands of American Indians will be coming to pay their respects. He is quizzed about the Indian organization CMA and what they hope to accomplish. A video of the new headquarters flashes on the screen. They show a clip of the immediate family coming out of the funeral home. The mother and father weeping strike a passionate chord in Charlie. When the interview is over, Charlie reaches for the phone and dials the CMA number given on the screen.

"Mr. Tall Bear, please."

"Just a moment," says one of the staff members.

"This is John Tall Bear."

"The deputies murdered those two boys. I overheard them joking about it. They busted me up pretty good, almost killed me. Please make sure they pay for it." Charlie hangs the phone up then buzzes his nurse for more pain medication. Tears are streaming down his face and he just wants to be numb.

Tall Bear walks over to the staff volunteer who had taken the call and asks, "Sara, do you know where that last call came from?"

"I can check for you, Mr. Tall Bear." She looks at the phone menu. "It came from Ada Indian Hospital."

Tall Bear walks over to Levi's desk where he's taking a call. John waits for him to finish the conversation.

"I just got an unusual call from someone at the Ada hospital."

"Who was it?"

"Don't know. But here it is word for word." John, leaning closer to Levi in a low voice, 'those two deputies murdered those two boys. I overheard them joking about it. They busted me up pretty good, almost killed me. Please make sure they pay for it.' That's all he said, then hung the phone up."

"John, we got to find this man! If it's true, and he got busted up overhearing a conversation like that, then his life may be in danger. I know a lot of people there. I'll going to run over there and see what I can find."

"That's a good idea. Call me if you find anything. And be careful."

An hour later Levi is walking down the hallway of Ada Indian Hospital, reminded of his bout with pneumonia years ago. He knows his way around and enters the admission office. As soon as he does, a middle aged Choctaw woman sitting behind the desk smiles, "Levi Tushka, what are you doing here?"

"Wanda Murphy, I didn't know you worked here. The last time I saw you was at that Pow Wow in Oklahoma City. What, two or three years ago?"

"Try four, and you promised you were going to call me the next day, and you never did."

"Hey, I'm sorry! I moved to Kansas and worked as a contractor up there for three or four years. Lost track of the time. You know I'm Indian. You're looking good, Wanda!"

"So, you using 'Indian time' as an excuse. That's pretty lame even for you Levi. Now, tell me what you're doing here?"

"You know me, just snooping around! No I'm just kidding. Looking for a friend of a friend, don't know his name. I forgot it. But I was told he got busted up a little. Just trying to find him and see if he is okay."

"Nobody's been admitted or come through the emergency room the last few days from fighting. You know if there's a fight the police would have been notified. A Hatak Lusa, one of the Chief's employees fell down a flight of stairs and suffered a concussion. He's upstairs on the 3rd floor. Could it be him?"

"Could be. Okay if I go up and see him?"

"Sure. When you get off the elevator, make a right and he's in the last room on the left at the end of the hall, room 317. Just so you know, I get off at 6 p.m."

"Thanks," Levi puts his hand on her shoulder, "but I'm helping out with the funeral of those two men who were killed. Let me give you a call next week. Good to see you again. Chi Pisa Lachike."

"Oh please, 'see you later', not that promise again. I'll invite you to my wedding. So long Levi."

As Levi steps off the elevator, to his right he sees two deputies coming out of the last room on the left. The deputies were there to make it very clear if Charlie said anything, his wife and daughter would pay the ultimate price. For some reason, instead of taking the elevator, they open the stairway door and disappear down the flight of stairs. Levi gets back into the elevator and goes down to the first floor and waits for them to reappear. The deputies come out the door to the stairway and continue out the front door of the hospital. Levi follows close behind and makes sure they get into their patrol car and leave the hospital grounds. He then goes back upstairs and steps off the elevator, walks down the hall to the last door on the left and looks in.

On the side of the door he sees the name Charlie White. He knows Charlie from way back when he worked at the Nation. He enters the small room and says, "Charlie White! What happened to you?"

"Levi Tushka!" says Charlie, recognizing an old familiar face.

"Charlie, it's good to see you. What happened to your eye? Your old lady pop you?"

"Still the same old Levi. No, I was working over at the Chief's place. He's got a big barn over there. I was on the second floor walking down the stairs and slipped and fell. Got a slight concussion, busted my eye open and sprained my hip. I'll be in here for a couple of days. What are you doing up here?" Charlie's obvious lie reflects the impact of the two deputies who'd left minutes earlier.

"I'm looking for one of my old lady friends," lies Levi in turn.

"What's her name? Maybe I know her."

"Wanda Murphy."

"I know her. She works in the business office."

"Thanks Charlie! Hey, it's been good seeing you. You take care of yourself," says Levi and leaves the room, exits the hospital and gets into his car. He checks for messages on his cell phone, then places a call to CMA.

"John, I found him. Got a little help from an old friend. I know the guy. Name's Charlie White, a Hatak Lusa. He's been working for the Chief for as long as I can remember. He's a pretty decent guy and got a nice family. There's a little cafe across the street from the hospital that serves some good home cookin'. Meet me in the parking lot, Ok? Just call me when you're 10 minutes out, and I'll be there."

When John arrives, Levi fills him in. There's no reason for Levi to go up again so he gives John directions to Charlie's room. John steps off the elevator, turns right and walks down the hallway to room 317. When he enters the room, he sees Charlie watching television.

"Mr. White, do you know who I am?"

"Yes!" says Charlie, his eyes almost popping out of his head.

"Mr. White, maybe you know something about a conversation I had this morning. The call was traced to this room, and I thought you might know who placed the call." John was stretching the truth, but he needed a little leverage.

"Mr. Tall Bear, please. You got to leave! You don't understand if they see me talking to you they'll kill me. They threatened to do something bad to my family!"

"Mr. White, I do understand. Please just give me a few minutes."

"No, get out of here and don't come back. I'm scared to death what they might do." Charlie is getting visibly upset.

"All right, I'm leaving. Mr. White, I'll have someone bring you a disposable cell phone that can't be traced to you or me. The phone will have my personal cell number stored in it. I'm your friend. Call me if you want to talk. Please be careful. Remember Levi and I are your friends and you can trust us to keep everything confidential."

John knows he's found an important ally inside the Chief's organization. He must find a way to keep him safe. Levi and John visit the nearest Wal-Mart where they pay cash for a disposal cell phone. They drive back to the Ada hospital, and Levi instructs Wanda to hand carry the cell phone to Charlie White. All they can do now is hope Charlie will dial John's number soon.

CHAPTER 20

Saturday dawns beautifully. The blue sky is dotted with large white puffy clouds. The high temperature will be around 74 degrees. John Tall Bear remembers preparing for his mother's funeral services at the same church many years ago. He is reminded of the sadness, the empty feeling the Taylor family knows. The loss of a parent forces you to consider your own mortality. The loss of a child, however, adds another dimension of pain because it feels out of order. Those left behind struggle to survive the day, then the next, one day at a time. Eventually, pain and loneliness fade and you tend to new life.

After John's mother passed, he began to realize in spite of his personal achievements, spiritual essence was missing. He began to visit church more regularly. There, he asked the Creator for guidance with which he'd set new priorities, and took charge of his destiny. He vowed to be a better person tomorrow than he is today. Death, he concluded will come soon enough for us all. We are here but for a short time. Therefore it's essential we conduct self with honor and integrity. Most importantly, he does not want to tarnish his mother's legacy.

Highway 78 is the only road in and out of Achille Indian Baptist Church. Traffic is bumper to bumper by noon, two hours before the service. Indian people are usually very patient. However those in larger cities are accustomed to a faster pace. John can only hope traffic doesn't create unforeseen problems. Upon arrival, he sees twice as many media personnel as the day before. Turning into the parking lot, he parks besides the white wood framed building with a steeple between two media tents. Roman and Tammy have a smaller tent set up in front of the church, an information headquarters to direct attendees. Several members of the media are interviewing them. Alongside and behind the church, the media have parked their vehicles with satellite dishes on top. Today Achille Indian is connected to the world.

John takes in a small stage erected on the north side of the church, under a huge tent that accommodates one hundred people. This tent is for the family and friends of the deceased. The staff has lined up three other tents behind the larger tent. These tents are not going to be enough to shade all, but should adequately cover the friends from the areas around Boswell.

John notices the Channel 8 Dallas television logo on one of the media trucks. Behind the church, for a hundred yards, a sea of people, cars, trucks, and tee pees dot the landscape. They have all come to honor the fallen young men. Only in their wildest dreams could Gary and Don Taylor have imagined so many would pay their respects. Since the previous day, John has received updates regarding arrivals every four to five hours. Still he is overwhelmed by the size of the turnout.

On stage, Buddy Mack Billey directs a small choir assembled from the surrounding churches. A good friend Willis Wallace leads the rhythm section. Another Dallas friend works sound. John has also invited Cassidy Alayna, a rising pop gospel singer from Caddo Mills, to perform Amazing Grace. Her flaming red hair reminds John of his beautiful granddaughter.

John and friends are ready to see this happen. Bringing these people, their communities, and churches together for a common cause, CMA can reverse a devastating tendency. Too many times Indian people are placed in the ground overwhelmed, even in death, by isolation. Though we are few now, all people are special. We are all God's children.

The service opens with a prayer, followed by a few gospel songs. A prayer in Choctaw flows from a Native Choctaw singer. The air is filled with song attesting the resilience of the congregation. When Pastor Jonathan Tubby takes the pulpit, the crowd is ready to receive his message. He keeps it simple, speaking in Choctaw at times to show respect and connect with the Choctaw elders. They hang on every word.

"Brothers and Sisters, we have all gathered here today to honor the memory of our fallen sons, Gary and Don Taylor. I am reminded of the passing of my own mother and father and I share the sorrow the family is feeling today. Life on earth is a continuing struggle, with pain and misfortune. But let us not forget the joyful times we had together, for that is the continuing legacy of these two young men. The brothers honored their parents with endless love. Their musical career was cut short, but had a powerful impact on many. Fans can only wonder what their future might have been. For some, memories of their image, voice and song will be timeless.

"In the grand scheme of the Great Mystery, we all are here on Mother Earth for only a short time. We are not promised tomorrow therefore we must live each day to the fullest. We should mature quickly and take God as our personal savior. We must do good work and wait for Him to take us home. We must have faith in knowing, when we get to the Promised Land there will be no sickness, no pain to endure. When we arrive at the Happy Hunting Grounds, food will be bountiful. Our loved ones, who have gone on before, will join us. Families, parents, children, friends, even precious pets will be united to savor every stress-free moment for eternity.

"For our ancestors in ancient times, confusion was unknown. They were strong, joyous, and filled with purpose. The feelings of alienation and detachment from the rest of humanity did not exist. Our people were free from diabetes, alcohol, and depression. Those evil things did not have a chance to take hold. They slept a sound sleep of good dreams, and awoke to plentiful days. They would stand at the Center with The Great Spirit and family. It was peaceful. Once again, this is the life that awaits us in the Great Mystery. This is, perhaps, the dream the Taylor brothers have seen and envision for all.

"Let us not forget Gary and Don Taylor were eager to serve the Indian people, to make our life better. They saw a need and forged into darkness not knowing when they might make the ultimate sacrifice. Their deaths are no different from ancient times, when our people went into battle against invading enemies. Our young warriors have fallen and those left behind must pick up the lance and continue on. Through this, we can keep their spirit alive, ensuring their deaths are not in vain. Amen, Let us pray."

John had witnessed Jonathan Tubby speak on many occasions. Today, his spirit soared and delivered one of his finest performances. His moving and uplifting sermon would stay etched in the mind of all who heard the pastor speak. The service concludes with another prayer and a final song. An invitation is extended for all to attend Sunday services at 10:45 a.m. the following day.

Pastor Jonathan announces at the conclusion. "Gary and Don Taylor will be buried in a private service for family and close friends only at the Achille Indian Cemetery a mile down the road. Those who did not receive an invitation are asked to please respect the family's wishes and remain on the church grounds. Dinner will be served in two hours. Amen."

Later that evening, the celebration continued with singing and Indian dancing until the wee hours of the morning. It has been a good day, one for this church and community to remember. There will never be another like it. Tragically, these young men owe their fifteen minutes of fame to atrocity. Their fond memories persist and Life goes on. There is much work to be done.

CHAPTER 21

Thomas ThunderHawk, a young man in his late thirties, half Choctaw and half Lakota Sioux, has traveled from Muskogee, Oklahoma in search of friends. Arriving in Durant, he got wind of the Friday night campsite activities at Achille Indian and decided to attend. Meandering, ThunderHawk spots an old friend July Tecumseh, a Choctaw/Creek who lives in Anadarko two hours north. They had formed a friendship while dancing the Pow Wow circuit throughout Oklahoma. July's wingman is Johnny Kick a Hole in the Sky, who is Choctaw and Apache.

None of the three knew the victims, yet they've been drawn to Durant. After dancing, drinking, roaming for available women, they realize they share a common bond. All are passionate about their Choctaw heritage, and tribal affiliations. Tribal pride among Natives is strong. Mind you, they are not looking for trouble, but some have a short fuse.

The three, along with dozens of new friends, attend the funeral services on Saturday. They partied Saturday night into the wee hours of the morning and agreed to meet on Sunday afternoon at the Sonic Drive-In on highway 69. Over burgers and hot dogs, a mission evolves. On Monday morning they will council with CMA, the only Indian entity in the city other than the Choctaw Nation.

John Tall Bear's temporary residence is a small motel several blocks west of the CMA office. Monday morning, as he drives down Main Street, something strikes him odd. Many of the Indian visitors are still in town, buying breakfast at cafes and fueling their cars at the local gas station. As he approaches the CMA office he can see a small group congregated outside the entrance. Closer, he sees the parking lot overflowing with cars, trucks and more people. He parks beside a television news crew from Dallas. A Chanel 8 reporter asks him for comments on the FBI's findings. Tall Bear politely declines, then pauses to consider. He notices Levi parking his car at the same time and waves him in.

He decides against an immediate statement until he has checked with Tammy and the office staff. Levi follows right after him and they proceed to an office where Roman completes a phone call. After the four are seated, they discuss the weekend over beverages and coffee.

Tammy says the Taylor family called last night to thank them for taking charge of the services. She also says the FBI released information late last night. Their finding, although excessive force is thought to have played a major part in the shooting, they could not find the deputies at fault. Until a more complete investigation is conducted, the shooting is deemed justified.

Lastly, Tammy informs them three individuals want a meeting with the CMA Executive Director and won't say why. One claims to be a spokesperson for several groups of Indian visitors still in town. Also, reporters from Channel 8 were requesting some comments.

"What do you think, Chieftain?" asks Levi, looking at John, respectfully playing with the title."

John, slightly amused, is getting used to answering to it.

"Channel 8 reporters aren't going anywhere, so let them wait awhile. Since they're here, let's see what the three gentlemen outside want. Afterwards we can call FBI agents Rivers and Jackson for an updated report. Levi, would you mind calling Senator Jim's office in Hugo? See if she's got any new information."

"My pleasure Chieftain."

"And Levi, please think before you speak, will you?"

"You never gonna to forget that wine commit are you?"

"No! We all know what CMA's agenda is, so lets not lose sight of that."

"Got it. I have a feeling others will look to us for answers and direction regarding the shooting."

"You're right Levi. The killing and CMA's agenda are now meshed together. We're going to have to walk a thin line here because the Taylor brothers were a part of our organization. Let's not make any mistakes. We don't want to jeopardize CMA priorities dealing with a myriad of issues. Tammy, would you ask the gentlemen to come in?"

Tammy reappears and says, "John, they would prefer to meet together and see you and the Executive Director at the same time. They are pretty adamant about it. We can use the coffee room since it's larger and has plenty of chairs."

"No problem. Tammy, you want to sit in?"

"No, too much testosterone in one room. I've got others things to do." Tammy escorts the three men into the coffee room, where Roman, Levi and John greet them.

It's obvious the three are passionate Indians. Hollywood costume design for these modern day Indian warriors would have been easy. Each wears faded blue jeans, bright colorful shirts, boots, belts, rawhide bracelets, and beaded necklaces hung around their necks. All three have their hair braided, tied off with beaded ties, carry themselves with commanding presence, and stand well over six-foot. Coffee and donuts are offered. After exchanging pleasantries, they all have a seat.

"I'm Thomas ThunderHawk. Can I ask who is in charge here?"

"That would be me I'm Roman Billy, the Executive Director."

"Mr. Billy, I'll get right to the point. We've all heard about the FBI's report not finding those deputies at fault for excessive force. Me and my two friends July and Johnny Kick think we need to send a message to the Chief of the Choctaws."

"A message?

"Yes, a strong message."

"And what would that be."

"Unified Indians are not going to take these killings sitting down. Those were white deputies killing Indians. These types of killings are happening all the time on reservations throughout Indian country. It has to stop! We think this is a good place to make a stand!"

'Represent! This Indian's got my attention.' John looks at Levi and knows he's thinking the same thing. It's no secret these types of shootings have persisted for the last hundred years on numerous reservations.

"With all due respect, the only unified Indians I know of are here at CMA," states Roman

"Not so, I'm July Tecumseh. My wife's brother was taken out off the Rez on a dark freezing night last year. They shot him in the leg and left him there alone. His frozen body was found the next day. They all know who did it. The local police department has been guilty of this type of killing many times. Our people could do nothing. They called the FBI, but they don't always investigate Indian shootings."

ThunderHawk adds, "This shit happens all the time up at Pine Ridge. More times than not, its white law enforcement killing Indians. Nothing is ever done to bring about justice. They just sweep it under the rug. If those two men where white, all hell would break loose!"

"Mr. ThunderHawk, we're all aware of those types of killings on reservations, so what is your purpose in sharing this information with us? What are you asking CMA to do?" asks Roman.

"We've decided we want to march to the Choctaw headquarters and demand the Chief fire those deputies and prosecute them to the fullest extent of the law!"

Roman looks at Levi and John, hoping one of them will jump in and say something.

"Mr. ThunderHawk, I'm Levi Tushka, I don't have any official position here at CMA except in an advisory position. Can I assume you want this office to assist you in this march?"

"That's right! We saw how you coordinated the funeral this weekend, and the march would have more impact if we had the support of CMA."

"Don't you see? It's perfect timing with the killings and all the Indians who turned out to see the services! The press is already here and we can take advantage of that. All we have to do is start marching and the television reporters will televise it," says July Tecumseh.

"Tecumseh, after what has happened this last week, that would blow the lid off this town," answers Roman.

"Gentlemen, Roman Billy is exactly right," adds Tall Bear. "As Mr. Tushka stated, we are advisors here. However, I speak for the three of us. This kind of action doesn't fit in our agenda."

"And what is your title here?"

"Tecumseh, titles aren't important here however, measured thinking is? Marching could be a strategy in the future, but this is not the right time. First of all, the city of Durant is probably going to require you to have a permit to march. The police dept. and Chief Wilson are pretty tight, so that ain't gonna happen. If you go ahead and march, some people may get hurt and some could go to jail. You should give this some serious consideration and perhaps find another way of expressing your views. Like you stated, the television people are looking for something to report. Speak to the reporters and perhaps they'll air your concerns."

"That sounds like a white man talking!" shouted angrily Kick a Hole in the Sky.

Johnny Kick is the oldest and most radical of the three. He is a history buff and a fan of Russell Means, an Indian activist leader in the siege at Pine Ridge Reservation in the 1970's.

"Mr. Kick look. I'm just trying to be rational here. We have lost two of our friends and wounds are raw. We don't want to create a situation where more of our people may be put in harm's way. I assure you CMA is going to do everything by the letter of the law to make major changes here in Oklahoma. I can't go into detail, but we need strong talented people like you and your friends to support us while we go through a growing process. We have some very powerful people behind this office."

"My brother was at Pine Ridge. They took that place over and busted some heads!"

"Mr. Kick, some of your people died there too. We don't want that to happen here in Durant."

"Come on Hawk, July, I knew they weren't going to help us! Ain't nothing here but a bunch of cowards!" says Johnny Kick as he gets out of his chair.

Roman rises quickly after hearing that comment, as if ready to jump in Johnny's Kick face. Tall Bear holds up his hand to Roman to "stand down".

"Mr. ThunderHawk, as I stated before, you and your friends should reconsider your plans. We live and work in this area and CMA is fully aware of the many injustices that are being done to our people. Without divulging our mission, I can tell you if CMA is successful, our actions will change the face of Indian Country. I would invite you to join us in these efforts and be a part of the solution and not the problem. Will you change your mind about the march?"

"We're marching this afternoon! We've made up our minds!"

"You're all crazy!" says Roman as he stands, growing testy and beginning to show more authority. "I want you to move your people away from the office and out of our parking lot. We don't want any part of this!"

"Hey, this is your town! Where do you suggest we move to?" asks ThunderHawk.

"There's an abandoned peanut mill across the street and two blocks east!"

The three men leave the CMA office and are seen directing their crowd east to the abandoned peanut mill. They are also spotted talking to a Channel 8 news reporter while its news crew loads up and follows the crowd.

"Sorry, John. I lost my cool there. What are we going to do?"

"Whatever we do, we need to do it fast," says Levi.

"Let's all take a deep breath and think for a minute. What happens if they march? Let's look at the situation from that angle. What happens when the police get involved? And I'm sure they will. What happens if they make it to the Capitol grounds? What will the Chief do?" questions John.

"Someone needs to call Senator Jim and inform her, suggested Roman.

"We should probably alert the FBI agents to witness whatever action the police take. We must let them know CMA is playing no part in this march," adds Levi.

"We probably need to call the Chief too. Levi, you know him better than anyone here. You make the call. I'll call Senator Jim," concludes John.

Tall Bear reaches Senator Jim as she is leaving her office for a flight to Washington. He describes this sudden march as a potentially dangerous situation. She agrees and will be in CMA's office within the hour.

Tammy alerts the two FBI agents who are now in route to the peanut mill. Levi says the Chief thought he was pulling a joke on him. Though Levi convinced him to take the threat seriously, the Chief didn't buy CMA was playing no part.

CHAPTER 22

John has sent one of his staff members down to the abandoned peanut mill to keep watch. She reports back four or five hundred Indians gathered to hear the three leaders speak. Levi and John walk to get a closer look and feel the situation. Excepting its leaders, the group as a whole looks harmless. No one is acting crazy, or carrying any kind of weapons. Nothing visible threatens the police. They head back to the CMA office.

Senator Jim and Agent Rivers arrive and both walk to the Mill for continued observation. They meet with police and the leaders of the gathering. ThunderHawk and the other two leaders convince them this will be a peaceful walk to the Choctaw Capitol grounds and back, a show of unity and respect to the victims. It is agreed no standing or shouting will be permitted in front of the Capitol.

From the Mill to the Capitol grounds is a fifteen to twenty minute walk. The return through a residential section of the city would be another thirty minutes. The complete event should last no more than an hour and thirty minutes, 2 p.m.–3:30, with a closing prayer. Levi, Roman and John, are less sure this design is what ThunderHawk, Tecumseh and Kick a Hole in the Sky intend.

Promptly at 2 p.m. the march begins, an omen itself, for Indian people are seldom on time. As they walk peacefully by the CMA headquarters, everyone looks happy and non- threatening. Perhaps John and the others were wrong for doubting their intentions. No visible anger, no drinking or weapons to be seen. How much trouble could they get into? All interested parties decide to wait until the walk is over to leave. Next-door, a small cafe serves old style burgers. Lunch is ordered, and they all sit down to wait.

———————

The Choctaw Nation Capitol encompasses a city block a half mile off Main Street. The two-story red brick building sits on the west side of the street facing east. Its white concrete front stairway is approximately twenty feet wide, a dozen steps to a landing and another dozen steps to the top. It's quite impressive. The large magnolia trees dotting the landscape give the complex a serene and peaceful atmosphere.

There are two Durant police officers stationed at the bottom of the steps leading up to the front entrance of the capitol. Two other officers are at both ends of the building. To park in front, you must park on the street. Most of the staff parks in a large parking lot behind the building. Twenty minutes into the walk, many begin arriving at the Choctaw Capitol. They're not moving away as quickly as planned and a crowd is forming in front. Within another ten minutes all arrive and the police officers are beginning to get nervous. This march is not going as planned, as seen by the Chief and his staff of twenty watching from windows on the second floor. They occupy every available window and are watching the crowd grow larger. ThunderHawk, Tecumseh and Kick a Hole in the Sky face the two officers at the bottom of the stairs.

———————

Two months before, if you had told Tall Bear he would be lunching in a small cafe in Durant, Oklahoma beside an attractive U.S. Senator, he would have thought you crazy. And here he is, with old friend Levi Tushka, surrounded by new friends, Tammy, Senator Jim and a couple of her assistants, enjoying a buffalo burger. Casual conversation about the Oklahoma University football team and the possibility of them playing for a national championship is the topic. Being from Texas, they discuss the Dallas Cowboys and their chances of making the playoffs.

Having played basketball in high school, John's a big basketball fan of the Dallas Mavericks. Naturally he throws their name into the conversation. To his surprise, Senator Jim is a huge fan and follows the Oklahoma City Thunder. Over burgers, she insists they call her by her first name. However when within earshot of her staff, John addresses her as Senator Jim. Halfway through their lunch, they notice some minor activity outside, but think nothing of it. All of a sudden cell phones are buzzing.

Tammy's rings first, then John's. Not wanting to be rude to their lunch guests, he ignores his and waits for Tammy to complete her conversation. He can tell by the expression on her face it is urgent. She quickly hangs up and, with a shocked look on her face, "They've taken the Chief hostage! The marchers overwhelmed the police officers and took their guns. They've stormed the capitol building and have taken over the whole complex."

"Was anyone hurt?" asks John.

"It appears no one is hurt badly."

"Gunshots?"

"Everything happened so fast, no shots were fired. That's all they were able to tell me."

"John, we have to go there and see what we can do," says Rachel.

"Senator, I don't think Durant police are going to let a United States Senator get anywhere near there. But, if we are to do anything, we have to move quickly, because they're going to secure that area very fast."

The Senator, looking at John and Levi, is pleading. "We.., we have to try! I helped arrange the march and feel somewhat responsible. Can't we try something?"

"John, I know a back way into the Capitol if we come in from the west side. But we've got to hurry. And, what the hell are we going to do when we get there?"

John pauses only briefly. "Let's go! We can decide what to do when we get there. We'll take your car Levi!"

The Senator, Levi and Tall Bear leave the cafe and speed west on Main Street. The dozen blocks takes only a few minutes. As predicted, Durant Police have blocked off 6th street, which leads to the Capitol. Levi knows the north side of the Capitol and the rear parking area will be guarded. Racing six more blocks, he turns right on a side street and approaches the Capitol from the southwest side. The only way to enter from this side is to park on a dead end street and jump a chain link fence.

Safe on the other side, they cross a grassy area that leads to several portable buildings. They were added when the staff outgrew the main complex. There is no one around. They cross a sidewalk and follow Levi to the southwest corner, the basement end of the building and a doorway. Levi and John, having spoken with ThunderHawk, Tecumseh and Johnny Kick, feel imminent danger is not a threat.

They breach a door left unlocked and all are safely inside. Quietly they approach a stairway leading up to the main floor of the complex. The Chief's office is on this floor at the far north end. Elevators are located there to the 2nd floor and the all-important tribal gaming offices. They can hear noise and activity from the front of the building. They can't see, but imagine, armed policeman, FBI and swat teams being put in place. John remembers Tammy saying they overtook the policemen and took their guns. Not knowing if they will face guns or rifles, they advance the stairs to a threatening double set of doors.

———

Durant Police Captain Sidney Johnson has trained for this situation most of his life. Never in his wildest dreams did he imagine this kind of event in Durant. Today could be the defining moment of his young career. Today he will get a chance to show what he has learned at the police academy. He and his team have set up a makeshift command center in a vacant lot across the street from the Choctaw Nation Capitol. He has surrounded the complex with his small police force and is deciding his next course of action.

With a bullhorn in hand and flanked by two of his Lieutenants, he begins formulating a plan. He has positioned squad cars at strategic locations to contain the coming and going into the Capitol complex. He knows including the Choctaw Chief, there would have been a staff of twenty-five to thirty plus visitors in the building. He determines the Indian marchers have at least three service firearms. He has been given what little information is available about the three leaders. It is too early into the siege to make any snap decisions.

An unmarked squad car is allowed into the area, and out step FBI Agents Rivers and Jackson. Agent Rivers flashes her badge.

"Captain Johnson, I'm Agent Rivers and this is Agent Joe Jackson. We just got the news. So you know, we met with the three leaders no more than two hours ago. None of us had any indication this might happen. Prior to that the leaders in question met with the personnel at the CMA offices on Main Street. From what we know, they were advised by the Executive Director to move their people to the abandoned peanut mill on East Main. That's where we met with them. One of your Lieutenants was present at that meeting and we assume he got authorization up the chain to let the march happen."

"Affirmative. That would be Lieutenant Smith, who's now at the police station in my place. He's one of my best officers and I signed off on the march based on his recommendation. Agent Rivers, do you have any more knowledge or information about these three leaders that we need to know? We just ran the only name we had–Thomas ThunderHawk–through our computers for warrants, and priors, and he's clean. Can you give us the names of the other two men involved?"

"July Tecumseh is one and, now you may find this amusing, but the third guy, his real name is Johnny Kick a Hole in the Sky."

"You got to be kidding! We don't hear too many Indian names like that around here. He's got to be from out of state."

"He's Choctaw and Apache, probably from Arizona."

Captain Johnson instructs his office to run the names. After waiting a short time, both names come up clean.

"Well I've got some good news. We're not dealing with hardened criminal types with a shit load of priors. The next thing we need to do is to find out what they want."

"Captain Johnson, can you tell us how many hostages we have in the building?" asks Agent Jackson.

"It's a guess right now. When they stormed the building some of the staff members escaped out to the back parking lot. Some got into their cars and drove north away from the complex. We've talked to homeowners across the street, and some witnessed thirty to forty marchers actually entering the building. A few went in and then left out the back of the complex. My guess is some of them had second thoughts, got scared and left the building. So we could have as many as sixty to eighty people in the building. And, we know among them there are at least three automatic weapons."

———

Levi knows the floor plan of the building, having worked here a few years ago. He enters first with Rachel behind, and John guarding her backside. Under any other circumstances John could have enjoyed the view more. He refrains and gives his attention to every move Levi makes. As they make their way down the narrow hallway for fifty feet, they encounter no one. There are several offices on either side, but empty. In another seventy-five feet, they come to a short stairway leading up six steps. Beyond, a set of double doors threatens. Levi turns the knob, opens the door, and the three of them enter into the main part of the complex. They take several more steps, and hear someone in front offices who hears them too. Two marchers come out of one office on their right, and one comes out from their left. Those three stand shoulder to shoulder, completely blocking the hallway.

The big one in the middle speaks up, "Are ya'll with us?"

Before they could answer, another one says. "Hell no. I saw him," pointing at Levi, "at that Indian office on Main."

John moves up alongside Levi, who is to his left, and positions Rachel behind both of them.

"Fellas, we work for CMA and we want you to take us to see ThunderHawk."

"Ain't gonna happen! We have orders not to let anyone in. You're leaving the way you came in, or I'm going to take your head off," says the big one in the middle.

"Sorry you feel that way big guy, but we're still coming in."

John takes a small step toward him. John knows what is coming because of the way the man is standing. As the big guy throws a right punch, John steps in to counter, shoves a heel of palm strike to the solar plexus, and launches it into a tiger claw to the throat. John can't linger, because of the two who are on either side of him. As he spins big guy counter clockwise, he pushes the one to his left in the direction of Levi, knowing Levi can handle him.

John then spins 180 degrees and catches the one on his right with a wicked left elbow to the mid-section. It knocks the man backward and down on the floor in the direction he came from. John turns in the direction of Levi and watches him spin his man around and choke him out from behind. Out of the corner of his eye he can see Rachel pressed against a wall, not frightened, but in a guarded position had they failed. The second one that was knocked to the floor gets up, runs for the hallway and disappears.

"I must be losing my touch," says John, as he takes a couple of steps toward Senator Jim, grabs her hand, puts an arm around her and asks, "Are you okay?"

"I'm fine. Wow, impressive! I thought I was a little silly coming in here, but I can tell I'm in good hands." She flashes big brown eyes and a warm smile at John.

John looks at Levi and says, "mine was the biggest, but I gave you the mean one, partner. You know they're coming back and they'll have a weapon, next time."

"We can count on that. What do you think Chieftain? So, you want to take point now?" He flashes a big grin.

"Levi, let's you and I have a look in those offices. Rachel, you stay here while we go take a look, OK?"

As Levi and John move forward, they pass a hallway to their left. John quickly glances down it to see if it is clear. He notices a small sign hanging above a doorway.

"Levi, look. Do you see what I see?" Levi looks at John, grins and nods. The small sign reads 'Tribal Membership'. They approach the door and through the window at eye level see no activity inside.

"Levi, you know what I'm going to do?"

"Yeah, I got your 6, go ahead."

"This may be our only chance to ever get a look at a voter list. Wish me luck."

Tall Bear quickly enters the room. Everyone had left in a hurry. The lights are on and softly a small radio plays Michael Jackson's 'Thriller'. John notices all the computers are still on, touches the mouse on one and the display comes alive. Surprise! On the desktop is a shortcut to the tribal membership file. John clicks on it, and the file opens. Holy Cow! There are over 180,000 names and addresses of Oklahoma Choctaws in this file. John looks in the first drawer, then a second, and finally a third before he finds a box of empty discs. He loads the disc into the drive and directs the file to copy. It's a large file, but it's data only, and it loads in under a minute. John retrieves the disc, puts the disc in a case, and places it in his back pocket. He is in and out in four minutes. This is a monumental find. With this information, they can really begin to create their own database.

John rejoins Levi at the end of the hallway. He gives him a slight nod to let him know he's been successful. They both move back down the hallway to rejoin Rachel. For a fleeting moment John feels like a thief in the night. They escape with something very valuable. However, John knows their mission to avoid another tragedy in Indian Country outweighs this misdeed.

CHAPTER 23

B ack at CMA headquarters, the office staff and volunteers are busy.
Some are taking and making calls, as Roman and Tammy, glued
to a small television set watch a live feed of the Choctaw Capitol. It
appears police have the building completely surrounded. One reporter
gives viewers an update from several blocks away using the complex
as a backdrop. What happens next is speculation. The screen switches
to a shot of Senator Cody in Washington being interviewed by the
Washington press.

"No, I don't have any information other than what is being reported.
Chief Wilson is a close personal friend of mine and I pray he's not
been harmed. I've just spoken to the President, and I'm leaving for
Oklahoma. I'm sorry, I can't say anymore. Thank you."

The screen switches to a shot of the President leaving the oval
office. Asked about the siege, he states, "This is a complete surprise.
Let's not get carried away. My Administration has good relations
with the American Indian Tribes. This is not a matter for Homeland
Security. I have some of my top people looking into the matter. The
distinguished Indian Senator James Cody from Oklahoma is en route
to assess the situation. He'll be reporting back to me as soon as possible. Thank you," he waves the reporter off.

The station switches to a live shot of the Channel 8 reporter and
FBI agent Karen Rivers. "Agent Rivers, can you give us an update?"

"As you can see the marchers have taken over the Choctaw Capitol.
They've taken Chief Wilson and some of his staff hostage. At this time
there have been no reported injuries."

"Have you contacted the leaders inside?"

"We're trying to communicate. They have yet to respond. That's all I can say at this time," and she walks away.

At CMA headquarters Roman's cell phone rings.

"Roman, it's John."

"John, where are you?"

"We managed to get inside the capitol."

"Great balls of fire, John the place is locked down. What part of the building are you in?"

"We're on the main floor of the southwest wing. We're trying to make our way closer to the Chief's office."

"John, be careful. Just so you know they have some firearms."

"Got it, I don't have much time. We already had a run-in with a couple of them. If we can make it up to the Chief's office, we can talk to ThunderHawk and try to defuse things."

"John, tell me Senator Jim isn't with you."

"Sorry Roman, she insisted on coming."

"Oh Lord! Take care of her, John. Good luck."

"Call agent Karen Rivers and let her know we're in here. I gotta go."

———

Back at command headquarters across the street from the capitol, Agent Karen Rivers hangs up her cell phone, turns and walks in the direction of Sid Johnson.

"Captain Johnson, I just received a call from Mr. Roman Billy, the Executive Director of CMA."

"And?"

"A couple of his associates are inside the complex."

"What?" Not believing what he is hearing.

"There's more, he also told me Senator Rachel Jim is with them."

"We have a United States Senator inside the building? What in the hell are they doing in there and how did she get in?"

"Captain, all he could tell me is they're inside, and are attempting to make their way to the Chief's office to try to talk ThunderHawk and his men into giving up."

"This situation just went from very bad to worse," mutters Captain Johnson.

Agent Jackson joins the two of them and says, "Captain Johnson, we just placed the first call to the Chief's office and no one is answering.

Captain, we need to make contact with someone on the inside. I suggest we go and get the CMA Executive Director, Roman Billy, and bring him here. He's the connection."

"Good idea Rivers. Make it happen," barks Captain Johnson. Agent Jackson gets into his car and speeds away to the CMA office to retrieve Roman Billy.

———

"Chieftain, they got to be coming pretty soon. If we're going to do this, we need to do it now."

"Ok, I'll take point. Rachel, stay between Levi and me."

Suddenly, the double doors swing open and July Tecumseh, pistol in hand, with two other men step through the doors.

"Tall Bear, I had a feeling it was you and your sidekick. Who's the pretty woman?"

"She's one of my assistants." John not wanting to divulge Rachel's identity, fearing they might use her as prime hostage.

"We invited you to march, now you show up after the dirty work is over. Cowards coming through the back door," sneers Tecumseh.

"July, we never dreamed you, ThunderHawk and Kick a Hole in the Sky would go this far. We're here to try and help you get out of this mess without getting yourselves killed. Let's talk about this and see what we can come up with."

"July, listen to Tall Bear," says Levi. "We don't have a lot of time. They have the building surrounded with Durant police and the FBI.

A swat team is probably on the way to take back the building. Those goons talk with their AR-15's."

"All right, start moving." July motions with the gun barrel pointing the direction he wants them to go.

Cell phones are confiscated. Tecumseh herds them toward the Chiefs office passing a locked door as Johnny Kick stand guards. Inside sits the Chief tied to a chair and his mouth duck taped shut. He's not going anywhere.

They proceed to the main office. ThunderHawk sits at the Chief's desk.

"If it isn't Mr. Tall Bear and his trusted sidekick, Levi Tushka!"

"ThunderHawk," John addresses him with a nod.

"Who's the pretty lady?"

"She's one of my staff members. You look very regal sitting behind the Chief's desk. In another place and time maybe you could have been Chief of the Choctaws. You've got everybody's attention now, clear up to Washington D.C. and the White House.

"It's about time somebody ready to listen." ThunderHawk puffs on an expensive looking Cuban cigar.

"Let's talk and figure out a way to get you out of this mess before someone gets killed?"

"Sure! I got time. Get Johnny," he briskly instructs July. He motions to the three chairs in front of the Chief's desk.

"Sit. Let's have a little Pow Wow! I do look good, don't I, Tall Bear? I could run this Nation!"

"Where's the Chief"

"I could do a hell of a lot better job than that idiot in there," pointing with a gun in his hand and looking at the closet where the Chief of the Choctaws sits in the dark."

"You haven't harmed him, have you?"

"Nah, he's fine. He can't talk right now, because we have his mouth taped shut."

"Hawk, I've been here from the beginning, when there was nothing. In spite of what you think, the Chief has done some good work," differed Levi.

"Doing what!"

"Building infrastructure."

"Well yeah we can all see that, he puts up buildings and sticks his fucking name on them."

"I agree with you there. He's a small man attempting to leave a legacy."

"The Choctaw Nation has a lot of cash from the casinos and look what he does with it. How many jets does one man need?"

"ThunderHawk, not going to argue with you, but a great Chief wouldn't have made the mistake you made today by commandeering the Choctaw Capitol," John says, as July returns with Johnny.

"Yeah, but we had to get their attention, Tall Bear. If we hadn't done something like this, they would keep doing the same old shit. We were just going to do a march by. Oh, we had talked about what it would be like to take over the Capitol, but it wasn't part of our plan today. When we got here, they just looked at us the wrong way. Like we were nothing! They didn't even take us seriously. We were invisible to them. They were laughing at us like always. Now who's laughing?"

"Thomas, I know exactly how you feel. Back in the 70's, Russell Means and the siege at Pine Ridge created awareness for our people. For a few years, the politicians listened because the siege created symphony. That's old news now. Today, the federal government doesn't give a shit about the Indians."

"ThunderHawk." adds Levi, "Hell, if I was thirty years younger, I would be standing right beside you. Those idiots out there have no knowledge of what the federal government has done to the American Indians. They could care less about how you feel and why you took over the Choctaw Capital. Eventually, they're going to start shooting and ask questions later, just like they do on the Rez."

"Thomas, listen. Listen to me. You and everyone else got caught up in the moment. Emotions are high because of the killing and the funeral. Why don't you consider ending this before somebody get hurt?" pleads John.

"You don't think they're going to let us walk out of here and go home do you?' asks July Tecumseh.

"No. You and I know that isn't going to happen. But we can get a damn good lawyer to defend you, and we can get you off without a lot of jail time."

"ThunderHawk, don't listen to that bullshit! As soon as we walk outside, they're going to cut us down. If we're going to have to go, let's take some people with us. I'm in this till the end!" shouts Johnny Kick a Hole in the Sky.

"Don't be a damn fool! You have too many of our people in here who stood behind you in the march. They trusted you and, if you play that hand, you're going to lose. What the hell are you going to accomplish by getting more people hurt or killed? We've already lost two and that's two too many!"

"ThunderHawk, why don't you let the marchers and hostages out of here? Show them you're willing to work something out," says Levi.

"Thomas, I have another suggestion for you to consider. It could be a win, win for everybody and nobody gets hurt."

"All right, John Tall Bear! You got the talking stick. Tell me what you have in mind."

───────────

Senator James Joe Cody is resting comfortably in his Lear-40 jet, cruising at 30,000 feet, passing over St. Louis, Missouri. The posh leather seats match the colors of his beloved Oklahoma Sooners. Cody often dreamed of owning his own Lear jet, but where would a young Senator from Oklahoma get $6,500,000 to buy one?

He is a lifetime away from his high school and college days in Norman, Oklahoma. His mother had worked at the local J.C. Penney for seventeen years. She was a caring, outgoing woman who taught young James to be social.

His Indian father was the strong silent type who prepared him for a future in athletics. The elder Cody had worked two jobs, so young James could prep for good grades and a scholarship to play football. Preferably, one of the skilled positions, quarterback, running back or wide receiver, are the glamor positions at the college level. If you could play one of those positions at OU, you were sure to make it to the pro level in the NFL.

Genetics and circumstance dealt father and son a different option. By young James' sophomore year, he was already bigger than most college quarterbacks. At 6 foot 6, 250 pounds; he was recruited to play left tackle. He tore up a knee his senior year, skipped the NFL and went into politics. Never looking back, he can buy and sell a dozen NFL quarterbacks today. If you every dream of owning a jet, you can make it happen by working in Washington. He purchased his two-year old jet from a sheik in Dubai last year.

His flight attendant arrives, "Senator Cody, we are about thirty minutes out. Is there anything you need before we start our descent into Durant?"

"I'd like another bourbon, please. And bring me a ham and cheese sandwich."

As the Senator sips the bourbon and wolfs down his sandwich, he considers the poor timing of this dilemma for his good friend, Chief Paul Wilson. Over the last ten years, they both have put away millions in off shore accounts. Both love the attention and limelight their positions provide. The Senator has been having great success in Washington circles. There is even talk of him running for the Office of President one day. To him it makes perfect sense. What other race of people deserves to run this nation? After all, this was the Indian's country before the 'white man' came.

He had thought of selecting Paul as his Vice-President. They could repay old debts to the Indian tribes and restore their people's dignity–two American Indians in the White House! Rulers of the free world! About time. Were he to make it there, what would jealous opponents call him, 'Blanket Ass' 'Drunken Indian' 'Savage'? Cody had been called far worse growing up in Oklahoma.

"Senator Cody, we'll be landing in Durant in five minutes." informs the flight attendant.

As the Senator steps out of the Lear Jet, a black limousine arrives to pick him up. The driver races toward the Choctaw Nation Capitol and, within minutes the police are waving his car through the perimeter. Durant Police Captain Sid Johnson and FBI Agent Rivers have been alerted to the Senator's arrival and are waiting when the black limousine pulls up. As Senator Cody exits the limo, Captain Johnson steps forward and extends a hand to the Senator.

"Senator Cody, it's an honor to meet you. I'm sorry it's not under better circumstances. I'd like to introduce you to FBI Agents Karen Rivers & Joe Jackson out of the McAlester office. They've been assisting me with this situation."

"Nice to meet you all. Bring me up to speed. What's going on Captain? I spoke with the President before leaving Washington, assuring he would be briefed soon."

"Senator, we've had several hundred Indians converge on Durant from most every county in Oklahoma. They came to attend a funeral of two of our local Indians that were shot to death by tribal law enforcement. After the funeral yesterday, several leaders encouraged a large group to march by the Capitol grounds in protest. The leaders gave assurance, it would be a peaceful march, and would last about an hour. When they arrived here at the Choctaw Nation Capitol things got out of hand, they stormed the building and took the Chief and his staff hostage."

"Do we know anything about the leaders of the group?"

"The leader, as far as we know, is Thomas ThunderHawk. We ran him through our computers for warrants and priors and he's clean. Another is July Tecumseh and the third guy is a character named Johnny Kick a Hole in the Sky."

"Sounds like we're dealing with some crazy Indians! Have they made contact to express demands?"

"We've had no communication with those three in the building thus far. I have a swat team on their way here now. A few minutes ago, I was informed, two members of a local Indian organization called CMA, Chahta Amoma Atokoli, had made their way into the building."

"How and why would they?"

"Your guess is as good as mine."

"Damn if I'm going to tell the President we're here guessing."

"Understood. One of the CMA members who's inside placed a call to their headquarters and spoke with their Executive Director. His name is Roman Billy," says Captain Johnson, looking at Rivers for confirmation.

Agent Rivers nods her head.

"Now we are getting somewhere. What was the nature of their conversation, Agent Rivers?"

"After receiving the call, Roman Billy called to advise us two of their staff members were going to attempt to convince the leader of the marchers to end the siege peacefully."

"Well, that's encouraging news. Maybe the hostage takers will listen to one of their own. We need to get that Executive Director Billy guy here, in case he receives another call."

"We have a car en route to bring him here. They should be arriving any minute," says Agent Rivers.

"By the way, what are the names of the two CMA fellows inside, and what do we know about them?"

"John Wilkerson Tall Bear is the main guy. From what my staff has been able to find out, he's a minor celebrity in the martial arts world. Our people say he's a capable individual, highly skilled in hand-to-hand combat. The Indian people we've been interviewing say he's going to be the next Chief of the Choctaws," answers Captain Johnson.

"What? Did you ask those people what they were smoking? Hard to believe considering the popularly of Chief Wilson! I've known Paul over thirty years and with the success he's had, He's unbeatable. Who's the other guy?"

"Another capable individual named Levi Tushka. He's well known throughout the state, a smart and crafty man in his late 50's."

"Well, it appears the odds may be in our favor. If our guys can talk some sense into the bad guys, maybe we can resolve this damn thing. It's going to be dark soon, I'd like to end this situation quickly."

"Senator Cody, aside from the obvious, we have an additional, very delicate situation to consider," says Agent Rivers.

"And?"

"Senator Rachel Jim is inside with Mr. Tall Bear and Mr. Tushka."

"What! Are you kidding me? How in hell is she involved with this mess?"

"That we don't know, Senator. We do know she has strong ties with the CMA organization. How she wound up in there is anyone's guess," answers Agent Rivers.

"So we are back to fucking guessing games again."

A car pulls up to the outer perimeter of the compound and is waved through. It makes its way up to the command center and parks behind Senator Cody's black limousine. Roman Billy emerges from the car and joins the Senator's group.

Watching from the Chief's office window, John Tall Bear is able to view the group standing beside a long black limousine. Obviously a very important person has joined the command team. He recognizes two of the four people huddled together, discussing what's going on in this very room.

"ThunderHawk, we've all seen this scene in the movies. They're going to want to start negotiations very soon, asking what you want."

"Okaso, I've been to the picture shows and right now, I'm in control."

"That's temporary and you know it!

"Hey, I'm a single Indian and nobody's at home waiting on me. So I got plenty of time."

"I've got a plan in mind. Could save the rest of the marchers jail time and a lot of unnecessary grief."

"Ok, let's hear it."

"At the appropriate time, I suggest you let the Chief's staff members leave out the front door. It'll be dark in thirty minutes, and when the hostages leave out the front, it will create a diversion, so your people can leave out the back under cover of darkness. There was no one guarding the back when we came in. You know, even if half of them get away, it's better than none."

The three Indian leaders move off to the side and huddle to discuss Tall Bear's suggestion. Johnny Kick is seen arguing against the plan and very adamant about it. After a couple of long minutes, cooler heads prevail, and they agree to the plan. No one asks what might happen next, but they're moving in the right direction.

Outside at the command center, Roman Billy has begun to brief the Senator and others when his cell phone rings.

"Sorry Senator. I've got to take this call. It's from John Tall Bear inside the Capitol."

As the Senator and others watch, attempting to listen to the conversation, John conveys the plan to release the hostages and gives him a time frame. John, knowing Roman is going to be quizzed, keeps it short and simple. If all agree and the plan is executed calmly, no one will get hurt. Not giving Roman time to question the plan, John abruptly ends the call. Roman repeats the conversation word for word and people begin to get into position. It's obvious to everyone John Tall Bear and Levi Tushka are in charge. Everyone else must wait.

Levi and Rachel move the marchers into place at the rear of the complex. John stays with the three leaders to coordinate getting the hostages in place near the front entrance. At about 6:30 p.m., they release the first pair of hostages out the front door.

At the same time a small group of marchers escape out the same back door, Levi, Rachel, and John entered. Every few minutes, a pair of hostages leaves out the front door while another group is escaping out the back. The plan works beautifully. Thirty minutes later a phone call is received from a marcher. Everyone got away. They will scatter to their homes across Oklahoma to watch the story unfold on the ten o'clock newscast.

Only the three rebellious Indian leaders, Levi, Tall Bear, Rachel, and Chief Wilson, still tied in the closet, occupy the Choctaw Capitol.

CHAPTER 24

Thomas ThunderHawk is sitting behind the Chief's desk leaning back with his boots on the corner of the desk. He savors another of the Chief's favorite Cuban cigars. His two lieutenants, Johnny Kick a Hole in the Sky and July Tecumseh, stand behind him. ThunderHawk enjoys what remains of his occupation. Levi, Rachel and Tall Bear, in the three leather seats face him, ready to negotiate. Many more decisions must be made before this event is over.

"I could never afford good Cuban cigars like this, Tall Bear. What do you think they're worth? Four or five bucks apiece?"

"More like two hundred," says Levi.

"Holy Shit! Are you kidding me?"

"No I'm not, those are Cohiba, Fidel's favorite."

"Well, the Chief may be a fool, but he's got good taste in cigars," as Thomas stuffs a few more into his jacket pocket and offers the box to July and Johnny.

"Tall Bear, you never told us the name of your pretty companion. I don't mean you Levi, you ugly Indian!" He and the other two break into laughter.

Levi smiles and knows it's a compliment. If an Indian likes you, they will kid and joke with you.

"She looks familiar. Where have I seen you, pretty lady?"

Before John can say anything, Senator Jim answers, "Mr. ThunderHawk, my name is Senator Rachel Jim."

ThunderHawk and the other two stop their clowning around and quickly become more attentive. During this conversation,

ThunderHawk has been messing around with the Chief's laptop computer, but stops abruptly at Senator Jim's answer.

"Senator Jim. Yes, I've seen you many times on the television. You're a very important lady. You've probably met the President and many other important people in Washington."

"I have met the President and others."

"Senator Jim, my question to you is this. Now we've done what John Tall Bear has asked, can you get us out of this mess without getting killed or sentenced to prison?"

"Mr. ThunderHawk, what you have done today carries grave consequences. If you release the Chief unharmed, getting you out of here without getting killed I can guarantee. But keeping you out of prison is going to take a small miracle."

"Senator Jim, I too have seen you on Capitol Hill working your magic. I know of some of the important bills you have pass for our people. I imagine favors are owed you. Don't let us rot in prison," pleads Tecumseh.

"Tecumseh, that's a possibility. I personally guarantee to do everything my office and position allow, short of breaking the law. With public sympathy a federal judge might consider a short sentence for the three of you. My question to you is, can we release the Chief now?"

It is obvious Senator Jim has got their attention. The three of them huddle over in a corner. After a few minutes, they agree to release the Chief. ThunderHawk wheels Wilson out of the closet. He instructs his men to leave the Chief tied, duck taped, seated. ThunderHawk tells John to make the call, the Chief is coming out.

Johnny Kick and July wheel the leader down the short hallway and out the front door to the top of the great concrete staircase. They quickly return, leaving Paul Wilson, still bound, for all to see. It is one last embarrassment ThunderHawk can impose on the Chief of the Choctaw Nation.

Television cameras are rolling and lights from flashing cameras illuminate the top of the staircase. Chief Wilson will be seen around the world, sitting in his great leather chair, his feet and hands tied, with duck tape over his mouth.

After a few minutes of discussion they all decide to exit the building together. Levi places a call to Roman to let him know of their plan. However, the command station says "No". They instruct Levi to send the three Indian leaders out together by themselves. Senator Jim is given the phone and she barks new orders.

"This is Senator Jim and I've given my word to these men they'll not be harmed as they exit the building. Mr. Tall Bear, Mr. Tushka and I will emerge first in front of the three Indian men. Should some idiot fire on us, they just might hit a United States Senator. This is the way it's going down." She closed the cell phone and snapped, "Gentleman, are you ready?" She is clearly in charge now.

"Tall Bear, one last thing. There's something I want you to see."

ThunderHawk motions for John to come behind the Chief's desk and look at the Chief's portable computer.

Tall Bear is stunned by the laptop's screen. Abruptly, his mind racing, he commandeers the keyboard, and sends an open file to a personal e-mail address. Quickly, copying it to a blank CD, he deletes the file from the hard drive and pockets the disc. ThunderHawk smiles.

"Tall Bear, you're good"

John looks back at ThunderHawk and whispers, "This might be the miracle we need to keep your sorry ass out of prison."

ThunderHawk, still grinning, says, "Achukma."

Six walk out of the Choctaw Capitol into the cool dark night and descend the marble stairway. At the bottom, in a sea of law enforcement personnel, they are forcefully separated.

The three Indian leaders are ordered to kneel down side by side with their hands behind their heads. Surrounded by a dozen members of the swat team, with TV coverage rolling and cameras flashing, ThunderHawk, July Tecumseh and Johnny Kick a Hole in the Sky have their fifteen minutes of fame.

While the media tend to the three young Indian leaders and Chief Wilson, Rachel, John and Levi disappear into the night.

CHAPTER 25

On Tuesday morning, the end of the Choctaw Nation siege is being covered nationally. All the morning shows use the siege as their lead story. CNN, FOX, and MSNBC's talking heads discuss the event. Much is speculation. What happened in Durant? A few older news types make the Pine Ridge connection and wonder what kind of impact it might have on Indian relations.

Why did the siege of the Choctaw Nation offices happen? Related topics report federal money owed to the Indians, Indian Health Care, alcohol and drug rehab centers, Indian casinos, Indian Chiefs, and Senators. Despite their seeming intelligence, news people don't have a clue about what caused the events.

The President, pleased the siege ended without any loss of life, has made a short statement. He has given Senator James Cody much of the credit for being on the scene, praising the Choctaw Tribal police, the Durant Police Department and FBI agents who assisted. He assured Chief Wilson the three renegade Indians will be charged and tried in federal courts and warns attacks on this nation and the Sovereign Indian nations within our boundaries will not be tolerated.

There has been tremendous interest in the three Indians who led the night's siege. It's obvious to those who witnessed the end, Tall Bear, Levi and Senator Jim played an important part orchestrating the surrender. Tall Bear and Levi are being hunted for a behind-the-scenes story.

John arrives at CMA headquarters around 9 a.m. to find a small crowd of news reporters camped out by the front door and across the street. He pushes his way through repeating "no comment". Roman, Tammy and Levi are already in their offices receiving and making calls. Seeing Tall Bear, they make their way into his office.

Tammy is first to speak. "John, the staff is too busy fielding incoming calls and not getting any work done. Senator Jim's office called a couple of times. Chief Wilson's secretary called and wants you to meet with the Chief at his office."

"I'm sure he does," says Levi.

"FBI Agent Rivers' wants to debrief both of you," continues Tammy. "ThunderHawk wants to talk as soon as possible. Sounds likes he's issuing orders. He said, 'Tell Tall Bear, I'm going to start talking if I don't hear from him soon.'"

"Who in the hell does he think he is?" asks Roman.

"ThunderHawk crafty. He's got a little leverage and he's beginning to assert some pressure."

"He's in jail and he's got leverage?"

"Can't give you the details yet Roman, but after last night, the game has changed considerably. First, here're a CD which contains the master mailing address list of the Choctaw Nation members," He hands the CD to Tammy. Her face registers a pleasant surprise."

"This will come in handy."

"It may not be as important as it once was, but have our staff go through it and print out a list of all the members who are at least one quarter or more Choctaw. Give me that number. I'll explain later."

"Chieftain sounds like we are going to play some serious poker. And you look like an NDN with his rent past due, dealing to an inside straight or a royal flush," chimes Levi.

"I imagine everyone here feels like we are in over our heads, but let me say this. After last night, we are stronger than ever. Yes, Levi, we have been dealt a different set of cards, but we got to play them correctly. We might forge CMA into a very powerful position. We have to be patient and play the hand."

"So, what's the priority?" asks Tammy.

"I must speak to Senator Jim to be sure we are all on the same page. Keep the staff fielding calls and taking care of business. This time tomorrow, we may need to plan a press conference. Let's just get through today."

One of the staff members joins them, "You may want to see this John. Chief Wilson is about to give a press conference." They all gather together in front of a small television in a corner of the office. A news reporter finishes the lead-in. Chief Wilson appears with his assistant chief and council forming a backdrop of support.

"Good morning, I will make a brief statement, and will not be taking any questions. Yesterday three of our people attempted to take over the Choctaw Nation Capitol office building and, for a short time, did. However, our purpose to serve has not been compromised. Today is business as usual. The President assures me the leaders of the siege will be charged and tried for a number of offenses yet to be determined in federal court.

"The Choctaw Nation is a sovereign nation serving nearly 200,000 members. We employ thousands and provide services to even more through our hospitals and clinics. I want to let our members, and the world know, Indian people are proud law abiding citizens. We will not let a few bad apples keep us from our destiny of returning our people to a life of dignity. As long as I am Chief, this is the way it will be. God Bless you and our Choctaw Nation," and he walks away.

"Sounds like he is campaigning," says Levi.

"I don't like his message Tonto. He's going to hang those three men. Can't let that happen. They made some mistakes, but they have potential"

John disappears into his office and places a call to Senator Jim. They discuss the past 24 hours, determining their next move. She has been inundated with requests from the news outlets and colleagues in the Senate for information, likewise, John and Levi. The bounce in her voice says she likes being part of an exciting and dangerous adventure. Last night was very different from her everyday life as a United State

Senator. Surviving the siege has created a bond among the three of them. John feels like Rachel is becoming a true friend.

He tells her the Chief called and wants to speak to Levi and himself. He asks her if she has seen the Chief's press conference. She says she has, and expresses concerns ThunderHawk and the other two are going to face too harsh a prosecution. She doesn't want some United States prosecutor trying to make a name for himself at the expense of the three Indians. John totally agrees, admits his counter strategy isn't completely worked out. John would like her to attend a meeting between Chief Wilson and himself this afternoon as an observer. He promises not compromise her position. She agrees and says she will be at CMA headquarters at 3 p.m.

Tall Bear calls FBI Agent Rivers and finds out ThunderHawk, Tecumseh and Johnny Kick have been moved early this morning to McAlester, Oklahoma, seventy-five miles to the north. In their short conversation, John agrees to allow her office to debrief him in due time. She gives him a direct number he can call to speak with ThunderHawk. John makes the call and convinces ThunderHawk to give him 48 hours to create some magic.

John's next call is to the Choctaw Nation and office of the Chief. The Chief's personal assistant confers with her boss and a 4 p.m. meeting is arranged. The CMA executive waits for Senator Jim's arrival from Hugo. His stomach growls, reminding him he hasn't eaten breakfast. He decides on a quick lunch next door to eat and relax. The morning had been taxing, emotional, and stressful. If his plan is going to work, he will have to be at his best this afternoon.

John makes his way through the waiting reporters and into the small cafe and finds a corner table in the back. A cheerful waitress in her earlier 30's brings him a glass of water and a menu.

"Now, Susan, you know I don't need a menu. I order the same thing every time I come in here."

"I know John, but if you keep eating what you order you're going to have a heart attack someday. Why don't you eat something a little healthier? How do you think I maintain this pretty figure?" she asks making a sweep of her body with her hands.

"Well I can't argue with those curves."

"Thank you. And you look pretty good for a man of your age, too," she giggles.

"You're darn right I look good! That's how I keep those young ones chasing me."

"All right, three eggs over medium, are you sure you want 4 slices of bacon?"

"OK, since you're concerned about my heart, I'll have two."

"Two slices of bacon, three slices of tomatoes, one avocado, no toast or bread, a glass of grape juice. And no we still don't have any walnuts and blueberries," she says as she smiles and walks away with an exaggerated sway of her young behind.

———

About ten years ago, Tall Bear researched the American Indian's 'hunter/gatherer diet'. An Ohio State University study had found the Plains Indians were once the tallest people on earth. John's tribes, the southeastern Choctaws, were not far behind. Their great Chief Tushkalusa was a towering man, built like an NFL linebacker, a magnificent specimen of athletic power. Only one hundred and fifty years ago they were the last to begin eating the European diet. For him, it made perfect sense to emulate his ancestors' eating habits of that era.

For the past few years, he's been practicing this Native philosophy of healthy eating. Like his Indian ancestors, he consumed more grass fed milk and meat. He tried to eat more fish and fowl not caged or injected with hormones. His pet peeve is genetically engineered strawberries. Working in the fields as a young boy, he had picked a more succulent berry. He remembered it to be smaller with a consistent shape and red throughout. Today it is much larger, deformed, the outer skin lighter red, whiter fiber inside.

John dug deeper trying to replicate how his ancestors had trained physically. He knows of course the Choctaws didn't go to the gym and lift weights. The American Indian was built for strength and speed. Burst strength and sprinting speed was more important than endurance, however, both were important chasing down wild game.

John tried to imagine what their historical physical exertion pattern might be. When in battle or play, any confrontation was intense, brief and infrequent. The hand-to-hand weapons were fast, quick and terminal. They were masters of projectile weapons like the bow, lance, spear, knife and blowgun. With a blowgun, the Choctaws could kill small game from eighty feet away.

The Choctaw created the game Lacrosse (Kabocha-toli-"stickball"). They practiced martial arts called "Itishi", Indian wrestling. Another sport they excelled at was foot racing. Like the Apache Indians, they could run for days if necessary.

John found a fellow Choctaw in Dallas attempting to emulate the same type of training he had researched and a friendship was formed. Together they began using vintage Nautilus machines from the '70's to replicate a weight-training program Indians might have experienced in everyday life. Almost every gym in America promotes two-hour training sessions three times a week. In the beginning, John emulated this. After experimenting, taking notes and seeing undisputable results, he now trains 12 minutes every five days. He keeps getting stronger producing more muscle mass and feels in the best shape of his life.

"I'm proud of you John, you didn't finish your bacon," says Susan, as she begins to clear his table.

"Someone hinted I was eating too much bacon, and one of my new rules is, if you're no longer hungry, stop eating. Always leave something on your plate."

"My momma taught me to eat everything on my plate and not to waste food."

"Your mother is a good woman. I'm sure she was just showing her love for you."

"Ok John, how do you eat like this and stay in good shape?"

"With exceptions, I usually eat what is called the American Indian Hunter/Gatherer Diet. Do some research and you'll find it stimulating. If you have diabetes in your family history, this philosophy of eating can eliminate the chance of your developing it," he says as he gets up from the table.

"Thanks, John. I'll check it out. I hear you're quite the celebrity, having rescued the Chief last night."

"Well, I can't take all the credit. I had a whole lot of help."

"Thanks to you, I've had a good day in tips. What's up with all the reporters out front?"

"I can't comment, but keep your eyes and ears open," John winks at her as he tosses a $5 tip on the table and walks out the door.

Reporters and news crews out front are getting anxious. The paparazzi camped across the street stay busy with minor action at CMA's front door. A few minutes before 2 p.m., Tall Bear enters. Tammy informs him Senator Cody has called and wants to speak. Levi and John have ample time to make plans for their 4 p.m. meeting with the Chief. It is a comforting feeling, having a United States Senator part of the CMA team. John is reasonably sure Senator Jim won't compromise the integrity of her office. Nobody can blame her for being sympathetic to her people and acting in their best interests. Politics is a dirty business. Most politicians have their own agendas and self-interest.

The USA, founded on faith-based ideals, has been tainted by greed for money and power from the very beginning. Time after time, indigenous people have met European colonialists with curiosity and open arms. In turn, generation after generation, century after century, United States forces have eradicated the Indians, people who occupied the land for millenniums. They took their land, even copied the Iroquois blueprint for democratic government.

The eagle, which once soared Creator's majestic skies symbol for all that was good and right, is nearly extinct. Washington DC has become the roost of hawks, sparrows and vultures. John hopes Senators Jim and Cody have their hearts in the right place.

CHAPTER 26

Waiting for Senator Jim to arrive, Tall Bear assembles his staff in one of the larger offices. Because of the meeting's serious nature, Levi opens with a Choctaw prayer. John silently asks for divine intervention to make his plan work as it could affect the Choctaw Nation and its people for decades to come. Next, John outlines a plan of action based on the information they have. Step by step, he lays out the 'what ifs' in a series of mind-boggling scenarios. It is decided only the principal people already involved, Levi and Tall Bear, along with Senator Jim will face this exchange with Chief Wilson. After much discussion, nearing the scheduled summit, everyone is on the same page.

As soon as Senator Jim arrives, she is ushered into the small office outside the conference. After exchanging pleasantries and small talk, it's time to leave for the meeting with Chief Wilson. John is sure the Chief does not anticipate Senator Jim's presence at this meeting. The Senator offers her town car as transportation to the Capitol.

Arriving at the Choctaw Capital promptly at 4 p.m. they are escorted into a small waiting room outside the Chief's office. The room is decorated with many American Indian artifacts. There are several paintings of past Choctaw Chiefs and one of Paul Wilson. There are older photographs of important events from the last fifty years. Five minutes pass, the inner door to the Chief's office opens, and his personal assistant invites them in. Chief Wilson offers the same three chairs the three occupied the day before. The Chief sits at his great mahogany desk, and behind him are the American and Choctaw

Nation flags on short flagpoles. On one wall are several autographed photos of past Presidents. It is quite impressive.

Before he has a chance to say anything, John speaks, "Chief Wilson, I want to thank you for seeing us this late in the afternoon. Before we begin, I want you to know Senator Jim is here as an observer to the meeting. At our request, she's been kind enough to drive in from Hugo to sit in. She has no knowledge of the nature of this meeting."

"Well sure, Senator Jim is always welcome here," replies the Chief with a big smile, but looking a little puzzled by John's remark. "First of all I want to thank you all for facilitating the ending of the siege. As I stated in my press conference this morning, those renegades will be punished by the federal government and sent to prison. Had it not been for the three of you, the situation could have been much worse. Senator Jim, I especially want to acknowledge you for your courageous action. I know the President and all your colleagues on Capitol Hill are proud of you and will appreciate what you have done. It's fitting to show the world we Indians take care of and solve our own problems and differences."

"Chief, I'm glad you see it that way, and if you don't mind…," John looks at Senator Jim and Levi for approval to speak first.

"As you must know by now Levi and I are heavily involved in a new organization called CMA, an acronym for Chahta Amoma Atokoli. This organization came about from Choctaws networking among Indian churches within the thirteen counties of the Choctaw Nation. Hundreds of elders have seen changes and are unhappy with the direction of the Nation in the last ten years. Enjoying undeniable success, CMA goal is to petition the federal government to be federally recognized as a separate tribe from the present Choctaw Nation. This new tribe is to be made up of full blood Choctaws, to better preserve the bloodline from being further diluted like the current tribe."

"A new tribe, you can't be serious."

"I assure you Chief, we are very serious. Here are several of the core ideas of CMA and the new tribe," as John begins to read from a sheet of paper.

"1. Elect a full blood Choctaw for Chief who speaks the Choctaw language, a requirement to hold the office.

2. Establish a new blood quantum for tribal membership, to be no less than one quarter. This will shrink the tribal membership and insure timely services to all deserving members.

3. Set aside at least 15% of revenue from gaming and casinos for cash dividends payable semiannually to tribal members every year.

4. Allow all members to have access to services, regardless of where they live and work.

5. We would like to see some of these changes implemented within the existing Choctaw Nation."

"Wait a minute!" shouts the Chief. "What the hell are you talking about, and what does it have to do with this meeting? I invited you people here to thank you for your help in ending the takeover."

"Chief Wilson," Tall Bear continues, "The spirits of our ancestors are not far from us. They know and understand our thoughts and feelings. Elders feel sorrow for the pain and suffering our people have endured the past six hundred years. We must live up to the privileges they granted us leading the way. Our young people are lost and divided as they go through life not knowing who they are.

"This is what I have endured in my fifty-five years on this earth. For many years I was lost. I never felt like I belonged anywhere. I always felt like I was on the outside looking in. We cannot allow our young people to suffer the same path. Many remain lost, for they are pulled both ways. We must share with them our knowledge to survive in both worlds.

"The white man's greed is his making and will be his downfall. You, as the Chief of the Choctaws, have taken his path. You have embraced the white man's religion, his political powers, and his greed for more money than can be spent in a lifetime. Some of you grow rich and fat while our people remain poor and suffer enormous hardships.

"We must teach endurance, educational prowess, honor, spiritual harmony and respect. We must insist on personal responsibility and teach pride in our heritage. We must recall and revive the old ways and, above all, teach and speak our language."

"You can stop right there. How dare you lecture me? Who the hell do you think you are coming into my office and laying this pile of shit on my table? I've given my life to building this Nation to serve our Indian people!" shouts an increasingly angry Chief.

"Levi, will you give the Chief the breakdown of blood quantum of his so-called Indian nation?"

"Chief, the blood quantum average of the 200,000 Choctaws you serve is roughly 1/64 on the Indian blood side. If the requirements to be NDN were to be say, one quarter, you would be serving only 17,000 Choctaws."

"Fuck you, Levi, and the horse you rode in on!" explodes the Chief.

"I'm not finished, Chief Wilson. CMA doesn't want Thomas ThunderHawk, July Tecumseh, and Johnny Kick a Hole in the Sky hung out to dry. We want them tried in tribal court, judged by Indian people."

"Like hell! This meeting is over!" the Chief announces, as he stands.

"Sit down, Chief! And please remain calm as I tell you I want your resignation within thirty days. In your own words, look at this pile of shit on your desk." Tall Bear's own voice is measured as he tosses a legal sized envelope on the Chief's desk. Levi is remaining quiet, but John can tell this verbal interaction between him and the Chief has rattled him a little and has shocked Senator Jim.

The proud Chief of the Choctaw Nation picks up the envelope, glances inside, and pulls out a photo then quickly shoves it back inside. The color drains from his face, his knees appear to buckle a little as he sits down hard in his chair. He bows his head, trying to regain his composure before speaking.

Before he can say anything, Tall Bear again speaks, "I want to make it perfectly clear Senator Jim has no knowledge of the contents of that envelope. She is only here as an observer. I assume you have security cameras rolling as we speak. Just so you know, Levi is filming this meeting with a small digital camera mounted inside his briefcase. The information contained in the envelope is an embarrassment to this office and the Choctaw Nation. It doesn't have to go beyond this room. As Choctaw elders, Levi and I wish to advise you."

"Chief," says Levi. "We suggest you replace your Assistant Chief and do it as quickly as possible. Schedule a press conference tomorrow morning at 10 a.m. to name his successor." Levi is thoroughly enjoying himself. Senator Jim is shell shocked and speechless. After a long minute, which feels like an eternity Tall Bear asks.

"Chief Wilson, one more thing. Is there any question as to who your replacement for Assistant Chief will be?"

The Chief looks at him and says, "No."

"Achukma, this meeting is adjourned." Tall Bear stands offering his hand to a stunned Senator Jim. He helps her from her chair and escorts her to the door with Levi behind. Tall Bear stops and glances back at the once proud and powerful Chief of the Choctaw Nation. *'How and why do powerful men go bad? Most have it all, but always want more. They all are such sad figures when they fall from grace.'*

CHAPTER 27

Tuesday morning, before Chief Wilson's scheduled 10 a.m. press conference, CMA staff members are gathered around the television. Most drink coffee, eat donuts or speculate on the outcome of overnight activities. Cars have come and gone well into the night at the Choctaw Nation Capitol. Senator James Cody was escorted in and out and council members from the thirteen counties have all been in attendance.

To news reporters, it seems odd the Chief has scheduled another press conference within 24 hours of his previous one. A local television news reporter describes what has happened in the past week. The camera pans to show other news networks doing the same thing. Vans and trucks with satellite dishes mounted on top surround the Capitol building. A reporter from Channel 8 news interviews a small group of Indians over to one side. They, too, wonder what the conference holds for members of the Nation.

Promptly at 10 a.m. a live shot from the office of the Chief of the Choctaw Nation fills the screen. Paul Wilson, half Choctaw, sits at his desk. Though well into his 60's, he still has a full head of hair. Today, he looks very pale and much older, as if he has been ill for some time. The members of his Council stand behind him.

"Good morning fellow Choctaws. These are changing times within the Choctaw Nation. Twelve years ago when I took office, this Nation provided jobs for 1500 people. Today we employ over 3,000. The Nation's gaming industry has made our Nation one of the richest of all the tribes. We have become big business. What transpired this past weekend is a reminder I must listen to the people and their needs.

"Although guiding our Nation into the new century required considering the big picture, I lost sight of an important part of the greater good. The Choctaw people have spoken to my Council members and they inform me, Indian people take care of Indian people, and we must solve our own problems.

"I have been advised by my Council to insist the Indian activists, Thomas ThunderHawk, July Tecumseh and Johnny Kick a Hole in the Sky, be released from federal custody and returned to The Choctaw Nation Courts. Their acts, for whatever reason, were carried out on the grounds of this Sovereign Nation, and should be tried fairly under its jurisdiction. Tribal attorneys have drawn up the necessary documents to facilitate transfers so these men are tried in our own Choctaw Tribal Court.

"The security system and the safety of our staff were compromised over the weekend. The philosophy and the people in charge must be held accountable. Therefore, it is regrettable, but I must ask for the resignation of my Assistant Chief, Newt Wallace. He will be reassigned to another position yet to be decided within the Choctaw Nation.

"To replace him, I have listened again to the recommendations of Council members. They suggest I recognize, and find an appointee in, a new organization recently established in Bryan County called the Chahta Amoma Atokoli. The Choctaw Nation has been following the progress of this new, dynamic organization and several of their leaders. Again, a good Chief listens to the people. Having their input will make our Nation stronger than ever. The core philosophy of CMA is to take care of the needs of the individual first, then family, and then Nation. This union of our philosophies seeks the best of both worlds.

"At this time I would like to extend an invitation to John Wilkerson Tall Bear to become the next Assistant Chief of the Choctaw Nation. I have not consulted with him, yet know, as a wise and courageous man, he will not refuse my request. Halito, and God Bless our people and Nation."

———————

While a few reporters remain, most are hurrying to their vehicles, making a mad dash to CMA headquarters two miles away. They create a minor traffic jam at the intersection leading to Main Street. In the office, after hearing the Chief's announcement, everyone is congratulating John. Though not the original design, ever-changing events compel pursuing this path and seeing where it leads. It may be a shorter route in their quest for a new nation. The possibility of overhauling the old one is inviting. It seems to be a win/win situation. Within minutes, news vans, reporters and photographers are filling the sidewalk in front of headquarters. John advises the receptionist to tell them he will be giving a press conference within the hour. Tammy, Roman, Levi and John return to his office to discuss his reply.

Roman is the first to speak. "Are you going to accept the Chief's offer to become Assistant Chief?"

"How could he not accept?" chirps Tammy.

"This is the way we all anticipated it would unfold. Yes, of course, he's going to accept. It puts our Nashoba achukma in the hen house," kids Levi.

All join laughing at Levi's 'good wolf' reference.

"Yes, I'm going to accept. It's obvious to me this is the fast lane to what we want to accomplish. We can bring about many changes, not just ours, but what the people want. With the Chief out of the way in thirty days, we can begin to make things right."

"What do you mean, the Chief out of the way in thirty days?" asks Tammy.

"I'm going to see if I can pull a rabbit out of a hat."

"Can you make that happen?"

"Tammy, I have learned not to underestimate John," says Levi.

"I have no doubt the Chief will be leaving within thirty days if not sooner. But lets not divulge that now. There's a more pressing matter to consider. Tammy, tell the reporters outside they have time to get lunch. I'll make myself available at a 1 p.m. press conference." His cell phone rings and he recognizes Senator Jim's personal cell number.

"Senator Jim, how are you?"

"My, aren't we being formal today? Now you're going to be the next Assistant Choctaw Chief, you're becoming a big shot."

"Now, you're being funny, Rachel! I'm quite a few notches below a United States Senator."

"Assistant Chief of the Choctaw Nation is a very important position. John, you knew this press conference was coming, so, how did you orchestrate that?"

"Rachel, I had no idea this was going to happen this way. It caught me by surprise, too."

"John Tall Bear, I don't believe you for one minute. I saw the look on the Chief's face when he looked in that envelope. Whatever was in there is causing all this today."

"Could be, but I didn't twist the Chief's arm. I'm thinking he sees the error of his ways and wants to make amends. In any event, it puts me in a great position. Now I can represent CMA's interests and the Choctaw Nation people at the same time."

"John Wilkerson Tall Bear, you should have been a politician. You can make things happen. Maybe someday you'll tell me what really went on in that meeting. Until then, I'll just have to wonder about you."

"As long as I have you thinking about me...," *'Now why did I say that?'*

"You are going to accept, aren't you?"

"I've scheduled a press conference at 1 p.m. Tune in and you'll find out."

"Ok, I'll be watching. Bye."

At 1 p.m. everyone waits for Tall Bear. John has never felt important enough to be the focus of a news conference. He remembers hearing his mother speak of Henry Belvin, principal Choctaw Chief from 1948 to 1975. She had met the Chief at one time and never forgot how approachable he was and able to mingle with the people. His mother would be beside herself to have her son accepting the office of Assistant Chief of the Choctaws. As they say in Washington, the number two position is just one heartbeat from the President. He gulps down a Dr. Pepper.

Stepping onto the sidewalk out the front door, he wades into a sea of reporters and people jockeying for position. Camera lights spark flashbacks to his boyhood walk down the gazebo stairs at the town lottery. Descending looking for support, he searched for a friendly set of eyes to no avail. Now all eyes are on him, and everyone is waiting for him to speak. Reporters have set up a make shift lectern fitted with microphones to catch and amplify his words.

Past the crowd, rustic buildings line the street. They are different shapes, sizes, and colors. Most are one story, over one hundred years old and some are empty. This is not a massive marble courtyard press conference. It's Indian country and John, a country boy who went to the city to make a living feels proud. For most of his life, he's felt out of place, but today, he is confident, coming home. Standing before the crowd, his mother's spirit with him, he stalls to find his rhythm, the intensity to make her proud.

"Thank you all for waiting for me. I know it's hot out here therefore I won't keep you long. This has been a difficult time for the Choctaw Nation and its people. Little more than two weeks ago we lost two of our young men, a tragedy we still mourn. There are many answers yet to be uncovered as to why two souls in the prime of their lives were taken away. As a Choctaw elder, I intend to ask the hard questions, get responses and deliver answers to their grieving parents. We will be working with Chief Wilson, the Durant Police, and the regional FBI office to investigate their deaths and bring closure so grieving hearts can heal. Why is it, when we lose someone in law enforcement, no stones are left unturned to find the perpetrators. That should be the order of the day for every tragic death, no matter the color of their skin, gender or field of endeavor. A life is a life and the value the same, is it not? This will be my first priority.

"Last weekend things got out of hand. During a peaceful march, a show of unity and respect to victims, unchecked emotions caused a takeover of the Choctaw administrative facility. Fortunately it ended peacefully without any injuries. I want to commend Chief Wilson for his swift action in demanding the authorities turn the men in question over to our Tribal Court. As he eloquently reported, we, as a sovereign nation, should have first jurisdiction in this matter.

"As some of you know, I have been one of the principal leaders of the Chahta Amoma Atokoli, a grass roots movement that began in many small Indian churches within the Choctaw Nation. Its principal goal reminds us of those with high blood quantum. All Choctaws owe gratitude to full bloods that survived the 'Trail of Tears'. These people are the direct link to our proud past. We must take advantage of their wisdom and knowledge of the old ways while they are here. I know each and every one of you knows someone like this. It is your duty to make them feel important because of who they represent.

"Chahta Amoma Atokoli will work within the Choctaw Nation and assist whenever asked. Falammichi is a Choctaw word, which means to defend and to restore. It behooves the Choctaw Nation to defend and restore the dignity of our people. Practicing Falammichi with family, friends and neighbors, I graciously accept Chief Paul Wilson's offer to become the next Assistant Chief of the Choctaw Nation. Halito and God bless you all."

CHAPTER 28

J ohn is sworn into office the next day with the Chief and the thirteen council members in attendance. For the next two weeks, he
begins to grasp the size and complexity of the Nation and its workforce. Too many employees with overstated titles put too little effort
in their positions. There is no chain of command or accountability
consistent from one office to the next.

Every publication of the Choctaw newspaper, The Bishinik, recognizes Indians graduating from college; photo captions and articles
thank the Nation for its financial assistance. Having paid for their
college education, one would think the Nation would take advantage
of this new workforce.

There is very little chance of landing a job within the Nation
unless you are kin to someone already employed. When positions do
become available, they not advertised to the outside. Many of its high
profile directors are not Indian at all. The lower positions are filled
with some who look part Indian. The Nation has become a dictatorship serving the Chief.

As any curious new employee, John is interested in gambling revenues. It is difficult to get anyone to give him information about this
area of the Nation's finances. People fear leaks might upset the Chief.

Another of the services the Nation provides, building homes for
disadvantaged Indians, is wonderful in theory, but corrupt in application. John is told mortgage payments are based on yearly income.
Some pay as little as $40 a month for a new home. Run properly,
this program could bring dignity to Choctaws in the autumn of their

lives. All you have to do is be full blood, live within the Choctaw Nation and put your name on the waiting list. However, it can be years before the rightfully eligible are moved into their new homes. Many die before receiving their entitlement. Yet, when a home does become available, if you know someone like the Chief, you can be moved to the front of the line. No one complains for fear of retribution, which would leave him or her without access to a future home or other services.

John appoints Levi his unofficial acting personal assistant. They plan to travel to each district and visit with the local councilman. In a casual setting, John and Levi will be able to exchange ideas concerning the Nation. Few will suspect they are speaking to the future Chief of the Choctaws. To date, they speak highly of Chief Wilson and the work he has done. John knows publicly all will take this position, but he often wonders how they really feel. Levi proves invaluable. Having lived in Oklahoma all his life, he knows several of the council members personally.

John is looking forward to visiting with the Nation's pastor, Randall Nohubby. He has to be in his early 80's, one of God's old warriors. John has known of him for many years, but never had the pleasure of meeting him. John's mother often spoke of the pastor, and he is excited to meet anyone who knew his mother in her early years in Oklahoma.

John and Levi arrive in Boswell just after 2 p.m. and sit down to visit with him.

"Halito Chim-achukma (Hello, how are you doing)? Chukma, Mr. Nohubby. It's so good to finally meet you," John says as he shakes the respected elder's hand.

"Um achukma akin-li (I'm good). John Tall Bear, I knew you when you were a youngster. You were about ten years old then and growing fast. You probably don't remember me, but I know this, your momma was proud of you."

"Halito Reverend Nohubby."

"And Levi, we go back twenty or thirty years, too. Good to see you are keeping better company," he laughs. What sounds like an inside joke completes the introductions. They sit down to get better acquainted.

Pastor Nohubby continues, "John, I've heard good things about you. I ran into Senator Jim the other day and she spoke very highly of you."

"Mr. Nohubby, she was very helpful in bringing the takeover to a peaceful ending. I have gotten to know her well and have the utmost respect for her."

"Yeah, she comes all the way from Hugo, just to have lunch with John."

John gives Levi an eye command to keep their visit more businesslike.

"Well, she's a lovely woman. She and her family have been dear to me for many years. You know, she has never been married."

John is beginning to get a little uncomfortable, so he steers the conversation to another topic.

"Mr. Nohubby, we are hoping to get some insight into what you think about the events of the last few weeks, and what sort of repercussions we might expect."

"Please, we are friends here, call me Randall. When Chief Wilson replaced his previous assistant with you, John, it caught us all by surprise. However, I'd known of your efforts and progressive work with your new organization."

"Randall, I can't take all the credit. CMA was growing long before I came on board. When I joined, I brought my trusted sidekick, Levi. I'm hearing jokes about us being the new Lone Ranger and Tonto."

"Well Tonto, glad to meet you," laughs the pastor, smiling at Levi. "Levi is a good man to have as a friend. I have watched him grow up, and he is well liked and respected among the old Choctaws. Of course, I knew both of your mothers, and y'all come from good Indian stock."

"John, I've called Pastor Randall on several occasions for guidance and advice. There were a few times in my life I had no hope and felted lost. This man would pray and counsel with me and lift my spirits. I don't mind telling you, Randall, you saved my life a couple of times."

"Levi, like I said, I knew your mother well. I'm glad, in her absence, I was able to step in and lift your spirits. In my lifetime, the elders did the same thing for me. You and John will do the same for others when they come to you for guidance and advice. It's the old Choctaw Indian tradition and we need to see more of it. Back in those days, we would never think of turning our back on someone no matter how good or bad they were. We were always trying to save someone. That's what appealed to me when I got my calling doing The Great Spirit's work, God's work. If I were a younger man, I would get more involved in politics to help our people. I'm old, but I am not blind to some of the things going on within the Nation. I envy both of you for what you are attempting to do and wish you great success."

John looks at Levi with surprise. *'This old warrior's spirit is still alive, and there is still some fight left in him. The fact he envies our work is an insight into the character of this great man.'*

"Randall, I'm glad we feel the same way. I knew our visit with you would be a fruitful one. You are a man of impeccable character so I won't hesitate in coming to you for advice and counsel in the future. That said I have no reservations telling you what I'm about to say. In fact you may find this hard to believe. We have solid evidence the Chief is not a righteous man. He has committed crimes I cannot speak of at this time. He will be held accountable to a higher power eventually. Because of this evidence, the Chief will step down from his office, and I will become the next Chief of the Choctaws."

As John reveals, he watches closely, looking for some reaction, but the pastor doesn't flinch in the least. The old warrior has seen it all.

One Chief leaves and is replaced by another. It is the natural order in life. We are born, travel the movement of life, and then we die.

"John Wilkerson Tall Bear, I expect this will happen because your word is iron. I have witnessed many Chiefs in my life. They come and they go. Some are great Chiefs and some are not so good. I have a feeling you will make a good Chief. I have but a short time left on this earth, therefore it is my wish to help you in any way I can. Like you, I have ideas and wishes for my people. Maybe I can see them happen through you."

"Randall, you have been the Nation's pastor for as long as I can remember. As you say, you have seen Chiefs come and go. As important, you have seen council members come and go. You know each of them that serve the Chief today. Levi and I, along with the members of CMA, have concerns about the direction of the Choctaw Nation. CMA's first priority is to take care of the legacy of our Choctaw elders, more specifically, Choctaw elder full bloods and those that have significant Indian blood. We don't agree with the present philosophy of allowing a person to become a member of the Choctaw Nation by proving they have, for a lack of a better term, 'one drop of Indian blood'. Because of this, the Nation has grown larger. Because of these large numbers, services the Nation offers are spread very thin and forced to take care of people who are undeserving. When they step in line in front of a full blood and demand services, it is a direct insult to the very people that got us here in the first place. I am speaking about your and my ancestors that survived the 'Trail of Tears'.

"There was a time, the federal government requirement to be Indian was at least one quarter blood. Eventually, the federal government gave in and allowed each tribe to define 'what is an Indian'," adds Levi.

"Randall, I hope you agree, Levi, CMA and I feel strongly we should revert back to the original requirement, maybe even half. The tribe will become smaller and the quality of life for each member will become far better. We can start giving cash dividends like some of the more progressive tribes. The federal government is not going to take care of our people forever. Far too many of our Choctaws are dying from obesity, diabetes, suicide, drugs and alcohol. Therefore we must do a better job providing jobs, housing, rehab programs and health care."

"Pastor, even though you are not a council member or a paid employee of the Nation, John and I know you are respected among the current council members. Do you have any insight as to how this council might react to a change in philosophy and reducing the tribe?"

"That's a good question, Levi. And, I don't know the answer. However, the majority of the council members are full blood. I'm guessing they might be persuaded to consider a change, given the right set of circumstances. John, Levi, I know you both to be good men and what you are proposing is a righteous plan. If you both don't mind, I would like to ask the Creator for guidance and assistance in this plan. Before you leave, let's pray."

CHAPTER 29

J ohn and Levi spend the next ten days visiting other council members in the thirteen counties. All are polite and receptive but he's sure some wonder where this Tall Bear character is coming from. He's lived in Texas for the last forty years and now he is the Assistant Chief of the Choctaw Nation. Some, with aspirations of rising in Wilson's ranks, are jealous.

John has been an outsider all his life. It didn't matter where he was, Oklahoma, Texas, the military–he never felt at home. For the first time he feels at the front door of a new home. Others will have to get used to it because he isn't going away. He will win them over eventually, or they will be left behind. His is not one voice, but the voice of the people from the churches and small towns, from the counties these council members supposedly represent.

John will fill in for the Chief at various functions, whenever he is away. Almost daily there is one to attend. Many times the Chief and he attend the same award presentation, the opening of a new clinic, gas station, or graduation. Everybody wants to have their photo taken with the Chief. If the Chief is not available, John is the next best thing. All these events and photos appear in the Nation's newspaper.

The Bishinik is nothing but promotional advertising, 'What is the Chief Doing for the Nation' as if he's running for re-election? There are the usual announcements of church functions, Pow Wows, photos of birthday celebrations, and obituaries. A long column was printed about the deaths of Gary and Don Taylor. Twenty or more others have passed away in the last thirty days. Most have been older Choctaws, but an alarming number of them were teenagers and young adults.

One obituary catches his attention, a young Choctaw girl who disappeared over a year ago. Her body was never recovered, there was evidence of foul play, and the courts have recently declared her legally dead. John didn't know Jeanie LeFlore, but the surname is familiar. He had played basketball against the LeFlore brothers from Calera when he was in high school.

As Levi has predicted, John begins to spend more time with Senator Jim. He has been attracted to her from the very beginning, but kept his emotions in check. She is a United States Senator, a little young for him and, for all he knows, they might be distant relatives. Now none of that matters, because everything seems so natural. They are both in the people business, in leadership positions, and spending time together is easy. She can be a powerful ally, and he doesn't want to let personal feelings to get in the way.

Meanwhile, Chief Wilson is going about his business as usual. To outsiders, everything looks normal. During the last two weeks, the Chief and his tribal attorneys have been able to hammer out an agreement to turn ThunderHawk and the two other leaders over to the tribal courts. That decision has been handed down as of Friday. Next, the first Tuesday of the month is a regularly scheduled meeting with the council members. Normally, these inform everyone of pending plans. Most major matters are discussed and voted on, but if the Chief really wants something, the council rarely opposes him. John has been looking forward to this month's meeting, but the Chief abruptly cancels it, announcing instead a Tuesday morning press conference at 10 a.m. The council members, staffs, all ask, 'Why?'

Roman, at CMA, contacts John, eager for details about the press conference. Tall Bear admits he has no clue. Rachel phones and he has to tell her the same thing. John is hoping to see Chief Wilson prior to the press conference, but the Chief arrives only ten minutes before the appointed time. John figures the council members don't know the purpose of the press conference either. At 9:55 a.m., they all assemble in the Chief's office with a few select news reporters.

Chief Wilson begins this press conference unlike most. He is not sitting behind his massive desk, but stands with a gallant effort to look strong and healthy. John doesn't think anything is physically wrong with the Chief, but he appears a little off mentally.

"I want to take this opportunity to thank you all for coming," says the Chief. "The last thirty days have been unusually challenging in this office. So much has happened in such a short time. I have given this much consideration and do what I must do."

"Today I am stepping down and retiring as Chief of the Choctaws. I have completed my vision here. My mother's doctors have made me aware of health issues she faces. They need to be taken care of as soon as possible. These are not major, but could be if we don't address them in a timely manner. As some of you know, she is in her late seventies. I am moving back to California to spend quality time with her."

"I have made this decision knowing I leave the office in the capable hands of my Assistant Chief. The people of the Choctaw Nation have been loyal to me during my service here, and I encourage each and every one of you to support my replacement. It is now my privilege, to introduce to you, the new Chief of the Choctaws, John Wilkerson Tall Bear." He faces John, shakes his hand, and turns the meeting over to him.

John has known it was coming sooner or later, but is still blind-sided by this bombshell. John assumed, when the end of the Chief's reign was in sight, they would sit down and discuss the transition. His brain scrambles for an acceptance speech and he has only seconds to do it.

"Chief Wilson, your retirement catches me and everyone by surprise. Considering the circumstances, I, of course, will accept the office of Chief of the Choctaws. It goes without saying we will miss your leadership and wish your mother a speedy recovery. If there is anything you need, the Choctaw Nation is here to assist. My first order of business as the new Chief is to call an executive session of the council members. After that meeting is over, I will have more to say. Until then, thank you, Chief Wilson."

The transition of one Chief to another Chief takes less than five minutes. After the conference ends, Chief Wilson is busy shaking the hands of the council members and staff and saying his goodbyes. Many of the council members are speaking directly to him. No doubt each is trying to get him to reveal the reason why he has made this decision so suddenly. They and the staff are stunned, but the out going Chief keeps his composure, smiling and wishing them all well. Within minutes, he picks up his personal briefcase, walks down the hallway to the door at the back of the compound, and leaves in a waiting car. An era has ended and a new one is just beginning.

After a few awkward moments, John and the council members make their way into a large conference room adjacent to the Chief's office. Levi and the Chief's personal secretary, Jackie Cummings, join them. John summons Jackie over. She has been crying and her eyes are red and puffy.

"Jackie, I'm going to need your help. Being the first time, I want to make sure everything is done properly. If there are legal issues, please help me address them. Can you do that for me?"

She quickly wipes her tears, tries to compose herself and says, of course, she will. John's position at the table is obvious to everyone. He eases into the leather chair at the head of the table and asks everyone to be seated.

"Please bear with me. I know this is a confusing and difficult moment for all of us here. With Jackie's help and yours, we can address the situation and your questions. I don't think there will be an objection if Pastor Nohubby opens this meeting with a prayer. Pastor Nohubby?"

The Pastor asks everyone to stand and hold hands as a sign of unity. After a very eloquent and moving prayer, they all sit down. Jackie quickly gets one of the staff to take the minutes and turns on a recorder to record the meeting. When everything is set up and in place, Jackie nods the meeting is now Tall Bear's.

"I have an idea as to how a typical meeting of the Chief and council members might have been handled. However, this is a very unusual day and this meeting will be a little different. I have many questions to ask of you, and I'm guessing you have that and more for me. So, I am going to open this meeting with a question and answer session. Your questions first."

Tom Folsom of the McAlester district #11 quickly fires, "When the Chief removed Assistant Chief Newt Wallace and replaced him with you, many of us were not pleased. Newt is a friend and a good man. We went along and didn't question the wisdom of our Chief. Now a new moon has not even come again and the Chief resigns leaving you our Chief." *'The old warrior doesn't waste any time,'* "Why so much change in so little time?"

"Mr. Folsom, you have a few years on me, but as an elder myself, I do not take change without question and some resistance. At this time I cannot explain the Chief's decisions of the last thirty days, or his resignation today. I have some ideas, but until Mr. Wilson reveals more about his sudden actions, and the reason for them, they are merely speculation. I prefer to deal with the facts as they are. Mr. Folsom, do you believe in fate?"

"Perhaps, but what has that to do with my question?"

"Mr. Folsom, the journey that led me here today, to this chair, with the title Chief of the Choctaw, was not my design. Still, I believe everything happens for a reason. What some label fate, I call the Movement of Life. Too many events beyond my control had to happen to get me here today. If Assistant Chief Wallace were sitting in this chair yesterday, he might be Chief, by design of Choctaw Law, for he was next in line."

"I was in Texas eight months ago trying to fix my golf game. However, when the Great Spirit presents a doorway we must have the presence of mind to accept responsibility and step through to the other side. Surely, some of you must acknowledge everything that has happened in the last thirty days was not one man's design. I feel, in due time, we will all have the answers."

One of the younger council members, Mike Frazier from district #10, jumps into the conversation, "Mr. Tall Bear, you say you are here today because of fate. I can't accept that. There are several of us on this council who wanted to become one of the Chiefs. It is only natural to begin first by working as a council member to assist and advise the Chief. That's why we all work so hard. Among us, it was common knowledge the Chief would look first to his council for a new Assistant Chief. Common sense tells us something is out of order. Why would he go against his own words and bring in someone from the outside without consulting us first?"

"Mr. Frazier, I can see how you would question some of Mr. Wilson's decisions, and sense the disappointment in the tone of your voice. Certainly as a young man you have had great expectations in your life, and for some unknown reason things didn't go your way. I have experienced that many times in my life. But looking back, in some cases, had I gotten what I wanted, I wouldn't have experienced something else much greater in its place."

"Mr. Tall Bear, I don't like you referring to the Chief as Mr. Wilson. It's condescending and disrespectful. He has been our Chief for thirteen years and was our Chief up until thirty minutes ago. Can you show the Chief some respect?" asks an angry council member from Wilburton District #6, Joseph Cole.

"Joseph!" says the only woman council member from district #5 Keota, Carolyn Red Hawk, "You need to show a little respect yourself. Regardless of how Chief Tall Bear got here, you are speaking to the present Chief of the Choctaws."

'Thank goodness, maybe Mrs. Red Hawk will be an ally. It looks like I'm going to need a few to get through this grilling.'

"Mrs. Red Hawk, Mr. Cole", he acknowledges both, "thanks for reminding me, 'Once a Chief, always a Chief'. Please accept my apologies for a lack of sensitivity. I will heretofore address the former Chief as Chief Wilson. It was a slip of the tongue so forgive me, I meant no disrespect."

"May I speak?" asks Pastor Nohubby. "I know each and every one in this room and some since you were kids. I have known Chief John Tall Bear since he was 10 years old. He was kind enough to pay me a visit a few weeks ago, along with Levi Tushka. We had a rather lengthy visit, and I found him to be honest, courteous and respectful. He enlightened me with his vision to bring about a sense of fair play in the Choctaw Nation. He may be an outsider, but I have a feeling he knows exactly what this Nation needs. For what's it worth, I share his views. I have known his mother and other family members for over sixty years. They are all good people, just like you and I. If we had any respect for Chief Wilson, we should at least have the decency to respect the man Chief Wilson chose as his replacement."

Mr. James Murphy from District #8 Hugo speaks up. "Pastor Nohubby, we respect your views. You have been the Nation's pastor for many years. I too know of Chief Tall Bear's family. Being from Hugo, I know of a tract of land the Chief's family owns. I found this when I went to Atoka to look up some land deeds. I came across his family name."

John wonders where Mr. Murphy is going with this line of conversation. He speaks like an old Choctaw, in short phrases.

"He is one of us. Chief Tall Bear was born in your Talihina district, Ken. He was raised here and speaks our language. Chief Wilson, born and raised outside of Detroit is half Na hollo (white man). I used to laugh when Chief Wilson tried to speak Choctaw. He really butchered it."

'*Thank you, Mr. Murphy for injecting a little humor into this meeting.*'

"I'm for giving Chief Tall Bear our support", says Mr. Murphy.

"I'm in agreement with James. We should just calm down, take a deep breath and give the new Chief a chance to explain how he will use the office to govern the Nation," suggests Mrs. Red Hawk. All eyes turn to Tall Bear.

"Before I go deeper with what I have in mind, I would like to get more input from you elders. A good Chief takes good counsel. It's past lunch therefore let us ask Jackie to order some food. After a bite to eat, we can begin in-depth discussions and act more cohesively as a unit. Is that agreeable?"

Everyone concurs. Jackie asks are sandwiches and drinks from George's acceptable? All approve, and one of the staff members is dispatched. John's favorite hamburger joint will serve lunch for everybody.

"While we are waiting for the food to arrive, I have a request for each of you. There is a pen and pad in front of you. Write down several things you would have the Nation do, likes and dislikes, or a wish list. You can be brief or in-depth, whichever you choose. I will do the same, then we can put everything on the table for all to see. The information we share will be the starting point of my Administration. Be creative and don't be afraid to dream big or go outside the box so to speak." Lunch arrives thirty minutes later. Levi and John sit in a corner and discuss the day's events.

"John, it looks like you're going to get some resistance before they accept you as their new Chief. What do you plan on doing?"

"I'm going to do like I've been doing, fly by the seat of my britches. All kidding aside, as soon as I get hold of those pads, I will know more about where I stand. Everybody wants something and if it's realistic and for the Nation, we can make it happen. One major problem, a few of them had their eyes on the Chief's office, and I can understand their disappointment. I'm not giving up this office, so they will have to get in line. They are not any more stubborn than you and I. When things don't go their way, people become resistant or uncooperative. Now Levi, if I had your gift of bullshit, I wouldn't have any problem winning them over." Levi laughs harder than John at this. John's cell phone is ringing, and it is Rachel.

"Hello, Rachel."

"John, what's going on over there? Everybody thought you were going to give a press conference an hour ago?"

"Well, I decided to have an emergency executive meeting and, for the time being, it's not going as well as expected. We are all taking a lunch break and chowing down on some burgers from George's. That ought to soften them up a little."

"John, you've got to be kidding. What's next and when do you think you are going to get out of there?"

"If you are thinking about taking me out to dinner, it'll have to be a late one."

"I've got work to do, so I will drive up after you're on TV."

"That sounds like a good plan for now. I've got to go." He hangs up the phone and finishes his burger. He wants to get a look at the pads before others finish their lunch.

"Levi, help me gather the pads up and let's have a look at them in my office."

Together they read all the information on the thirteen pads, plus one from Pastor Nohubby. Among the requests were more health clinics and diabetes programs and more funding for higher education. There were several requests to ramp up building of Indian homes. Only one suggested the Nation give cash dividends back to Choctaw members. One wanted to put aside a program to restore old Indian churches and to assist in building new ones in the thirteen counties. John knew that was Pastor Nohubby's request. An attention getter was job placement and vocational training for those without college educations. Most were pragmatic proposals with applicable solutions.

John is most interested in cash dividends and vocational training. These two ideas are going to be his bargaining chips. They are going to play poker. John has a feeling his previous number one priority, re-defining 'what is an Indian', will be more difficult. Not one of the council members came close to it.

John calls Rachel and predicts his meeting might go later than expected. The press conference will have to wait until tomorrow. They decide to postpone their dinner engagement until the following night. John tells her he will give her a call if the meeting ends early. She wishes him good luck and is back taking care of senatorial business.

John was looking forward to their dinner date, perhaps a little too much. He enjoys being around Rachel, and he feels like some kind of connection is being made. Only time will tell. 'Just be patient,' he thinks, 'and time will give you the answers, some good, and maybe some bad.'

The meeting goes well into the evening as they discuss the needs of the Choctaw Nation. Council members saddened by their beloved Chief Wilson's sudden resignation have unanswered questions. Some, lost in the shuffle, don't know where they stand. Angry discourse about small items not worth a hill of beans eats up valuable time. The young ones are the most vocal and argue longest. Elder Council members are more patient, skilled negotiators biding their time. The loudest are not always heard or taken seriously. It is the cool, calm and calculating that gather attention and pick their time to speak. Tall Bear lets everyone vent their displeasure.

As John watches them interact, he sees more leaders than followers in this council. They are able catalysts, facilitators, and planners. As members challenge him, he draws from their wisdom and leadership skills. Successful leaders have egos but smart ones keep it in check and allow your contemporaries some latitude. Later, he will assert himself and become a Chief they can stand behind.

Discussions linger beyond the dinner hour therefore they send out for more food. This time they work while they eat. An hour or so later, everyone is getting tired. There is no more fight left in them. The room is getting quieter and its time for Tall Bear to make his move. He takes control and for the next two hours he lays out his plan and goals.

Levi has brought solid information and facts to the table. He details everything John proposes. Several times, sensing what John needs he asks pertinent questions. Just after 11 p.m., they reach a working agreement. All will be available for a press conference the next day. They adjourn for the night.

Tomorrow's 2:00 p.m. press conference has been scheduled so elders can get some much-needed rest. John's night however, is not over. He and Levi will work well into the morning hours putting together an agenda for the next six months. John also fine-tunes his presentation. Before they leave the office around 2:30 a.m., John e-mails Roman and Tammy at CMA so they can make whatever plans they feel are necessary. John leaves a message on Rachel voice mail asking her to call in the morning. The executive meeting has broken their first dinner date. John doesn't want to exclude her from the process or tomorrow's press conference.

He finally gets to bed around 4 a.m. but doesn't sleep. His mind plays out 'what if' scenarios, then realistically concludes only some of what he proposes will be well received. He will rattle peoples' cages, make some uncomfortable, and some angry. He enjoys the process. John's ideas are sometimes outside the box, certainly not mainstream. But then he tells himself, *'You can't do that, it makes too much sense and is too logical.'* Before dawn unmotivated by power, money, or fame he asks Creator for a sign he's on track. At one with the Great Spirit, he journeys the Mystery of eternal life. Asleep, Tall Bear dreams his grandfather.

The ancestor speaks, *'Sometimes in life, when you chart a new course, take a path not travelled it can be lonely. A good warrior relies on all his wisdom and courage stepping into the unknown, where past, present, and future meet. The Choctaw have survived on the wrong side of a frozen river for a winter lasting over two hundred years.*

'You know there is more to the river than ice. You feel the melting water. Filtering noise of the city and daily cares, you hear the distant rushing, you have never seen it, but you feel it rumble beneath your feet. The thaw is

coming, the Movement of Life flows again for the Choctaws. The Great Spirit hears your questions, 'Why am I here? What is my destiny? How will my legacy be perceived when I leave Mother Earth?'

By 11 a.m. the next day, Durant is choked with thousands of folks interested to hear the new Chief speak. The crowd is mostly Choctaw members whose blood quantum ranges from full blood to nine generations (1/512). By previous law all qualify for services the Nation has to offer. Naturally, they want to know how the new Chief and his Administration will affect them. There are non-Indians who do business with the Nation, the newspaper, printers, banks, food and clothing industries. A few, the Mayor of Durant, Senator James Joe Cody, Senator Rachel Jim, and others are politicians.

Rachel had called John earlier in the morning and asked can she be part of the supporting cast that stands behind him. She expresses disappointment when he declines her offer, suggesting it would be better for her not to be associated with his presentation. By 1:30 p.m. people are gathered in front of the Choctaw Nation Capital, awaiting the arrival of the new Chief. At a quarter to two, Levi strolls inside John's office and takes a comfortable leather chair near his desk.

"Chieftain, it's a big day for you and the Choctaw Nation. You and I have come a long way since we first met at that bookstore in Dallas. I never told you this, but at one time I had dreams of being the Choctaw Chief. I want to personally thank you for making my dream come true. Being your Assistant Chief is good enough for me. I'm in this for the long haul and I will support you every step of the way. I'm sure most of the council members, after last night, feel the same way. You were like a great conductor orchestrating a classic piece of music the way you took over the meeting last night. That was a brilliant piece of work. You were born to do this job. You are going to make a great Chief, and history will remember you for doing wonderful things for our people."

With that he gets up, shakes John's hand, and gives him a big brotherly hug.

Moved by Levi's kind words, John smiles and responds. "Levi schmoozing up to the Chief already? Don't sell yourself short. You could have done just as well last night. I get most of my ideas from you anyway. Ready to go, Tonto?" John motions for them to leave the office.

"Lead the way, Kemosabe!"

Tall Bear emerges into the bright sunshine and the crowd comes alive. Setting his stage are large puffy white clouds dotting a vivid blue sky. In the front row he sees the mayor, Senators Jim and Cody and Choctaw church elders he has known for years. He even spots high school friends he has not seen in ages. He cannot remember being this happy in his life. John knows in his heart his mother's spirit is near and smiling.

"Halito Chukma, fellow Choctaws, ladies, gentlemen and distinguished guests. I want to thank you all for coming out on this beautiful summer afternoon. Yesterday, as most of you know, Chief Wilson resigned his position and turned the office over to me. His departure caught everyone by surprise, and prompted my initial obligation to the distinguished group that counseled him. Like you, they had many questions therefore we addressed those first. In an executive session that went well into the night, every suggestion and idea from every council member was put on the table and discussed. New and important unanimous decisions were made. Should any council members have second thoughts, I invite them to step forward and voice them now."

John pauses for a moment, no one steps forward.

"The decisions made last night are today, the new laws of the Choctaw Nation. Give this presentation your full attention. At its core, our program has four talking points; health care, higher education, the work force, and blood quantum."

"First and foremost, the health of every Choctaw member is important. We will continue to make available the finest health facilities we can offer. Whether you live inside or outside the thirteen counties, if you are a member of the Choctaw Nation, services will be available to you."

The crowd, with a huge roars shoots to its feet.

"One of the new programs within the health and wellness department deserves your special attention–the Falammichi Project. Sadly, our people are ravaged by an epidemic of obesity and diabetes. It must stop. As the Native Choctaw 'Falammichi' suggests, we can change our lifestyles to 'defend and restore'. I am a living example of this philosophy, following the healthful ways of our ancestors prior to the arrival of the 'white man'. While it is obviously impossible to reproduce the traditional diet and lifestyle of the 1400's, it is possible to emulate it."

There is little reaction from the crowd during this part of his presentation. *I'm sure many are confused as to how they would implement this new/old health concept into their daily lives.'*

John continues on. "Proper foods combined with brief sessions of high intensity exercise can eliminate excess body fat and prevent the onset of many common sicknesses. When the English explorers and settlers arrived on the northeastern coast of America in the early 1400's, they attested the towering height, powerful physiques, and robust health of the Woodland Indians. Obesity, diabetes, high blood pressure, heart disease, and other so-called diseases of 'civilized' man did not exist among them.

"The Woodland Indians diet, combined with infrequent but very intense exercise, like bringing down large dangerous game, and engaging in warfare against interlopers, stimulated the body to grow in strength and lean mass. Today, we call this the 'fight or flight' syndrome. These people experienced full function in good health even into old age."

Still no reaction from the crowd. John feels like a standup comedian that is fast losing the room, yet he forges on.

"'High intensity training' works both the anaerobic and aerobic pathways. This stimulates increased muscle mass by provoking the chemical and respiratory reactions of the body's 'fight or flight' response to a perceived threat. As late as the 1870's the Plains Indian Tribes still enjoying a natural diet of buffalo, deer, wild turkey, fresh fish, fruits, berries, and vegetables, were among the tallest people on earth. These people were virtually free of the maladies associated with a grain and sugar based European diet. The 'Native Hunter/Gatherer' way of eating will be reflected in the menus of every restaurant and diner owned by the Choctaw Nation and available to all members."

The crowd gives a lighter roar, some clapping, but still there is confusion. Why does their new Chief lecture them on their health?

"With prospects of living longer from a healthy lifestyle, higher education is the second important plank of our platform. We will continue to invest heavily in anyone who wants to attend the college of their choice. In addition, we intend to fund and implement vocational training programs in Durant and the surrounding counties. These will teach support personnel in the medical and dental fields. We will offer programs for the performing arts, video and film production, for work in front of and behind the camera. We want to grow and nurture our own talent to headline at the Tushkahoma annual celebration and the showrooms of our casino and resorts. These programs will be available to all Choctaw members regardless of where they live."

The crowd shows some life and gives their approval with extended clapping and enthusiasm.

"Our first Council and Chief session reflected both traditional and progressive lightening rods of legislation. It was an opportunity to update legislature and systems. Though we felt charged to serve the needs of all Choctaw, it was important not to lose sight of even one tribal family member, in the process.

"We were deeply moved upon learning of Debby Jean Billey (53) a church-going full blood Choctaw who lived and worked in the small town of Wewoka, Oklahoma, outside the thirteen counties. She was on dialysis with the Chickasaw Nation providing her heath care. She died a year and half ago. A Choctaw bureaucrat couldn't or wouldn't help her because she lived out of the area of service. The Chickasaw paid for her burial in Achille, Oklahoma Bryan County, home of the Choctaw Nation.

"Her 19-year-old son, a full blood Choctaw teenager troubled by drugs and alcohol abuse, could not get the help he needed from the Choctaw Nation. His mental health was unstable from the loss of his mother, and committed suicide a year later. The Chickasaw Nation paid for his burial in Achille, next to his mother.

"Redman Jack, a 3/4 Choctaw living seventeen miles south of this Capital, lost his house to a fire. The Chickasaw helped build him a new home in Achille. Where was the Choctaw Nation in these three cases? You will never hear stories like this as long as I am Chief. We will take care of our people and, whenever possible, come to the aid of other tribes."

Another roar of applause follows.

"Tribal government's promise should always be, 'We will invest millions of dollars to assist each and every one of you to restore yourself.' Alcohol (the white man's drug) kills more people than all other stimulants and wars combined every year. It is not the Choctaw way to be greedy and held hostage by an almighty dollar. Past administrations have copied the colonizer's way of doing business far too long.

"I know tobacco is ingrained in Indian culture, but we have become addicted to the commercial brands of cigarette manufacturing and marketing. It is their purpose to make sure you are a customer for life and continue to purchase their products. Though legal, use of these substances only impoverishes Natives and profits U.S. corporations. Those who continue to purchase these dangerous products risk alcoholism or smoke related addictions, often losing both physical health and a personal psychological sense of control.

"The Choctaws can not be party to this any longer. We will remove ourselves from the tobacco and liquor businesses. No longer will we sell these items in our establishments. It may cost us millions in revenue each year, but it is the right thing to do. If our Nation is to survive, we must take drastic measures to promote healthy lifestyles."

Nothing but silence from the audience is intimidating. A struggling standup would be yanked from the stage, yet the new Chief forges on into darkness.

"Rather than building new wasteful facilities and infrastructure here in Durant like the former Administration, we have decided to streamline our existing program and facilities. No one will lose his or her jobs. However, no longer will we tolerate people just drawing a paycheck. We want our employees to produce. We will be professionals and work efficiently in all departments. Fail to do so, and you will be replaced by someone who can. Any new positions will be advertised in both Durant papers. Sending Choctaws to college, we will increasingly create positions for them when they graduate.

"The most significant change in this new Administration will be its membership qualifications. Even though numbers are at an all time high, just short of 200,000, we are a dying race. Reliable research has determined the average Indian blood quantum of our membership is 1/64th. That is seven generations removed from a full blood. Statistically, 1/64th of anything is seldom considered significant. This trend shows no sign of reversing itself therefore we must encourage an about face.

"Past administrations let too many with diluted lineage enjoy tribal membership. More precisely, if you were able to prove you had one drop of Indian blood in your family tree, you could become a member of the Choctaw Tribe. Years ago, this practice was instituted to fabricate a larger tribe and acquire more federal funding from the United

States Government. Our nation is self-sufficient today so it can and will survive without federal dollars.

"Unchanged, the inflated numbers will eventually threaten the sovereignty of the Choctaw Nation. The federal government will look at our Nation and say, 'you people look just like us, blonde haired and blue eyes. You are no longer Indian.' This will happen! And they will be correct. All tribes continue to struggle with the states that want their own casinos. Let's not kid each other. The federal government has been trying to eradicate all the Native tribes from the very beginning.

"Hundreds of Indian boarding schools were built in the early 1900's for this purpose. My mother Ada Wilkerson, one of thousands who attended these deplorable institutions, was not allowed to speak her Native language, and denied her traditional heritage. The federal government's slogan in those days was 'Kill the Indian, save the man'. Bureau of Indian Affairs called it 'civilizing', but Indians who survived knew it to be another, 'cultural genocide'!

"Most recently, in the mid 50's, my family participated in the federal government Relocation Program. They promised to relocate Indian families from rural areas and Indian communities to large cities like Dallas, Los Angeles, Minneapolis and others. New jobs, new housing, new furniture and a new way of life were the selling points. They sounded like use car salesman's, for it sounded too good to be true. These families didn't envision the destructive effects of displacement. Natives were divided into smaller isolated groups. The federal government knew what would happen. We would die from loneliness and alcoholism. Many would commit crimes and go to prison. We would marry outside of our race and dilute the Native blood of our people.

"The federal government has broken thousands of treaties with the American Indian. The few treaties they are forced to honor today are costing them billions through federal programs like Indian Health Services. This is all about money and one day in the future, the federal government will say 'No more! You look just like us. Thus we revoke the sovereignty of your 'Nation'. And then the Choctaw will be no more.

"Therefore, the Choctaw Nation must preemptively redefine 'What is an Indian?' We are setting a new required quantum, at least ¼ Choctaw blood, for membership. As of today, existing members not meeting this requirement will have their membership revoked. By our count, this new requirement will reduce our tribe to approximately 20,000. With this new apportionment, we can offer better care and increased services to deserving members.

The crowd is agitated. A volley of boo's continuing to muddy the air. Palpable high anxiety in the audience has security personnel very concerned.

As Tall Bear waits for the crowd to simmer down, he scans the expressive faces of Roman, Tammy and Rachel in front, and the council members who stand behind him. He knows they are nervous and his next statement will make it even worse. John waits a moment that feels like a lifetime.

"In addition to the requirements of the existing 20,000 members, the amount of free services you will receive will be directly related to your blood quantum. A fair market price will be placed on every service we offer so you will know its cost from the start. For example, if you are a full blood, you pay nothing and all services are free. If you are half Indian, you will pay one half, or like most, if you are one quarter, you will receive a 25% discount on the service.

"Every living Choctaw today rides the backs of full blood during the Removable Act in 1832. Were it not for the brave and courageous that survived the bitter Trail of Tears, you and I would not be here today. Our position is anyone less than 1/4 and claiming Choctaw, is not as deserving as the full blood Choctaw ancestor. Pretending one drop of Indian or Black blood makes you Indian or Black is illogical and is simply not true."

Another round of boos and cat calls leads John to believe the crowd is just short of wanting to start throwing things at him, like their worthless membership cards. The more demonstrative are beginning to leave. He waits another long moment for the crowd to settle down before continuing.

"I'm sure many of you feel this is harsh treatment, since you have been receiving these services free of charge. Even though you remaining members may have to pay a portion for services, we have initiated another program to help you pay for these and more. As of today, we have decided to put 15% of our annual revenue from gaming and other Nation businesses into a fund to be distributed semi-annually to every member of the Choctaw Tribe."

The roar and applause is now deafening and lasts for several minutes. Elvis Presley once threw expensive jewelry into the crowd to get his fans motivated to love him. Hundreds of Indians whoop and holler as if emulating a 'rain dance'. Like Elvis, Chief Tall Bear has a parting gift for his fans.

"Choctaw members will be receiving their first dividend checks next month on December 1st. By our calculations, each of you should receive enough funds to purchase a new home or at least buy a car and take a vacation. These new laws and financial entitlements should encourage our tribe to become more Indian tomorrow than we are today. Halito and thank you."

And with that, he leaves the podium to return to his office. Departing, he hears the thunderous approval of the more heavily gifted Choctaws drowning out the cat calls and boos from those who feel slighted.

The last line of Tall Bear's presentation is profound. Members who are on the cut line, so to speak, at 1/4 will soon recognizes if he or she marries anyone less, their children will not be eligible for tribal membership. In fact, it will encourage everyone to marry his or her equal or marry up to someone who is more Indian. In doing so, they will have access to more services and financial entitlements. It will not be long before all Indians are experts in math. It is a numbers game now, and Choctaws will learn to work it to their advantage. The tribe should get more authentic, richer and stronger than before. Change is coming.

CHAPTER 31

———

Gunter and Angelina are lip locked trading spit. JBL speakers hung from the rafters of a popular Chicago dance club blare Led Zepellin's Whole Lotta Love. They gyrate, not on the dance floor, but beside the bar, where four empty 'vodka on the rocks' glasses wait to be refilled.

Tonguing Angelina's luscious lips, bumping and grinding her mid-section, Gunter, at 6'5", towers over the crowd of dancers. Many are dressed in biker gear, studded leather, boots and white skin. Though Gunter's attire is the epitome of what these yuppies pretend, they have no idea a wolf is in the hen house.

His keen eyes finds what he looking for. Despite near freezing temperatures outside, the long legged blond wears a short black mini skirt, red leather boots and matching red leather biker jacket with nothing on underneath. A strobe light high in the ceiling spins, hurling slabs of light onto the dancers. The intermittent flashes expose her breasts, small pink nipples, and flying strands of waist length hair to those who stare.

"Gunter my darling, you are not paying attention to me," says Angelina as she runs her fingers through his short white mane.

"Sorry, but I don't want to loose them."

"Honey, they're are not going anywhere, they just got here. We have hours to watch them. Kiss me and fuck me hard here at the bar," she says as she unzips his fly and pulls out his cock.

Gunter with one massive hand grabs her ass, "listen my little bitch we're working tonight. No mistakes."

His Johnson finds a wet opening up her scant attire. Satisfied, she clings to his broad shoulders, shuts her mouth and begins to moan. Few here care unless she's thrown on the bar, free for all.

Over Angelina's shoulder he watches the blond for a couple of minutes. He can see warm beads of sweat on her forehead and in the valley of her breasts. He imagines her hot sweaty pussy and smell of her perfume. Without a care in the world, she grooves to the music. Soon, he dreams her with a red rubber ball wedged in her mouth, arms and legs tethered. Targeting completed, he cums inside Angelina, gasping, 'You're next, bitch.'

––––––––––

Gunter's great grandfather Kurt Werner was born into a family of musicians in Germany. In his 20's, feeling lost, unable to find suitable work, he wandered the streets of the city. Beneath shabby clothes and a bearded face he thought himself a proud man. He could never accept charity, but everyday he would scavenge a few scraps of food from a wide array of trash bins that lined the street.

After months of homelessness and sleeping wherever he can, he finds refuge at a dance hall. There a woman has pity on him and takes him home. The woman is a reader of books and begins teaching Kurt the ways of the world. One winter day, when she is out looking for work, Kurt finds Herman Hesse's Der Steppenwolf in her collection of literature.

The title refers to the novel's protagonist who fancies himself half man and half wolf. The character hates his middle class lifestyle, but is incapable of conforming. Kurt in his delusional state identifies with the wolf man and adopts its personality. Not impressed with this dual and volatile nature, the woman kicks him to the street to fend alone again.

One winter morning while on his daily tour of searching for food, he falls to his knees in the street in a suicidal trance. The bitter cold will take him soon, but before he meets his demise, he thinks to himself.

'Is it me behind this cold and dusty face
Was I born to lie here dying, in disgrace
People passing on the street
Don't hide their shame for me
I would beg for the lend of a hand
If I could only stand
Please God, don't turn away
I'm so afraid, for when I'm gone
There'll be no one, to weep or mourn for me
Now it's time, for me, to close my eyes.'

As the bitter cold comforts him, he slides into darkness but hears a familiar voice in the distance, "Kurt, I'm here. I'm here to take you home. Please Kurt, wake up. I can't live without you."

Grateful the woman who reads books has saved him from death, he agrees to obey all her commands. She informs Kurt, she will make him fall in love with her. Knowing the dark corners of his mind, she will ask him to kill her. He and the woman live together for three years and they have a son. Kurt Werner changes his name and becomes Hans Steppenwolf.

Gunter Steppenwolf is a reincarnation of his great grandfather. His mother committed suicide when he was a boy of seven. His father paraded women in and out of his life until he was seventeen. Most were women of the night and unable to nurture him as a loving mother would. When his father was away or in a drunken stupor, the women took advantage of his youth and raped him. Left alone to fend for himself, he became isolated and troubled.

Inwardly, turning to his dark side, he began experimenting with killing and torturing animals that roamed the neighborhood. He enjoyed the sense of power it gave him. He was arrested numerous times for petty crimes before he turned eighteen. He becomes a willing participant in the drug scene of the 1970's while managing a punk rock band. He, like many of his relatives, is mentally disturbed, a borderline psychotic. Yet through it all, he was resourceful, because he was not afraid to try anything. Finally, he was given the ultimate test of killing someone and he liked it. Now, murder is just part of his resume. Those who hire Steppenwolf accept his expensive services, because he is good.

———————

Steppenwolf watches his prey. The blond and her companion who have been dancing and drinking for two hours gather their coats and make their way to an exit. The doorman introduces them to a cold and windy night. The streets are unsafe and not drivable, but her townhome is but a short two blocks away. Wet snowflakes dance on their faces and cover their coats.

Gunter and Angelina track at a safe distance under cover of darkness and flurries. They watch as she slips and falls into a snow bank piled along the curbside. She laughs, and then attempts to make a snow angel as her partner reaches her and helps her to her feet. Together, they weave left and right planting distorted footprints in the snow. It won't be long now.

———————

The blonde's soon to be ex has hired Steppenwolf. They are involved in a nasty and expensive divorce case. She along with her lover has planted false and incriminating evidence against the husband. He stands to loose millions in divorce court along with his two children. The millions he can do without, but he refuses to have his children taken by a heroin addict.

Steppenwolf smiles. There is no foot traffic to get in the way at the midnight hour. There is only a three-step walk up to the entrance of the townhome. As the prey nears the steps, the wolf silently closes the gap. Slowed by alcohol and the cold winter night, the blond fumbles with her keys before inserting the right one into the lock. On the second attempt, the wolf hears the latch slide open. Like a sail catching wind, the door flies open and crashes against the interior wall.

Using the sound as interference, the wolf leaps out of the cover of darkness and blinding snow and rushes the two. They never see him attack. A back of the neck hand sword knocks out the male and he falls to the floor. Gunter spins the blond around and applies a chokehold. She refrains momentarily, arms flailing but looses consciousness and slides down his legs. Angelina begins to apply zip ties while Steppenwolf closes the door and locks it. This was all too easy.

Touring the countryside, Gunter and his punk rock band played a bar in Hayden, Idaho. A few skinheads in the audience took exception with the group's song selection. A fight breaks out. The band and a dozen members from the audience were arrested. Steppenwolf shares a bench with one of the skinheads who claimed to have founded the Aryan Nation.

A friendship was formed and Steppenwolf and his band began playing at many of their secret functions. Through this alliance the band was included in a network of dozens of white supremacist chapters scattered throughout the states.

While in Tulsa finishing a job, Steppenwolf gets a call one night from a member in Des Moines, Iowa. He was offering a seventeen-year-old girl who was half German and half black. Iowa, a stronghold of white supremacy didn't do 'black' and wanted her gone.

"Why would I want her?"

"She's an exotic beauty, drop dead gorgeous. She brings too much attention to us up here."

"Beautiful women are dime a dozen."

"She got one brown eye and the other green/blue. For a little Native flavor, mixed in with her black roots is Cherokee."

"Every degenerate that's ashamed of their true race swears they're Indian just to be 'somebody'."

"Not following you, man."

"The largest Indian tribe in America!"

"Cherokee?"

"No, you stupid fuck, the 'Pretenders'."

"Don't be ugly, Step, I'm trying to give you something."

"Not interested."

Knowing Steppenwolf favors short women with big tits. "She's got a killer set of young tits. Stands about 5'4"."

"C's?"

"C plus for sure, but you're the tit man. With your twisted mind, you could love one and hate the other," said the man with a belly laugh.

"Funny animal man, no woman in her right mind would let you get close to her tits."

"I admit I'm an animal. I love to eat pussy."

"Pig! She got small feet?"

"Yep! Got a nice ass and legs to match too. So get your evil ass up here."

Steppenwolf made the six-hour drive and was given the girl. She became his slave companion and stayed because she wanted to. He didn't like the name Angelina, so he calls her 'Sugar', sometimes 'Brown Sugar'. After confirming she was more Indian than black. That was four years ago.

Alex brain cells snap. He comes out of darkness, lying on a hardwood floor in the center of a large living room. His hand and feet are zip tied together and there is silver duck tape over his mouth. He watches a tall muscular man with short white hair giving orders to a woman who helps secure his beloved.

Ava is stripped naked and standing inside a doublewide French door entrance to a den. Her hands are tethered at 10 and 2 o'clock. Plastic bracelets, fixed in the same fashion to her ankles, allow her a wide stance in a ballerina's second position. Alex remembers her spread eagle in the snow, making snow angels on a weekend getaway as tears give way.

From behind Ava, a woman's slender hand appears, seductively teasing the firm mounds of her torso. The other hand attempts to place a red rubber ball into Ava's open mouth.

"Please, please, I don't want the ball in my mouth."

"My pretty bitch, its either the ball or this," as he drops his leather pants to the floor. She nods that she has chosen him.

"Well, well, well we have a player here," as he removes the rest of his clothing. "Dance for me like you did at the club. Then I'll give you this."

Sugar lovingly rubs her hands over her new Playmate's body. One caresses a breast gingerly, pinching its delicate pink nipple. The other tickles her navel before sliding south to her vagina, to stir that moist cauldron round and round like a magic stick, enticing Ava's clitoris, and then returning northward to fondle Ava lips and penetrate her mouth. In Ava's ear, a whisper so soft, only Ava can hear, Sugar coaches, "plié, plié".

Steppenwolf motions for Sugar, who crawls then scrambles on her knees and forearms to lap his testicles.

"Dance bitch," commands Steppenwolf. Ava and her sister respond. Both engaged in roles, which please the alpha wolf. Alex watches with tears in his eyes.

"Are you ready bitch?" The fated Ava signals her desire.

Steppenwolf, his hand on the back of Sugars head, violently tosses her aside, ramming cock into his angel.

Well-prepared pleasure seldom tarries. They pump and roll, jerk and glide, in spasms of canine passion, till both peak and slide into an ecstatic release. Finished, Gunter's cell phone rings. With a long slender finger, he selects the speaker button.

Catching his breath while trying to slow his heart rate, "Chief, I'm a little busy here, can I call you back a little later?"

"Hell no. I don't care if you got your cock up some blonds ass, you make time."

"Well that's close enough," as he motions for Sugar to find him a towel. He struts across the room in front of Alex and collapses on a sofa as Sugar returns and begins cleaning him. He then signals with a hand gesture to Sugar for something to drink and she leaves.

"Ok Chief, I'm sitting down. I was working out in the gym. I'm in between reps. Now what can I do for you?" Sugar returns with a drink and presses it to his lips as if caring for a toddler.

"I'm dying here, I need some fucking help. I was just forced to resign. I don't want to go back to California with my tail between my legs."

"Trouble with the same man."

"Him and a U.S. Senator dug up some shit on me."

Steppenwolf howls with laughter. "I'm so sorry Chief," trying to show contempt. "So, after I burned his church down, it didn't scare him off."

"Fuck no, you evil piece of shit. He's got my job and sitting in my office."

"Testy, testy Chief. So what do you want me to do?"

"I want the son-of-a bitch to ride off into the sunset and never come back."

"That's going to cost you."

"Before he rides off, he has something I need badly, to become Chief again."

"You already resigned. How can you possibly return?"

"You forget, Oklahoma is Red country, I'm a fucking Republican, and 'the end always justify the means.'"

"Then I suggest you save yourself a lot of money. Shoot him your-self in downtown Durant at high noon."

"That, I can't get away with, just yet."

"I get the picture. Fill me in later. I have a job to finish tonight. I'll leave in the morning."

After a few more reps Steppenwolf is finished. The two are injected with enough heroin to kill a dozen. This crime scene will be a puzzle for the locals however to a few it will be obvious. A bag of cash to the right connection and the case will be closed as an overdose.

CHAPTER 32

I n life and the martial arts Tall Bear knows for every action there
is a reaction. In a nano second, 180,000 people were cut from the
tribe. Within twenty-four hours, the trouble begins. John had anticipated this possibility, but underestimated the anger and frustration
of those whose privileges were revoked. Regardless of their passion
for Choctaw heritage, this is about money. The pretenders are angry
because they no longer have access to free services.

Throughout the thirteen counties, come reports of fights and ram-
pant vandalism, bricks thrown out of cars at Indian businesses, half a
dozen attempted arsons at buildings owned by the Nation. There have
been some minor injuries but no one has been badly hurt. Employees
and customers are unnerved by the sheer boldness of these activities.
John's team of advisors discusses this at length and decides to hire and
assign more security personnel to trouble spots. They hope these temporary emotional flare-ups will soon subside. Two weeks go by and
the incidents continue to happen. They have a big problem.

Rachel and John's Friday night date begin at a Mexican restaurant
called Desperados. The twosome settles into their favorite booth and
orders dinner.

"John, I'm so glad you talked your friend into opening this restaurant here. It's the best Mexican food north of the Red River."

"Well, I have known this guy for twenty years and I knew he wanted to expand into Oklahoma. What better place to open than where his good friend can share a meal?"

"I love the decor."

"I promised to send him all the people I knew. He didn't need any help from me. Good food, outstanding service, a wonderful atmosphere and the word got around fast."

"The place is packed tonight. Every time I drive by, the parking lot is full."

Their dinner arrives and the conversation turns to how great the food looks and taste. They are ready to order dessert when John catches Rachel, her fork halfway to her mouth, looking over his shoulder with a startled expression.

"What's wrong?"

"One of those guys at the table behind you just gave me the finger and made a kissing motion with his mouth."

"Are you serious? Which one?"

"The one at your '6'," as John begins to turn around and gets up from his chair.

By now Rachel is steaming. "John, sit down. I don't need you to fight my battles!" He sees her standing and walking to the table behind him. Rachel approaches the table where five men and two women dine.

"Young man, why did you do that? I don't even know you."

"Hey lady, I don't know you either, but I know the asshole you're having dinner with. I was hoping to make him mad so I could kick his ass," the arrogant man at the table replies.

"What do you have against John Tall Bear?"

"He kicked my momma out of the tribe and now she is sick and can't go to the hospital!"

"I'm sorry to hear of your mother's medical difficulties, however I'm sure you know, no hospital can deny your mother emergency care should she need it. And as for kicking that man's ass, I've seen him in action and I can truthfully tell you, you're going to need more men than you have at this table. Now back to me, I'm offended and you should be ashamed. I'm positive your mother would be, too. FYI, I'm United States Senator Rachel Jim and I can have your ass kicked without even raising a finger."

Rachel returns to her chair and John says, "Rachel, you are a force to be reckoned with!"

"John, I just gave him a piece of my mind. If you don't mind, I've lost my appetite. I would like to leave."

John pays their tab and follows Rachel out the front door into the parking lot. He sees several groups of men clustered by their pickups. They snap to attention when the party of five men and women follow John and Rachel out of the restaurant. As they get into Rachel's car, the truck gang and their buddies from inside converge on them. The leader begins shouting obscenities at them, and John starts to open his car door to get out.

Rachel grabs his arm and says, "John, don't go out there. There are too many of them."

He has just gotten his door half open when one of the men body slams it shut. The car is now surrounded with almost twenty men shouting obscenities. Rachel retrieves her cell phone and calls 911.

As she completes the call, one of them busts the windshield on the passenger side. Another one attempts to smash the back window with his fist. The enraged mob pushes and rocks the car, trying to turn it over. John is essentially helpless, an unusual feeling for him. Even if he wanted to get out of the car, he can't. They are trapped. He looks at Rachel and sees she is truly terrified, hanging on to her seat and bracing her feet on the floorboard, but not making a sound.

The activity attracts a group of onlookers standing around watching the men try to turn the car over. The car is rocking precariously, on the verge of going over, when four men show up and begin to bust some heads. Three Indians and a white man fight the crazed brutes. John is now able to get his door open and join the four rescuers. He begins fighting with two men who come at him. He takes a couple of shots to the back of the head and kidney area. Turning around, Tall Bear scuffles with the guys who blindsided him. John dismisses one with a flurry of punches, then sweeps and takes the other to the ground.

A Durant Police car pulls into the parking lot with lights flashing. Two uniformed officers join in the melee, and begin cracking heads with their nightsticks. Another squad car pulls in, more officers jump out. Right behind them are Levi and Roman in a Choctaw Nation Tahoe. They join the others apprehending as many of the offenders as they can. Within minutes it's all over. People are running to their pickups, squealing tires, and leaving the parking lot. Durant police are able to detain several of them and note license plates of those turning tail.

As things settle down, Police take witness statements. Levi and Roman walk over to John.

"Chieftain, you and Rachel okay?"

"Yeah, we're fine. I'm glad you guys got here in time. They almost turned the car over."

"Well, what happened?" asks Roman.

"Rachel and I were having a quiet dinner and all of a sudden she gets huffy and says something to a group of guys at the next table. She must have pissed them off, because they followed us out to the car and things got out of hand."

Levi and Roman's eyes get big and their jaws drop. John turns and looks at Rachel. She is stewing.

"Boys, John is lying! Only a silly man could interpret what happened that way."

"Gotcha!" John laughs. Levi and Roman are trying not to join in.

"Rachel, since John can't tell the truth, will you tell us what happened?" asks Levi.

Rachel begins telling the true story. The local news reporter is already questioning witnesses, writing his story for the 10:00 o'clock newscast. John can see it, *'Senator Rachel Jim and Choctaw Chief John*

Tall Bear assaulted in restaurant parking lot.' The news goes national. *'Here we go again.'*

———————

The next morning the phone wakes John from a sound sleep.

"John, you awake? I've got a little surprise for you."

"Levi, what's my little surprise? You going to quit chasing women?" John asks, still in the process of waking up.

"Not a chance, Chieftain. Look out your front door."

"My front door? Ok, give me a minute. I'm not even dressed! There's not something out there that's going to embarrass me is there?"

"No! Just look out the front door and come back to the phone."

Tall Bear puts on a pair of jeans and walks to the front. He looks out and is puzzled by what he sees. He opens the door, and walks out into the yard. There are two men with rifles stationed at the entrance of his driveway. Approximately fifty yards down the street two more men stand with rifles.

"Morning Chief," says one of the two men guarding his driveway.

"Good morning gentlemen. How long have you been here?"

"We've been here since about midnight."

John looks down the street in the opposite direction and counts about a half-dozen men in all. He notices the two men at his driveway wear matching red caps with 'Choctaw Nation Security' printed on the front. They wear matching t-shirts with the photos of four Indians with rifles, the great Apache Chief Geronimo, his son, brother-in-law and 2nd cousin. 'Homeland Security' is printed underneath. Around their necks hang photo IDs with CDIB cards from the federal government, showing them all to be Indian. All are dressed in blue jeans or dark pants, and each has a rifle in hand. John returns to the house and picks up the phone.

"Well, I can see you've been busy all night. What brought this on?"

"John, after what happened last night hit the 10:00 o'clock news, Roman started getting calls from all over offering to help protect their Chief! We used one of the offices at the casino for interviews and about a hundred men showed up. Roman and I screened all of them and put together an official uniform. A small team is going to follow you everywhere until this settles down. Pretty cool, huh?"

"Levi, don't you think that's a little over kill? You've got a dozen men stationed outside my house."

"Aha! There's 24, Kemosabe! You just can't see the rest of them. Them are real Indians out there!"

"Well, we need to talk about this."

"There's nothing to talk about. I don't want your job so we're going to keep you safe whether you like it or not. Roman and I decided this is the best way to protect you. John, these men volunteered because they support you and what you're doing to make this Nation better for them and their families. So when you get dressed and ready to come to the office, they'll escort you. Chi Pisa Lachike (see you later)."

The Black Mercedes AMG sits in the parking lot in front of Last Chance Pawn Shop on State Hwy 75 north of Durant. Steppenwolf sits in the passenger seat counting out $100 dollars bills, securing each stack with a rubber band. Angelina sits behind the wheel wearing a bored look and white leggings. A peach colored bikini top secures her 'C pluses'. The AMG is surrounded by a half-dozen pickups sporting white nationalism decals. Several men in each vehicle are fixated with lurking eyes on the AMG's driver.

"Step Honey, I don't like all those men gawking at me. It's making me nervous."

"Could be those hicks have never seen anything like you in Oklahoma," as he continues to create thick piles of $100 bills.

"The goofy looking guy in the Ford looks like he playing with himself. He hasn't taken his eyes off my chest"

"Stupid men like him go ape-shit when they see a '10'."

"Am I really a '10', Step?"

"Sugar, you are the north side of '10' with a perfect set of tits."

"I love it when you tell me my tits are perfect. How do you know my tits are perfect?"

"Sugar, because I have nursed and played with a thousand pair of tits and yours are perfect. That's why they call me the Tit Man."

"I wish I had worn a sweater, I'm chilly and my nipples are perking up. See."

Steppenwolf stops counting and slides his right hand under her top and squeezes her left nipple.

"Take the bikini top off."

"Step, no!"

"Angelina, I said take it off, now!"

Angelina unbuttons the top in the back, exposing her perfect 'C pluses' as the top falls into her lap. Steppenwolf out the corner of his eye watches the men become animated. The power he has over these men arouses him.

"Now, very slowly, and I mean very slowly with both hands, untie your hair in the back. Not so fast," director Steppenwolf. "Now tilt your head back and shake your hair from side to side. Aha, just perfect," as he takes her left breast into his hand and gently caresses it. He pulls it up and sucks on it for a moment. Then he leans in and kisses her long and tender. He finishes by pinching her nipple as she jumps and let out a soft squeal.

"We'll continue this later, now put your top back on," as he switches from movie director to bank teller counting bills. When he completes the stacks of $100, he stuffs them into a gym bag and signals his contact to the passenger door.

"Good work the other night. I see some of your men got tagged pretty good. There's a little extra in there."

"Yeah, a couple of those Indians were pretty good, see," flashing a smile with a missing tooth. "I got off light, a couple of my guys got busted ribs and one broken leg, but it was still fun. I'd like to rid the world of those darkies."

"You leave that to me. Have your people keep on doing the same shit. I want to maintain tension in the air and make this whole town uncomfortable. That frees me up, so I can do the big shit. We on the same page?"

"You can count on it boss."

"All right, go pay your men, I'll be in touch,"

He passes the gym bag through the window.

Assigning the right people to implement and maintain programs keeps Chief Tall Bear's staff busy. Summer has turned into fall and the first dividends to Choctaw members are only a few months away. Everyone is upbeat about this year's end and the beginning of a new one. Blueprint and foundation are laid in place. John has an idea what the Choctaw Nation will look like in ten years. It has come at some cost over the last few months. He has received numerous death threats. Many still fear for his safety.

John creates a new position within the Nation–Special Assistant to the Chiefs–and offers it to Roman Billy. At Levi's insistence, Roman and a small entourage of Roman's Choctaw Nation Security Team travel with Tall Bear everywhere he goes. Whether speaking engagement, dedication, or miscellaneous event, Roman and John's personal guard are nearby.

They are able to satisfy their tribal court and close the case against Thomas ThunderHawk, July Tecumseh and Johnny Kick a Hole in the Sky. John creates a little drama by assigning them positions within the Choctaw Nation, but it dies down quickly. They are still investigating the murders of Gary & Don Taylor. John fires the two deputies, Ray

Cross and Jeffrey Irwin, and has their tribal lawyers and prosecutor interview them both on several occasions. He even asks FBI agents Karen Rivers & Joe Jackson to interview them again to see if they can get them to trip up. They don't have any luck either. They have no solid evidence against the deputies to put together a case for the wrongful death of the Taylor brothers.

One late afternoon, Levi and Roman ask for a meeting with Tall Bear.

"Chieftain, thanks for making time today to discuss some security concerns that Roman and I have, said Levi.

"Anything new that I don't know about?"

"Chief, we knew you were going to take some heat when we downsized the tribe. We thought that would go away, but every week something else happens. Nothing big, but people are still uneasy," adds Roman.

"Chieftain, when you look at the big picture starting with the Taylor brothers killing, the burning of Macedonia, Mary Holden's murder, and the Mercedes running up your ass on the way back from Talihina. That's a lot of freakish things."

"Chief, don't forget the fight at Desperados and the smaller things that persist. But damn, we are missing something."

"Guys, I hear you, but what more can we do? You got a small army following me around everywhere I go. It's embarrassing."

"I got one more idea, discussed it with Roman and he agrees we should try it."

"What far out scheme have you drawn up this time?"

"Chieftain, I'm your second in command so give me a little respect here."

"Ok, lay it on me."

"Chieftain, no need to make your entourage any larger, something a little more covert."

"All right, you got my attention."

"We need somebody to mix and mingle, not established employees of the Nation with Choctaw stamped on their forehead. Let's turn Thomas ThunderHawk, July Tecumseh and Johnny Kick a Hole in the Sky loose on the town as average citizens and let them operate undercover. You got to admit, those guys are crafty and resourceful."

Levi and Roman watch John for a moment as he considers their newest plan.

"I like it. What do we call them, 007, 8 and 9?"

"That's my wise Chieftain."

Because they are three, the Choctaw word 'Tuchina' is unofficially assigned to them. Team Tuchina is born.

After Chief Wilson resigned, the one man who might have helped build an airtight case against the two deputies disappeared from the area. It's a cool fall morning, when John gets a call.

"Hello, Chief Tall Bear."

"Mr. Tall Bear, this is Charles White."

"I know. I recognize the cell number to the phone I gave you. How are you? And, where are you?"

"Mr. Tall Bear, I'm fine, don't want to say right now, but I am in Louisiana."

"Charles, not sure you know but much has happened since we last spoke. You have nothing to fear. The two men in question have been fired and no longer work here.

"That's good news."

"We're still trying to build a case against them and so far we have had no luck. We could use your testimony. Then we may have a chance of putting them away for a long, long while."

"Mr. Tall Bear, I'm sorry for taking so long to call you, but I felt my family might be in danger. You know they threatened me when I was still working for Chief Wilson. I have not been sleeping well and my conscience is getting the best of me. I have talked it over with my wife, Beverly, and I am ready to talk. I don't have a job, so I cannot afford to come to you."

"Charles, don't worry about coming here. I'll come to you. By the way, when I come, I will bring your last month's employment check with me. You left so suddenly no one knew where to send it. I'm sure you can use it."

They make arrangements to meet at a small hotel outside of Alexandra, Louisiana. Levi and John leave the next afternoon on one of the Lear jets owned by the Choctaw Nation. They rent a car and drive south out of Alexandra. This is beautiful country. John can see why Charles and his wife would want to come back here to live. They arrive at a small hotel thirty miles south of town. Adjacent to the hotel is a small cafe, and they find Charles and Beverly in a booth drinking coffee.

After they exchange pleasantries, Tall Bear inquires about their daughter. Beverly says she has moved to New Orleans to stay with relatives and has enrolled in college there. She is doing fine, has met a young man and plans on getting married soon. John congratulates them on the impending marriage and promises a position with the Nation should she ever need a job.

"Beverly, Charles, I'm glad you called and decided to help us. I'm hoping your information might bring closure for the Taylors. When I became Chief, I vowed to see justice done for the family and the Indian community. Do you mind if Levi records our conversation? His recording might not suffice in court, but it will clarify the case for me. Later, a sworn deposition or your testimony in court might be required."

Charles nods yes to Levi.

"Mr. Tall Bear, we both decided to do this. We have prayed to the Lord Almighty about it. I go to church every Sunday and Wednesday night and my conscience is still clouded. Beverly and I will do whatever you ask, whatever is necessary."

Charles recalls the conversation he witnessed regarding the Taylor brothers. Listening to his account, John feels the two deputies could be indicted with Charles testimony. He probes further, asking Charles about other VIP guests who visited the former Chief's home. Charles searches him mind and provides a long list. One in particular got their attention, Senator James Joe Cody.

John has brought along a small Sony video player. He asks Charles to view some video clips. John cautions Beverly one clip is of a sexual nature and advises her not to watch. Charles looks at John as if to question why he should look at it. John tells him he will recognize one person in the clip. He tells him it is the other person's identity John is interested in. As he turns on the small video player and cues the clip Charles is to view, John angles the screen in his direction, away from Beverly. He pushes play and the clip begins.

"Oh my God," says Charles putting his hand to his mouth. "That's Senator Cody." He turns his eyes away from the screen.

"Please look again and tell me if you recognize the young girl in the clip."

"I'm sorry, the plastic bag over her head makes it difficult to see the young girl's facial features. Where did you get this?"

"This clip and others was found on the personal laptop of Chief Wilson, along with hundreds of still photos of Senator Cody in unflattering positions. There are several video clips of Wilson as well. This information is damaging to the Chief's office and is the reason Wilson was forced to resign. We can only guess the Chief filmed the Senator and others for leverage. No one other than my closest team members has seen this footage. The authorities have not seen this DVD. At the proper time this DVD will be turned over to the authorities. Charles, will you look at the clip again?"

On the clip Senator Cody is seen having sexual intercourse with a woman who looks to be in her early 20's. She appears to have long black hair. A see-through plastic bag was tied over her head and she was hanging partially off the bed. John had heard of this type of sex, breath play, designed to heighten the intensity of orgasms. It is also very dangerous and many who have played the game have died.

"Take a closer look at it again and see if anything triggers your memory."

Charles views the clip once again, "Stop! Can you freeze the frame?"

John does, and then tilts the screen back in Charles' direction.

"That's little Jeanie LeFlore. Look at the outside of her left ankle. You see the small dream catcher tattoo?"

"I see it," says John. "There is no question it's a Native dream catcher."

"She was such a sweet little girl. I often kidded with her I was going to get one of those dream catcher tattoos on my arm. I wasn't serious, but it was fun kidding around with her. She was there many times. Most of the time, it was when the senator was there too. But then after one weekend, I never saw her again."

"Are you suggesting she and the Senator spent a lot of time together?"

"Yes, I hope she's all right. She had no business being around those people in the first place. She talked about leaving Oklahoma one day and attending school in California."

"Charles, do you remember the approximate date of the last weekend you saw her?" asks Levi.

He thinks a moment, and then he turns to Beverly. "Do you remember the weekend you're brother Les called?"

"I'm thinking it was the last weekend in March."

John could have almost guessed the date himself. He remembers reading the obituary of the young missing girl, never found and declared legally dead.

"Charles, do you remember what kind of clothing she was wearing the last time you saw her?"

"I sure can. She was always wearing tight blue jeans and a red tight fitting button up shirt. Come to think of it, I never saw her in anything but that getup. Red was her favorite color."

Charles bows his head as if to ponder and gather his thoughts. He doesn't say anything for over a minute. John can see a tear begin to flow down his cheek. Beverly begins to feel his pain and places her arms around him to give him comfort. Charlie regains his composure, wipes his tears away, looks at John and says. "Mr. Tall Bear, that's all I have to say."

"Charles, Beverly, thank you for inviting us down and giving us this information. We have to dig for more information. We'll call as soon as we have more details. Before I leave, here is the check for your last month's work. Plus, it includes an extra six months of severance pay. Anytime you want to come back to work, just let me know."

They say their goodbyes and Levi and John begin their trip back to Durant.

While driving to the airfield, John calls Roman to tell him what they have learned. John remembers the girl's name in the obituary was Jeanie, but isn't sure of the last name. In tune, Roman says he will retrieve a copy of the Bishinik obituary and try to locate family members. As expected, Roman was able to confirmed same girl, still no next of kin.

Over the next several weeks, the two deputies are brought in and questioned again. Separately, both are asked about a girl named Jeanie. After several hours of interrogation, Jeffery admits knowing the girl. Ray Cross says he never saw the girl at all. John and Levi know he's lying, and sense they are moving in the right direction.

They have a credible witness stating the two deputies killed the Taylor brothers in cold blood. They just can't corroborate it. They know Senator Cody had contact and a sexual relationship with a missing, and presumably dead girl. They need solid evidence, a stroke of luck to connect everything. Experience tells Tall Bear time has the answers they seek. What a man can't know the Eagle sees.

CHAPTER 34

T all Bear is scheduled to make a dedication speech at the ground-breaking ceremony for a new drug and alcohol treatment wing in Talihina. The tribe has managed to finance the millions necessary to expand the four year old existing facility. Instead of a 28-day treatment program, the initial visit will be changed to 90 days. A second option will extend care, to six months and as much as one year, depending on the staff's recommendation. In the past, shorter programs, like revolving doors, cycled sick patients to the streets.

John eagerly anticipates this return to his birthplace. Inquisitive by nature, he will search for insights at his first Ceremonial Sweat as Chief. He asks Levi and Roman if they would like to join him. They jump on his invitation to get out of the office and go to the country. The trio piles into the car and begin their journey to Talihina. Following tradition, they'll fast the rest of the day.

Upon arrival, the three take care of tribal business and Choctaw Nation fanfare, and then prepare for their evening sweat. Several other employees will be joining them. They meet up and drive a red dirt road through a forest of pines, which tower 70 to 80 feet into the sky. They stop at a clearing, exit their vehicles and wait for the one who will guide them to the Sweat Lodge.

John was last there some ten years ago with his elder son, Randy, who was going through the 28-day alcohol program in Talihina. His son was an Airborne Ranger in the Army, which asked him to do things against his moral code. While serving, he developed the need to drink to mask the horrors seen on unknown conflicts directed by the military. He was eventually diagnosed as suffering from Post Traumatic Stress Disorder. Tall Bear had spent a memorable afternoon walking through the tall pines, listening to Randy speak about the substance abuse program.

The son had already conducted many Sweats and shared his knowledge, giving father insights to their importance. John had marveled at Randy's attention to detail. He was an ancient Indian wanting to live by the old ways. Randy found it difficult to maneuver through the white man's world and stay true to the morals and values of ancient ancestors. John envies his sons conviction to stay true to himself.

Jojo Wetumka, a Choctaw elder assigned to the Tall Bear sweat emerges out of a hidden trail and surprises the waiting group. Wetumka is well into his 80's yet moves like a man half his age. Somewhat of an icon in these parts, he's built and taught the traditional sweats for ages. His close friends with respect and affection call him Gap because of a missing front tooth. He has been known to take a swing at some who mistakenly thought they were part of his inner circle. Most call him Mr. Wetumka to be on the safe side.

After a very brief introduction, the old Indian enters the trail and everyone follows. Wetumka sets the mood. As they walk in Creator's Cathedral, no one speaks. Halfway to the top of their climb, they begin descending and cross a small creek with crystal clear water. There is no bridge. They watch as Wetumka gracefully jumps from rock to rocks protruding above the running water. The water is ice cold. Arriving at the other side, they begin to climb even higher among the pines. They hustle to keep up with the 6' 175 pound Wetumka.

"Pisa." Against a magnificent blue sky, the old Indian points out two eagles soaring close to the Heavens.

"This is a good sign. We will have a successful Sweat."

After a short climb, they come upon a flat plateau, and fifty yards in front of them John can see the Sweat Lodge. It hadn't changed much, if at all, since he last saw it. Wetumka exchanges instructions with the fire keeper and several helpers who have a sacred fire going. John feels as though they have stepped back into another place and time. It is such a peaceful and tranquil setting, truly majestic.

"I built this lodge years ago and it has served us well."

"Mr. Wetumka, is this a typical lodge?" ask Levi.

"Yes, most traditional Sweat Lodges are dome shape in structure. As you can see, I stabbed slender limbs into the ground in a circle approximately ten to twelve feet in diameter. Then I bent the limbs together toward the center to form a dome framework. It's tall enough that most can stand once we get in. In the old days, we tied the limbs together with rawhide. Nowadays, we use rope from Home Depot or Wal-Mart."

"Very interesting! What's going on inside?" ask one of the employees.

"We have a fire pit dug out in the center about the size of my momma washtub. The dirt floor is swept clean and covered with a mat of sweet grass, soft cedar boughs. Sometimes, we use sage leaves for comfort and cleanliness. These can catch fire pretty easy, so we positioned them away from the pit. When you sit down, be careful not to kick anything into the fire."

"How do you keep from choking to death inside?" asks another.

"We leave an opening at the top for ventilation. In the old days, the lodge was covered with the hides of buffalo, bear or moose. For you modern day NDN's animal skins have been replaced with plastic sheeting, old carpet, or heavy gauge canvas sheets to retain the heat and steam. The lodge entrance always faces east for traditional reasons. Warriors would greet the rising sun and asks the Great Spirit for guidance. The sun represents the source of life and power and the dawn of wisdom. The fire heating the rocks is the undying light of the world and eternity. We seek a new spiritual beginning in the Sweat Ceremony."

"Great information," says one.

Outside and to the east of the lodge, Wetumka and the fire keepers have built the sacred fire pit where the stones are to be heated. There, an altar-barrier prevents participants from going beyond this area. It also keeps anyone from falling into the fire pit if they emerge from the Sweat lodge disoriented.

Traditionally this altar consists of an animal skull, such as buffalo or other large beast, sitting atop a post. At its base is a small raised earthen mound where items sacred to the group or clan are placed. Such items include sage, sweet grass or feathers, and a pipe rack for the ayanalli haloka.

The purpose of these traditions and the Sweat is spiritual cleanliness. Randy taught John, to fast for an entire day prior to the Sweat, avoiding caffeine, alcohol and any other unhealthy substances. Personal items such as Eagle feathers and medicine pouches are allowed and welcomed. Many cultures do not allow a female on her moon into the Sweat. Some do.

"All right listen up! In Choctaw tradition, before you enter the Sweat Lodge you should have some tobacco to offer to the sacred fire. We have brought some for you. This is a time to say a prayer or ask a question. The smoke from the tobacco will carry your request to the Great Spirit. When you enter the lodge, I, Jojo Wetumka will smudge you with the smoke of burning sage and waft the smoke over you with my eagle feather. Then you can crawl into the lodge in a sun-wise (clockwise) direction, bowing in humility to Great Spirit and Mother Earth. You will take your place in the circle, sitting cross-legged upright against the wall of the lodge."

The seven remove all things not natural to the Sweat and strip to their underwear. A few wrap themselves in a towel. They all come prepared, give their offering, and say a prayer as they toss their tobacco into the Sacred Fire. When everyone is seated inside, Wetumka closes the entrance to the lodge opening. The lodge becomes dark.

Wetumka speaks, "You are free to leave anytime during the Sweat if you cannot endure any longer. But try to leave between the rounds. We will start by passing the 'talking stick' so each of you can say something about yourself, where you are from, your clan or tribe. You may offer a prayer to family members or loved ones who may have some kind of illness. Tell all what you hope to accomplish from the sweat. This is a time to be honest and ask forgiveness from the people you have hurt or neglected. If your heart is good, the Creator will forgive. Each will speak the truth in the honor of Grandfathers, Mother Earth and the Spirits."

After all are seated, Wetumka asks for the fire tender to bring in the heated stones from the sacred fire. One at a time they are set in the shallow pit inside the lodge, first the stone on the west, then north, east, south, and in the center to Grandfather. Additional stones are then placed to Grandmother and The People. After four to seven stones are in the pit, the entrance is closed and sealed by the fire keeper. The red-hot stones light up the inside of the lodge. The soft glow from the stones bounces off the bodies inside as the ceremony begins. Wetumka sounds the water drum and calls forth the spirit guides in prayer from the four directions. He then dips water and pours it onto the hot stones in the pit. This produces large amounts of steam, usually one dipper for each of the four directions, until he is told by the spirits to stop. He begins his prayers, songs and chants.

As the steam and temperature rise, so do their senses. Viruses and bacteria cannot survive above the temperature of 98.6F, and photons are released into the air. Messages and visions from the Spirit World are received through the consciousness of everyone inside. Typically a Sweat will last four sessions, or rounds of endurance. Each round will last twenty to thirty minutes and ends when the lodge leader opens the door.

Each of the rounds has different meaning and focuses on one of the four directions. After the second round, they all leave the lodge and jump into the cold stream just down the hill. It is exhilarating, going from one extreme to another. None of them say very much. John gets the feeling most are experiencing something and don't want to disrupt the moment with idle conversation. They go back in to complete the last two rounds.

Into the beginning of the fourth and last round, John becomes very light headed. For a few moments, he feels like he is floating above the ground. The steam is intense, and at times it is difficult to breathe. Sweat drips from his body. Everyone is drenched. Their perspiring bodies glisten from the glow of the red-hot rocks. As Wetumka pours more water onto the hot rocks, the steam creates an image against the animal hide backdrop that covers the lodge. Borderline delirious, John reaches to touch it. Before him is a Sacred White Buffalo, with strange red slashes across its face. John knows this is not coming from the hot red rock, because the water has cooled the rocks. He imagines something red in color flowing from the buffalo's eyes and mouth. For a split second, he sees another image. A snarling white wolf leaps toward the white buffalo. As quickly as it appears, the wolf falls into the fire pit. Simultaneously, John feels himself lowered to the floor of the lodge.

Wetumka announces the ceremony is over and instructs them to exit very carefully as not to stir the spirits lingering in the lodge. One by one they leave the Sweat Lodge in a clockwise manner. They all make a mad dash for the clear cold waters of the nearby stream. After cooling off, they all go back to an area close to the lodge. Large boulders and rocks are positioned around another fire pit. Food and water are brought to them, and they celebrate the ceremony's end.

Wetumka speaks. "This has been a good day. If any would like to share their feelings, this would be the time. I'm interested, has anyone experienced a vision?"

All revisit their thoughts and sensations. Everyone seems interested in Tall Bear's vision of the Sacred White Buffalo. John didn't mention the white wolf. It was only a nano second and he thought it less important. One suggests Talihina located in Buffalo Valley is the connection. Another suggests many years ago a white buffalo was born in this very valley. John accepts these suggestions, however, no one expresses a clue or insight about the red color streaming from the face of the buffalo.

"Tall Bear, I'm told you were born here in Talihina. That could explain your connection. Also it's interesting that you have seen a white buffalo with a red face. Perhaps you should seek counsel from the medicine man Ironhorse who lives in this area," offers Wetumka.

"Mr. Wetumka, I will look into your suggestion about Ironhorse. We all have heard of your wisdom and you have taught us much. We appreciate your part in making this sweat successful and pray for the opportunity to return."

"You are all welcome anytime, and, call me 'Gap'."

John remembers ten years earlier, his son had foreseen much of what he just experienced, and concluded, "Dad, if you ever do a Sweat here, you will experience something very significant. You will be looking for answers and find some of them here. This is your birthplace."

CHAPTER 35

Three Indians strut down Main Street searching for the Atoka Bar & Grill. Heads turn as they step in a strange rhythm. Their Saturday Night Fever slide is closer to reservation cowboy.

"July, do you know where in hell you are going," questions Johnny Kick a Hole in the Sky?

"The hotel flyer said 3434 Main St."

"Did it say, east or west, 'cause we are on West Main?"

"He doesn't know, hell, we could be 34 blocks away," complains Thomas Thunder Hawk.

"July Tecumseh never gets lost. See the flashy neon sign across the street a half block up,

'Atoka Bar & Grill'."

Team Tuchina enter Atoka's only bar and grill featuring live music. They find an empty booth by the pool tables opposite the dance floor. Beers are ordered over 8 ball protocol, challenges and trash talk. They agree on 'cut-throat' so all three can play. Johnny Kick insists on playing for $5 a game convinced he'd play better with something on the line. July wins the first three games, shaming Johnny into quitting. He sits down to give his beer company.

While July and Thomas make war on the table with a game of 8-ball, a vision on the dance floor catches Johnny's eye. The band plays a two-step and redneck couples flock to their places. Johnny stands and joins the two at the pool table, motioning them to check out the sensuous sway of the Atoka's hottest young lady.

"Fellows, I've been around the block a few times and I can tell you this. She's the finest number I've seen."

"Amen to that Kick. She looks out of place for this joint," offers July.

"She looks to be part Indian too," adds Thomas.

Tuchina watches as the song ends and another slow one begins. Four or five guys rush her to take her for a spin. The lucky one grabs her and marries his body against hers. His pressure on her chest pushes half of her ample breast out of her top. She pushes him away to regain her form and another takes his place. She decides she has had enough and attempts to walk away. The redneck knowing he will never have another chance in life with someone so stunning grabs her wrist.

"Stop it! I'm through dancing for the night."

"Come on baby, I saw how you were looking at me."

"It was disgust, not lust, you pig, so leave me alone," jerking free.

"Kick, you and July, watch my 6," commands Thomas, almost sprinting around the table and across the dance floor. His two wingmen follow.

"Hey guys, this is my cousin. I heard her from across the room, she's through dancing." July and Kick make threatening bookends for Thomas, as Team Tuchina stares down the small group of hounds.

"Why didn't you tell me you were coming out tonight, I would have come by and picked you up?" offers Thomas.

"Spur of the moment decision, cousin," as she slides over to Thomas and hugs him. "Next time I'll call yah."

Not wanting to mix it up with three imposing Indians, the men retreat to their table and beers.

She makes eye contact with all three and slides into her booth, lowering her volume, "Will you sit with me. We can make this look real."

"Absolutely. I'm Thomas Thunder Hawk, Johnny Kick pointed you out and that's July Tecumseh.

"Angelina."

"Pretty name, you're not from around here, are you?" questions Thomas.

"No, I'm from up north."

"You look part Indian. What tribe," muses July?

"I'm quarter African American, quarter German on my father's side and half Seminole from my mother."

"Well, we're a little Indian too," says Johnny and they all laugh in unison.

"You guys should be in the movies, sooooo handsome."

"Johnny Kick too?" Another round of laughter at Kick's expense.

"You're the one that needs to be in the movies. Drop dead gorgeous like Elizabeth Taylor," gushes Johnny Kick.

"I'm a big fan of Seminole Indian women. I've been telling my partners for years how pretty Seminole Indian women are," gushes July.

"Who are you," questions Thomas as he eyes July? "Seriously, what's a beautiful young women like you out alone in a dump like this?"

"My boyfriend's away on a job for a couple of days. I just got bored looking at four walls and watching mindless television."

"Where's the job located?" asks July.

"A little town northeast of here, called Talihina."

"We know Talihina. So where you staying?" inquires Thomas.

"A small town north of here."

A waitress stops by and asks if drinks are needed. They order and conversation continues. When the drinks are emptied, the Seminole angel says she must leave and asks the three to walk her to her car parked curbside. Like puppets on a string they reluctantly express goodbyes. She teases, hopes to see them again, and drives away in a black Mercedes AMG with Tennessee plates. Team Tuchina ends the night playing pool and throwing back more beers.

CHAPTER 36

J ohn sleeps like a newborn baby Saturday night and wakes to a
cool fall morning. Pulled in so many directions prior to coming
here, he thought he had focus, but the Sweat has a way of allowing
things to fall into place, defragging the hard drive. At the drug and
alcohol treatment center in Talihina, this tiny, Buffalo Valley town, a
new chapter begins.

Expanding the treatment center was not a difficult decision. One
life lost to addiction is one too many. John has witnessed hundreds
of American Indians, friends and loved ones, travel down alcohol's
destructive path. He is here to open a new wing of the center and
proudly dedicate and re-name it in honor of his mother. She died
from complications of diabetes twenty years ago, hence his second
most important project, stamping out obesity and diabetes. These
two projects are the cornerstone of his legacy in the Choctaw Nation.

Before the ceremonies, John invites Levi and Roman to have
breakfast with him at Norma's Place, one of the three diners in town.
They arrive around 8:30 in the morning, sit down and place their order
with a friendly waitress. They share the space with a natives drinking
coffee and exchanging local gossip. No one knows who John is. He
has been Chief for only a short time and he happy to go unnoticed.

The three of them discuss the Sweat from the night before. Though
all had been thoroughly rejuvenated by the trip, John's haunting vision
reminded him of the sweat that prompted his visit to his mother's
church and first meet Roman. The buffalo's injuries in this vision
differ from the first with the Roman soldier and the Indian warrior.

He knows the meaning will reveal itself in time and keeps these thoughts to himself for now.

He tells Levi and Roman about the last time he had dinner here with Mary Holden, reminiscing about the boxing match he had with her brother, Blackie. They found it amusing, after all these years, Mary was still mad at the young Indian boy who gave her brother a few bruises. John tells them he regrets never taking the time to look Blackie up and laugh about old times. They all express disappointment her murder is still unsolved. Roman had some boxing experience in the military and shares a few of his stories. John kids that Levi's boxing skills came from fighting off jealous husbands.

A pleasant breakfast turns serious when John receives a call from ThunderHawk. Thomas had mentioned Tuchina Saturday night outing in a casual conversation with Tammy. When the Mercedes AMG was mentioned, Tammy made the connection and insisted he phone.

"Thomas, I can't begin to explain how important this is. Did you get a name?"

"Angelina, but we didn't get a last name."

"I've got you on speaker, so Levi and Roman can hear. What else can you tell me?"

"Chief, we kind of rescued her from an awkward situation and she invited us to sit at her table. We had one round of drinks with her, so it was a pretty short get-together."

"Thomas, Levi here, good work. Did Angelina tell you where she was living?"

"She said she was staying in a small town north of Atoka."

"That could be Stringtown, maybe Kiowa, probably not as far as Savanna. Damn, I wish we could pinpoint where she might be holed up," Levi complains.

"Sorry Levi, we were all a little off our normal game because the way she looked. You had to be there. She could stop traffic in downtown Hollywood."

"A pretty Elizabeth Taylor," adds John.

"For damn sure."

"Anything else?" questions Levi.

"This could be important. We didn't get the boyfriend's name, but she said he was on a job in Talihina."

"That's a little scary. Thomas, tell July and Johnny thanks and I owe them one. Halito."

"So what do you think Chieftain?" asks Levi.

"Not much we can do except stay alert and we would do that anyway."

"She's driving the AMG, so that put the dude in another vehicle. That's not good for spotting him," added Levi.

"It's a long shot, but I'll call Tammy and have Team Tuchina drive up north as far as Savanna and look for Angelina, suggested Roman.

"Can't hurt."

"I got a bad feeling about this Chieftain," complained Levi.

"I hear you, let's get out of here, I have a dedication to give."

———

It's only a five-minute drive to the site of the dedication, south for a quarter mile, they turn right onto 63A. Pine trees, forty to fifty feet tall, line the two-lane road to the Talihina Recovery Center. The road splits and to the left is the new state of the arts hospital. Since February 1995 the hospital has provided all health care for the surrounding area. The Choctaw Nation under the auspices of PL 93-638, the Indian Self Determination Act, manages it according to a contract between Indian Health Services and the federal government. Federal dollars are earmarked for tribal use each year and Indian Health Service personnel provide technical assistance.

The split to the right takes you to the existing Recovery Center. Across the street sits the old red brick hospital, where John was born. The older building, no longer in use, stands at the base of pine-covered Buffalo Mountain. IHS still owns and controls the property. Tall Bear decides to check with IHS about the possibility of restoring it. In the old days, before he was born, it was a tuberculosis sanatorium. John has heard stories people in this area think the old hospital is haunted. Some say the incinerator lights up at night and you can see figures roaming around outside making moaning sounds. Surely the building can be made useful again without tearing it down. Like the human body, and personal relationships, left unattended, they wither away. This will be another way to practice John's Falammichi philosophy, to defend and restore.

To the right of the existing Rehab Center, several acres of pine trees surround an open area. At the site chosen for the new wing stands a makeshift stage with a podium. Today they will break ground and work will commence the following Monday. Well over a hundred people are gathered waiting for the dedication to begin. At 10 a.m. John, Levi, and Roman join a small group of VIP's already seated on the small stage. John is pleasantly surprised to see Senator Jim and several other politicians representing nearby governments. Tammy has brought a small group of CMA staff members. In all, there will be a little over a dozen people on stage. The Chief of Staff of the new hospital, Dr. Red Cloud Wolf, serves as MC. After Rachel and several others speak, Tall Bear is introduced.

"Halito Chukma to all." John extends both of his arms in welcome. "I want to thank our special guests, Senator Jim and her distinguished colleagues, Mayor Dixon, Dr. Red Cloud Wolf, and others. If there is a common denominator in all of us, it is we are here to serve. Because of federal funding, not only will this facility treat our Choctaw people, but anyone in the county who needs this kind of health care.

"Today's dedication is special for me personally. As some of you know, I was born in that old red building across the street. It was never my design to come back and do this. I had other plans, but the Creator intervened, and brought me here. It is the Great Spirit, working to make this happen.

"There are many theories as to why our Indian people fall victim to alcohol. Stories are told, prior to the 1400's, American Indians relied little on grains, sugar or alcohol. The white man introduced these items to our people and we have yet to recover. Grains and sugar produce obesity in our people, while alcohol has wreaked mass destruction on Indian families. The white man had been drinking alcohol for thousands of years, and many learned to tame the evil drug and demons it provokes. Indians have had a much shorter time to adjust. Dr. Red Cloud Wolf and his colleagues in the medical field suspect heredity and imbalances in genetic material causes Indians to be susceptible to addiction. Had we had this information years ago, perhaps we would have put something in place to shield our people. Education makes a world of difference in everyone's lives.

"It's fitting, a new drug and alcohol center carries my mother's name. She lived and raised ten children in a home with an abusive, alcoholic husband. I saw firsthand the destructive force it had on a family. Time and wisdom have taught me not to be bitter, and I have long since forgiven my father. Still, I share this story with you to let you know no one is immune to tragedy once alcohol is mixed. My mother was not alone in this experience. She and every other mother fought this battle as only they could, with love and compassion. I thought the Creator took my mother far too early, but I'm sure He decided she had suffered enough.

"It gives me great pleasure dedicating this new facility in honor of my mother, 'The Ada Wilkerson Recovery Center'." John raises his arms to the heavens and says, "Momma, I feel your presence. I love and miss you."

As John begins lowering his arms, he feels a hot stinging sensation between the left side of his chest and the inside of his bicep. The first thing he thinks is 'heart attack'. Then he hears a thump in a tree behind him. This rip turns him slightly to his left, where he sees Rachel still clapping and smiling in his direction. He thinks it odd, knowing he is in harm's way and feeling immense pain, however

Rachel hasn't processed what is happening. Instantly, John feels something hammer into his lower chest wall. Everything is happening in slow motion now. In seconds, everyone has registered the sounds of two gunshots. John now sees Levi reacting and beginning to move in Rachel's direction to shield her from danger. John hears Tammy and others screaming in the background and he fears for their safety. He begins to fall and can see Roman rushing in his direction and shouting.

"Chieftain hit! The Chief is down!"

Tall Bear watches Roman leaving his feet and flying through the air to shield him. He shouts again in the direction of the tribal police who are there in abundance. "The Chief is down, get an ambulance!"

They hear two more bullets hit a different tree. Another hits the golf cart parked behind the stage, there to transfer VIP's to and from their cars. Two final gunshots hammer eardrums, and then there is silence.

"Momma! Momma!" cries Tall Bear. Then everything turns black.

CHAPTER 37

A flat screen television mounted in the corner of the room is alive with information of the shooting. Across the bottom of the screen is text tape. 'The Chief of the Choctaw Nation cut down by unknown assassin's bullet, is still in surgery at the Talihina Indian Hospital. Sources say he is in grave danger.' The newly appointed Chief, John Wilkerson Tall Bear was there to dedicate a new alcohol treatment center when he was hit by sniper fire. Witnesses say they thought as least half-dozen shots were fired. The Chief was hit twice, first in the upper arm, secondly just below the heart. At this time there are no suspects and they have not confirmed where the shots came from.

A CNN reporter onsite used the stage as a backdrop and reported the attempt could be some kind of conspiracy.

"There has been much drama coming from the Choctaw Nation over the past eight months. First, there were the shooting deaths of two unarmed Indians by the Choctaw Tribal Police. Thousands attended the funeral of the two young men in protest of then Chief Paul Wilson. The day after the funeral, a few hundred Indians marched to the Capitol grounds and rushed the compound, taking the staff and Chief Wilson hostage.

"Members of a local Indian organization called the CMA, including current Chief John Wilkerson Tall Bear and United States Senator Rachel Jim, managed to slip inside the Choctaw Nation building under cover of darkness, and initiate the end of the siege. Four days later Chief Wilson fired his Assistant Chief and appointed Tall Bear to the position. A short month later Chief Wilson abruptly resigned and John Tall Bear became the Chief of the Choctaws. Finally, the new administration, under the leadership of Chief Tall Bear, cut their tribal membership by 90%, redefining 'what is an Indian?' requiring a higher blood quantum to be a member of the tribe, and greatly expanding the persons of interest in the search for today's shooter."

Attempted assassinations typically are top news. Support for the fallen Chief is over-the-top, and catches the newsmakers, reporters and networks by surprise. Facebook and Twitter sites are swamped with commentary and opinions. An overwhelming numbers of ordinary people travel to Talihina, a town that can barely accommodate a few hundred, let alone several thousand travelers.

Huddled together on two couches, and occasionally glancing at the flat screen televisions, are Roman, Tammy, Senator Jim, a couple of the Chief's immediate staff members, and several doctors. Among them is the new Chief of Staff, Dr. Red Cloud Wolf. Tall Bear himself researched and recruited Dr. Wolf, a half Choctaw, from one of the top hospitals in the nation. Dr. Wolf and the medical team are attempting to address some of the immediate health issues the Chief is facing.

"The second bullet is giving us some concerns. It missed John's heart, traveled through his left lung, nicked a couple of organs, and is lodged just to the left side of his spinal cord. At this time, the surgeons are attempting to stop the bleeding the bullet has created. Surgery could go well into the afternoon and quite possibly into the evening hours.

"Had this happened eight months ago, the Chief wouldn't have made it out of this valley alive with these wounds. Prior to my coming on staff, the Chief and I evaluated this hospital and found it to be totally inadequate to handle even a basic emergency.

This kind of frankness and his unbelievable talent as a surgeon, characterize the kind of man Chief Tall Bear needed to head the Choctaw Nation Hospital. He had wanted the best talent available to take care of his people. Dr. Red Cloud Wolf is someone the Choctaw people can identify with and place their trust in. And now the Chief himself is in ICU, under the care of Dr. Wolf and the very team he helped assemble.

"This hospital was built state-of-the-art, but staffed with marginally committed people just drawing a paycheck. At his insistence we assembled great medical teams and they now gives him a chance to make it through the night. All anyone can do is wait and pray."

"Roman," says Levi, pulling him aside. "I can't just sit here and wait. I want to find that son-of-a-bitch!"

"Levi, I know how you feel, but for now you are the acting Chief of the Choctaw Nation."

"There isn't going to be any Nation for me if John dies. Reading between the doctor lines, it could be hours before we know anything. Roman, you know there aren't many roads leading out of Talihina we can't cover."

"Two maybe three if you go off road. What are you getting at?"

"It would take someone considerable time just to get out of this valley. We've got to find out where those shots came from."

"Levi, if you think back, those bullets hit several seconds before we heard the gun shots. It could only be a rifle and was fired from a great distance."

"Roman, you're right! Yes! And the direction they were coming from…the shooter would have to have been in one of those trees a hundred yards away!"

"I don't think so, they came from further away."

"You think it came from the mountain bluff! Hell, the bluff is almost a mile away."

"Who could make that shot?"

"A professional hit man. The person who hired him has got to be well connected, with deep pockets."

"Well, that narrows it down from a few thousand suspects. Tammy, Roman and I are going back to the stage. If anything changes, good news or bad, you call us. Let's go, Roman."

Outside the waiting room, stand two men eager for word about their fallen leader. Police Chief Charlie Two Crow and Cody Simpson, one of his assistants, greet Levi and Roman. Two Crow has lived and worked in Talihina for the last nine years. He started as a patrolman and through the years worked himself up to Police Chief.

Two Crow is everybody's friend, but takes his job very seriously. He is a recovering alcoholic who had come through the Talihina Recovery Center twelve years before. He has been clean and sober ever since. He raises a sixteen-year-old daughter and loves country and western music. The town knows Two Crow's patrol car by the driver's sing-a-long to the C&W that drifts from its Bose speakers.

"Two Crow, we're going back to the stage," states Levi.

"How's the Chief?"

"They won't know anything for hours. All we can do is wait and pray. Two Crow, I want to know where those shots were fired. We can't sit by and wait for the FBI to get here."

"Chief Levi, I'm going where you go."

"Then let's get moving."

The four men jump into a waiting tribal police car and, within five minutes, they're back at the stage, the site of the shooting. The tribal police have everything seemingly under control. Authorities have taped off the entire site.

Standing on the stage, officer Cody Simpson, a younger Choctaw, asks, "What are we looking for?"

"We're looking for the slug that hit the tree. That's the first thing I heard out of the ordinary," says Roman. The other three pick out the tree nearest them and begin to search for a rifle slug.

"I got it," says Levi. Roman and Two Crow join him at the base of a massive pine tree.

"Cody, would you mind going up there and stand at the podium where the Chief would have been standing?" Within seconds, it becomes obvious which direction the rifle had been fired from.

"Holy Shit! You think it was fired from up there?" asks Two Crow, pointing his finger in the direction of the mountain. Roman is crouching down near the base of the massive pine where the bullet entered the tree.

"If you visualize the line of sight from where the bullet hits the tree and line it up with Cody's shoulder and extend it out, it's the only possibility. There're no trees, buildings or other sites to perch a rife between here and the mountain."

There's a rock bluff up there," says Levi.

"That was my first guess, too."

Eagles Nest is the name of the rock bluff overlooking the Buffalo Valley floor. It is also an alternate location hang gliders jump from. When the best site is overrun with other gliders, thrill seekers will use this jump site, even though it is far more dangerous. Plus, it's more difficult to haul their equipment up this part of the mountain. It takes an experienced climber over an hour just to carry his hang glider gear up to the top. At the top, he will then have to descend another hundred feet to the rock bluff. After arriving, there is ample area to do just about anything you want, short of playing flag football.

"We need to get up there as quick as we can to see if the shooter left any clues. I'd bet an Indian taco he's long gone," says Levi.

"Chief Levi, who could make a shot like that?" asks Cody Simpson.

"Someone very skilled… Roman, you would know more about that kind of talent."

"I'm guessing only a dozen people in the world could make that shot. The Army has an elite team of men, but only a few could execute the same shot. It would have to be someone from a special unit, the best of the best. My guess is CIA or covert team."

"We need a tracker," Two Crow declares.

"Two Crow, is that old Apache Indian still alive?" asks Levi.

"You talking about Tommy YellowHawk?"

"That's him!"

"That old man must be in his eighties. He's nothing but an old drunk. I have to lock him up a couple times a month. He ain't no tracker though."

"The hell he ain't! He's one of the best trackers I've ever known! I could tell you some stories about YellowHawk. I wouldn't want him tracking my ass if I was trying to get away."

"I would've never guessed he had that kind of talent."

"Can you find him and bring him here?"

"Sure, no problem. He lives in a small shack about a mile outside of town."

"Roman, will you and Cody get whatever supplies you think we will need. I've decided to go with Two Crow to get YellowHawk."

"Consider it done Levi, we'll meet back here in an hour," says Roman.

CHAPTER 38

———

YellowHawk's home is barely visible from the rocky dirt road a hundred yards off the main highway. Actually, it's a wooden shack standing in the middle of a small grove of pine trees. You had to be looking to see it. Behind it is a huge rock boulder twice as tall as the shack. It appears the bolder stands in place of a back wall. Levi and Two Crow make their way toward the shack on a path littered with beer cans and empty whiskey bottles.

As they get closer, a thin trail of smoke escapes a small chimney. The walls of the shack are made of rough 1x12 slabs of pine lumber. A badly rusted corrugated tin roof keeps the rain and sun out. An old bicycle with a flat tire leans up against the building. To one side of the shack is a fire pit with a large cast iron pot to boil hot water for cooking and bathing. Nearby are two large poles, stuck in the ground about five feet apart. The poles are about six feet tall, with some kind of animal skin stretched between them. The scene is picturesque like a modern old west movie lot or stepping back fifty years in time.

Approaching the shack, they interrupt a playful tussle between a shaggy looking dog and a bobcat. The bobcat give a signal playtime is over. The dog alerts his owner with a bark, someone is invading their space. He is a mixed breed of some sort, not big but not small either. The black & brown dog approaches the two men with the bobcat trailing behind, stops, and stands his ground. Ofi flashes his teeth and growls a low rumble. The dog makes it known this is as far as Levi and Two Crow are going to advance. Ofi has back up with big cat off his right shoulder. Two Crow feel a little nervous, as he places his hand on his 44 Glock, ready to draw if necessary.

"Don't do that. The dog's not going to do anything unless we do something stupid," as Levi puts his hand on Two Crow's arm.

"Who's worried about the dog, it's that Bobcat that's scares me."

"I hear you! That's why I'm standing behind you... Hey Peaches! You in there?"

"Peaches?" Two Crow, looking at Levi as if he was crazy.

"The YellowHawk I know, loves canned peaches."

On the way to YellowHawk's, Levi asked Two Crow to stop at a local convenience store. Thinking he might need some leverage, he makes a purchase for Tommy. Levi shows the can of peaches to Two Crow.

"I hope you brought something for that dog and bobcat too."

"Nope, didn't know about the guardian's."

"Damn," as Two Crow slides behind Levi.

"Hey Peaches! It's Levi Tushka. Come on out."

"Levi Tushka, is that you?" quavers a voice from behind the old shack.

"Yeah, it's me and Two Crow."

"Ofi chilosa (dog quiet)," shouts YellowHawk, and the dog quiets. The bobcat doesn't move and stands her ground.

"Binilichi (you sit)," and the dog sit down on the ground while the bobcat ignores.

Naturally, Levi and Two Crow recognize the Choctaw commands YellowHawk gives the dog. Both look at each other and laugh. By now the old man is half way down the path holding a small rifle in his hand.

"Halito Chukma Levi, Two Crow. I thought it was some young kids snooping around."

"Here Tommy, I brought you a gift." Levi tosses a small can of peaches to the old Indian.

"Big Levi, you are the only man in the world I let call me Peaches," he playfully points the rifle at Two Crow.

"You crazy old Apache! Don't point that old Winchester in my direction."

"What the hell are you doing, teaching your dog Choctaw?"

"Hey, You know what they say. When in Choctaw country, do what the Choctaws do."

"I hope you taught that bobcat a few words too," manages a still nervous Two Crow.

"I ain't crazy! You can't teach a cat to do anything. All she does is sleep and tear up the place."

"Every Apache I ever met was a little crazy," laughs Levi as he extends his hand.

"Big Levi, what brings you up to see me?"

Levi fills his old friend in about what has happened the last few hours, and asks if he will come and help. They need someone with his tracking skills.

"Big Levi, my old friend, I will come and do whatever I can on one condition."

"What's that?"

"This young buck," pointing at Two Crow, "must buy me some whiskey, two half pints."

"I ain't buying you no whiskey, you old drunk."

"Yes, you are," says Levi.

"And one for Ofi. He's coming, too," laughs YellowHawk.

"No way!" shouts Two Crow.

"I'll get my gear. If its ok with you guys, I'll leave the Big Cat here."

"Hell yes!" both men reply in unison.

Within minutes the three men and Ofi are speeding toward the liquor store in town. Reluctantly, Two Crow buys two half-pints of whiskey for the old Apache. It is a small price to pay to for an expert tracker on their trip up the mountain.

Back in the car, YellowHawk gets acquainted with his bottle of whisky, Two Crow asks about the Bobcat. Ofi had brought the cat home one rainy night. It was undernourished and probably an orphan.

Together man and dog took care of the cat and restored it. NDN's kinship with all creatures of the earth, sky and water is a real and active principle.

Animals have rights. The right of man's protection, the right to live, the right to multiply, the right to freedom, and the right to man's indebtedness. YellowHawk merged himself with the land without destroying the natural beauty, except for a few whiskey bottles and beer cans. He made a home for himself and any animal that was without one. Levi admired and loved his old Apache friend.

Within minutes they join Roman and Cody Simpson and are off to the base of Buffalo Mountain. Arriving at the site, YellowHawk and Ofi begin to look around the entrance to the trail leading up the mountain. Ofi is lively and jumping about.

"Binilichi," commands YellowHawk, and Ofi sits down. YellowHawk doesn't want Ofi stirring up dust and destroying fresh tracks. The old tracker spends several minutes looking over the path where Ofi got excited. Levi, Roman and Cody stand around watching the old Apache and his dog do their work. It's like watching a scene out of an old movie.

When YellowHawk had gone back into his shack to get his gear, he came out wearing leather moccasins, tight fitting old blue jeans, carrying a Winchester rifle in one hand. He wore a Ghost Shirt made of elk skin with the sleeves cut off at the shoulder. There are several patches the size of bullet holes hand stitched with leather lacing in front and back. Ghost Shirts of the Lakota Sioux were thought to be able to defend against bullets and have Spiritual powers.

A beaded leather band was tied around the tracker's head to secure his shoulder length black hair from flying about. Attached to the leather band, a couple of yellow and white eagle feathers dangled down the back of his head. Beaded bands of leather were also tied around one of his biceps and on both wrists. Slung over one shoulder was a leather strap attached to a beaded leather pouch. Perhaps this pouch was to carry his bottle of whiskey.

As YellowHawk and Ofi got in the car, Levi and Two Crow had looked at each silently amused, but in a more serious mood, knowing, to comment on the old Apache's dress was not important.

"Big Levi, I see two sets of tracks going up the trail but only one coming down. One is a big man, larger than you and taller. The other one is the size of me. The big man was carrying a lot of weight."

"You think only one came down. Who was it?" asks Roman.

"The big man came back down not long ago."

"How does he know all that," marveled Cody.

"He's Apache," assured Levi.

"Is the shooter is still up there?" asks Two Crow.

"I don't think so," says YellowHawk.

"How can you be sure?" asks Levi.

"Big man still carrying same weight. Levi, I'm thinking other person was a woman. My guess, she's not the shooter. She was leading the way, maybe a local guide. Don't know until we go look," replies YellowHawk, who is still studying some of the tracks and trying to keep Ofi still.

"Let's get going. If there is someone still up there, I want to find them before dark or before they find another way down," says Levi.

"Kanali," YellowHawk commands the dog to move, then turns to walk up the trail behind Ofi. The searches fall in behind. It's a winding trail among skyscraping pine trees and large rocks and boulders. High above, you can see the blue sky peering through the treetops. A bald eagle soars about the sky. Advancing a hundred yards, Ofi begins to wander off the main trail to a smaller one.

"Atany a," commands YellowHawk, and Ofi returns to the main trail.

It's amusing to hear the old Apache speak to his trusted companion in Choctaw. It's obvious they have done this many times, as

Ofi understands every command and reacts accordingly. In this day and age, there are many Choctaws unaware of these words. The team of men and animal continue climbing another hundred yards, and as they approach a clearing the blue sky opens up. Ofi stops and begins to growl in a low tone.

"Issa." YellowHawk holds up his closed fist for all to stop. YellowHawk moves forward into the clearing to make sure there is no danger.

"Minti." YellowHawk motions for the men and dog to come to him in the clearing.

"Big Levi, this is where the tracks stop." He points to numerous footprints cluttering the edge of a rock plateau. This is where it gets more difficult for the average person to continue to track. YellowHawk, though, is no average tracker. He continues to walk, examining the rocky area in front of him.

"They came this way." He motions everyone to follow him. YellowHawk begins to descend to a rocky area amid more trees. After a short descent, they arrive at another, smaller plateau overlooking the valley floor. Behind them was a natural rock cave large enough to keep four or five people out of the elements.

YellowHawk walks to the cliff's edge and examines markings in the rock. "This is where they mounted the weapon." He points to gouges in the rock made from a tripod with something heavy mounted on it.

"There's no one here now, so what's Ofi growling about?" asked Two Crow.

"Not sure, but if there's something mysterious here, Ofi will find it."

Ofi is in the back of the small cave sniffing around. He comes out and wanders about over the small plateau. More excited, he walks dangerously close to the cliff.

"YellowHawk, you better watch that dog or you're going to lose him over the cliff. I've seen him run and jump and he understands Choctaw, but I don't think he can fly," says Levi, with a laugh.

"Ofi issa binilichi." YellowHawk walks to the cliff's edge where Ofi has stopped what he is doing and sits. YellowHawk looks over the cliff's edge. His eyes find an object about a hundred feet below.

"I found what Ofi was growling about."

Everyone gingerly walks to the cliff's edge and peers over. Below is the lifeless body of a woman. She is lying next to a small pine tree, which has kept her from falling further down the mountain. She has landed in a small area jutting out from the mountain, about fifteen feet wide sloping downward. Without the tree, she would have fallen another hundred feet and never been found.

"One of us has to go down there to check if she is dead and look for some kind of identification," says Two Crow.

"I'll go," says Cody Simpson.

"Thanks Cody, but this is a job for me. I've got a little first aid experience should she still be alive.

All we have to do is figure out how." Two Crow retrieves his cell phone and calls dispatch to send an ambulance, giving instructions about the location of the body and the difficulty in retrieving it.

"We have plenty of rope here. We can tie it to that large pine over there for a safety anchor. Levi and I will lower you down. Have you ever rappelled before?" asks Roman.

"Hell no, but I don't want to be responsible for lowering one of you big guys down there."

As a precaution, two lines are tied to Two Crow and secured to a large tree. A loop is tied at the bottom end of the rope to place one foot in, leaving the other foot free to manipulate the jagged wall of the cliff. A loop is then placed just above his head, to slip one hand through to clutch the rope. No one in the group has any climbing or descending experience. Getting the body up will be left to the professionals.

Two Crow is strapped into the makeshift harness and gently lowered over the cliff's edge. After bouncing off the rock wall a couple of times, he arrives safely on the narrow shelf below. He quickly confirms the woman is dead. An execution style gunshot to the back of her head was made before she was pushed over the cliff. Two Crow didn't recognize the woman as being from this area. She is Caucasian, in her mid to late forties, a small woman, as YellowHawk suspected. She is about 5' 4" and weighs around 125 lbs.

He checks the back pocket of her tight fitting jeans and retrieves a leather credit card holder that contains a driver's license and five crisp hundred dollar bills. The license reveals she was much younger than she looks. Her name is Christina James, age 38 from Durant, Oklahoma. She was a bleached blonde and had her nails done recently. The front of her shirt is partially torn, exposing one of her breasts. There appears to be an entry wound, made by a bullet to her chest, nears the heart. Two Crow guesses she had implants, because the bullet appears to have ruptured one, causing it to deflate. She looks like she had been very attractive at one time, but suffered hard times in a short life.

"She's dead. Cody, will you go back to the road and guide the recovery here?"

Two Crow, defending the body, his eyes searches the crime scene for any useful evidence. Soon the recovery team and FBI investigators arrive and begin to do their work. Two hours later the four men watch as the body of the woman is lifted up the cliff and carried to the ambulance to take back to the morgue. There is no more they can do here. The trip back to the hospital is a somber one. This day was supposed to be a happy occasion, but within a moment it had turned tragic. Their friend has been shot and fights for his life in intensive care. The shooter's partner, or guide, has been executed. The shooter is long gone. Back under the rock he crawled out from, leaving no clue as to who he is or whom he serves.

CHAPTER 39

A crowded waiting room outside the second floor intensive care unit is packed with friends of Chief Tall Bear. Levi and Roman huddle and acknowledge their concern for the fallen Chief. Tammy looks at her husband with tears streaming down her cheeks, and they embrace. Levi walks over and hugs Senator Jim, whispering words of encouragement softly into her ear. This is all they can do, for nothing has been reported to them from the doctors.

Levi tells Tammy and Rachel what they discovered this afternoon. The ladies gasp when hearing of the dead woman found on the mountain ledge. Men discuss idle details when there's nothing else to say. Tribal officers, with the help of state law enforcement agencies, confirm the woman was indeed Christina James formerly from Dallas, Texas.

After attending high school in north Dallas and working in several gentlemen's clubs, she had moved on to drugs, prostitution, and methamphetamines. Favoring Native men she frequented the Indian bars in Durant. Her family had disowned her many years ago. Anyone who knew more was unlikely to speak for her. She probably knew who the shooter was, but had taken that information to the grave.

It was nearly 6 p.m. when Dr. Wolf and an assistant appeared to make a statement to those who filled in the room.

"Good news. Mr. Tall Bear is now out of surgery and resting comfortably. The bullet pierced his left lung and the surgeons were able to repair the damage. He is now on a ventilator to assist his breathing and will be for a couple of days. One of the bullets is lodged near his spine. We have decided to leave it in place for the time being. It is dangerously close to the spinal cord and quite frankly we want to see if Mr. Tall Bear is able to move his lower body when he comes out of the anesthesia. For now, I suggest you go home and get a good night's rest. We'll alert you if there are any changes in his condition."

It is decided several members of the staff will take turns waiting throughout the night and will alert everyone if any changes occur. Tammy and Roman decide to spend the rest of the evening with relatives, and Levi decides to spend the night in one of the hospitality rooms available to visiting staff members. Senator Jim asks if they will make one available to her as well.

Levi settles into his room, and attempts to watch some television while waiting for his food to arrive. Every news station within a hundred mile radius is reporting the story of the shooting. There has been genuine reaction from around the country. The FBI is concerned about a conspiracy to kill the leader of the Choctaw Nation. An agent is posted outside Levi's room for guarded measures. Not long after 8 p.m., there's a knock at the door. It is Senator Jim.

"Levi, can I come in?"

"Of course! Senator Jim! Please come in. I was finishing dinner. Can I get you anything?"

"No thank you, Levi, and please call me Rachel."

"Ok, Rachel. You look tired."

"Thanks for making me feel at home. I am tired but I'm also worried about John. Everything was going great. He's doing a wonderful job, getting important issues completed. I'm sure you must know by now we have some sort of connection."

"You don't say," mused Levi trying to lighten the mood.

"Nothing serious, he's very cautious and moves slowly. I know he's been very busy with the duties of the Chief's office. I just wish he would make more time for us. Sorry, I must sound like a silly jealous wife."

"Rachel, I know John cares big time."

"Why would anyone want to do such a thing?"

"Well, don't worry. John's a tough Indian and he's going to pull through. He hasn't confided in me, but he definitely perks up when your name is mentioned."

"Oh, Levi thanks for telling me that. It's nice to know. By the way, I've made several calls to Washington and called in some favors."

"What kind of favors?"

"I have some contacts at the National Security Agency in Baltimore, and I've called them to see if they can assist us."

"How can the NSA help us?"

"Satellites! At any given time there are several satellites sweeping the earth. You remember the movie Enemy of the State with Will Smith and Gene Hackman?"

"Yes I do. Good film, I've seen it several times on cable. Can they really do what they did in the film?"

"That and more. They can read the license plate on your car, providing they have a good angle. They can even see the color of your eyes."

"Is it possible they could have seen what happened on top of Buffalo Mountain?"

"That's what I've asked my contacts at the NSA to check. I've been told there's a good chance one of the satellites photographed the mountain side and would have captured some images."

"Well, what do we do next?"

"We need to fly to Baltimore, and I want you to go with me. I know you may feel the need to stay here, but I don't want to make this trip alone should something happen to John while I'm away."

"Rachel, John is going to be fine and everything at the Nation is on hold for the time being. My assistants at the office can take care of everything. When do you want to leave?"

"As soon as possible. I can have a car drive us to Muskogee and have a private jet ready to fly us to Baltimore."

"That's pretty country up there. I know a part Cherokee woman, Cindy Two Eagles who lives in that area. I was a guest in her home about five years ago. Fantastic cook too. She cooked everything Indian style the way I like it. Her home is like a museum filled with wonderful, hard to find Indian artifacts. She's well respected among the real Indians and the Pow Wow scene."

"Levi, is there any state in the union you don't know some woman? When did you have time to do all that? From what I understand, you're still friends with most of them."

"Well, not entirely true. When I was a young man travelling around, I would stay with kinfolks and do odd jobs. They would tell me about their kin elsewhere and I would go and stay with them. I'd do a little work for them and learn about the old ways. When they got tired of me, I would take off to visit somebody else. I wanted to see all this country. You know, the Indians in the old days would follow the game and wander north and south. I guess it's the restless Indian in me that kept me on the move. I had to jump out of a few windows a couple of times to save my backside, but for the most part, I am still friends with most of them."

"Levi, I don't know what to think about you. But I do want to stop by and check on John before we leave."

Before leaving, Rachel speaks with Dr. Wolf. He assures her John is resting comfortably and doing well. He promises to alert both should there be any changes in his condition.

After an hour's drive, Rachel and Levi board a small jet and are on their way to Baltimore, Maryland, home to the National Security Agency. They arrive around midnight and a car is waiting to take them to meet Rachel's contact. A staff member whisks them through all the security and they go deep into the Command Center. At Major Eric Harper's office, his second-in-command greets them. Major Harper knows they are in the building and within minutes joins them.

Senator Jim, it's an honor to meet you," As he shakes her hand, "I'm sorry it's not under better circumstances."

"Assistant Chief Tushka, I want to extend my deepest concerns to both of you for the harm to your friend, Chief Tall Bear. My people tell me he's in stable condition and resting well. While you're here, we'll be in constant communication with the hospital. If anything changes, we'll know about it."

"Major Harper, thank you for seeing us at this late hour. You know what has happened and the problems we face. We can't imagine why anyone would want to harm Chief Tall Bear."

"It's fair to say, we've ruled out the obvious, disgruntled ex-tribe members. We think this was a professional hit," says Levi.

"Chief Tushka, from the information we have, I'm inclined to agree. When I received Senator Jim's call, we began to look back at the satellite sweeping images of that time line. It's a little time-consuming, but we are getting closer. If you will follow me, we can visit the control center and see how they are progressing."

They are about to leave the office, when one of his aids knocks and enters the room. "Excuse me, Major Harper. We just found it. I knew you would want to know ASAP."

"That's great timing. Shall we go?" as he motions for them to follow the aid.

They are led down a series of hallways, through several security checkpoints and finally into a large room. They climb a short stairway to a control center overlooking an enormous room with seven huge television screens mounted on the wall. The control center is like a small theater with big comfortable chairs lined up behind the computer engineers. Their top engineer is working on this project, using the center screen as his personal workstation. They all take a seat. The Major explains. We found the right satellite, and programmed the land coordinates and timeline. The engineer zoom in on the targeted area, Talihina and the mountainside due west.

Due to the enormous search area, this has been a time consuming task. Given the name Eagles Nest, they focus on the mountain. Within a few minutes, the young computer engineer locates two people walking to the shooting site. As suspected, the woman leads a large man to a clearing on the mountainside. They watch as he sets up his equipment a few minutes before the time of the shooting. There is no sound but watch the animation of the two. They can only guess what's being said. Approaching the appointed time, the shooter secures a rifle on a tripod and takes his position. The woman stands behind him and looks back from time to time as a lookout. Watching the stillness of the shooter, they sense the shots would be coming soon. They don't hear the shots or see any muzzle fire, but they have an adjusted timeline of when the shootings occurred.

"He's a big man, looks like about 6'5" or 6' 6"," observes Levi.

"His hair looks so white and wild, maybe an older man?" adds Rachel.

They now see both become more animated, as he begins to tear down his equipment. The shooter motions for the woman to assist him and she does. As she crouches down on one knee, the shooter quickly stands up and moves behind her, and they see him pull an automatic pistol from inside his jacket. They watch in horror as he puts the gun near the back of her head and fires. She falls to the ground near the edge of the cliff. He takes one step toward her and fires again into her chest. He holsters the weapon, kneels down and pushes her over the cliff. They watch her fall, lands on the flat area, then rolls, tumbling another twenty feet where she comes to rest at the base of a pine tree. He stares at her body for a minute, then finishes disassembling his equipment, loads it into a carrying case, hefts it on his back and begins to walk away.

Suddenly he stops. He turns and walks back to the cliff's edge, looks down at the body, and then in the direction of his original target. Because of the angle, they don't have a clear image of his face, so his identity is still unknown. They already know the identity of the woman. Something in the sky catches the shooter's attention, and he looks up as if he is looking straight into the lens of the satellite. They know this is not humanly possible, but see what he is looking at, a bald eagle. The majestic bird soaring high in the afternoon sky, has given them a clear image of his face.

Levi is reminded of a song written by a fellow Choctaw. *What a man can't know, the eagle sees.*

Rachel comes out of her chair with her hand to her mouth. *'I've seen this man before.'* Before leaving NSA, Major Harper gives Senator Jim a photo of the shooter and tells her all agencies involved will have the same image in their systems within minutes. He assures her the shooter cannot stay under cover long, and when he reappears, one of their agencies will find him. Silently, the two are led through the hallways, past offices–security checkpoints–to the front entrance of the building. Rachel and Levi step out into the cool, damp Maryland night, and walk briskly down the marble steps leading to the parking area where their car is waiting. Before entering the car, Rachel stops and turns to Levi.

"Levi, I know I have seen this man before."

"Where do you know him from and what is his name?"

"I don't know his name."

"Why didn't you tell the Major you recognized the man on Eagles Nest?"

"Levi, I wasn't sure because it caught me by surprise, but now I'm sure I have seen him before."

"Well, are you going to tell me or not?"

"I'll tell you when we get on the plane. I want to leave this place now."

Rachel turns away and gets into the car. Levi throws his arms up, showing a little annoyance, but knows when not to argue with a woman, especially when she's a United States Senator.

———

Senator Jim and Assistant Chief Tushka board the small private jet in the wee hours of the morning. They settle into their seats, and Rachel waits until the jet has taken off and climbed into the sky to their cruising altitude. She then turns to Levi.

"I'm sorry to keep you waiting, but I needed some time to let this all sink in. So much has happened in the last twenty-four hours, and it's gotten me a little off balance. I wanted to be very sure before I said anything. I have seen the man in a photo in the company of Senator James Joe Cody. I don't know what his position is or how he is involved with Senator Cody, but I'm sure it's the same man."

"Senator Cody? Rachel, you got to be sure about something like this."

"For a moment back at NSA, I was in denial. I didn't want this to be true, because of who it involves. Senator Cody is one of our people. We are talking about implicating a U.S. Senator in an assassination attempt on the Chief of the Choctaws. If Senator Cody is somehow involved in this, it will be a catastrophic scar on all American Indians."

"Rachel, if what you say is true, it's not hard to believe. Senator Cody and Paul Wilson have been friends for over thirty years. John has just gotten the Senator's best friend forced out as Chief, so it's not a stretch to imagine his involvement."

"Levi, being forced to resign as Chief of the Choctaws is huge, but to conspire murder? There has to be more to this than we imagine. Both are intelligent, seasoned men of public office. I have worked alongside Senator Cody on more than one occasion. I just can't imagine he's mixed up in something as treacherous as this. Now, I'm tired, and going to try to get some sleep before we land. Then, I want to go straight back to Talihina and look in on John." Rachel snuggles down in her chair, closes her eyes and falls into deep sleep.

Levi is left alone to consider all the options. As he studies the grainy photo, he begins to feel he has seen the man too, but where? Was he the man at the gas station in Durant? He only got a passing glimpse of him. Could he be the same man that burned Macedonia Indian? As Rachel stated, much has happened in the last twenty-four hours.

John Tall Bear has is done a tremendous job in eight months, as Chief of the Choctaw. There were even whispers of him running for Governor or President some day. Now, he lies in intensive care

fighting for his life. What the hell is going on? Are Indians trying to kill Indians? Levi had met Senator Cody once, and he didn't like him then. He was a loud-mouthed politician saying what the people wanted to hear. If Cody has any involvement in the shooting of John Tall Bear, the Senator can run, but he can't hide.

CHAPTER 40

A
s the plane lands in Muskogee, Levi and Rachel's phones ring.
Tammy report John, has awakened and feeling good. The better
news is he exhibits no sign of paralysis in his arms or legs. Dr. Wolf
expects him to spend the morning in a battery of extensive x-rays and
further tests. Naturally, all are relieved.

Tammy estimate it may be late afternoon before John can have
visitors, and advise they take their time driving back. Up most of the
night, Rachel and Levi opt to eat before returning to Talihina. They
make their way east, near the outskirts of Muskogee, and find a mom
and pop cafe still serving breakfast.

Settling into a booth and ordering their food, they wait, listening
to a TV newscast from a flat screen mounted high in one corner. John
Tall Bear's shooting and recovery is still the lead story. An outpouring
of support and well wishes arises from the President to blue-collar
workers of America. Thousands of Indians throughout the state continue to converge on the tiny town of Talihina to honor the injured
Chief. Social media sparrows praise him. Some characterize the major
changes in the Choctaw Nation as 'revolutionary'.

"Senator Jim, have you decided what you're going to do with the
information you have?"

"Oh please Levi, Rachel. We are way past standing on formalities.
Yes, I've decided to call FBI agent Karen Rivers' office and give her a
statement of what I know and suspect. This is going to get nasty, and
I want no part of what they might have to go through to find the
answers. However, I would like to be a fly on the wall when she and

agent Jackson question Senator Cody. I'll be so disappointed if any of this is true. We Indians have so few people to look up to and emulate. I hate to see one of us go up in flames. But if he had anything to do with John's shooting, I'll light the match myself."

"That's the best way to handle this. You don't want to expose yourself and your office by withholding information about the identity of a high profile fugitive. I'm sure agents Rivers and Jackson will keep your office informed. As long as this guy is out and about, John is still in danger. Roman and I will add more security at the hospital until this dirt bag is captured."

On the television, a CNN reporter in Washington D.C. catches their attention, a questioning Senator Cody, emerging from a building.

"Senator Cody, Tony Green with CNN. What can you tell us about the shooting of Choctaw Chief John Tall Bear?"

"I'm disgusted!" shouted Senator Cody as he continues to walk. The reporter follows along with him. "Chief Tall Bear is a good man and has done great things since he has taken office."

"I know you were close friends with former Chief Wilson. There has been speculation your friend Wilson was forced to resign," mentions the reporter.

"There is not an ounce of truth in that statement! My good friend Paul Wilson felt it was time for new leadership, and his return to private life. I know for a fact he wants to move back to California where his ill mother lives and play more golf."

"With all due respect, Senator Cody, my sources say otherwise, that he's a bitter man."

"You can respect all you want, you piece of !*#*!*#*! ('white shit' in Kiowa)." Senator Cody mumbles inaudibly under his breath and jumps into a waiting car.

"That was Senator James Joe Cody, the powerful Kiowa Indian Senator from Oklahoma. He appears to have a little problem with the English language this morning. I'm guessing he was wishing me a late Happy Birthday. This is Tony Green, CNN, reporting from Washington. Back to you, Kyle."

"I understand a little Kiowa, and didn't sound like a birthday wish to me."

"I heard what he said, and I understood it. He disgusts me. I'm ready to leave." Rachel abruptly slides out of the booth and walks out the door. As all good men do, Levi quickly pays the bill and follows her.

Levi has called ahead and discussed with Roman what is needed to secure the hospital. It appears they are short of skilled security personal. Roman calls back to Durant to get more of his security team to assist in Talihina. However, it better to have too much than too little. Securities check points have been placed at all roads leading into the hospital. It is even tighter inside the hospital, where armed teams roam the hallways, constantly checking to see who needs to be in certain areas.

Outside of John's, room near the elevator, fans and supporters await his arrival from upstairs. Most know they will not be allowed to visit the Chief in his room. They just want to see him and wave as he emerges from the elevator and makes the short trip back to his room.

As the elevator doors open, the first person John sees is Rachel. What a pretty sight! Behind her are Levi, Roman, Tammy, several staffers and a dozen others. He's wheeled into his room and, after getting situated into the bed, the medical team leaves, except for Dr. Wolf. A few moments later Rachel, Levi, Roman and Tammy are permitted into the room.

Dr. Wolf addresses the visitors. "The Chief has been through as much as anyone should have, in the past 24 hours. We've had him up for most of the day running tests and what he needs now is rest. You can all stay 15 minutes. Tomorrow morning we want to have him up and walking, so tomorrow is going to be a big day in determining where we are in his recovery."

"John, the bullet in your back is not as threatening as we thought. In my opinion, if it's not causing you discomfort, we should just leave it alone for now. If you want, we can go back into surgery in a couple of days and take it out. The decision will be up to you."

"If you take it out, will it help my golf game?"

"Apparently, still be a little delirious from your pain medication?" Dr. Wolf, as seriously as he can emphasizes, "No, removing the bullet will not help your golf game."

"Well, hell, leave it where it is."

"Now that's the John Tall Bear we all know," says Levi.

"John, you take your golf game too damn seriously," mutters Rachel.

"Quite frankly, another one of my concerns is the slight concussion he received in the fall," says Dr. Wolf.

"When and how did he get a concussion?" asks Tammy.

"It happened as the shooting started," recalls Levi, when Roman threw his 240 pounds on the Chief."

"Are you telling me Roman gave me a concussion?"

"That's the only time it could have happened. When he threw his body on top of you, the force of the tackle caused your head to hit the floor of the stage."

"Roman, I'm going to trade you in for a middleweight bodyguard. You're too damn dangerous!" Now everyone is in stitches. "Ohoo, my head hurts just laughing."

"Chief, you are probably going to have some headaches for awhile. Remember, a concussion is a bruising of the brain. That's not good," says Dr. Wolf. "I hate to cut this party short. Let's all let John get some rest. I'm prescribing a mild sedative to help him sleep. John, tomorrow we'll get you on your feet, and maybe out the door in a few days."

Next day, as promised, Dr. Wolf gets John on his feet and moving again. For precautionary reasons, he is kept at the hospital until the end of the week and possible release Friday afternoon. Levi's gone back to Durant to run the Nation's business. They speak several times a day.

Roman and his security squad stay behind and continue to do what they do best, look after the Chief. Roman is going to make sure no one takes another shot at John. Rachel takes some vacation time to watch over John. After a couple of days, she gets around to telling him about her trip to the National Security Agency with Levi. John doesn't tell her Levi has already told him of the trip and what they found out. Levi felt it was important John know what was going on. The motive for the shooting is still anybody's guess.

Rachel passed the information she had to FBI agent Rivers. Agent Rivers commended her for a great piece of investigative work, saying it will be very helpful in finding the shooter. Major Harper and his team at NSA are able to identify the marksman on the mountaintop, and send it back down the chain to the McAlester FBI field office and Agent Rivers. Two days later, Rivers tells Rachel, Senator Cody has been questioned about the shooter. Senator Cody insists he hardly knew the man.

The NSA believes the man seen in the company of Senator Cody and the shooter, are one and the same, Gunter Steppenwolf, a German arms dealer. Steppenwolf had been working as a lobbyist, attempting to secure a counter intelligence contract with the State Department. It's believed he has already left the country, and all agencies are on high alert should he resurface.

During the next few days, Rachel and John spend quality time together. So much has happened in the last eight months. John feels caught up in a fast moving river, unable to swim against the current, on a mystery ride.

'There I go, giving myself too much importance.' Hey, I am the Chief *of the Choctaw Nation, and that's pretty good for someone who just barely made it out of high school with a 'C' average.'*

He doesn't want to think about the problems looming ahead. The Nation is in good hands with Levi at the helm. Lately, John has begun to feel Levi is more qualified than he to be Chief. John's philosophy is, if you are going to be successful at any endeavor, surround yourself with good people. John has made a good choice in Levi. Perhaps he will get his chance one day. And then there is Roman Billy. What a great find he is, and a credit to the Nation with his hard work and intelligence. And behind good men are even better women, like his wife Tammy Lynn.

Hospitalized in the town where he was born, John feels inadequate and unneeded. He must leave, swim in the fast moving waters and see where it takes him. There are many mysteries and a strong need for answers. First, 'Why did a German arms dealer named Steppenwolf shoot me?'

CHAPTER 41

John returns to Durant and takes the weekend off anticipating the work ahead. Letters, e-mails and phone calls, wish him a speedy recovery. Repeatedly, they mention a great grandmother who was full blood Indian. There are hundreds of requests to do searches for people and lost relatives, as the world re-discovers the Choctaw Nation.

What the people want, the media delivers. American people are hungry for more about the Indians and their Chief, John Tall Bear. He is asked to appear on several of the major talk shows and popular news programs. When producers of Brian Williams's The Eleventh Hour invite John for a feature interview, Rachel, a fan insists he accept. He too, likes the TV talk show host's quick wit, and no nonsense approach. Williams respects his guests, yet is willing to ask the hard questions. The Eleventh Hour is a good forum to remind the public 'Change is coming'.

Huge success can bring bad press for Indians when billions of dollars pour into their casinos and enveloping states want part of the action. Never mind laws that give Indians the right to run casinos on Indian lands. Some states favor pending legislation, which could allow non-Indian interests to compete with them. John considers this and various policy matters that deserve MSNBC treatment and accepts The Eleventh Hour invitation to represent the Choctaws.

Two weeks later, an executive producer of The Eleventh Hour leads John back stage. After a brief stop in makeup, they position him just off camera. An associate producer, who couldn't have been more than twenty-five, with a head set on and clip board in hand goes over a checklist of topics Brian might want to talk about. She asks John for matters he wishes to address as well. She cues him at thirty seconds. They wait as Brian Williams completes his introduction.

"Tonight we have a very special guest, Mr. John Wilkerson Tall Bear, the Chief of the Choctaw Nation. After taking office ten months ago, he caused a storm among his 200,000 some members, by changing a major membership requirement in his tribe. His ethical philosophy 'What is an Indian' generated a much smaller tribe, with just under 22,000 members. A recent assassination attempt thrusts him again into the greater public eye and made him front page national news."

By this time, they have seated John in a comfortable chair across the desk from Brian yet out of the tight camera shot of the host.

"Like the Hollywood people say, this is an exclusive, his first network television interview since the shooting. Chief Tall Bear welcome to The Eleventh Hour."

"Halito, and thank you for having me on your show. Please, call me John or Chief."

"Chief, my producers tell me you are on the road to full recovery. I want to personally wish you continuing success."

"Thank you, Brian."

"Your quick rise to Chief of the Choctaw's is a fascinating story in itself. But, first let's talk about the assassination attempt. I understand, to-date, no shooter has been apprehended. Can you tell my viewing audience why anyone would want to shoot you personally, or as Chief of the Choctaw Nation?"

"Brian, our first impression was it might have been a former disgruntled member of our tribe. Our tribal membership went from 200,000 to fewer than 22,000 when we put our new blood quantum requirements in place."

"I'm told Senator Rachel Jim of Oklahoma was very helpful."

"Within hours of the shooting my security team discovered evidence this was a professional hit. Senator Jim and Assistant Chief Tushka working with NSA were able to determine the identity of the shooter. Within 36 hours of the shooting all other agencies were notified. Gunter Steppenwolf is a wanted man."

"Pretty impressive work. That would account for the security team escorting you. Three of them checked out my staff pretty well and made some of them a little nervous. Somehow they missed me."

"You're speaking about Team Tuchina, my personal security. One of the three, Johnny Kick a Hole in the Sky can be a little intimidating to some. We tease him about his fan base of women in every state. And Brian, they know you to be a respected journalist and they trust the bond you have with your audience."

"With your rapid rise into the position of leadership, by any chance are you thinking about going into politics?"

"No, I've got all I can handle being Chief of the Choctaw Nation. Politics is too much like taking a moonlight walk in a cow pasture."

"You're not thrilled to mix and mingle with Fox News and assorted sycophants of the radical right?" Brian and John both share a laugh.

"Sycophants, I'll have to add that ten dollar word to my repertoire. Brian those named are staunch Republicans, however there are many Democrats who are just as misinformed."

"Thank you for reminding me, there are bad apples in almost every group. Chief Tall Bear, when you became Chief, one of the first and most controversial things you did was tightened the membership requirements of your tribe. Can you tell us why?"

"Well, Brian, first let me say this. We moved the requirement back to one quarter, as the federal government originally set it. However, in 1975 the Indian Self-Determination Act allowed tribes to set their own standard."

"Given the choice, why would the Indian Tribes change from the original one quarter standard? Knowing how proud Indians are of their heritage, I would have guessed they preferred more stringency."

"Very astute of you Brian. However, over the years, the former Chiefs who reduced the blood quantum requirement were creating larger tribes. This was a numbers game to get more federal dollars and grants to subsidize their programs."

"Now I'm beginning to understand, but I imagine diluting the requirements had repercussions."

"Right again Brian, this produced a group of 'whiter' Choctaws lining up for the services to the point of exhausting them. In my opinion, the one-quarter requirement for 'what is an Indian' is extremely liberal. The 'one drop of Choctaw blood makes one a Choctaw' assertion disrespects the sacrifices of our ancestors. With booming casino monies and health services in the balance, living full bloods were rightfully insulted."

"Chief, are there any other tribes insisting their members be full blooded Indian?"

"No! Most do not know this, but out of all Native Indians in the world, only 1% percent is full blood. Several tribes like the Mississippi Choctaw require members to be at least one half-Indian. Their requirements promote stronger bloodlines. Personally, I would prefer the requirements of the Mississippi Tribe. My staff of advisors talked me out of that."

"Correct me if I'm wrong, but I understand the previous Chief, Paul Wilson, was half Choctaw. Was his administration responsible for 'diluting' the blood quantum requirements for Choctaw tribal memberships?"

"Yes, Brian, his and other Chiefs before him. Ten months ago, the requirement to be a member of the Choctaw Tribe was essentially one drop of Indian blood. My team had done extensive research in the thirteen counties we service, and this is what we found. The 'whiter' the tribe got, the greedier they became. Bottom line, it's an insult to our brave Indian ancestors who made that tragic journey, the Trail of Tears, in 1832. They were forced to walk from Mississippi to Oklahoma during the harsh winter months. Three thousands of elders and small children died along the way. For anyone with small amount of Indian blood to feel entitled to full services in the Choctaw is offensive."

"Chief Tall Bear, that's pretty straightforward. I can tell you shoot from the hip and tell it like you see it. I understand your passion for your people, however the public perception is tribal members are getting rich from the casino revenues. You must have a lot of rich Indians out there in Oklahoma. My staff tells me your casino brings in millions..."

"Billions! I apologize for interrupting you, Brian, but the Choctaw Tribe has never given a penny of casino proceeds to individual tribal members before I took office. That's about to change at the end of this month, when Choctaw members will receive their first dividend checks. Our new plan is to re-distribute 15% of gaming revenue among our entire membership on a quarterly basis. This money will be enough to take care of basic necessities, pay mortgages, purchase a decent car and send their children to college. They aren't going to get rich as you say. It's not our nature to acquire great wealth."

"Chief, I find this fascinating. Obviously there are many misconceptions about the Native Americans? How is it 'not our nature (that is, the Native American) to acquire great wealth?'"

"You mentioned one in your question. Anyone born in this country can be called Native American. The US government has used that term most since the latter half of the 20th century to maintain a white male hierarchy. It's not specific enough. It's not guessing, most 'Indians' defined this way prefer something else. Choctaw language can be traced back 12,000 years before Christ. More educated individuals understand, though no one knows what the indigenous people of this land first called themselves. Common sense acknowledges

Choctaw people would have been called 'Chata'. Now, back to your last question about acquiring wealth.

"The 'white man' has generally despised the Indian for the way we lived in (relative) poverty and simplicity. Our ancient philosophy forbids the accumulation of great wealth and enjoyment of luxury. The burdens of a complex society are needless peril and temptation. It is the rule of our life to share the fruits of our skill and success with the less fortunate members of our family, clan or tribe. Love is wonderful, but lust destroys. The building of great cities, creating crowded and unsanitary dwellings, causes the loss of spiritual powers. Those who live in the Creator's Cathedrals know magnetic forces accumulate in solitude, but are neutralized by life in a crowd."

"Interesting and very eloquently stated, Chief Tall Bear. You have also said, 'When the tribe starves, the whole tribe starves. When you eat, the whole tribe eats.' That sounds a little like a socialist government."

"Now you mention it, it does. However, I see it more as democratic socialism. I can vision a small body of Chiefs, War Chiefs with an elected Supreme Chief ruling a group of tribes. This body would not own property, but would insist tribal wealth be evenly distributed."

"Sounds pretty simple."

"Brian, we live in a complex society and this type of government would not work today, because capitalism and greed is ingrained in man and society."

"Chief, makes you wonder how we went from simple governments to today's enormous wealth disparities?"

"I read the daily papers and watch MSNBC and occasionally FOX for information. Correct me if I'm wrong. Four percent of the American populace have more money than the other ninety six percent combined. The majority of that four percent are members of the Republican Party. Capitalism created the disparity. If one's life missions in to acquire all the money he or she can, so be it. As a good man, I'm sure Creator would frown on this accumulation of wealth without sharing. That kind of wealth is spiritually worthless. Look at it this way. You can't spend that kind of money in a lifetime and you damn sure can't take it with you. If these four percent refuse to share, they are no different than the rich dictators of the world who live in luxury as their people suffer. It's a sad situation when forty percent of Americans cannot handle a $1000 emergency crisis. A simple government, like our ancient American Indians used, is one that looks after all its people, not just a few."

"Chief, this is embarrassing to ask, but we know 'the drunken Indian' stereotype, can you tell us how you deal with that ugliness?"

"Brian, running a casino is all about the money. We know there will be gambling and drinking addiction. We will spend great sums of money for education and treatment. The day I was shot, we broke ground for a state of the art alcohol treatment center at my birthplace Talihina, Oklahoma.

"Thousands of treatment centers tout the 28-day treatment program, but we know it's just a revolving door. Therefore, our minimum stay is six months and can extend it to one year. We know there will be casualties. But, the casualties and the slow death of our race began over 600 years ago. When the 'white man' introduced alcohol and tobacco to our ancient warriors, they overthrew the honor of our men. The warrior was no longer able to protect his wife and children from the 'white man's lust. When she fell, the whole race fell with her. The 'white man' had centuries to learn how to drink alcohol, however the Indian has only had 600 years to learn how to deal with it. Alcohol and tobacco products are no longer offered in our establishments. It's costing us millions, but it's the right thing to do. It has done too much damage and yet, as we announce, 'Change is Coming', we are challenged to save as many as we can."

"Chief, I studied American history in college and very little of it traced the American Indian timeline. I'm sure you have pearls of knowledge to share with us. Let's talk about them on the other side."

CHAPTER 42

"We are back with John Wilkerson Tall Bear, who's agreed to guide us with the keen eyes of a Native Warrior on an Eleventh Hour journey. He speaks with the wisdom of an elder's counsel, in the bold voice of a man elected to serve the Choctaw Nation as Chief. Before our station break, I asked him to give me a remedial crash course in American Indian History."

"Brian, for you and many, who belong to a powerful majority (i.e., rich white American men) has a common oversight. Whether you defy or deny the existence of white privilege, much of what I'm about to say shouldn't offend anyone personally."

"All right Chief, though I do find those who deny their pigment, or stubbornly refuse to differentiate obsolete mythology and working science, boorish."

"Pleased you feel the same way. Think about this Brian. Rich white men who catalogue their achievements and crank out others they've appropriated, stack-self serving lie on top of lie. People like myself are invisible because we are Indian, not white.

"Studying and teaching martial arts, like others in the United States, I felt immersed in an 'Eastern' art. Having seen enough, I began sharing warrior movements taught by my father, uncles and grandfathers in the 1940's. Having resurrected them, I was met with a good bit of skepticism because what they witness and studied where seen through blue eyes not brown. Through subsequent research, I have been able to extend a warrior system developed in America systematically throughout time, at least since the end of the last Ice Age."

"Chief Tall Bear, can you give us a big picture number for that time?"

"Certainly, Early American Indian history begins near 12,000 B.C., determined by the archeological discovery of projectile points (arrowheads) found in the Mississippi Valley region. Now, these are your scholars, and scientist, not mine. Making points is a very sophisticated process even with modern tools. The purpose for mass production of points was warfare–protection of family, cities, territory, and way of life. Prior to this, early Natives would have first defended themselves with empty hands. This leads us to the natural order, for the learning progression of martial arts. First there were empty hand, second, weapons in hand, and then, refinement of both."

"Does this book (holding The Apprentice Warrior authored by Chief Tall Bear) explain?"

"Somewhat Brian, but that book was basic common sense self-defense for those that didn't want to attend a martial arts school. In the book, I share the Seven Sacred Feather and its Native philosophies."

"Chief I did a quick read of the book and it enlighten me into a mood to appreciated all we neglect about our environment. I'm a fan. Continue on about your study."

"Let me be a little more in-depth then. Collective knowledge leads to principles of strategic warfare. I named the whole process 'Red Warrior' in defiance of the 'white' man's prejudice. The Choctaw subtitle is Falammichi Ibbak Chukillissa, to "Defend and Restore with the Empty Hand.""

"Chief, that's fascinating, thank you for teaching me and the audience a bit of Choctaw history and language. My staff had told me you're a master of martial arts. I too have my own security team. Producers Barbara and Diane always run interference and keep me out of trouble. Chief don't test me, I've got both of them as backup. Right?" teases Brian, glancing their way.

This cues a cameraman to break the fourth wall and catch two side stage managers shaking their heads 'no' in mock terror, comically defying their boss.

"No? Okay, I guess I'm on my own. In many ways it's been one of Eleventh Hour's most wide-range investigations. Chief, tell us about Indian religion, if you will."

"I can't speak for all Indians, though I know something about the ancient religious ways. Some of what I am about to say is personal theory. No one religion has all the answers about the Great Mystery. 'God' or 'Creator' is not a big enough word to describe All He/She is. For lack of a better word, I use Creator. I believe in Creation.

"Creator/Lord/God didn't write the Bible, He was its inspiration. Man wrote the words and is subject to misunderstanding–flawed, built to make mistakes, coded for error. The Bible tells us Creator made one pair of man and women. Could He/She not have made many pairs to multiply Mother Earth, thus the different skin tones, ethnic groups and languages?"

"Sounds like Comparative Theology which allows for diversity of beliefs."

"Well said Brian, the problem is many are narrow minded and will ignore other opinions and options. My mother brought me up in the church. However, this will trouble some, I no longer believe in prayers or miracles. I have suffered great losses and prayed thousands, if not millions of times and none were answered to my knowledge. As I previously stated, I believe in our Lord, God, or Creator. We are put on this earth to find ourselves, make our decisions and suffer the consequences without divine intervention. Oh, I still pray or speak to Creator out of habit, but its more venting to myself without grand expectation. Ask yourself this, 'why would Creator answer your prayers and not others praying for the same thing who have a greater need'? To be fair to all is not to intervene in the natural order of the universes. Miracles are moments in life when everything falls into place for someone or something and creates a positive outcome. We were all created sons of the Creator and we stand tall, conscious of our divinity.

"I question why man spends millions on grand buildings to worship, collects millions to support the pastor and his jets. Shouting God's name in a grand building is not our way. What better place to have a conversation with Creator than among the natural elements of the Creator's world. Is there no greater cathedral than walking among the tall trees, or walking in the moonlight? As an elder, I have come to know and understand more about my personal beliefs and the Creator."

"Chief, I'm curious, was this theory taught to you by your parents?"

"No, Brian, my mother was a Christian. However, I have a little more information than she did. Native history tells us thousands of our people died at their hands. I believe Christianity and other religions among modern civilizations are contradictory and have irreconcilable differences. It is my personal belief after all these years; there is no such thing as a 'Christian civilization' today. This is why I was confused for so many years. However the Spirit of Christianity, most other religions and our ancient Indian religion of the Great Mystery/Creator are essentially the same."

"Chief Tall Bear, that was very interesting and eloquently stated. Hearing your theory is a first for me and I'm sure for most of our viewers. It's obvious you have a distrust of politicians. So how do you balance that when you go to Washington?"

"I have never been to Washington on behalf of the tribe, and hope I never have to go. We have programs in place jointly funded by the federal government. We will continue to keep those in place as long as federal dollars are available. My goal, however, is to become independent of Washington in the near future. We will eventually stand-alone."

"Chief, the old time views of your people is refreshing to hear. We've elected a black President, now how about an American Indian President of his own country. Indulge me, what might this country gain from an American Indian President."

"Brian, Indian's have come a long way from being considered savages without souls. The Standing Bear Trial of 1879 found us to be human. Hard to imagine, that was not long ago! We were made citizens and allowed to vote in 1906, some thirty-six years after the black man was allowed to vote. Voting was state regulated and recently as 1957 Natives could not vote in some states. Do I need to remind all, this was our country first?

"First of all, it would be difficult to find someone who's qualified. The Indian man today has been stripped of his identity for several hundred years. Many never find their way back, and those who do are mentally wounded and would want nothing to do with the office of President. A modern Indian of today could take the values of our ancient ways and begin to influence those values in America. However, it would take just as long to restore it as it has taken to get us to this place. Brian, it's nice to dream, 'what if', but it's not likely to happen in my lifetime."

"Chief, okay, as long as we're dreaming, let me ask you this. Knowing your distain for politics, I'm sure you wouldn't be afraid to step on anyone's toes. I assume you have no intention of running for office. I'd like to ask you this. What would be some of the things you would do first if you were the President of the United States?"

"Brian, now that would be a fun day at the 'Red House'."

"I like it already. And how about having the corporately owned politicians, and other misfits, painting the White House red? Maybe even some 'Illegal' Mexican immigrants could supervise and give orders," says Brian. "Now there's a lesson in human rights recognition!"

"Brian, I can see you're getting into this, but I was kidding about the Red House. In spite of what the White House image might mean to some Indian people, I still consider it sacred ground, better leave as is."

"Sorry, Chief, I couldn't resist and got carried away. Please continue."

"Back to my day at the White House. First, it's common knowledge, substantiated by Bills in Congress, the U.S Government with guns forced approximately 500 treaties on American Indians. In the end, all of these treaties were broken. I would insist the Federal Government honor all these broken treaties. The very characters of the US founding fathers are in question until they are made to stand behind and honor their own agreements. If America is truly going to be the leader of the free world, then its government must stand true to its word."

"Second, I would instruct the liquor & tobacco industries to cease manufacturing today and find another way of doing business. We have become a society of too much tolerance and apathy. Every day in every major city you read in the papers or watch news stories of alcohol and tobacco products taking people's lives. Alcohol is partly responsible for the downfall of the American Indian. His history is ignored for it threatens whiteness."

"Whew, Chief, for a guy that eschews politics, that was a heck of an inaugural blast!"

"You haven't heard the better half. Simply put, I would insist on universal health care for all. Those who've fallen to bad health and disease appreciate, if one is healthy, you are wealthy. A healthy society is a productive society.

"America is a land of immigrants, therefore I would open our borders. Why should we turn away the very people we once were? The Europeans fled their homeland for ours running from injustice.

"Last and as importantly, I seriously think we should revise, not abolish the 2nd Amendment. We preach to the world as a powerful, just, and intelligent nation, but aren't smart enough to recognize, much of the law we are governed by is obsolescent. The American male no longer needs to hunt and kill game for the table. One person doesn't need 47 handguns and rifles and the average citizen doesn't need to own an assault rifle fitted with huge magazines.

"The NRA is largely a group of men who, without their guns, are not men. Their delusional members put food out, sit in blinds, shoot animals with high-powered weapons and call cruelty and murder 'hunting'. To kill the Creator's animals just to hang their mounted heads on a wall is shameful. An American Indian President would be a humanitarian first and Mother Earth would be his church."

"Chief I'm sure the NRA won't be sending you a Christmas card."

"Brian, here's the tragedy. The data shows there are 10,000 deaths due to homicides in America every year. Mass shootings have become normalized. Everyone needs to consider this. If there were a total ban on assault rifles like the AR-15 and a partial ban on other weapons, with the exception of law enforcement and those who protect our borders, how many of those 10,000 could be at home sharing a meal with their family?"

"Well Chief, you just took on half the country. But, what the hell! It's been entertaining listening to you rattle some cages. Chief John Tall Bear I respect your opinions. I know these are passionate concerns of yours from your experiences as an American, and most especially, as an American Indian. It's been an enlightening visit and, the way the switchboard is lit up, you struck a chord in the heart of many and the behinds of many others. Chief, it's been a pleasure." Brian extends his hand and the interview is over.

CHAPTER 43

T he Eleventh Hour appearance creates a busy two weeks for Chief
Tall Bear. After the show, his office is inundated with requests for
interviews from newspapers, guest appearances on other programs,
and overall interest in the Choctaw Nation. Following a particularly
long day at the office, dinner at home, and an hour on the phone
with Rachel, John decides to turn in. It's almost 11:30. He's about
to pull the covers back and jump into bed when the phone on the
nightstand rings.

'*This can't be good*', looking at the caller ID and seeing its Levi.
Picking up the phone, "Levi, what's up?"

"John, I'm down at the casino."

"I thought so. I can hear the slot machine noise in the background.
This better be important. What did you do, lose your pay check?"

"John, I know this is going to sound strange, but we have some
kind of phenomenon going on down here. I haven't had anything to
drink and I know it's late, but trust me, you're going to want to see
this with your own eyes."

"Levi, it's almost midnight. Just tell me what it is."

"John, no, you've got to come! All I can tell you it has something
to do with the Buffalo statue in the main lobby. I'll tell you more
when you get here."

"Ok, I'm on my way."

The casino is a short ten-minute drive. If everything goes well,
John can be back home and in bed by 1 a.m. He trusts Levi's judgment.

It must be something of great importance to insist he come to the casino at this late hour.

The Sacred White Buffalo sculpture in the main lobby of the new casino is a magnificent showpiece, with a cascading waterfall as a backdrop. American Indians view the white buffalo as a sacred symbol, like other significant prophetic signs, the weeping statues, bleeding icons, and crosses of light prevalent within Christian churches. Some see these as a renewal of God's ongoing relationship with humanity.

The odds of the birth of a white buffalo calf are estimated at 610 million to one. One was born near Caddo Mills, Texas a few years ago. Casino designers thought the sculpture would be the symbol of a new beginning for the Choctaw Nation.

As Tall Bear approaches the casino, he can tell it is a busy night from the overflowing parking lot. Rather than park his car and take a shuttle to the front door, he decides to drive up to the front entrance and park. After all, who is going to tell the Chief of the Choctaws he can't park there?

As he walks through the front entrance, he can see a small crowd viewing the showpiece in the main lobby. Levi, Roman and several of the casino staff are standing and talking amongst themselves. As John gets closer, he can see the problem. At first, he thinks it must be some kind of prank, but quickly dismisses the thought. This is far more serious. When John approaches, Levi turns to acknowledge him.

"How long has this been going on?"

"The staff noticed it about an hour ago and brought it to the attention of the night shift manager, Gary Holt."

"Sorry to get you out so late, Chief," says Roman. "The staff called maintenance to come and see what they could do. They tried to wipe it away and figure where it was coming from but as you can see, to no avail. Gary called me, I called Levi, and now you know why Levi got you down here."

"Gary, let's get this area petitioned off from the guests and see what we can do about this."

"Sure thing Chief." He and one of his assistants, hurry off to get the necessary equipment.

"John, there's something really strange going on here. The maintenance crew got a ladder up there to see where it's coming from and they saw nothing. There's no hole. It just appears out of nowhere, and now the water is beginning to turn pink," says Levi.

At the base of the White Buffalo is a large pool of water. The design of the centerpiece is made to look as if the statue is standing on water.

"Chief, the pool was clear when I got here an hour ago," says Roman.

"A marble statue with blood red tears streaming down its face, and dripping into the water pool, that's a first for me," puzzles Levi.

Chief Tall Bear, with his gaze fixed on the Sacred White Buffalo, mysterious red tears flowing from its eyes, takes charge.

"Someone call Pastor Nohubby and get him on the phone. And see if we can locate a medicine man or two. Call Two Crow in Talihina and have him tell YellowHawk our buffalo statue is crying blood tears. I've seen this in a vision in the Sweat in Talihina a few months ago. When I was shot, I thought the shooting was related to the vision. Now I know I was wrong. The vision was preparing me for this and an event of tragic significance. It's pointing us to a path or doorway to uncover an unknown secret. I need answers now!" Feeling the urgency, but knowing he needs some sleep before facing what is ahead, he turns and leaves.

———

John wakes up in a troubled mood a little before 6 a.m. He immediately calls the casino night manager, Gary Holt, and is informed nothing has changed except the deepening color of the water pool. Per instructions, Gary has closed the room off to the general public, by posting construction notices. No one is allowed in the area. All employees have been sworn to secrecy in fear of losing their jobs. For the time being, the media has no knowledge of what is happening behind the walled off casino lobby.

John calls Levi and Roman and schedules an 8 a.m. meeting at his office. Levi informs him YellowHawk is on his way from Talihina, bringing with him a medicine man. Tall Bear waits till 7 a.m. before calling Rachel to articulate the happening. She wants to attend, but he stalls her off until they know more.

He arrives at the Choctaw Capitol around 7:30 to find everyone already in place so the meeting begins early. Levi has picked up coffee, breakfast snacks, donuts and has everyone seated in the main conference room waiting for John's arrival. On one side of a boardroom table sit Roman, the Pastor, Two Crow, YellowHawk, and Ironhorse, a medicine man from Talihina. After introductions, the medicine man stands and offers a firm strong hand to Tall Bear.

Staring into friendly, dark brown eyes, this man is clearly in his early 70's, well over 6' 3", 225 lbs., and in great shape. Mind you, Roman, Levi and John are not small men but Ironhorse dwarfs them. He looks like a prototype NFL quarterback. His faded Levis top Ostrich boots which display scuffmarks from a stirrup. A colorful red shirt flashes out from under an elk leather vest that shows wear. His salt and pepper hair is pulled back into a ponytail reaching the middle of his back. A silver feather dangling from one earlobe along with a leather choker strung with bear claws make it very clear, he is Indian.

What becomes obvious to all, as they stand shaking hands, is Ironhorse could pass for John's older brother or, maybe even his father. Eyes cannot ignore the unspoken connection between the two. Shaking hands, John can feel the energy begin to flow between them.

On the other side of the table, sitting beside Levi, is a strikingly beautiful medicine woman named Tish-ah-yah-hanah. Choctaw County, Mississippi is her home. She is visiting relatives in nearby Tishomingo. Levi, having heard of her reputation, invited her to sit in on the meeting. Beside her are a couple of surprise guests, Thomas ThunderHawk and July Tecumseh, two Indian leaders of the Indian march and takeover and now members of Team Tuchina. Their third member Johnny Kick a Hole in the Sky is visiting New Mexico

"Halito, I want to thank all of you for coming at this early hour. I assume all of you know of the event at the casino or you wouldn't be here. You're a collection of Indians filled with wisdom and knowledge of our culture. I've asked you here for your advice. I want to share with you a vision. I need your experience and interpretation. As I told some of my staff last night, whatever is happening with the White Buffalo sculpture was presaged in my vision. Assistant Chief Tushka, Roman Billy, and I attended a Sweat in Talihina several months ago. When I was shot, I thought the shooting was part of the same vision in Talihina. Now I know I was wrong. That was not the event the vision was pointing me to. When I saw the sculpture last night crying red tears, I made the right connection. I didn't say so, but I'd also had an earlier vision but dismissed it. Now I believe it may have a connection as well. Last year, prior to getting involved with CMA and the Choctaw Nation, I participated in a Sweat. It was my first Sweat in twenty years.

"In my vision, an ancient Roman solider and an American Indian Warrior are riding horseback, side by side, on a mountain top. In a valley below I see a herd of buffalo led by a magnificent White Buffalo. At the time I believed the two warriors were on a buffalo hunt together. In this vision I saw red streaks running down the side of the White Buffalo as if he had been wounded. I now believe this vision was trying to tell me something, perhaps reveal a doorway to the past. I have reached some conclusions, but I wish to ask for your interpretation first."

Roman Billy, analytical and extremely organized, begins writing on a notepad in front of him.

Levi says, "Both of your visions have the white buffalo. The red could signify our People."

"The red could stand for blood too," adds Thomas ThunderHawk.

"It could stand for death as well," July Tecumseh says.

"Two different warriors, anybody?" asks Tommy YellowHawk.

"This is just a thought, but the Chief said the first time he met Roman Billy was at the church. Roman was a soldier in the military and the Chief is an Indian warrior from the martial arts," says Charlie Two Crow.

"That's something to consider, two warriors from different eras sitting on horseback," says the medicine man, Ironhorse.

Roman who is feverishly writing down all the comments says, "Now we're getting somewhere. I can see a connection."

"The Creator states many events are by his design. You put these two visions and current events together, a story begins," says Pastor Nohubby.

"Chim ma aiyua achafa," says Tish-ah-yah-hanah.

John had been waiting for this interesting woman to speak up. "What do you mean 'the chosen one'?"

"Tall Bear," Tish-ah-yah-hanah stands and walks over to John who is still seated. Tall and slender, she moves with a quiet grace. As she glides, her athletic legs push a cotton dress cut just below the knees decorated with beaded feathers. Her long black hair, cascades over soft shoulders and hangs down the middle of her back. The hem of the dress gently touches the top of a magnificent pair of leather boots. Her elk skin boots are covered with intricate braiding. They were old and showing some wear, but he imagines they were once very expensive.

"I have a small gift for you." Tall Bear stands to receive it. She gently holds his hand and places a small object wrapped in very old piece of deerskin into his hands.

"Thank you Tish-ah-yah-hanah. I am honored to have your gift." He wants to give her a hug, but is respectful and chooses not to. He unwraps the small object and is puzzles. It looks familiar, but he doesn't know why.

She turns and says, "Gentleman, I believe Tall Bear was chosen to rescue the Choctaw Nation. As far away as Mississippi, I have heard many negative comments from our brothers and sisters in

Oklahoma. The Choctaw Nation has lost its way and has become more like 'white man'.''

"What you say is true of the past," responds Levi. "However, Chief John Tall Bear has made many changes since he came into office. I know of his plans for the future of our Nation and they are righteous. With the changes already in place, and those to come, we will restore our image of a caring Nation. Our people will be proud to call themselves Oklahoma Choctaw."

"Tish-ah-yah-hanah is a wise woman and I agree," says Ironhorse. "The spirits are restless and are working together to bring about some sense of order. They see in Tall Bear someone whose heart is good, one who possesses the values of the ancient ways. They are channeling their energy through him. He is the messenger. He surely is Chim ma aiyua Achafa."

"Chief, I've put everything said into my impression of the events," says Roman. "Your first vision motivated you to attend Achille Indian Baptist to meet our group, dissatisfied with the direction of the Choctaw Nation and looking for new leadership. When two of our young members died senselessly, anger and sympathy caused Indians to speak out, and insist on being heard. This motivated many to march in the protest led by Mr. ThunderHawk, Mr. Tecumseh and Mr. Kick a Hole in the Sky."

"How do you relate ThunderHawk and Tecumseh's involvement in the march, to the Chief's visions and what is happening at the casino?" asks Charlie Two Crow.

"Well, it might be a stretch, but the two ancient warriors could signify ThunderHawk and Tecumseh too."

"Roman, you could be on the right track. Can you connect the loss of the brothers, Gary and Don Taylor with any of this?" asks Two Crow.

"Two Crow, I'm not sure. I'm just guessing, but Gary and Don Taylor could also signify the two warriors, as they were fighting for the cause of Chahta Amoma Atokoli."

"What does Chahta Amoma Atokoli have to do with all this?" asks Tommy YellowHawk.

"YellowHawk, don't you see? The Chief came to the church to meet me and I was sent to the church by our organization, which eventually became known as 'Chahta Amoma Atokoli'."

"Okay, now I follow you. Your name is Roman and you were a marine soldier and Chief Tall Bear is a martial arts warrior, so two warriors," says YellowHawk. "I thought I was going to need my partner Ofi, to follow your tracks." Everyone laughs at his comment, which lightens the mood in the room.

"Is everybody in agreement with this train of thought?" John asks. All nod their heads. "Does anyone have any suggestion as to what we should do next?"

"We are in search of answers not in this room," states Tish-ah-yah-hanah. "It would be a good idea to go to the spirit world and seek guidance. The information came by way of two visions the Chief experienced. I suggest we all attend another Sweat Ceremony and participate in a vision quest as soon as possible."

Where did Levi find this woman? She looks to be in her seventies, yet has a youthful air and shows great wisdom. She has spoken only twice but makes perfect sense.

"Ironhorse, John asks. "If you were in my position, what would you do?"

"I would follow the words of Tish-ah-yah-hanah. Her accent is like beautiful flowers, each adds splendor to our ears, hearts, and minds. Her talk offers comfort to the weary, music for the soul. Her eyes see beyond the great desert and past the mountaintops. She is wise beyond her years. Ironhorse would walk beside her any day and anywhere."

Listening to Ironhorse assessment of Tish-ah-yah-hanah, John too was reminded of her accents and special rhythm in her speech pattern of Mississippi Choctaws. "Ok! I stand with Tish-ah-yah-hanah and Ironhorse. Is everyone else in agreement?"

"Chief, ThunderHawk and Tecumseh have performed hundreds of Sweats. They may be young, but they are old school when it comes to the Indian tradition of holding a Sweat," says Levi.

"Chief Tall Bear, I would like to volunteer my property down in Bokchito. We've held a few down by Muddy Boggy Creek. Everything you need is already there. I can make sure everything is in place to have it tonight," says Pastor Nohubby.

"Thank you Pastor Nohubby. It's settled then. Let's meet there at 6:30 this evening and begin the Sweat soon after. Pastor Nohubby, will you lead us in a closing prayer?"

John spends the rest of the day meeting with different program directors, planning functions, making, taking calls. He phones Rachel to tell her of their plans for a Sweat later in the evening. She's never been to one and asks if she can join in. John is pleased to have her company, and gives her directions, agreeing to meet her at Pastor Nohubby home at 6:30. He checks in with the day manager at the casino, and nothing has changed.

He calls Levi to his office and questions him about Tish-ah-yah-hanah. Did he know more about her than what he had disclosed this morning? John is intrigued by her presence. Her spiritual essence is greater than her physical appearance, her inner strength and power astound. There is more to her than meets the eye. John asks Levi to tell him about Ironhorse the medicine man.

Ironhorse is thought to be in his early seventies, maybe more, no one knows for sure. Levi has heard stories about him since he was in his late teens. Ironhorse is a legend all over the state. It seems everyone has a story to tell about the old Medicine Man. There are tales how he could hit powerful home runs on the baseball diamond, score a hundred points in a pickup basketball game. He had beaten several men in a bar fight, killed a grizzly bear with his hunting knife. The stories went on and on.

No one knows for sure if any are true, bottom line, everyone knows not to go up against IronHorse. The odds of meeting two such extraordinary people in the same day are like being struck by lightning at the golf course on a sunny afternoon. John feels time will reveal the mystery behind their true personas.

CHAPTER 44

Levi, Roman and John leave for Bokchito around 5:30. Passing by George's Hamburger Drive-in tests their discipline, for they know they should fast the rest of the day. The drive east on the winding Highway 70 to Bokchito is pleasant and uneventful. Bokchito is a small town named after a large creek near the eastside of town. It is a typical small Oklahoma town, with a population just over 500, barely large enough to support a U.S. Post Office. The town is mostly non-Indian, with the Native population only around 15%. There is a gas station, one mom and pop family restaurant, and no fast food chains. The town closes up shop at 7 p.m.

After 45 minutes of discussion and anticipation, they arrive at 6:15. Everyone else begins to arrive. ThunderHawk and July Tecumseh have everything prepared for their Sweat. The lodge is a little small and won't accommodate everyone. It is decided only Roman, Levi and John, plus Rachel, YellowHawk, Ironhorse and the lady Tish-ah-yah-hanah, will participate in the Sweat. John is concerned that Tish-ah-yah-hanah has not arrived yet. The Pastor will sit out, and Charlie Two Crow will assist ThunderHawk and Tecumseh. The men are wearing running shorts and t-shirts. Rachel is decked out in sweat pants and a matching top from Neiman Marcus. John teases her about being somewhat over dressed, so she strips down to running shorts and a tank top exposing her well toned body. That was a mistake, now he cannot keep his eyes off her. The light of the moon illuminates her tan skin, flaunting a college girl aura. She obviously works out and eats the right kinds of food to maintain her youthful appearance. The Senator is quite a package.

ThunderHawk and July Tecumseh are giving final instructions for this Sweat. It will be only one round instead of the customary four. This is a special ceremonial, because of the urgency, and Tecumseh says he has a surprise in store. It will be a Sweat of endurance as well. Just as he finishes speaking, the elusive and somewhat mysterious Tish-ah-yah-hanah suddenly materializes.

It is already dark, and she emerges out of a wooded area east of the Sweat Lodge. As she approaches, her image is backlit by a bright full moon. The low bottom area near Muddy Boggy Creek has created a lite fog. It is a little eerie seeing a beautiful woman in deerskin Indian regalia appears out of fog. Her dress is adorned with magnificent beads and bone work. Her hair cascades down her shoulders and back, and she looks much younger than she did this morning.

John did not hear her car drive up, but because they are anxious to get started, he dismisses the thought. Thought to be the eldest, therefore she enters the lodge first. John doesn't expect her to enter as she is dressed, but she does. He wonders to himself how she will survive the high temperature in the lodge, so decides to keep an eye on her in case she should show signs of distress.

Medicine Man and YellowHawk follow Tish-ah-yah-hanah into the Sweat lodge, in a clockwise manner, and take their seats. ThunderHawk and Tecumseh have filled the floor with red cedar chips. It has a wonderful aroma. John guesses this is Tecumseh's surprise. Red Cedar is considered a sacred wood, and this is the first time John has experienced the use of it in a Sweat. He is excited, looking forward to a good adventure.

Together, they all begin to pray softly to themselves. As in their ancient way and customs, prayer to the Creator is of a personal nature and not for the ears of many. They are given a 'talking sticking' and begin sharing with each other something of themselves, beginning with the last to enter. Tish-ah-yah-hanah's, 'talking stick' in hand begins to chant in a Choctaw dialect unfamiliar to John. He can understand some of the words, but it is still confusing. *'I wonder if Levi is confused too, but he speaks the language better than me.'*

ThunderHawk begins to bring in red-hot glowing rocks. After a couple of trips, he begins pouring sacred water onto the rocks, and the steam and temperature begin to rise within the lodge. Outside July Tecumseh begins to drum slowly, calling for the spirit world to come forth. As the temperature rises, so do their senses. They are fifteen minutes into the Sweat when ThunderHawk comes in and sprinkles something on the hot rocks. Sparks begin to fly, and a strange aroma springs forward, further triggering the senses. He leaves and John begins hearing someone playing the flute as Tecumseh intensifies the drumming.

He looks at Rachel to his left, and sees her skin glowing from the light of the hot rocks. She looks like something magical. She is surely experiencing something, as her eyes are closed and she is slowing swaying to the rhythm of ThunderHawk's flute. The heat and steam are beginning to affect all inside. Levi directs John to looks at Tish-ah-yah-hanah. Everyone is sweating profusely except her. She looks like she is ready to go for a midnight walk or dance in the sacred circle at a Pow Wow. Surely she must be feeling the effects of the steam. John can see her clearly, not sweating and very composed.

The drumming intensifies and everyone appears to be floating in mid air about a foot above the floor of cedar chips. John feels the presence of the Spirit World and feels the Spirits are channeling insight to everyone inside. They are now thirty-five minutes into the Sweat, and John begins to feel light headed. It is difficult to breathe because the steam is so intense. Everyone is drenched in sweat. Their bodies glisten from the glow of the red-hot rocks, everyone, except Tish-ah-yah-hanah, the mysterious one.

"Chosen one, my great, great grandson, do you not see?" beckons Tish-ah-yah-hanah. John hears. *'Is my hearing deceiving me. Did she say great, great grandson? I'm confused.'* Suddenly, he sees the vision before him.

"I see a Hatak Lussa," (black man). He is an older man. Just like the last Sweat, John is feeling delirious, and wants to reach out and touch his vision.

Then suddenly Rachel grabs his arm and says, "I see him! He sits on a great black horse!"

"What is he doing, my children?" asks Tish-ah-yah-hanah.

"He is riding through the swamp. He is running from someone or chasing someone," says Levi, as everyone begins to get involved and sees the same vision.

"I see a different horse," says Ironhorse. "I see a beautiful Indian girl riding a spotted Indian pony. She is wearing a red Ghost Shirt and she is crying. I see her teardrops flying in the wind. They look like white pearls and they explode when they hit the ground."

"I see the Indian girl," says Levi. The heat and steam is staggering. Those making comments look as if they are about to pass out. Still Tish-ah-yah-hanah unaffected by the heat and steam looks calm and composed. Her body is swaying to the music of ThunderHawk's flute. The drumming is deafening and much faster now.

"YellowHawk, you are the tracker. What do you see?" asks Tish-ah-yah-hanah, as if she is orchestrating the vision before her.

"I see the girl on horseback racing away from something. No, she is racing to something. It is a white buffalo as it stands beside a small watering hole. The buffalo wants to drink, but cannot for the water is tainted. Beyond the watering hole is a sand desert as far as the eye can see. There, all I see is darkness."

"I see the dark desert, and I see vultures circling about. It appears as if many have landed near something dead," says Roman.

"Aiyua Achafa, see and hear what is before you and restore. You were Aiyua before you were born. You are Falammichi (defender, restorer), and we are proud you are from our clan," says Tish-ah-yah-hanah. She is staring at John, and he looks straight into her eyes.

As he is looking into her eyes, he is looking into eternity, the past and the present. He sees a small village, in a clearing, near a river of crystal clear running water. Smoke is coming from the individual tee pees and he sees many people. They are friendly people of all ages and genders. They are not smiling, but he can tell they are happy and with full bellies. The adults are going about their work. He can see several young braves being counseled by old Indian men. The elders are privileged to say what and how they please without contradiction. Their words are like iron and never questioned. They are revered. This is the way it once was. John sees a great warrior, who would inspire terror in the hearts of his enemies, playing with his grandchildren.

There was no religious ceremony connected with marriage among them, however the relationship between a man and woman was regarded as mysterious and holy. The warriors of that day, prior to the coming of the 'white man', were strong but the women stronger. The secure position of the Indian woman is a test of their civilization. They set the standard of morality and protected the purity of their blood. The wife did not take the name of her husband or enter his clan. Their children belonged to the clan of the mother. She held all the family property. The honor of the house was in her hands. A woman who attained the ripeness of years, wisdom, and in some way displayed tremendous courage, was sometimes invited to set at the council. She was strong until the 'white man', the soldier and trader, who, with strong drink, overthrew the honor of the Indian man. The 'white man' exerted power over a disempowered husband, and purchased the virtue of his wife and daughters. When she fell, the whole Indian race fell with her. Tall Bear is seeing bits and pieces of ancient Indian ways.

The children are running and playing. He sees several dogs jumping about with the children, and one looks very familiar. He is a large black and white Dalmatian. He stops jumping and stands majestically, acknowledging John. John knows this dog! He has not laid eyes on him for half a lifetime. His name is Boy. Beyond him,

John sees Tish-ah-yah-hanah sitting on a wooden stump. Before her is a beautiful little girl who appears to be four or five years old. Tish-ah-yah-hanah is braiding her long, silky black hair. The little girl is happy to have the attention of her great grandmother. The young girl looks and smiles at John, and suddenly he feels a calming, motherly sensation, as when his mother put her arm around him and gave him comfort when he was a young boy. The more John sees and hears, the weaker he becomes. Tall Bear is at the height of his vision.

July's drum and ThunderHawk's flute sound like hundreds of instruments. John knows this cannot go on much longer. His eyes pierce the steam, and once again fix on the little girl. She has a warm smile and John can see her lips moving, but her soft voice is barely audible. He hears her say a name from his youth, "Sonny", and he then loses consciousness and falls to the floor.

He comes out of the darkness and hears Roman say, "His body hasn't fully recovered from the shooting. He's still a little weak."

Tall Bear is lying on the ground outside of the Sweat lodge, cradled in Rachel's arms. She is caressing his forehead with a cool damp cloth.

"Should we call 911?" asks Pastor Nohubby.

"I don't think so, he's coming around. He will be all right as soon as we get some fluids in him."

"He fasted all day and that's a factor too," says Levi.

"I don't want to take any chances! I want to call 911! John! John, can you hear me?" shouts Rachel.

As John opens his eyes, he can smell Rachel's perfume. Her face is so close her shoulder length hair is caressing his cheek and forehead. He stares into her soft brown eyes, and she begins to smile. Everyone is standing around with concerned faces. He sees a full moon against a dark blue sky, with millions of stars dotting the heavenly canvas. He sees everyone except Tish-ah-yah-hanah. He tries to get up quickly, but Rachel and Levi hold him down.

"Tish-ah-yah-hanah."

"Whoa boy, you just stay there for a few minutes and drink some water," says Levi.

"Tish-ah-yah-hanah, where is Tish-ah-yah-hanah?" he asks once again. He can see everyone looking about and not having any success finding her.

YellowHawk leaves the circle. "I'll go and find her."

John relaxes for a few moments, closing his eyes and trying to recapture what he has witnessed. There is so much to digest and try to comprehend. Had he seen what he thinks he saw? To be sure, he thinks the vision of his childhood companion "Boy" was unmistakable. Who would forget their first dog? He had seen photos of his mother, as a little girl, seated on the running board of an ancient model T Ford. Did he see her and her great grandmother? Did he see a vision of Tish-ah-yah-hanah? The insight into the culture of the old Indian ways, what was that all about? Was it a message? As the 'chosen one,' as Tish-ah-yah-hanah had referred to him, does he have unfinished business? Pastor Nohubby has brought a chair from the kitchen table, and the guys lift him up and sit him down. A glass of ice water is placed in his hand, and Rachel orders him to drink.

"I'm feeling better. What happened in there?

"You passed out and fell to the floor. And this time I had nothing to do with it."

"Are you sure? I have a splitting headache," John says and grins at Roman.

Levi looks around, getting acknowledgement from everyone, and says, "I think we all have a headache. That was pretty intense in there."

"ThunderHawk, what did you sprinkle in the fire when you came in?" asks Roman.

"I didn't put anything into the fire that didn't belong there."

"The drum and music was so loud and intense," observes Rachel.

ThunderHawk and Tecumseh look at each other as if they were all crazy.

"We didn't do anything out of the ordinary, except add hotter rock and more water to keep it to one session," says July.

YellowHawk joins the group. "Chief, there's no sign of her. Security says no one left by way of the street or they would have seen her."

"She just didn't disappear in thin air. She's got to be around here somewhere," says Charlie Two Crow.

"Let's go inside the house where it's a little cooler and John can be more comfortable," says Rachel.

"YellowHawk, will you take a couple of the security guys and walk the creek back of the house?" says Roman.

"I'm on it. I'll backtracked to the creek and walked the banks too."

"Did anybody see her come out of the lodge," asks Rachel.

"I didn't see her after you guys dragged the Chief out. Most of our attention was on him. July, did you see her come out?" asks ThunderHawk looking at July.

"I never saw her."

"Chief, you feel like getting up and going into the house?" asks Levi. With John's nod, Levi reaches under his arm, and he and Roman help him to his feet and walk him to the back door, leading to the kitchen. Everyone sits down here, and ice tea is served, along with a light snack.

Pastor Nohubby has lived a very simple existence. His wife Ida died many years ago. The house is small, a two bedroom wood frame built thirty years ago. It is clean and orderly, but lacking the finishing touches a woman would give. Pastor Nohubby is a busy man. Visiting churches, doing God's work and working closely with the Choctaw Nation is his priority. But make no mistake; this is the home of an Indian, filled with artifacts, blankets, DreamCatchers and numerous gifts bestowed on a respected man. The kitchen is small, but large enough to accommodate a simple wooden table capable of seating eight. Levi and the Chief are seated at each end, with Roman somewhat in the middle. Once again Roman retrieves a tablet of paper and begins to write down what he saw in his vision.

"I saw a dark desert with vultures circling above something dead. Did anybody see anything else?"

"I saw a man riding through a swampy area," contributes Levi.

"Chief, what did you see? I saw you reach out as if you were trying to touch something."

"I saw an old black man on a horse in the swamp," John says, still trying to shake off the effects of losing consciousness.

"I saw the same thing! He was on a great black horse," says Rachel.

"So far, I've got a black man on a black horse riding through a swampy area, and vultures in a dark desert near a kill. Anything else?"

"I saw a different horse," says the medicine man. "And a beautiful Indian girl was riding it."

"I saw nearly the same vision! An Indian girl with long black hair. She was wearing a red shirt and crying. She looked as if she was in distress," says Levi.

"I saw the girl on horseback too. And a white buffalo near a small watering hole. Beyond the watering hole a great sand desert. There, all I saw was darkness as if I was looking into the face of the Great Mystery," says the medicine man.

"Chief, the black man on the horse has got to be Charlie White. He was the caretaker of Chief Wilson's stable of horses for many years." Looking at everybody, Levi continues, "Now this can't leave this room, but we visited him somewhere in Louisiana a while back. He was so scared he didn't want anyone to know his whereabouts."

"Levi, I got the impression he wanted to tell us more when we spoke with him the last time. I wanted to pressure him to say more, but I didn't want to scare him off."

"I got the same impression. I could see the fear in eyes and hear his voice shaking on occasion."

"OK, we have the white buffalo beside the small pool of tainted water. And, what about the Indian girl wearing the red shirt on the other horse? Didn't you say she was crying? What does she have to do with the white buffalo statue at the casino?" asks Rachel.

The medicine man, Ironhorse, speaks again, "When I was told of your buffalo statue crying red tears at the casino, I knew this sign had great significance. The spirit of the buffalo is sad. He will not stop crying until there is justice. There is a connection between the young Indian girl and the statue. The vultures in the blackened desert are on a hunt. It is the sign of someone's death. Perhaps the death of the young girl?"

"John, in your vision, did you see any other signs or miss something?" asks Levi.

John sits and stares at a centerpiece on the kitchen table. It is a small wooden statue of an Indian warrior on horseback with his lance thrust high into the air, a sign of defiance and victory. John is in deep thought for sometime before he answers.

"Yes, I did, however they were insights of a seemingly personal nature. There may or may not be a connection to the statue. My personal visions seemed of a much broader nature. I feel it was a messages from the ancient world giving me insights of more work for me to do."

YellowHawk enters the back door. "Big Levi, I took some of your security men and searched out back and down by the creek. Tish-ah-yah-hanah never went down there. I could find no tracks. She never left out the front, as the security men would have seen her. I have seen this before. The Apache have a word for it. I do not know the word in your Choctaw."

"She is a Shilombish (ghost). A friendly one. She was present to pass on great insight and wisdom to someone. I have seen this only a few times. She was visiting someone here in this room. She was perhaps an ancient relative. She was visiting you, Chief," says Ironhorse, as he looks at John.

"You are a wise old man, Ironhorse. I hear your words and I appreciate your wisdom. You are from the valley where I was born and perhaps it is no coincidence you were the right medicine man to share my Sweat. I saw visions of our ancient world when our people were happy and free to roam wherever the food was plentiful. Our neighbors allowed us to walk their land without fear. I saw the respect given to our elders. The old ones are our history and much can be learned from them. I saw great warriors, feared by many, but showing gentleness in the presence of their children. The great warriors were leaders and teachers. The women were even stronger, and their words were iron. I saw a village with many people of all ages. Children and animals were dancing about among the tall trees. There was peace and harmony and a sense of balance between man and nature. I saw the customs of our people no longer practice and I am saddened. I know what I must do."

CHAPTER 45

A rriving at the Choctaw Nation Capitol, at 7:00 the following morning, John Tall Bear finds Levi and Roman in the small break room down the hall from his office. The office doesn't open for business until 8:30 A.M. but his small squad of security personnel is already in place. Since the shooting, security has been taken to a higher level. Tall Bear doesn't like the look and impression it gives, but honors advice to take extra precautions.

He has never been a coffee lover, but the aroma of freshly brewed Columbian gets the best of him this morning. The three men thrash the details of what transpired the night before. The Sweat had been exhilarating, moving and confusing. After a good night's sleep, things seem a little clearer. Further discussion favors contacting Charlie White again. Tall Bear directs Levi and Roman to concentrate on the phenomenon at the casino. He will locate Charlie.

Tall Bear returns to his office and places a call to Agent Rivers for any progress finding Steppenwolf. Almost six weeks a shooter at large has kept everyone on edge. Were any new information available, surely, Rivers would advise him. He makes the call.

"Chief Tall Bear, you are on my list of people to call today. You must be psychic."

"No Agent Rivers, just impatient."

"Chief, I don't blame you, but we're doing all we can."

"Let me ask you this. Have you spoken to Senator Cody?"

"Chief, I'm not at liberty to speak about that."

"Agent Rivers let me remind you Senator Jim stated the man in the photo at NSA was seen in the company of Senator Cody. NSA confirmed him as Steppenwolf. Now, are you telling me you can't speak about the information we gave you?"

"Ok, Chief are you on a secure line?"

"Hell no, I'm on my cell."

Both know not all personal phones are secured. She answers anyway. "The question has been put to the Senator and he has denied any involvement with him whatsoever. Clearly he's not being truthful, but he is who he is and we have to give him latitude. We need more evidence to move forward. The Senator has not been sighted lately. Between you and me, if you see the Senator, the other isn't far behind."

"Can you at least confirm that Steppenwolf is in fact the shooter?"

"Yes Chief, we're pretty sure it's Gunter Steppenwolf."

"So, Whitey was named after the Hesse protagonist?"

"One and the same, but this guy may be more messed up than a character in a German novel.

Chief, it gets worse. Steppenwolf is a highly skilled, trained assassin, an arms dealer, willing to operate for any country with the money to buy. This is no boy scout. He's a pro at the highest level."

"Great! Let me know when you get any new information."

"You'll be the first, and, he doesn't like to be called 'Whitey'. We are told he slit a man's throat in a bar for that."

Did Agent Rivers suggest Steppenwolf might still be state side? Every government agency has his profile, and if he resurfaces somewhere, they'll get him. He'll take care of the things he can. As he hangs up the phone, his secretary walks into his office with a small brown envelope in her hand.

"Chief, this came in the morning mail. As you can see, it's marked 'urgent for Chief Tall Bear'. Normally we open everything, but I thought you might want this yourself."

"Thanks Jackie, I appreciate that," as Jackie hands him the envelope and leaves the room.

Tall Bear anxiously opens it, and the only item inside is a single photo. He can tell it was taken late at night. A full moon spotlights recognizable faces. Another door opens, the conscience of Charles White. *'The spirits are working for us today, and this is already a good day.'*

Levi walks hurriedly into Tall Bear's office.

"Levi, I thought you and Roman were down at the casino checking on that situation."

"We were Chief, but one of our tribal deputies spotted a black Mercedes at the Love's gas station on Main Street. He thought it might be important, so after the car pulled away, he went into the station and questioned the attendant. Guess who purchased the gas?"

"I have no clue."

"The Honorable and reclusive Senator James Cody."

"Interesting, Levi. I got a little surprise this morning in the mail. I had a feeling this was going to be one of those pivotal days. Did the deputies follow the car?"

"No, but they saw the direction the car was moving in and called ahead. The Mercedes was seen by another one of our tribal patrol cars. They were instructed to follow the car and guess where it was headed?" asks Levi, smiling like a cat that ate the canary.

"Tell me it was heading out to Chief Wilson's place."

"You're right. This calls for one of those big fat Cuban's Chief Wilson kept in the closet."

"Now Levi, you know I don't smoke. I tossed them out a long time ago."

"Damn John, why didn't you give 'em to me? You know every now and then I enjoy a good Cuban cigar."

"Just practicing a little Falammichi, looking after your lungs. Tell you what. We need to give those deputy's a bonus. Radio them and tell them to watch from a distance, and let us know if they start moving. As soon as it gets dark, I've got a plan. Go get Roman and I'll tell you both what I have in mind."

Darkness begins to fall as the three of them leave the office en route to the home of former Chief Paul Wilson. John can't forget Rivers' statement, 'If you find Senator Cody, the shooter's not far behind.' The three are packing heat, as legitimate law enforcement officers for the Choctaw Nation. The traffic is light so they'll be there in fifteen minutes. *'Am I ready to find Whitey?'* He's wearing his best kick ass ensemble, his 9 inside the pocket of his jacket. Now, he doesn't propose to be in the same league as his adversary, but he's got two able friends as backup, and a score to settle. Not knowing what they will discover, they term this 'a tribal intervention'. The three of them have completed the necessary tribal police training. Two tribal patrols cars stationed to watch, can notify Durant police in a moment if needed.

Levi and Roman have both seen light action in the Marines. Tall Bear has been in many fights and a few dangerous situations, but he had never been in a gunfight. He isn't scared, but he's nervous as hell.

Only Levi had been to Chief Wilson's compound, to look at his stable of horses several years ago. Before they left the office, Levi sketched out a small map of the compound and house. There are three simple entrances, mainly in the front, one on the side and one in the back. It's a crapshoot which entrance is the most dangerous. Not knowing, who's inside and where they might be, it's decided, Levi will go through the front door and Roman will enter from the back. The side door is John's.

There are two driveways into the Wilson property. A tribal patrol car is parked near the entrance to both, thus sealing them off. They decide to go in under cover of darkness through an opening in a fence that borders the compound. Roman parks the car, and they find a house with no side gate and enter there. Jumping a narrow drainage ditch, they are inside the compound, in a wooded area with forty to fifty hundred year old pecan trees. The lawn is freshly mowed and immaculately groomed. As they huddle down behind a massive tree trunk, Roman gives brief instructions. All three of them have cell phones with wireless headsets. It takes a second for all of them to get connected, and they are ready.

John is thinking, *'This is going to be a piece of cake.'* Maneuvering through the pecan trees, it should be easy to make their way up to the main house.

"When you get to your door, test it first to see if it's locked and report in. If you find it unlocked, you'll enter first. We'll wait 10 seconds then, on my command, the other two will bust in," instructs Roman.

The three of them carefully move from tree to tree until they get close to the house. Levi is the first to separate and finds his way to the front door. Roman and John watch him settle into position, and then continue. John can easily see the side door, his point of entry. He slips in between two rose bushes lining a sidewalk leading to a small patio. Arriving, he kneels to survey. Glancing to his right, he sees Roman disappearing behind the pool pump house. He knows Roman will be in place in a moment or two. It is eerily silent and quite dark.

The moonlight peeking through the pecan trees gives off a very soft light. Tall Bear stands and like a dancer in seven short steps he's at the side door. Standing to the right, he tries the handle as he attempts to look inside a small curtained window, and gets lucky. The knob turns freely, without making a sound.

"The side door is unlocked."

"Front door is locked."

"Back door is locked."

"All right, we're all ready. Safeties off! Chief when I say go, you enter. Levi, count to 10 slowly and make your move. We all set?" They all acknowledge they're ready.

"Chief, chukoa!"

Tall Bear opens the door and slips inside. Shutting the door behind, it makes a slight click, as the door latch slides into the strike plate. In the silent room, it sounds very loud, as there is nothing else to hear except for the pounding of his heart. He hears the opening and closing of his heart valves. The room is dark, as his eyes are beginning to adjust. He's in a kitchen. He can hear the sound of the refrigerator humming softly and can hear voices straight ahead and to his right. With Walter in his right hand, he begins walking slowly into darkness, and jumps a little at the sound of the icemaker dropping ice into its bin.

Approaching a hallway, he turns right. Two steps further, and peeking around a doorjamb to his left, he looks into a large dimly lit room. The first thing he can make out is a long leather sofa about ten feet away, with a large man sitting on the far right end. His back is to Tall Bear, who guesses this might be the shooter, Steppenwolf. Facing him, across a coffee table is Senator Cody. To the left, sitting on the same sofa as Cody, is former Chief Paul Wilson. He puffs a cigarette, a hard fall from Cuban cigars.

Roman, at the back door, pulls a large bowie knife out of its sheath and silently pries open the back door.

'The Chief's in there alone already. What the hell was I thinking, exposing him to danger? I should have gone in first.'

He slides inside, and closing the door, finds himself in a rear hallway and silently steps the length to another door. He can hear voices coming from the far side and can tell by the conversation nothing has happened yet, so he stands down.

———

Levi is eyeing the massive door. He leans on it, to see if it has any give. It's solid, doesn't budge. During his football years, he could move a 300-pound lineman. Surely he can pop this door.

'My peoples are inside and they're counting on me. Nothing's going to keep me from going in, even if I have to blow the damn door lock off. Dang, ten seconds is an eternity'. He steps back four paces, lowers his shoulder, and readies to assault the oak door.

Tall Bear gingerly steps inside the large room, with his back to the wall and his eyes glued to the three men. Walter is in his right hand, hanging beside his leg, hammer cocked and ready. He listens intently to the conversation going on in the room.

"Paul, what the hell were you thinking leaving incriminating shit on your laptop?" asks an angry Senator Cody.

Paul Wilson, with his head hanging low, stares at the carpet between his feet, takes a long draw off his cigarette and says nothing.

"When Tall Bear found that shit, it was the end of your career as Chief of the Choctaws. Without that information, they could never have put any pressure on you to resign. On top of that, an investigation will be able to find you and I tucked away millions in the Caymans!"

The white hair man with his back to John says, "Paul, you just make damn sure you send the rest of my money to my Zurich account."

"I'm not paying you another fucking dime until the job is finished!" Paul Wilson answers, not looking up.

"I agree with Paul. We paid you to kill that bastard in Talihina. Killing the girl and woman wasn't part of the bargain. Like I said, Paul and I have millions sitting in accounts in Grand Cayman. I know we agreed on a set price, just finish him off and you can write your own check."

"I killed the old woman just to rattle Tall Bear's cage. The big titty bitch on the mountain bluff was just a causality of the business. She saw my face and could identify me. I couldn't leave her alive. I had a little fun with her, though, before her luck ran out."

"Hoowah, now you're the one who's shit out of luck Steppenwolf."

John steps forward into the light, pointing the Walter PPK at the back of Steppenwolf's head. Senator Cody and Paul Wilson's eyes are almost popping out of their heads at seeing John, and the color is draining from their faces.

"Steppenwolf, don't turn around! There's some German made whoop ass aimed at the back of your head! Put your hands behind your head and lock your fingers!"

"Do as he says," orders Roman as he enters the room from John's right, with his weapon pointed at the three men. Surveying the situation, Roman comments, "Well, well! Look what we have here. Nice work John!"

Bam! Levi busting the door and splintering wood from the jamb startle everyone. The room explodes with movement. Steppenwolf dives to his left on the floor, shielding himself with the sofa. Tall Bear can't see what he's doing but instinctively mimics him diving, pointing Walter in Steppenwolf's direction. Steppenwolf fires the first of two rounds where he anticipated Tall Bear to be standing behind the couch. He adjusts to Tall Bear sliding across the floor and gets off a second round but misses.

In between Steppenwolf's two rounds, Tall Bear has an idea where his target will be and gets off a blind shot, but misses, shattering glasses sitting atop a portable liquor cabinet on a far wall. Steppenwolf appears, and Tall Bear's second round catches him in the left ear, blowing it off. Tall Bear sees the blood splatter on his white hair, but doesn't know the extent of his injury. Steppenwolf doesn't react to the damaged ear as both lie on the floor, eyes locked on each other. Weapon smoking and leveled at Tall Bear, he squeezes off what would have been his third round. It jams as Levi bursts into the room and with his foot, traps Steppenwolf's malfunctioning weapon to the floor.

"Move and I'll blow your ugly Nazi head off!"

"Nice timing, Levi."

Senator Cody and Paul Wilson sit frozen as they stare down the barrel of Roman's gun. Tall Bear scrambles to his knees as Levi allows the big German to sit up. Steppenwolf holds his hand to his missing left ear while blood flows freely down his neck, soaking his shirt.

"So Indian, how'd it feel when my slug thumped you in the chest?"

"A little worse than that missing ear. I owe you one. Move Whitey and I'll blow your little dick off."

"Now don't do that, I couldn't fuck your pretty Senator. Never had a Rachel."

"Shoot that son-of-a-bitch John, if you want," shouts Levi.

"No, I want his ass to rot in prison."

"You two on the couch, lock your fingers behind your head. Try anything and I won't hesitate to shoot you. I'm actually hoping one of you will. It would make my day!" says smiling Roman.

"Is that a bathroom?" Tall Bear asks Paul Wilson, as he points to a door several feet from him. He nods. Tall Bear opens the door, keeping Walter pointed at Steppenwolf sitting in the middle of the floor. He reaches in, grabs a hand towel, and tosses it to the German.

"I want to take care of you so you and your ass can service all the 'studs' in prison."

Roman places a call to the tribal patrol cars outside and instructs them to call Durant Police and send an ambulance.

"Levi, you made such a ruckus coming through the front door you scared the shit out of everybody," Roman says with a big grin on his face.

"Represent! I do make a grand entrance, don't I?"

"Chief Wilson, you're in some deep shit now. Amazing, you had it all, and still greedy for more. Don't you wish now you were in the Catfish business with me instead of thieving with the crooked Kiowa Senator? Now both of you are going to spend the rest of your lives in prison," says Levi still pitching his catfish-farming venture.

"School him Levi!" Tall Bear walks over in front of the disgraced former Chief. "I have a very incriminating photo of both of you. From the looks of the photo, you two could be facing the death penalty."

"What the hell are you talking about?" asks Senator Cody.

"He's knows what I'm talking about."

"I had nothing to do with that," says Paul Wilson.

"Paul, you keep your fucking mouth shut!"

"John, what are you talking about?" asks Roman.

"I was going to show you and Levi earlier, but this came up. I've acquired a photo of our two friends here, along with Deputies Cross and Irwin, loading something into a construction truck. I believe it's the body of Jeanie LeFlore wrapped in a rug."

"Holy shit!"

"Cody killed her! I had nothing to do with it!"

"You little coward! I told you to keep your big mouth shut! They have nothing on us! I don't think this photo exists, so shut the fuck up!"

"John, why do you think it was the LeFlore girl?" asks Levi.

"You remember being told about the dreamcatcher tattoo on her ankle? Well her left ankle is visible hanging out of the blanket and if you look close, you can see it clearly."

"Hot damn, we got both you assholes now, and Whitey too," says Levi.

Roman begins walking toward the middle of the room, "I'm going out front to see what's holding everybody up."

As he sidesteps Steppenwolf, he lunges, grabbing the Bowie knife strapped to Roman's leg. Shoving Roman on top of the Senator and Wilson, Steppenwolf leaps to his feet, squaring off at the east end of the room where Roman had come in. Levi quickly moves toward him pointing his gun at him.

"Don't shoot him Levi! We need him alive. He can testify against the other two," Tall Bear says.

"I'm going out the back door and nobody's stopping me!"

Roman quickly gets to his feet and runs between Steppenwolf and the door.

"You're not going anywhere, Whitey," Roman standing his ground pointing his weapon at Steppenwolf's head.

"You timber niggers are no match for me!" He turns and lunges at Levi, who has lowered his weapon. The knife travels diagonally from Levi's left shoulder, across his chest, and down to his belt on his right side. It has sliced through Levi's jacket, creating a cut across his chest.

Tall Bear moves Levi out of the way and tosses Walter to Roman, who now has a gun in each hand.

Cutting Levi has Tall Bears adrenalin pumping. He squares off in a warrior stance and commands, "Roman, if he somehow gets lucky, shoot the son of a bitch! Until then, he's mine."

"Chief, you sure you want to do this?" asks Roman, his voice under control and very matter-of-fact.

"Ro, I know what I'm doing. He's mine! I've waited long enough for this asshole to show his face. It's payback time. Like I said, if he gets lucky, unload both irons on him. Get the picture, Whitey? If you want to leave this room alive, shut the fuck up or do something about it."

Steppenwolf realizes he's not going anywhere, and what he was hired for is about to go down. He has one last chance at John Tall Bear, his only failed hit. He begins to posture in a fighting stance, moving the knife from side to side in a figure eight pattern.

The ancestors have taught Tall Bear to see the big picture in three layers. The first evaluates how you and your opponent match up and subconsciously creates another specific layer to focus on. The second 'defend and control the weapon' focus on the shoulder, not his eyes as other knife instructors teach. There is a third layer as well.

Steppenwolf got lucky with Levi. Tall Bear calculates he might attempt the same 45-degree angle pass on him. Inside the first layer, seeing the second clearly, movement in the right shoulder alerts Tall Bear. The knife is coming in from the left side. Tall Bear steps slightly to the left, to the outside, and parries Steppenwolf's wrist as it moves into Tall Bear's centerline chest high. The knife is traveling too fast. Tall Bear misses and for a split second chases. He knows this might happen, and is ready for his attacker to come back with his horizontal move. Tall Bear captures his right wrist with his own right hand and explodes with a left inward forearm block into Steppenwolf's elbow.

Normally, Tall Bear would be able to gain control of his opponent with this move, but Steppenwolf is strong and exceptionally fast. He pulls out of Tall Bear's grip, but it's not a concern, for Tall Bear knows the possibilities. His 6' 5" frame creates challenging angles for Tall Bear too. They square off again. Tall Bear knows what's going through Steppenwolf's mind, and this is the third layer. Tall Bear has defended Steppenwolf's best maneuver, and he's got to be thinking about that. The last layer is creating doubt in your opponent's mind and restoring a dangerous situation with confident and superb execution. As knife fighters do, they set up again.

"Is that the best you've got, Whitey? It'll be a cold day in hell when a stinking German can best an Indian in knife fighting!" Yes, Tall Bear is baiting him. Tall Bear squares himself up and slaps his own stomach as though inviting him to stab there.

"Come on Whitey, put it right here," Tall Bear pats his stomach again. Pissing Steppenwolf off, Tall Bear knows what's coming, just what Tall Bear wants, a linear thrust toward his mid- section. This is the easiest attack to defend. He's seeing all the layers now. The knife is on its way. Tall Bear steps forward and to the outside of the center-line, captures Steppenwolf's attack hand with his left while twisting his wrist counter clockwise while stripping the knife with his right. This turns Steppenwolf's upper body counter clockwise and takes his left hand out of play. Still clutching Steppenwolf's left wrist, Tall Bear spins clockwise underneath Steppenwolf's arm and pounds his opponent's right kidney with the knife's hilt. The German's lights dim, his knees buckle.

The clockwise motion has also created a left wristlock. Tall Bear drops on to his left knee and slams Steppenwolf to the floor at Tall Bear left side. The next sequence would be the kill shot, pivoting to his right knee and burying the knife in his opponent's throat. The decision is made in a millisecond. Tall Bear shuts the movement down. Steppenwolf is unconscious from the kidney shot, loss of blood and his head hitting the floor.

Many years ago, when Tall Bear created this movement, he named it Dance of War (Chepulli Tanap in Choctaw). He now hears the sirens from approaching ambulances and police cars. The paramedics take care of Levi's long, but superficial, wound. Though he has lost a considerable amount of blood, he's a tough old Indian and will be fine in a few days.

The Durant police come in and quickly take control. The tribal police are sent out to direct traffic and help contain the immediate area. Two Durant police officers take John, Levi, and Roman to another part of the house, where they begin to ask some preliminary questions. During the questioning, John's cell phone rings, and its Rachel. They were to have had a dinner date tonight, so she is surely wondering where he is. One of the police sergeants sternly asks John not to take the call.

"Am I under arrest?"

"No."

"This call is important, "I'll be brief."

"Rachel, I'm sorry, something came up and I couldn't call. It's a long story, but the short version is Senator Cody was spotted in town and trailed to Chief Wilson's house. Having probable cause the shooter would be in their company, Levi, Roman and I surprised the three of them inside the home. We're still here. Steppenwolf is wounded and on his way to the hospital. Durant police on the scene are in charge until FBI agents take over shortly. I'd like your help here. No, we're all ok, but I'd like for you to take care of the media. Good, I'll see you when you arrive."

John closes the phone. He faces the police officer and says he is not going to answer any questions until FBI agents take over. The officers let the three of them sit while they wait. In a short time the agents from the FBI arrive and the Durant police turn the crime scene over to them. Within twenty minutes, news involving an unknown U. S. Senator is breaking on all the major networks. Within an hour, the whole neighborhood is crawling with news reporters, photographers, and police officers trying to contain the people. The Durant police are sent out to help direct traffic and assist the tribal police.

An FBI crime scene team arrives to control the area. John watches them go through their routine and they looked nothing like his favorite crime show, The Closer. Kyra Sedgwick and the cast of characters make her show entertaining.

The federal agents in their black suits and black Tahoes are here to take names and kick ass. John, Levi, and Roman are loaded into one of the Tahoes and driven to the Durant Police station. There, they are separated and two agents are assigned to each of them, and the interrogations begin. Within minutes their tribal attorneys arrive on the scene, and negotiations follow.

The tribal attorneys argue the three are members of tribal police and were acting in the jurisdiction of their sovereign nation. Whatever the alternate viewpoint, the three were completely within their rights to act upon the situation as they saw fit. John knows the photo in his possession gives probable cause to act as they have. When the information and evidence they have is passed on to the investigators, their actions are justified. FBI Agents Rivers and Jackson also appear and provide pertinent information from their investigation. After about thirty minutes of questions asked and statements taken, it's determined no crime was committed on their part. They are free to leave.

The three are escorted into the front lobby, where Rachel and Tammy wait. It's late night as they walk out, into a sea of reporters, lights and cameras converge on them. Microphones poke their faces left and right. A shield of Durant police officers whisks them into Rachel's car. The Choctaw Nation headquarters is just a stone's throw away. They anticipate a pack of reporters camped there too.

The CMA headquarters, a few blocks east on Main Street, becomes the destination. Roman has installed a remote controlled gated iron fence behind the headquarters to secure employees' personal cars. After quickly maneuvering a few city blocks, they lose the last reporters attempting to follow them. Once inside the building, they collapse into the comfortable chairs of Roman's spacious office and breathe a collective sigh of relief. Tammy begins brewing a fresh pot of coffee, and another bombardment starts.

"John, I'm so angry with you! Why didn't you just call Durant police or the FBI?"

"Rachel, Senator Cody was not a wanted man. He's free to visit anyone he chooses. Without someone actually seeing Steppenwolf with him, they wouldn't have reason to investigate."

"Well, why didn't you call them when you saw the shooter was in the house?" asks Rachel, sounding like a prosecuting attorney.

"Hell, we were already inside and it was too late by then! When we discovered Steppenwolf with Paul Wilson and Senator Cody we couldn't chance being discovered making a call or waiting for other law enforcement."

Not giving up, Rachel continues, "Levi, I'm mad at you too for letting him do this."

"Rachel, ah, let me remind you, he's the Chief and my boss. How am I going to say no to him? I could lose my job!"

"Yeah, right!" replies Rachel sarcastically.

"And, I had to be there too, to bust the front door down!" smiles Levi. The three men burst, laughing so hard they are almost crying. The two women refuse to lose the puzzled looks on their faces.

"I'm glad the three of you think this is funny. You could have all been killed!" says Tammy.

"I'm sorry, Honey. You would've had to be there to understand." The three of them start laughing again.

"Well, why don't you tell us little women what's so damn funny then?" Tammy tries to look and sound tough. The three men look at each other and start laughing again.

"Now, what are you laughing about?"

"We're laughing at you, Tammy! We've never heard you try to act so tough using cuss words," says Levi.

"Well, I'm mad, as hell." She sits down beside Roman, puts her arms around him, and kisses him on the cheek.

"OK, so.., now.., when are you boys going to tell us little women what is so funny?" demands Rachel.

"John, you want to tell her?"

"No, you go ahead."

"Well, after John and I got inside, we had the place secured, but it was pretty tense. Levi was the last to come in and I thought to myself, 'What's taking him so long?' But when he busted the front door down and made his grand entrance, he made such a ruckus it scared the shit out of everybody. Bodies started flying, gunfire started popping and gun smoke filled the air." The three men begin laughing again.

When Roman and Levi begin their narrative of the knife fight, the room gets serious and quiet. The five of them sit, talk, and drink coffee for another hour. The nagging questions, 'who shot Tall Bear, and why?' were answered. With the information revealed tonight, the Senator and former Chief will be charged with conspiracy to commit murder, attempted murder, along with wire fraud and the embezzlement of millions of dollars from the Choctaw Nation and U.S Government. Charlie White's testimony will indict the two deputies charged with the murders of Gary and Don Taylor.

However, without the body of Jeanie LeFlore, additional murder charge cannot be brought against the four of them. Senator Cody and Wilson were at the top of their game when, greed caused them to disgrace their Nation and, more importantly, their tribe. This was a sad and tragic ending. There is still unfinished business left to attend to, but those problems will have to wait until tomorrow.

The night is not over as they receive bad news. In route to the hospital, Steppenwolf over powered a guard, takes his weapon, and escapes. FBI agents found the ambulance north of town with the officer and two EMT's shot to death.

It is almost midnight when they say goodbye. Whenever John's had a difficult day, he feels his dreams will calm angry spirits and give him valuable insights. Visions are sacred. The night is filled with good and bad dreams. No hand weapon can defeat the forces of evil during sleep. The dreamcatcher protects him while he rests. This is an American Indian tradition, but like many other things, the practice has been taken, and used by everybody. Non-Indians have little or no knowledge of how to use the dreamcatcher.

The dreamcatcher produces visions of good hunting, success in battle, happy memories, and a healthy life for all family members. Good dreams love the spider-like web and travel softly through the sinew threads and through the center of the web. Bad dreams are caught and trapped in the sinew web, and perish with the first light of day, never to bother the dreamer again.

As the dreamer tonight, John hopes to see good visions and receive answers to assist him find his adversary Steppenwolf.

CHAPTER 46

J ohn wakes up the next morning feeling rested for the first time in many moons. He's had several dreams during the night. Tish-ah-yah-hanah and Ironhorse were featured players. Perhaps it's because only a few days ago they experienced the Sweat together. His rejuvenation breakfast is fresh blueberries, a banana, strawberries, a handful of walnuts, two teaspoons of honey, and a cup of fresh grass-fed milk blended into a smoothie.

He retrieves family papers from the desk and begins to examine his birth certificate. Written on the back of it, in his mother's handwriting, is a family tree. On his mother's side, his fingers find the name of his great, great grandmother. Under her English name, in very small letters, is 'Tish-ah-yah-hanah'. He wonders how he could have missed it. He stares at the name for a long minute, in amazement. He remembers the vision from the Sweat, when he saw his mother sitting before her grandmother as she was braiding her hair. Tish-ah-yah-hanah had referred to him as great, great grandson and the 'chosen one'. Had he shared a Sweat with his great, great grandmother? John feels this is one of those mysteries best left alone. He had asked Levi to look for her, but she was nowhere to be found. No one will believe him anyway, except the people who were there in the Sweat.

John begins his day at his office taking care of tribal business. His mind wanders every now and then thinking about his mother and

Tish-ah-yah-hanah. He has to discipline himself to get through the morning. Every Thursday at 10 a.m., he is available to see anyone who wants a little time to speak to him personally. This includes those with problems that can't be solved by the program directors. Elder Choctaw who prefer privacy want to discuss projects they feel are needed. This is a great time for John to listen and learn.

Earlier, John had placed a call to Charlie Two Crow in Talihina and asks he bring the medicine man Ironhorse, and Tommy YellowHawk, to Durant later in the day. He tells Two Crow to tell YellowHawk he has a bottle of Jimmy for him and one for Ofi, if he will come. He finishes around 1:00 and calls Rachel. She is visiting Tammy at Chahta Amoma Atokoli headquarters and agrees to a late lunch. They agree to meet at a barbeque restaurant down the street. Before leaving for his date, he places another call to Two Crow, to check on his whereabouts.

"Charlie, where are you now?"

"I'll be arriving with YellowHawk around 2:30."

"Did you find Ironhorse?"

"Chief, I went by his house and his neighbor told me he left early in the morning because you needed to see him. And, if anyone calls, he would be at the pool hall on Locust St in Durant."

"That's strange. I never indicated to anyone I might need to see him today. And what is Ironhorse doing at a pool hall?"

"Probably taking all the hustlers' money."

"What?"

"You didn't know that old Indian was a legend on the pool hall circuit 40 years ago? His game is snooker and he's a magician with the cue ball. He probably needs some money to buy more feed for his animals."

"Then, I wish him laser eyes and a smooth stroke. Charlie, when you get here, will you pick him up and come over to the casino. Meet me in the lobby by the buffalo statue. I'll see you a little after 3 p.m. Levi, Roman and several others will be meeting us there."

"Achukma."

'Ironhorse is indeed someone very special'. 'How would he know I needed him today? Maybe he is one of those medicine men who has a special gift'. John suspects he is one of those rare men who can make contact with those from the past. Many questions are left unanswered in the Great Mystery.

———

Rachel and John talk long over lunch, about the sweat the night before last. They discuss her office and politics. They talk about the future of the Choctaw Nation. They muse on everything except their personal lives as though nothing need to be said. No promises, desires or plans for their future are ever made or spoken aloud. John had been married twice and isn't rushing to make it three.

Long seconds pass and minutes rush ahead to 3 p.m. John tells Rachel of the casino meeting and who will be there, but not what it's about. He asks if she wants to come along. She says she is definitely coming, just to keep him from trouble or doing something stupid.

"Are you carrying a gun today?"

"Of course not." John looks at her with surprise. She's having a little fun. Moments and words like this prove their connection. If John could program his counterpart, she would be the right person. Does he want her there? Of course! She knows when to say yes, no, or whatever. Sometimes when things are too good to be true, they're not. This is why John is determined to move slowly in their relationship and let everything play out.

———

All gather in front of the Sacred White Buffalo statue at 3 p.m. This is the first time Ironhorse, YellowHawk with Ofi and Two Crow have seen the strange phenomenon. John wants the three of them to witness what he and others have seen for the past few days.

"I want you all to know I'm close to making a decision. You're all here to convince me otherwise if I'm wrong. All of you experienced the Sweat with me a few days ago, and you have the same information I have. We have not talked about it, and now is your chance to speak. I'm betting we are all on the same page."

"I have an idea what you have in mind as I have seen it in a dream," says Ironhorse.

"Ironhorse, that's exactly why I want you here. You're the eldest of the great medicine men alive today. You're from the valley where I was born, therefore creditability is acknowledged."

"I feel a spirit here in the building," contributes Two Crow.

"When Two Crow and I walked through those doors, I could feel a spirit moving about. Ofi gave me a heads up," says YellowHawk.

"YellowHawk is right! The Shilombish is in a transition period and will remain here unless something is done to free it. I have seen this many times before. The spirit cannot go to the hereafter because a great injustice has been done. The spirit is angry," says Ironhorse.

"John, Roman and I know exactly what you have in mind and we agree with you. We're ready," says Levi.

"John, what are these men talking about?" asks Rachel, looking very puzzled.

"Rachel, with all the information we have, I'm going to give the order for a demolition team to come in and remove the buffalo statue and dig below it. In fact, I feel so strongly about the decision I have a demo team waiting in the parking lot. There are thirty men out there with all the equipment needed to start. Let's do this!"

Tall Bear summons Roger and tells him of his plans. Roger doesn't question John's authority, but states the noise will certainly cause a lot of complaints. John says he's prepared to shut the casino down if necessary. The lobby is already shut off from the public. Roger asks John to let him section off the entire north end of the casino. Within ten minutes, everything is in place. The demo team begins working.

"Chief, whoever built and planned this casino, should have put the entrance on the east side of the building just like a Sweat lodge."

" I like Ironhorse's suggestion Chieftain," says Levi.

"Done! Put on next week's agenda to find a new architect for renovation. The northeast side of this building will be tainted if we find what we are looking for."

With two large forklifts, the demo team grasps the statue and moves it to a location outside. Those watching witness another phenomenon. The Sacred White Buffalo quits crying as if the spirit knows something is being done on its behalf. John is certain when he sees Ofi becoming agitated and jumping. He calls Roger back, explains the situation, and asks him to shut the entire casino down. The demo team rips the carpet out and brings in compressed air tools. Jackhammers bust up the concrete where the statue once stood.

"Chief, if we are right, this is sacred burial ground. It would be wise to acknowledge this before we progress any further. We want to honor the person, using our burial customs," says Ironhorse.

"Ironhorse, take charge and do what you think is necessary."

Following the brief ceremony, tracker YellowHawk instructs the men to tear up the concrete where Ofi first sat down. In less than twenty minutes, the men have broken through to dirt cover. Next they dig with pick axes, shovels and finally hands. Ofi is franticly digging along with the men and finds a corner of a blanket. John recognizes the pattern from the photo and orders everyone to stop. He asks Levi to call the FBI office in McAlester and make sure Agents Rivers and Jackson are notified. This is now a crime scene.

The casino is shut down, the parking lot is emptied and, in a little over an hour, the FBI team is in charge. There is nothing more for the rest of them to do but go home and await the outcome. Later in the evening, Jeanie LeFlore's body is recovered and taken to McAlester. There, an autopsy will determine cause of death.

Ten days later, it is revealed she had, in fact, died from asphyxiation. Another murder and or accessory to murder is added to the growing list of charges Senator Cody, Paul Wilson, and the deputies face.

Time, in most cases gives us the answers good and bad. At least the families touched by these crimes will have some sort of closure, knowing justice is being served. The word 'closure' is seldom enough when you lose a loved one. There is only arrival at a different level of acceptance. Eventually you learn to accept and tolerate the pain. The book of life is brief and once a page is read, there's just memories. This is all the LeFlore and Taylor family have left. But if there is a thread of life within, you hang on until….

CHAPTER 47

O ver the next several weeks, the casino remains closed. Millions are spent on renovations. It's important to get things right. A new architect establishes an entrance on the east side of the building. John's team of designers introduces a Native theme to be used throughout the remodeling process. The Las Vegas style of glitzy glamour is gone. Instead, Indian men and women in full Native regalia will greet and interact with the customers. John hopes this new image and emphasis will appeal to Indian and non-Indian alike.

The casino restaurants are given a Native makeover. American Indian dishes are added to their menus. A small museum that sells jewelry, fancy beadwork and souvenir items with Native designs is included. Items sold come from Indian arts and craft makers within the thirteen counties. A line of Native clothing and t-shirts is being introduced in the small shops. With this new marketing philosophy the casino produces jobs outside as well as inside its walls. The refurbished complex is being given a new name, The DreamCatcher Casino.

Already in the works is a theme park with an authentic Indian village. Upon completion, the village will feature Native actors showing how a real Indian village functioned 600 years ago. A new entertainment division recruits Indian entertainers, offers training and showcases talent at the casino. The house band has a Native look and sound.

A young Indian man from Dallas with an Elvis voice and stage presence is brought to John's attention. Reagan Lee uses an Indian stage name, Sky Walker, a reminder of the King's ancestry and inspiration. Women love him and men like his style. John hears his songs, watches him perform, and signs Sky Walker to an exclusive contract. Six weeks later, he headlines the new grand opening. His show is a huge hit. DreamCatchers first star is born! Within a week, the show is booked solid for another three months. More people come from out of state and leave their money.

Over the next six months, major improvements to the adjunct golf course highlight Native themes and a respect for nature in the layout and landscaping. Attractive young Indian men and women hired as caddies will be attending college on golf scholarships. Those who take advantage of these opportunities will move on to positions in pro shops, teaching on the golf range, and course management. When word gets out about these changes, high rollers book rooms and tee times, golf all day and gamble all night.

The positive effect of dividend checks issued to tribal members is visible in Durant. The Choctaws are coming out of their shells, traveling to town spending their money. You can see the peace and contentment in their faces. Many who once struggled exhaustively for mere survival, can manage and enjoy a more equitable economy. As the money is spread around, more shops begin to open, creating more jobs for the general population of Durant. Indian families are sending their children off to school. Enrollment at Southeastern State College is at a new high. More dormitories and small apartments are being built to accommodate the new students.

John reflects on the accomplishments of the past year. A noble movement brought them from small Indian churches to where they are today. They had a vision for their tribe and families. They needed access to good health care focused on eating healthy foods, exercise, less alcohol and tobacco. More importantly, they wanted to be recognized as good, honest people working hard to have a better future for their children. The tribe is no longer invisible. Choctaws are up front and getting involved in community affairs and self-government.

John decides to schedule a press conference. On a beautiful Thursday morning, Tall Bear takes the podium, glances to the east where Father Sun always rises, and silently asks the Creator for guidance and wisdom in his words.

"Halito, and I thank you for coming. Though every day is a new beginning for each of us, it is time for me to reflect back on the past two years. We have come a long way. Once the invisible tribe, we stand tall in full view of the entire world. We have done many good things in a short time. However, something is missing in my life. Having asked the Great Spirit, our Creator, for guidance, I must take charge of my own destiny. Unrealized dreams require my full attention."

"When we set off together, I held the Chief of the Choctaws should be full blood and speak our language. Saddened by evidence emerging I am less than full blood, I must step down."

John pauses until the stir of protest in the crowd quiets. "Today I am resigning as the Chief of the Choctaws." Another groan arises from the crowd, and again John waits for it to subside, "It has been an honor and privilege to serve you."

John taps his right fingers to his mouth, and then both hands tap his heart and execute an intricate movement ending with his right hand forward and open, as if setting a butterfly free.

"There is good news! I turn the duties of this office over to a very capable individual, my Assistant Chief, Levi Tushka. He is unquestionably full blood Choctaw and speaks our language fluently."

"I leave you with these words. 'As we journey the movement of life, we're all a work in progress. My Falammichi philosophy is to defend whenever possible and to restore someone every day. Share your wealth and knowledge, till there is no more. If your heart is good, Creator will smile graciously down upon you and give you a long, healthy life. Do this good work and you will become Hatak Achukma Falammichi," (a good man who defends and restores).

By the end of the day, the transition is complete. Levi Tushka becomes Chief of the Choctaw Nation. His first item of business is to select Roman Billy as his Assistant Chief. This is in keeping with John's vision, and he is pleased. They will take the Choctaw Tribe to places John cannot. Tall Bear's mother is surely proud of her son, and to him that's all that matters. Levi offers to create a special lifetime position for John as Special Advisor to the Chief. John requests time to consider. He doesn't say no therefore the door is left open. Levi asks John what he will do next. John tells him he wants to play more golf and teach his granddaughter how to speak Choctaw, plus, he's always wanted to write a book.

John dreams of walking into a store, like Barnes & Nobel, and seeing a stack of his books on display. He doesn't consider himself a writer, but with hard work and perseverance, perhaps he will become an author. He has taken a new mistress, writing, and she will not share him with duties as Chief of the Choctaw Nation.

"Achukma," responds Levi, "I can't wait to read your first novel."

EPILOGUE

As John begins to clean out his desk, he finds the small gift Tish-ah-yah-hanah had given him and begins to examines it. Then, closing his eyes holding the small object, he begins to search the corners of his mind for a connection. He gently caresses it turning it over and over in his fingers. It's a miniature copper six-shooter he treasured as a young boy. John had never wanted to be the Indian when he and his friends played 'cowboys & Indians'. Therefore his parents gifted him a pair of copper colored six-shooters with leather hoisters and gun belt. The treasured set of guns came with a miniature copper six-shooter strung on a neck chain. As young boys do, he eventually lost it and forgot about it. He now holds the same miniature copper six-shooter in his hand. This is powerful evidence Tish-ah-yah-hanah is not of this world.

He inspects the envelope with the incriminating photo, thought to be from Charlie White. He is stunned to see the postmark is not Louisiana as he thought, but Talihina, OK.

'This can't be right.' He examines again the image of men loading Jeanie LeFlore's body into the pickup.

John begins to wonder again. *'Just who is this man, Ironhorse? Did he take the photo? What was his relation to Tish-ah-yah-hanah? Did Ironhorse, the Medicine Man, orchestrate my rise to the position of Chief of the Choctaws and if so, why?'*

Again, John remembers, his son Randy's premonition. *'Dad, if you ever do a Sweat here, you will experience something very significant.*

You will be looking for answers and you will find some of them here.' The statement had seemed confusing to John then.

He wonders again. *'How could Randy have known I would return to my birthplace searching for something? What other mysteries the Medicine Man Ironhorse, would reveal in Talihina?*

Last, where is Steppenwolf?

The End

AUTHOR NOTE

———————

Three pivotal characters in The Invisible Tribe embody the spirit of Team Tuchina.

ThunderHawk is modeled on my youthful self. The cool and measured July Tecumseh reflects my elder son Randy, hence his nick name Cat Daddy. The brash talking Johnny Kick a Hole in the Sky represents my younger son Reagan Lee.

The collected personality, strength, and mannerism where used to mold the characters in the book. Though my sons have passed (as so shall I), this book honors the memory of three warriors.

BIOGRAPHY

Adrian Roman was born at the old Indian hospital in Talihina, Oklahoma on January 26, 1942. He is 4/4 Choctaw Indian and has a Certificate Degree of Indian Blood (CDIB card) issued by the Bureau of Indian Affairs. He attended elementary and high school in Kiowa, Ok until 1957. During his formative years in Kiowa, the Chieftain as he was known, a gifted athlete, excelled in basketball, baseball, track and boxing. His was the only Indian family in a prejudice town and Chieftain was forced to fight for wounded pride. It was during these early years he began to appreciate and create self-defense movements. As he continued his quest for manhood and acceptance, he became a teacher of self-defense. Eventually he would become the Grandmaster.

In 1957 Chieftain and his family were forced to move to Dallas, TX by the BIA Relocation Program. After finishing high school and a tour in the United States Air Force, he settled in Dallas got married, divorced and discovered American Kenpo. He began his formal training in the martial arts under the legendary Grandmaster Edmond K. Parker through the seminar circuit, and would receive his 5th Degree Black Belt from Parker in October 1990.

In 1995, he began training under another legend, Grandmaster Remy Presas, the Father of Modern Arnis. Presas eventually offered to proclaim the Chieftain his protégée to assume the leadership of Modern Arnis when Presas retired. However, he respectfully declined his offer for he was on another journey of his own to resurrect his Native system.

With the encouragement of Ed Parker and Remy Presas, Chieftain began to create and resurrect the fighting movements of his Choctaw Indian ancestors. In 2000 the Red Warrior martial arts system was born. The last and final version is simply called IronHorse.

In May 2000, the Chieftain was inducted into the Texas Martial Arts Hall of Fame. In August 2003, the International Martial Arts Head Founders and Grandmasters Council awarded the Chieftain with the rank of Soke/Grandmaster, 10th degree in Red Warrior. Black Belt Magazine, Dec 2004 issue, showcased Chieftain and his Red Warrior system in a six page article. It's the first time a premiere magazine acknowledged Americans Indians had a system of their own.

He also worked on the hit television series "Walker, Texas Ranger" as an extra. His first book 'The Apprentice Warrior' is about practical self-defense for the beginner. His first novel is a murder mystery thriller called 'The Invisible Tribe'. He has finished the sequel 'Ironhorse, the Medicine Man' and preparing it for publication. The Chieftain now single resides in Irvine, CA with his daughter and granddaughter. His hobby is golf and carry's a single digit handicap. Another is performing Elvis tunes as an Elvis Tribute Artist in Seniors Citizens Homes and clubs. He offers Distant Learning Programs/Rank in American Kenpo (Ed Parker System) and his Native system Red Warrior.

Contact Adrian Roman aka Chieftain
adrianroman42@gmail.com
chieftain1942@gmail.com

CPSIA information can be obtained
at www.ICGtesting.com
Printed in the USA
FSHW022047241020
75137FS